NARCISSISTIC
Tendencies

DATING BY DESIGN
BOOK THREE

JENNIFER PEEL

Jy Peel xoxo

To My Fans,
I love and adore you all.

Special thanks to Lincoln Hoppe
for all the insider information about Hollywood.

Chapter One

I LOOKED BETWEEN THE profile on my screen and the man who sat in my office, twisting the gold band around his finger. There were several similarities between the two hotshot playboys, except the one in front of me had surprised me.

"How's Meg?" I asked.

I missed her in the office. But it made sense for her to focus on finishing school and finding another job now that she and Zander were married. Even though the client dates in our office were professional and platonic in nature, I didn't think it was a good idea for a married person to go on them. Why open the door? It looked like Meg and Zander agreed. Zander, too, was no longer playing the role of relationship manager. He now filled the position of executive vice president. He took over several of Kenadie's duties, including running the connection meetings and assigning clients to their respective relationship managers.

Zander looked up from his phone. He had been staring at it while playing with his ring. He seemed anxious. "She hasn't been feeling well since we got back from Punta Cana last month."

"Oh. Is she okay?"

He looked down at his phone again. "I'm sure she's fine; she's at the doctor right now."

I had never heard him sound worried. I was happy I was wrong about him. I mean, he was still conceited, but Meg had gotten to him somehow, and it was apparent how much he cared for her. We were all shocked when they showed up married last month after eloping over Memorial Day weekend and an impromptu honeymoon. Not all of us, exactly. Kenadie, who we were waiting on to start our meeting, had attended the spur of the moment wedding in Wyoming where Meg's family lived.

"I hope she feels better soon," I offered.

He ran his fingers through his hair. "Me too."

Kenadie appeared. "Sorry I'm late." She shut the door behind her. "I just got off the phone with the marketing firm to finalize our campaign. They're reaching out to Nicholas today to schedule filming for the first commercial. And they are sending over the pictures from his photo shoot. I can't wait to get those up on our website. This is going to be big for us."

I cringed internally. This wasn't a good idea. I got that it was going to be huge for Binary Search and why Kenadie, the CEO and owner, would agree to such an idea, but Nicholas, or Nick, as he'd asked to be called, was the wrong man.

In my evaluation of him, it had been clear he had narcissistic tendencies. He seemed unable to handle criticism, like when we met yesterday and I politely suggested he put away his phone he was obsessed with, he only glared at me and kept right on checking it. He was obviously self-absorbed and had no regard for others' feelings. Not unlike Zander, but at a more pronounced level. His Hollywood lifestyle, I'm sure, had contributed to it. He was used to constant admiration.

Not only that, the answers on the questionnaire we had each potential client fill out were unbalanced. His values and preferences were all over the place. On one hand, he checked that he was not looking for a long-term relationship, yet the traits he wished for in a partner had everything to do with wanting that person to be loyal to him in every regard, as if they were in a lasting relationship.

If only that were the most off-putting piece of information. He clearly thought highly of himself and wrote down more achievements than any client I had ever seen. Perhaps I could excuse the Emmy and People's Choice Award, but he mentioned three times that he had been *People's* Sexiest Man Alive. And there were a dozen other awards listed. I swore half of them sounded made up, like Most Overlooked Actor. Self-importance was a huge red flag.

I had to voice my concern. "Kenadie, I asked to speak to you and Zander so we could discuss Nick's evaluation."

She was now seated next to Zander. She looked at me, surprised, I'm sure, by my tone. Zander looked mildly interested as well, but his phone stayed his main point of focus. He must really be worried about Meg, which worried me too, but first I needed to deal with the Nick situation.

Kenadie's pretty brown eyes narrowed. "Is there a problem?"

I straightened in my seat. How did I put this after only meeting with him once? Well, once in my capacity here. "I'm concerned about his...attitude...and how he will come across to any of the women he may date using our service. It might bring in more bad publicity than good."

"Any women we choose for him will have to sign a non-disclosure agreement before they can go out with him. Nick's lawyers made that a stipulation in the agreement," Kenadie was quick to answer.

"Unfortunately, I can see why."

Kenadie now had a slight look of panic on her face. "What are you saying?"

"I'm saying I've never met a man more egocentric than him." That wasn't exactly true. There was a bigger ego maniac in my past, but no one here knew about him and I liked to keep it that way. Both Kenadie and I looked at Zander.

Zander looked up. "Why are you looking at me?"

Kenadie and I both turned away from him and faced each other.

"As I was saying, as far as I can tell, he cares about no one but himself. At least Zander usually places Meg's feelings above his own."

Zander's head popped up. "Why do I keep being brought into this? I told you both he was a player. And I'm happily married now, thank you."

"He's more than a player. He doesn't seem to have an emotional attachment to anyone—maybe he's incapable of it, I don't know. I would have to spend more time evaluating him to know for sure."

Kenadie sighed and bit her lip. "Kate, this is a done deal. We've signed. I've hired several more relationship managers to handle what I'm sure will be a huge increase in business when people find out that Nicholas Wells is using our service. Can you fix him?"

"People aren't like cars; you don't take them to a repair shop and 'fix' them. It takes a willingness on the patient's part and a desire to change."

Kenadie looked at Zander for support. They were more than business partners. They had been best friends since high school.

Zander shrugged his shoulders. "Kenz, this is your call."

"Kate." She faced me, desperate. "I need you to work your magic on him."

"I'm a psychologist, not a magician."

4

"Please. Maybe he was having an off day. I'll tell his people that you need to spend some more time with him."

"Don't you think that will sound a little strange? We don't offer therapy here."

She slumped in her chair. Despair was etched in her features while she thought.

"What if Kate became his relationship manager?" Zander suggested.

Kenadie's eyes lit up and she perked up a bit. "Yes, yes. We can say we are giving him specialized attention since you evaluate each of our clients. And this way it would reduce the amount of people here that would have to sign an NDA. He was worried about people having access to personal information about him, so this could actually play in our favor."

"Oh no, no, no. I don't do narcissists outside my office." I had gone that route before. All I'm saying is annulment is an ugly word.

"Is he really a narcissist?" Zander eyed me. "You used to say that about me."

"I said you had tendencies and I stand by that. Nick is...well..."

"Please?" Kenadie's entire body begged.

I looked at Nick's headshot on my screen. It was professionally done. It looked so perfect I would have said it had been touched up, but I had met him in real life—twice, actually—and I had to hand it to him, he was gorgeous on the outside. At forty, he still had thick, sandy brown hair and eyes of blue that looked like a daydream. He worshipped his own body, so he was in perfect shape, and his chiseled features wore his eternal five o'clock shadow like they were meant to be together.

Besides his looks, I couldn't think of a redeeming characteristic about him. Not even the memory of our first meeting helped his case. But I looked between his picture and Kenadie. Kenadie, whom I admired and respected. She was intelligent, and I agreed whole-heartedly with her approach to relationships. I was happy to help her grow her business. I felt like what we did here was important. People should be more selective about who they dated. I wish Binary Search was available to me back when…well, back when I didn't know better. I would hate to see anyone ruin what she, and the rest of us, had worked so hard to create here.

I looked one more time between Nicholas Wells and Kenadie. I knew I would regret it, but I would regret the demise of Binary Search more.

"Fine," I breathed out.

Kenadie didn't waste a moment and jumped out of her seat, making her shoulder length, curled, dark blonde hair bounce. "I'll call Nick's people now." She gave me a relief-filled smile. "Thank you, Kate. Hopefully, he'll surprise us." She made a beeline for the door before I could respond.

Zander bolted for the door, making a call to his wife, I'm sure. I really did hope Meg was all right. Zander had me worried, as did the man staring back at me on my screen. I let my hair out of the messy bun I had thrown it in early this morning and ran my fingers through my long hair.

My mind drifted back to the first time I met Nick. No one but me would ever know it wasn't yesterday. Not even Nick, though he did mention during his eval that I looked familiar. It was the only decent remark he made the entire time. I felt it better not to mention our run-in fourteen years ago. He didn't need to know I had at one time idolized him, and I'd like to think that naïve twenty-year-old woman no longer existed. How could she after everything she had been through?

Now, more than ever, I was glad I didn't share my brush with fame with anyone. At the time, I hadn't spoken of it because it seemed like the magic of that moment would have lost some of its luster. I used to think it was fitting that it happened at Serendipity, my favorite bookstore. A chance meeting in a place named for happy coincidences. Ask me back then, I would have told you it was fate. It had been the only time that summer I was able to visit my beloved bookstore—normally I was there every Saturday, a tradition I still kept up with. But that summer I was home from college for only a week before I left to work as a counselor for a specialized camp in Tennessee for disabled children.

I had to admit that I was kind of bummed I was leaving for the summer after I met him. Everyone knew Nicholas Wells was from Georgia. I'd even plotted with some of my high school girlfriends how we would meet him. On the Edge, the crime drama he'd starred in as Talon Fox, was all the rage. I had planned to name my first son Talon, unless I married Nicholas. Which was my first choice. I didn't think he would want a son named after his character.

Sadly, I'd never been happier to hear of someone getting divorced—other than myself, of course, except my situation went one step further: annulment. Not dwelling on it. I'm ashamed at the shouts of hooray that went on in my dorm room when it was announced on every major network and gossip site that Nicholas Wells and his model wife, Alessandria-with-no-last-name, split up. I never understood the no-last-name trend. My roommates and I shamefully made fun of her, but really, we were only jealous of the European beauty with long legs, mesmerizing emerald eyes, and flawless features. What a gorgeous couple they made. Of course, my friends and I never thought she was good enough for him. We all cursed her when it was reported that she left him for one of the extras from On the Edge. It was quite the scandal back in the day.

I foolishly thought I could nurse Nick's heart back together, given the chance.

Then life handed me a moment. One I had never forgotten. I was walking out of Serendipity in the quaint Emory Village near my parents' home in Druid Hills—where I live now, too—not watching where I was going. My nose was in one of my favorite books, *Les Misérables*. I had purchased a new copy since I'd given my previous copy to a roommate who thought reading paperbacks in the rain was a good idea. I was already so into it that I barely knew I was walking out the door. That's when I felt the bump and watched my book drop. When I bent down to get it, I was met with the most enigmatic blue eyes. The bookstore magically transformed into its namesake and I froze for several seconds. His penetrating gaze held me, that was, until our hands touched while we each tried to pick up the book. It was more than a tingle, it was like reading a torrid love letter, but without words. His touch was scorching. I had never known a heat intense enough to cause shivers.

"I'm sorry," I managed to stutter. "I wasn't watching where I was going."

I couldn't believe I was face-to-face with my honest-to-goodness fantasy. And I was kicking myself for looking grungy in yoga pants with my hair in a ponytail and ball cap.

The brittle smile he was famous for that gave nothing away appeared on his sun-kissed face. "Lucky for me."

Never had three words excited me more. I stood up straight, he followed. We both held the book between us. He acted as if he didn't want to let go. Neither did I.

Nick's gaze drifted toward the title of the book. "*Les Misérables.* I enjoyed the abridged version."

"You're missing out," I told him without thinking.

His eyebrow arched like the character he played. Just enough to make me catch my breath.

"Is that so?" The question danced out of his mouth.

I adjusted my hat and bit my lip, embarrassed I'd been so bold. "You have to read the unabridged version for the beautiful history and to see what happens to the doll."

He leaned in closer. I still remember the way he smelled, like amber and vanilla. "Care to fill me in?"

I wanted to, anything to talk to him longer, but my personality came through. "I wouldn't want to do you the disservice."

He tilted his head and studied me for a moment, as if he was surprised by my response. "What is your name?" He didn't introduce himself, he knew by my reaction to him that I knew exactly who he was.

I opened my mouth to tell him, but I wasn't the only one who'd recognized him. A group of women walking past rushed us. My book fell again and I was left to pick it up in the chaos, trying not to get stepped on. The women didn't even care that they had interrupted my serendipitous moment. They pawed at him while preening themselves, pushing him farther away from me. I walked away with my book but looked back to see if there was any chance he noticed I had gone. I couldn't even see him in the sea of women.

It was the first time I ever questioned if being with someone that popular and attractive was a good thing, because on some level, you would always feel like you were competing for his attention. I should have listened to that voice. Sadly, that's exactly what I ended up with. That relationship was abolished, null and void, I reminded myself.

I stared back at the present Nick on my screen, shaking off memories of long-ago days. Thankful on one hand I'd had the moment. Everyone needed a magical moment, to experience the kind of heat his touch produced. If only I could meet someone to recreate it with. I'd often wondered why I never had. To be honest, that memory had carried me through some dark times. But I'd learned my lesson and

I was thankful I was no longer the woman who could be seduced by a pair of alluring blue eyes. The question was, how was I going to save the women I would pair him with from losing their heart to the possible narcissist staring back at me?

Chapter Two

ZANDER SHOOK ME out of my contemplation when he rushed by my office door, ashen faced, muttering, "That damn bearskin rug."

What did that mean? "Is Meg okay?" I called out.

He didn't respond.

I would call Meg later. I prayed she had nothing seriously wrong with her. Zander's behavior had my insides brewing with unsettled feelings.

Kenadie poked her head in on her way out for the day. I still remember the days when she was the first one in and last one to leave. Married life suited her. I was happy she had found a good match in Jason, even if he went about getting to know her in an unconventional way, reckless, even. I thought back to when I evaluated him here in my office to use our services. There was something off about it. Not to say there were any red flags, but his questionnaire didn't accurately depict him. It was apparent from talking to him that he was the kind of man who valued commitment and family. He was someone who wanted a life partner, despite marking he wasn't looking to be in a serious relationship. I was right about that, but I had no idea he and Zander had cooked up the idea so he could get close to Kenadie. Zander managed to get Kenadie to be Jason's relationship manager and as they say, the rest is history. Jason dated other women so he could woo Kenadie. Not the brightest idea, but if you thought about it, it was kind of romantic. Though professionally I would advise that deceit was never a good way to begin any relationship, even if the intention was pure.

"I heard back from Nick's people and Nick is in favor of this new direction," Kenadie said uneasily. Her creased brow said she was worried about what I'd previously disclosed.

I did my best to keep my sigh in. Part of me, like ninety-nine-point-nine percent of me, was hoping he wouldn't agree. The tenth of the percent was only okay with it because I felt like I was sparing my coworkers any heartache. There was mass swooning in here yesterday when he arrived. The speculation through the office was rampant. Kenadie had yet to announce that Nick was using our services.

There were still aspects about how this partnership came about that I didn't know, but Kenadie assured me that despite the fact that he was to become the face of Binary Search, he would be a real client in every sense of the word. Of course I thought our services could help everyone, but I had a hard time buying that Nick would find our services useful. Zander was right, the man was a player, if the tabloids from years gone by were to be believed. After his divorce, he didn't seem to lack for female companionship. On his questionnaire, he stated his last relationship lasted two days and was only ten days ago. When I asked him about it, he smirked like it was a joke, or perhaps he thought I was. Why did I agree to be his relationship manager again? The answer was easy. I believed in what we did here, and I wanted to continue to help people avoid the earth-shattering pain I endured. The tools we gave people here to enter healthy relationships were priceless.

Kenadie stepped into my office. "Kate, you don't have to do this. I know it's a lot to ask outside of your role here. An invaluable role, I might add."

I gave her a small smile. "You don't need to butter me up. I hope I can help, or at least mitigate any disasters."

"Disasters?" Kenadie gulped.

"I'm sure it will be fine." There was no hiding the uncertainty in my voice.

She took a deep breath. "I hope so. He agreed to give you his personal number. I'll email his contact info to you. And you know the drill, since you created most of the questions our relationship managers ask during the dating phase. I'm hoping by tomorrow to announce on our website that he's using our service. Perhaps we could pair him with someone during Friday's connection meeting?"

"So soon?" I wasn't sure I was ready to go on the client date with him, or ever see him again.

"It's been in the works for several months already, so yes."

"I suppose that means you want me to contact him."

Her button nose scrunched. "As soon as possible, if you would."

"I'm thinking a raise is in order," I teased.

"Done." Her shoulders relaxed. "Thank you, Kate. I had no idea when I agreed to...well...let's just say I thought I'd done my homework. And after talking to him several times, I'm surprised by how he came off in the evaluation."

"I've been wrong about people before," I tried to ease her angst.

"We were all wrong about Zander," she grinned.

"Speaking of him, is Meg okay? I saw Zander flying out of here looking upset."

She pressed her lips together in a thoughtful manner. "To be honest, the newlyweds haven't wanted a lot of company. And Zander has been surprisingly attentive to Meg, as well as guarded with what he shares about their relationship."

"That's a good thing. He's matured."

"I never thought it would happen, but I'm happy for him and Meg."

"Me as well."

Kenadie checked the time on her phone. "I'll text Zander to see if anything is amiss. But I need to get going. Jason and I are meeting my momma for dinner."

"Tell your mom hello for me."

Kenadie gave me a sly glance. "You know, Momma still thinks you and Dylan would make a great pair."

Dylan was her older brother who lived in Boston. We'd shared a few nice dances at Kenadie's wedding on New Year's Eve and he had called a couple of times, but I had rules against dating cops and engaging in long-distance relationships. While I admired and respected law enforcement officers, their divorce rates were staggering, and long-distance relationships didn't have good odds either. I couldn't afford to make another misstep, so I only dated those who fell within my parameters. It had severely narrowed the field, but after Douglas, I had to put guidelines in place for my own well-being.

"As good of a matchmaker as your mom is, I don't think it's a good idea to date my boss's brother." It was another rule that fell in with no dating coworkers.

"Momma will be disappointed to hear that, but I understand. Besides, I already lost one of my best employees to Zander. I would hate to lose you, too."

"Enjoy your dinner."

"Knowing my momma, it will surely be interesting and most likely be her lamenting the fact that Rick and Renee got married at the courthouse and are still refusing to have a reception. Same with

Zander and Meg. She and the Nanettes are itching to throw someone a reception. They still can't believe both couples basically eloped. You would think that was an unpardonable sin in their book. If only Jason and I had been so brave." She gave me a wave. "Anyway, I better go before Momma has something else to complain about. Have a good night, Kate."

"You too." I smiled to myself as I watched her go out. Her mom and friends, dubbed the Nanettes by Kenadie and Zander, were the most meddling, lively, and adorable women I had ever met, except for my own mother, but she had her own eccentricities. Dad too.

My parents were some other people I should check on. Since Dad's heart attack and subsequent retirement, they were either going to kill each other or separate. Either would devastate me, and more than likely leave me with my mom living with me. Yes, Dad would be the one to die in that scenario. Even though my mom was against killing animals to eat them or to wear them, she seemed to be on the verge of making an exception where Dad was involved. Especially since he was no longer going along with her new health fads and diet of the week. We'd been subjected to every diet imaginable, from the macrobiotic and Mediterranean diets to vegan and alkaline diets. She was currently on a vegan kick.

Since Dad's heart attack, he decided, unfortunately, that all the healthy eating throughout the years had done him no good, so he was going against his doctor's and my mother's orders and eating anything he pleased. He brought home a bacon cheeseburger last week that had Mom staying the night with me until, as she put it, the animal's spirit, which my father massacred, vacated the house. I hadn't mentioned to her the club sandwich I had eaten earlier.

Although it all might be a moot point if Dad finally burns the house down with one of his home improvement projects. The man had no idea what he was doing, and the house looked like a tornado had come through and no one thought to call their insurance agent for repairs. Mom said that is was affecting her chi and Zen. Next week it would probably be her mana.

All I knew was I wanted my loving, albeit quirky, parents back. It was like Wars of the Roses over there now. And as much as I loved my parents, I didn't want to live with one of them. That would put a damper on my already anemic love life. Nothing like bringing your date home and having your mother waiting up for you. That would definitely not help my plan to get married before my ovaries and skin shriveled up. I could picture my mom now, asking any potential husbands if they wore boxers or briefs and admonishing them that, if it was the latter, they were killing their sperm count. Mom once told one of my dates his voice was too low, which didn't bode well for his sperm count. I had to get my parents to make up ASAP or I was never getting married.

I sighed and dialed Meg's number before I headed out of the office. One worry at a time. It went to voice mail. I'd try back later.

Perhaps I should head to my parents' for a little marriage counseling session. Or maybe I should drown my worries in a milkshake. Decisions, decisions.

Chapter Three

MEG SAVED ME from the empty calories of a milkshake and trying to fix my parents' relationship by calling me on my way home and asking me to meet her at our favorite juice bar, which made killer smoothies. I asked how she was feeling and she said she would explain it all when we met, but that all was well. I had a feeling by the tone of her voice that she was looking for more than a friendly chat. In my line of work, I was used to it. For some reason, people thought since I had a doctorate in psychology I had magical answers to give. Unfortunately, there were no magic fixes. I could give insight, even offer treatment plans, but either way it required work. I was surprised how many people wanted answers and solutions yet were unwilling to make changes.

Meg was not one of those people. Not that she needed to change anything or looked to me to fix her problems. She mostly liked to hear my take on things, especially when she was dating Zander. For good reason, she had some trepidation about dating a man who proudly used to declare he was never getting married and had dated more women than there were days in a calendar year.

Maybe Meg had some supernatural power. She certainly had an effect on Zander. He was still Zander—as in, he still made inappropriate comments and he had a high opinion of himself—but I had watched him the last several months with Meg. He seemed to be in awe of her. Like she offered him a new way of thinking about life. A life he never knew existed, but now couldn't get enough of it.

Not to say they didn't have any disagreements. There were a few times the office got a little interesting when they had tiffs, like Meg called them, but they were quick to make up and move on. Zander, surprisingly, was the first to apologize. He was also usually the one to cause the issue, but he didn't like it when things weren't good with Meg. It was as if a piece of him was missing when Meg was unhappy with him. Flowers would be delivered, and PDA abounded in the office when she worked there. It was nauseating but admittedly cute. And honestly, it made me a little envious.

I had to remind myself to turn to all the good in my life to combat those feelings, and there were plenty of things to be grateful for. Despite not having the family I'd always hoped for, I was educated, made a good income, owned my own townhome, and when my parents were sane they were amazing people. I had a feeling I would be telling myself this a lot with my new responsibilities at work. I couldn't believe I agreed to be Nick Wells's relationship manager and that I would have to go on a client date with him this week. He would probably look at his phone the entire time or stare at me as if he couldn't believe some mere mortal was speaking to him. He had done that a lot yesterday. I tried not to let it unnerve me. Not sure how well I did.

I arrived at the juice bar not too far from my place in Druid Hills. I'd landed in the same community as my parents. When they built some new townhomes in my price range there, I couldn't resist. I loved the small-town feel in the middle of Atlanta. I could walk to my favorite bookstore and favorite places to eat. The parks and the overall sense of community were amazing. Maybe someday my children would even get to take advantage of the great schools. You know, before my ovaries died a slow, painful death waiting for the ideal candidate to make use of them.

I arrived before Meg and got us a bistro table with high-back chairs by the window. The juice bar didn't see a big crowd around dinner time. During breakfast and lunch, this place was packed. I normally didn't drink my dinner either, but I was looking forward to talking to Meg. I had connected with her more than anyone in the office and missed her daily presence. Most of my coworkers thought I kept to myself, and I did. I was one to sit back and observe. I was interested in their lives and getting to know them, but life taught me to be cautious about forming attachments. Funny, I was happy to help others form them and keep them. Or was that ironic? Since being in Kenadie's wedding, I had tried to engage more in the office and even outside with Meg and sometimes Kenadie, but I knew I could be better. I suppose my new role would help with that. So perhaps that was the silver lining?

Meg pulled up to the front of the shop in her old truck. She slowly exited and when I caught a full view of her, I could tell even from a distance that she didn't look well. Her olive skin that was normally darkened this time of year from being in the sun was pale, and the usual bounce in her step was gone. Worry crept in again.

With the jingle of the bell, I waved to her. It was there I caught her red eyes. I stood, more worried than I had been. She took labored, deliberate steps to me and we greeted each other with an embrace.

"Hi, there."

That was enough to invite her to cry on my shoulder. She was a few inches shorter than my five-feet-seven. A few of the other patrons glanced our way, but they did the decent thing and didn't linger on the scene.

I patted her back. "I thought you said everything was okay."

She tried to compose herself before stepping back and wiping her eyes. "I'm sorry. I'm fine. Really, I am. I think." Tears filled her pale green eyes.

Everyone always commented on Zander's bright green eyes, but I thought Meg's outdid his.

"Why don't you sit down, and I'll go order for us. Do you want your usual?"

"Actually, I think I'll go with the raw banana ginger one."

I tilted my head but didn't press; instead, I squeezed her hand. "I'll be right back."

She nodded her thanks and took a seat while I headed to the counter to order. Maybe she was nauseous, that's why she wanted the ginger. A light went off in my head. No. That couldn't be. They hadn't even been married two months. I held my flat stomach. It hadn't taken that long for me either, I remembered. I always remembered. Why did I feel so empty still? Annulment was an ugly word, miscarriage was vile. *Positive thoughts. I was here for Meg.*

I walked back to her as soon as the order was placed and paid for. They would bring the smoothies to our table. Meg was staring wistfully out the window as if she was hoping for someone to arrive.

I took my seat across from her. "You can begin anytime," I said, using a little therapist humor.

She gave me a tiny smile for my woeful comedic attempt. "Thanks for meeting me."

"Anytime. What's going on?"

She tucked her short dark hair behind her ear. "Well...I finally got all my things moved into Zander's apartment."

"Uh-huh."

"I'm still on track to graduate at the end of next month."

"All good news."

"And," her voice cracked, "I'm pregnant."

My training kicked in and I showed no signs of shock or envy. I gave her a gentle smile. "Congratulations. How do you feel about it?"

"Me?" She wiped her eyes. "I'm so happy, as you can tell." She laughed.

I reached across and took her hand. "Are you really?"

"I am. It definitely wasn't in the plan right now, but I can't think of anything I would want more than a baby with Zander." She pressed her lips together and tried to stave off any more tears. "But, Zander...he is..."

I held my breath and tried to repress my memories of when I told Douglas I was pregnant. It was the beginning of the end of something that should have never even started. I hoped Zander wasn't so callous.

"Well, I don't know what he is. He came home when I told him over the phone. I wanted to tell him in person, but he thought since I wouldn't tell him over the phone it was bad news and I didn't want him to worry more than he has been. I've been so tired, and then I started throwing up. Not every day, thank goodness, but enough to know something wasn't right. And then my period was late. I think he was in denial about what that meant."

"Did he say anything after you told him?"

She bit her lip as if she was embarrassed. "You know him and his colorful vocabulary, but basically, he cursed the bearskin rug at my dad's place and blamed our months of, uh...celibacy."

My training went out the window with that surprising bit of news; my eyebrows raised.

"I made Zander wait until we were married."

21

I sat back, stunned and impressed. And proud of Meg for holding her ground.

"I know it's shocking. Zander being the most shocked of all. But I guess it made us both more anxious and neither of us were really thinking about birth control."

"So is the news unwelcome to him?" I tried to ask delicately.

She shrugged and the tears reappeared. "He wouldn't say. He came home and paced and paced, sometimes he stopped and stared at me, but he said nothing until he left to go to the gym. He said he needed to think."

Our smoothies arrived, but neither of us made a move to taste them. Instead, I leaned forward and rested my hand on hers. I tried my best to wear the hat of friend more than clinical psychologist. Most importantly, I had to remember that Zander wasn't Douglas, so it didn't cloud my advice or the comfort I tried to offer. Though I had my worries, given Zander's behavior and how much his lifestyle had changed in the past several months since he'd entered into a relationship with Meg.

"It's not uncommon for men to be afraid about impending fatherhood."

Meg sat up straight, her eyes brightened.

"For many, it means facing their own mortality and fears about whether they can be a good father and provider. Given what you've told me and what I witnessed at Kenadie's wedding about Zander's parents, I could see why he might feel inadequate since he didn't have a good example. And men worry that their wives will no longer be their lovers, but instead only a mother. For Zander that might be especially hard to deal with right now since he's barely had you to himself."

She nodded her head. "That all makes sense, but what if he doesn't want the baby?"

I felt a stabbing pain in my heart for her and myself. Douglas's words shouted in my head that I'd tricked him and I was on my own. I took a deep, cleansing breath. "I hope that isn't the case. But you are one of the strongest women I know, and you will handle whatever life throws at you and come out better in the end. Besides, I think the Nanettes and Kenadie will kill him if he doesn't."

She laughed. "That's true." She thought for a moment. "But I want him to be happy."

"If he can't find happiness with you and the new little life you carry, he doesn't deserve it. With that said, give him some time."

She sighed as if relieved and took a sip of her smoothie. "Enough about me. How are you? Have you seen Nicholas Wells yet?" Even Meg sounded enamored with him. Not that I could blame her. For anyone who had never met him, I could see the appeal. He came in a very pretty package. Just ask him or *People* magazine.

If only I could really talk to her. Not that Zander wouldn't. Now that she didn't work there, he shouldn't, but Zander did a lot of things he shouldn't do. I gave her a close-lipped smile. "I met him yesterday."

"And?" She was dying to know.

I thought about what I could in good conscience divulge. I twirled some of the loose strands of my hair that had gone back up in a messy bun. "I'm reserving full judgment."

Her eyes widened then narrowed. "That doesn't sound good."

"Let's just say he gives your husband a run for his money with how much he loves himself."

"That bad?"

"I'm going to be his relationship manager, if that says anything."

"What?" She almost spit out some of her smoothie.

"I'm sure Zander will fill you in."

Her solemn demeanor was back. "Hopefully by the time I get home he'll be speaking to me again."

I was about to answer her, but it was unnecessary. A harried Zander came crashing through the door. The few patrons and employees all focused on him. He was still in his workout clothes, with sweat-drenched hair.

The weight of the world fell off him when he zeroed in on Meg and took long strides to our table.

"Darlin', there you are." He sounded out of breath, which was saying something. By the way his workout clothes fit him, he was obviously in prime shape. Not like I was checking him out, but I imagined Meg must be very pleased.

Meg sat up, pensive. "How did you know I was here? Is everything all right?"

Zander took his wife's hands and pulled her up, holding her as close as he could. He kissed the top of her head.

She melted into him.

"I came home and you weren't there. I've been trying to call you. You mentioned a smoothie sounded good earlier, so I thought I would check here first before I started calling our friends." He leaned away from her and his eyes landed on her abdomen. "I was worried about you and..." he swallowed hard, "the baby."

Meg flung herself back against her husband and clung to him.

I had a feeling they would work it all out. It looked like Zander would surprise me once again.

Chapter Four

MY FINGERS FELT numb. They were refusing to dial Nick Wells's number. I knew I had to. His gorgeous face was plastered all over our website now. The phones hadn't stopped ringing and the online inquiries for more information on how to become a client were overwhelming. Kenadie had been smart to hire more relationship managers and an additional admin assistant. My life was about to get more chaotic, and not only because of my new role, but because I evaluated each prospective new client. Not all applicants made it to me. It was surprising how many people didn't pass the background check or wrote in questionable, bordering-on-frightening, answers on their questionnaires, like fetishes and dark fantasies. We had called the authorities more than once.

I was stalling. The connection meeting was in two days, which meant I should try and see him tonight so I could do my research tomorrow and choose three unlucky, I mean potential women to suggest as his first victims, oops, dates.

I must have picked up my phone a dozen times. I organized my already neat desk. Sent a few emails. I needed an if-then strategy to motivate me. If Kenadie emailed me one more time asking if I called him, I'd do it without delay. That was good. A thoughtful, mature way to deal with procrastination. I wasn't buying it either. I picked up my phone and, unfortunately, my fingers worked this time.

One ring. Two rings. Three rings. Four rings. I was hanging up.

"Who is this?" his deep voice growled.

No! I was taken aback by the gruff manner in which he answered, so I paused.

"Who is this?" he repeated.

"Kate Morgan." I tried to keep the bite out of my tone. But really, who answered the phone that way?

"How did you get my number?"

"I googled it." Okay, so that was a little biting, more like a nibble, but he deserved it after being so rude.

"That's impossible."

"You're probably right. Kenadie from Binary Search gave me your number. We met Monday."

He paused for a moment. "You're the psychologist."

"That would be me. I will also be acting as your relationship manager, which is why I'm calling."

"Right, the date phase."

I swore I heard a hint of mocking. "It's an important step and part of our process."

A heavy breath came through on his end. "Fine. When should we have our date?"

"If you're available tonight I can make reservations at Atlas in The St. Regis." I knew one of the sous chefs there. It was a high-end place, at least for Atlanta. I'm sure there were pricier places in LA.

"That won't work."

He couldn't know how happy that made me. "Perhaps tomorrow?"

Please say no.

"Meet me at Jack's on the River tonight at seven. I'm doing some workshops at the performing arts centre nearby. I'll try to be on time."

Who was this guy? His rudeness was off the charts. If this were a real date, it wouldn't be happening. But since I was getting paid to go out with him—wait. That sounded awful. Maybe Zander was right, being a relationship manager was akin to being a pimp. I couldn't think like that.

"Can I give you some advice?" I felt if I didn't I wasn't doing my job.

Silence on his end. Not surprising.

"I hope when you start to see the women who have not only paid a nice sum of money to use our services here but have an expectation that we are pairing them with someone they deserve, that you treat them with more deference than you just showed me. I'll see you at seven." I hung up.

I was going to get myself fired at this rate, or at the very least removed as his relationship manager, which wouldn't be awful for me, except my evaluation of him seemed to be spot on. I was determined to protect the company from him. How? I had no idea.

....

I ran home to change into something more dinner appropriate. Not because I was trying to impress Nick Wells, but because I would do my best to represent the values we aspired to at Binary Search. Nick Wells was the last man I would ever want to attract. He went against almost every rule on my list. Being a possible narcissist at the top, not to mention he was a celebrity. Two of the biggest rules broken right there. Celebrity divorce rates were some of the worst. And that lifestyle was a breeding ground for selfish behavior. Not that I was too concerned that a celebrity would ever want to date me, much less marry me, but I had to add it to my list just in case. I liked to cover all my bases.

Atlanta traffic was alive and well, so I had to rush to change. I climbed the steps to my main level from my first-level garage. I took a moment though, before I headed to my third level, to admire my home. It was the first place I had owned. I didn't count my brief six months with Douglas. That was all a lie anyway—he never owned the place like he said. One of his many, many lies. It made me even more grateful as I looked over my piece of heaven that it was truly my own. I was in love with the openness and the dark wood with taupe doors and crown molding. The built-in bookcases that framed the fireplace were my favorite. They overflowed with my trusted friends.

I hustled up to my bedroom and headed to the section of my closet that I had designated as "dating" clothes. These were clothes that spoke to the kind of person I wanted to attract and represented how I wanted to present myself. Most importantly, they were clothes I felt good in. I had a feeling I would need all the help I could get being around a man who worshipped himself and undoubtedly had a following of worshippers. Thankfully, he was well past the height of his popularity, but judging by the women in our office, people still recognized him and would love the chance to fawn all over him.

This could be a long night.

I chose a red wraparound dress that accentuated my waist and showcased my legs, but still fell nicely just above the knee. It was classy with a hint of fun. Exactly the kind of person I hoped to attract and strived to be. I knew I fell short, especially in the fun department, but I was trying to be better. More outgoing. More like the me before Douglas, though I could never be the same after what he did to me.

I let my caramel hair down and added a few waves to it before giving it a little volume. For makeup, I went with a bronzy neutral look to bring out my blue eyes. When it was all said and done, I felt nowhere near ready to face Nick. Not only did he bring up bad memories for me, but I felt so foolish—once upon a time, it was my dream to be Kate Wells. Thankfully, my frontal lobe was fully attached now, and I was smart enough to know that men like him should be avoided like white after Labor Day. Which reminded me, I should probably throw away the six seasons I owned of *On the Edge* on DVD. I remembered squealing every time a new season came out. Sometimes I missed that naïve young woman and the innocent way she used to look at the world.

I slid into some beige pumps to match my skin tone and hustled back out to my car and traffic. Maybe Nick didn't care, but I planned on being on time. The traffic on 75 had abated, making my goal more realistic. My nerves had not quelled. I wasn't sure why I was so nervous. I had zero interest in him, but there was something intimidating about him. He made me feel like I had to keep my guard up, and that wasn't really my style. I was by no means a laid-back person, but for many years now, I felt most comfortable observing, only engaging when I had to. Like my mother was quick to point out, it was probably why I wasn't married or even in a relationship, that and she thought I was too selective. My problem was I hadn't been selective enough.

I put on some Etta James and ran through a checklist that I might give a patient. Try to find positive meaning in the unpleasant task, control my negative thoughts, reward myself when it was completed. I liked that last one. The question was, how would I reward myself? Maybe that new handbag I wanted, or comforter? Depending on the night, maybe both.

By the time I made it to the restaurant off the Chattahoochee River, I still wasn't looking forward to it, but I was calm. Thank you, Etta James, you've yet to disappoint me.

The charming restaurant reminded me of a quaint chateau, with blooming azalea bushes adding to the ambiance. Nick got a point for that. If the food was half as good as how beautiful the exterior was, I would have thought I'd found a new favorite place. Assuming he didn't come here ever except this once. Dean Martin could be heard on the sound system for the patio diners enjoying the river view. I was already in love with this place. If only I wasn't meeting Nick.

I took a deep breath and steadied myself as I entered ten minutes early. I was ready to fall more deeply in love with the interior, but I couldn't believe what was surrounding me in the waiting area. On second thought, I shouldn't have been surprised. Nick was everywhere. It was like a homage to him and *On the Edge*. He was staring at me at every turn. His brooding persona jumped off each picture, whether he was in a police officer uniform, his signature tight jeans, let's not forget shirtless, or holding his TV partner and love interest. There I stood looking at each photo on the surrounding walls before I ever made it to the hostess. I wasn't even sure why. Perhaps I was astounded at his arrogance to have dinner in what could easily be called the Church of Nicholas Wells, or maybe because that's what several other people waiting to be seated were doing.

Sadly, I recognized each episode where the shots of him were taken. Like the one where he saved his partner, Samantha, from a fiery car crash. He did his own stunts, something else he bragged about on his questionnaire. I'm ashamed to admit I still got a little fluttery remembering that scene. It was sexy and sweet and we'd all been rooting for them to get together.

His character Talon Fox was brooding, yet sweet and attentive to his partner's needs and wants. There was even a humble quality. One I had found endearing. Thoughts of Nick in my office easily

30

vanquished any lingering feelings for his character, Talon Fox, out of my mind. Talon Fox was an illusion. I was a fool to ever believe that Nick was like the character he played.

In the midst of what I would call my horrified fascination, I was approached by a man.

"Hello."

His smooth deep voice with a hint of Southern charm turned my head. I was caught by a pair of oddly familiar enigmatic blue eyes. They were framed by crinkles and belonged to a distinguished older gentleman with the finest head of silver hair I had ever seen. He was dressed impeccably, too, in a gray button-down and dark slacks. If only he were younger, were my first thoughts. I didn't date anyone more than ten years older than me. Divorce rates for wider age gaps were too risky.

I stopped my ogling long enough to say, "Hello."

His eyes took me in, in a way that I hadn't experienced for a long time. His smile said he liked what he saw.

I was both flattered and cautious. And I couldn't shake the feeling that I knew him.

"I'm Jack." He held out his hand.

I placed my slender fingers in his capable hand, refined by time, and tilted my head. "As in Jack-on-the-River Jack?"

His deep melodic laugh rumbled through me. "The very one. And you are?" He kept my hand firmly but gently in his own.

"Kate Morgan."

His mysterious blue eyes lighted. "Ah, Kate, we've been waiting for you."

I slid my hand out of his. "You have?"

"You're on our reservations list."

"Oh." I was surprised Nick had made the effort.

Jack gave me a grin that stirred familiarity again.

"Have we met before?" I asked.

He stepped intimately close and revealed how fantastic he smelled. It was as if I stepped outside after a good rainstorm. "Believe me darlin', I would have remembered you."

Wow. A shiver ran down my spine. Who was this man, and did he have a younger brother? Son perhaps? Oh my gosh. A thought crashed into me. I looked at the nearest photo of Nick and then back at the debonair man next to me. They couldn't be. Could they? I took another peek of Nick.

"Are you a fan?" Jack asked.

"Not particularly, no," I blurted before I thought.

Jack's laughter once again consumed the space. "I like you, darlin'."

I was going to ask Jack how he knew the man who adorned his establishment's walls, but it became painfully apparent who he was when the doors opened and in strutted his son with the loveliest teen girl by his side. There was no question it was Nick's daughter, Skylar; she was the spitting image of her model mother Alessandria, right down to the long legs and emerald eyes. Except her eyes had an innocent quality to them. She had an aura of a guileless creature. Even the way she braided her long blonde hair to the side spoke of her purity.

She noticed us first and ran straight into her grandfather's open arms. "Grandpa."

"There's my girl." Jack held her tight.

Unfortunately, that meant her father joined us too. Or he attempted to. He had some fans in the waiting area. He paused and chatted with a couple, even took a picture with them. He flashed his signature brittle smile and made the woman swoon and giggle.

I noticed Skylar roll her eyes. I liked her already.

Jack chuckled and caught my eye. "Skye, I want you to meet someone."

I liked her nick name.

"This is Kate Morgan."

"It's nice to meet you." I smiled at the beautiful girl.

Skye gave me an appraising sort of look. "You're the one having dinner with my dad." She didn't sound very fond of the idea.

I imagined it must be hard for her to see her dad date. Even though this wasn't at all that kind of date. "If you had plans with him, I'm happy to reschedule. Or you're welcome to join us for our dinner meeting." I wanted to make sure she knew it wasn't a date and I was no threat to her. Also, I really didn't want to be alone with Nick. Besides, seeing how he interacted with his daughter could give me some more insight into him.

Skye's demeanor went from scrutinizing to surprised. "Really?"

Jack gave me a smile of approval. "I think we should all have dinner together." His focus shifted behind me. "What do you think, Nick?"

My head turned, and I was met with those Wells eyes. They captured mine before they roved over my body, exactly like the pair that belonged to his father had. Was he perusing me or judging me? He wore a look of discontent. He probably wasn't happy with the way our phone call ended. But he was on time. My body, unfortunately, had mixed reactions to the way his eyes seemed to x-ray me. A hint of excitement ran through it, as well as a heavy dose of loathing. I berated myself internally for the small lapse of judgment in my neurons. Not that I could entirely blame them. I used to have posters of him on my wall. No one ever needed to know that.

Nick's eyes stayed on me, but he spoke to his father. "Think about what?" The timbre of his voice matched his father's, but his had an air of conceit.

A mischievous smile appeared on Jack's face, showing off his laugh lines. He had plenty of them, unlike his progeny, who may have never laughed a day in his life judging by how taut his jawline was.

"I've decided I can't bear to part company with our gorgeous new friend, so Skye and I are changing our plans and dining here with you. You don't mind, do you?" Jack didn't give him a chance to answer; he held out an arm for me and one for his granddaughter. "Ladies, let me show you to the best table we have here."

Nick's scowl said he wasn't on board with the new plan, but he didn't object.

Relief flooded me. I happily took Jack's arm, as did Skye. Her mood lightened with the change of plan. Mine did, too. Part of me felt guilty because I knew I wasn't technically fulfilling my duty as a relationship manager, but who was I to come between father and daughter? And I liked Jack. Not in an I-would-date-him sort of way, but there was something about him. He was a throwback to days gone by, where the man wasn't afraid to show his interest. It was refreshing. And he was keeping me from being alone with his son, so I blessed him.

We strolled through the crowded main dining area that was decorated to match the outside. Cottage and French country dining tables and chairs dotted the restaurant in hues of antique white. Crystal bronze chandeliers set the mood. Several patrons stared as we passed by, or should I say, as Nick passed by, trailing behind us.

Jack led us out to the covered patio that had a gorgeous view of the river. The breeze off the river and patio ceiling fans made it comfortable to be outdoors in the warm July evening. Pots of flowers in a variety of colors overflowed the cozy space. Jack seated us near the edge where we could get the best view of the river and the trees that lined the body of water. Several patrons greeted Jack like they were old-time friends.

Which made me wonder. "When did you open this place, Jack?"

Jack pulled out my chair for me. "I've been in business about five years. Retirement was too boring."

I took my seat while watching Nick pull out Skye's chair next to me. He earned another point for that gesture. "What did you do before you retired?"

"I was in the Navy for years, before I managed this kid's career for a while." He nodded toward his son. "But Georgia is more my pace."

I had no idea his dad was his manager. I'm sad to admit how much I did know from reading several articles about Nick when *On the Edge* first came out and the subsequent years after. Like I knew Nick's mother, Barbara, died during the fifth season. My roommate and I mourned for him like we actually knew him. Okay, so I'd had a brush with him by then. Now I'd like to brush him away.

Nick took the seat across from me but had yet to say a word to me. Not like I had greeted him either. I wasn't good at real dating, much less this awkward scenario. Let's not forget I had serious reservations about the man. I had to remember, though, I was there to help Binary Search and mitigate any potential disasters.

"Hello, Nick."

His eyes connected with mine, which was another point for him. Making eye contact was a good thing, but he was too good at it. His gaze was so penetrating I physically felt it. I remember Meg once mentioning that's how she felt when Zander looked at her. I had never experienced such a sensation until now. Why couldn't he just return my greeting instead of making me feel exposed? But that's what narcissists did. They fed off your vulnerabilities.

I tore my eyes away from his. I refused to be vulnerable again, at least not in the presence of someone who couldn't be trusted with it. No relationship ever worked unless both parties were willing to be vulnerable.

"I made it on time." It was hard to tell if he was being sarcastic or if he wanted praise.

"I'll add a star to your chart in the office," I deadpanned.

The corner of his lip may have twitched, but his eyebrow arched so fast I wasn't sure.

Jack, on the other hand, chortled from the seat next to me. "Beautiful and quick witted. Where do I sign up?" He gave me a wink.

Nick's famous eyebrow arch now hit his dad.

Jack took it all in stride. "I may be old, but I'm not dead, son." Jack patted my hand. "I suppose I should ask if you're single."

"Grandpa, you're too old for her," Skye stated boldly.

I smiled at Skye and was pleased she returned it. "I think your granddaughter's right."

"I hate to argue with beautiful women, but in this case, I might make an exception."

He had me wishing he was younger while Skye shook her gorgeous head at him.

Nick apparently didn't like the direction of the conversation. "Where's our server?"

"Patience," Jack reprimanded his son.

"I already know I'm having the spinach and cheese crepes," Skye said.

"That sounds delicious," I addressed Skye.

"They are," Nick spoke, surprising me.

I shifted my gaze toward him. "Perhaps I'll order them then."

"You won't be disappointed." Nick's tone was smoldering.

Unfortunately, I usually was.

Chapter Five

WHILE WE WAITED for our food, there was no lack of conversation. Jack was unlike his son and liked to talk.

"So, darlin'," Jack turned his attention toward me, "Nick tells me you work for the matchmaking service he's got himself all tangled up in. What is it you all do there?"

I took a sip of water out of my goblet and set it down. "We use a blend of technology and human observation to help connect people in a meaningful way."

"Are you observing me now?" Jack flirted with me.

"Yes." I leaned in and played along.

"And what is your conclusion?"

"You're trouble."

Jack tapped my nose. "You're right."

Nick cleared his throat.

Jack leaned back and grinned at his son. "You're here to observe Nick, then?"

"In a matter of speaking, I suppose."

"What do you think of him?"

Both of Nick's eyebrows skyrocketed up.

"I'm not allowed to discuss our clients."

Nick shot me a thoughtful look.

"He's practically an employee, doing advertisements for you," Jack pressed.

"Be that as it may, he's still a client." One who I'd signed my life away for. The NDA his lawyer sent over for me to sign made me afraid to even call him a client in front of his family, but since Nick had already told them, I hoped I was staying within the lines.

Jack clapped his hands together. "If you can't talk about him professionally, at least tell us why you aren't a fan of his work."

I was right. Jack was trouble. I rubbed the exposed part of my chest. "Did I say that?" I reached for my water.

Skye was giggling to my right while her father was waiting for my reply.

Jack's eyes danced to a devious tune. "I think you did."

Nick was laser focused on me.

I met his stare. "What was the name of your character again?"

"Talon Fox," Skye giggled some more. "Dumbest name ever."

"Yes, and so broody," I added.

Skye smacked her dad's arm playfully. "I told you, Daddy."

Nick surprised me and caught his daughter's hand and gave it a gentle squeeze.

The father-daughter pair were obviously comfortable with one another. The affection he showed Skye gave me some pause. It was genuine.

Skye faced me. "It's so embarrassing to watch that show."

She made me laugh. "What do you like to watch?"

"Mostly YouTube, but I love the home design show, *This is My Place*. Oliver Ren is the hottest. I want to be like him and host my own show someday."

"I love that show too." The show's basis was to go in and pick one room for a deserving person and make it over, making it their "place." "Do you remember the show last year where he made a headboard out of old hardback books?"

"I loved that episode. He did it for that retired librarian who donated all the money she won in the lottery to the library," Skye responded.

I placed my hand across my heart. "That was so sweet. I was so inspired by it, I made the same headboard."

"Ooo. I'd love to see that."

"Me too," Jack said seductively. He really was trouble.

"You know my dad produces that show?" Skye informed me. "And I got to meet Oliver."

"I didn't know that," I glanced quickly at Nick, who looked between Skye and me with interest, before I asked, "Is Oliver Ren as good looking in person?"

"Even better," Skye sighed, "but he has a girlfriend."

"He's too old for you and off limits." Nick sounded like a dad.

Skye waved her hand at her dad. "In ten years when I'm twenty-five and he's thirty-five, no one will care. And the last woman you dated was young enough to be my sister."

Tension arose like a tidal wave, as did the scarlet tint in Nick's cheeks.

All her dad had to say was, "Skye," and she said not another word on the subject.

The arrival of food was good timing. After a few bites, the delicious food worked its magic like only good food could. The mood at the table shifted back to being more lighthearted. Jack was back to asking me more questions.

"Are you from around here?"

I swallowed and nodded. "Mostly, yes. I grew up in Durbin Hills but attended college in Pennsylvania and then Iowa."

"What did you study?"

Nick obviously didn't tell him what my role was at Binary Search. Interesting.

"For my undergrad I received a degree in sociology. Then I earned a masters and a doctorate in psychology."

"I didn't know we were in the presence of a doctor. Nick, you never mentioned it."

Nick wiped his mouth with his napkin. He too had ordered the spinach and cheese crepes. "I didn't know."

"Should we call you Dr. Morgan?" Jack teased.

"No." I smiled. "I don't usually advertise it in the office. I want people to feel comfortable around me. The only time I ever use that title is Monday nights when I volunteer at one of the counseling clinics near my place. The people there are my only true patients now."

"Smart, beautiful, and generous." Jack was liberal with compliments.

I tried to take the compliments for what they were. Even tried to absorb them. Since Douglas, I was wary of them. Douglas had laid them on thick when we first met, and I bought into it. But by the end he made me feel like the most worthless person who had ever lived. I still had to fight against those feelings. And I was always afraid that when someone complimented me, it wasn't genuine, or they had ulterior motives. I didn't want to feel that way. It was tiring, to be honest.

"I don't know about that. I only want to give back where I can."

Jack beamed at me. "How someone hasn't snatched you up yet, I can't fathom."

Someone had snatched me, devoured me, then spit me out. "I do my best to make that difficult." The ease to which I owned that surprised me.

"I like a challenge, darlin'." I don't think he was teasing.

"Dad," Nick's voice warned.

"Ah, let your old man have some fun." Jack stood up and held his hand out to me. "Take a spin with me."

A few couples who had too much to drink had started an impromptu dance in the corner. I had enjoyed watching them on and off. One couple were spectacular swing dancers. I looked at Jack's hand and reminded myself I wanted to have more fun in my life. My hand landed in his. "I would be honored."

He pulled me up and close to him. "The honor is all mine."

If only he were younger. Though my mom was right, I would probably find some reason we couldn't be together. For now, though, I would enjoy the moment with the distinguished gentleman.

Just in Time by Dean Martin was playing over the restaurant's sound system.

Jack led me to the corner and held me close, but in a gentlemanly manner. He was tall like his son, and even in my heels I had to tilt my head up to look at him. He made me wonder how such a carefree man had raised such a brooding son.

Jack's eyes sparkled before he leaned in to whisper in my ear. "If I were a younger man, I would be asking for your number right about now."

"If you were a younger man, I would be giving it to you."

His playful laugh rang in my ear. "I do enjoy vexing my son. And this is doing the trick quite nicely. Don't you think?"

We both looked his way and, sure enough, his eyes were shooting daggers at his dad.

"He needs to lighten up a bit. But that said," Jack's tone took a more serious turn, "I don't know what in the world he is doing using a dating service. Maybe he's tired of all the piranhas in Hollywood. Or he's finally realized how horrible his taste in women is. Skye's mother, and I use the term lightly, has put them both through the wringer, so I'm begging you for Skye's sake to make sure he's matched with someone who won't hurt him or her."

I wanted to ask what had happened, but it wasn't my place. "I promise." For his daughter's sake I would do my best. The question was, would Nick hurt whoever I set him up with?

Relief washed over Jack's face. "Are you available for him?"

"No." I had to keep the shock of horror off my face at such a notion. "Employees aren't allowed to date clients."

"Too bad." Jack swung me out, making my dress twirl. We both laughed as he pulled me back in. "You are enchanting, darlin'. You remind me of my Barbara."

No one had ever called me enchanting before. I wanted to believe him. I almost ached to. "I'm sorry for your loss."

"Don't be. We lived five lifetimes together. I only wish the same for my son. For you too."

"Thank you, Jack."

"For what?"

"For reminding me what this is like and giving me some hope."

He pulled me closer and we swayed together. "Anytime, darlin'."

As if the evening hadn't already been so unexpected, Nick and Skye joined us on the dance floor. I leaned on Jack's shoulder and watched father and daughter. Skye talked and talked, and her dad listened as he held her tenderly. It was as if I could see in his eyes that he wished the moment would never end. If I ever did marry, I hoped my husband would dance with our daughter like Nick danced with his. And, as always, I wondered if my baby would have been a little girl. She would have been nine now. I could picture her standing on her father's feet, dancing and dancing. Well, not *her* father's, he was awful, but I planned to do so much better the next go around.

Amid my contemplation Nick's eyes locked with my own. They made me pause. His eyes asked the same thing I was thinking, *Who are you?*

I left with more questions about him than answers.

I had no idea what type of woman to pair him with. I didn't even get to ask him one question. Confusion swirled in my brain. I was having a hard time reconciling the man in my office and his egregious questionnaire, to the man who treated his daughter like a princess. Mind you, he hardly said a word to me or anyone else. Perhaps I should pair him with someone who didn't mind carrying the conversation, but even a person like that wanted some reciprocation.

I said my goodbyes to Jack and Skye, each giving me a hug. Nick hung in the back, not saying a thing. But while I was walking to my car, I was stopped by the sound of the man with nothing to say.

"Kate."

Startled, I stopped in the middle of the parking lot, but didn't turn around.

It didn't take long before Nick was close behind me. "Kate," he repeated.

I turned slowly. I was caught off guard by how near he was and how easy it was to think that never had a pair of jeans looked so good. I'd been trying hard all night not to allow myself to have thoughts about how physically appealing he was, especially when he danced with his daughter, but some of my barriers had failed and suddenly my mind was consumed with how attractive he was. I closed my eyes and took a breath hoping that would help. When I opened them, he was still there and looking as beautiful as he did before. His eyes looked good in the soft glow of twilight. Stop it, Kate.

"Did I forget something?" I stuttered.

"You seemed to forget this was a date."

I stepped back. "Client dates aren't real dates."

"Regardless, you still owe me one."

My breathing was becoming shallower by the second. "I have to research who to pair you with tomorrow so I can connect you with someone on Friday. There isn't any time," I rationalized.

"Do you eat breakfast?"

I nodded, finding it easier than speaking.

"Name a place and time tomorrow and I'll meet you there."

"I don't think—"

"I expect to get the full experience." He spoke with an air of authority I wasn't used to.

"Fine. There's a café near my place. I can text you the address. It will have to be early."

"Like I said, name the time."

"Does seven work?"

"I'll try and be on time." He paused as if he was waiting for me to offer him some advice. When I didn't, his lip upturned the slightest fraction. "Don't forget to text me. See you tomorrow, Kate." Without another word, he turned around and strutted back to the restaurant.

I stood there astonished at the turn of events. The least of which was I didn't know he could talk so much. The greatest being how fast he made my heart beat. I should probably get that checked out.

Chapter Six

IT WAS ONE of those nights where I kept saying only one more chapter, but the next chapter would come and go. I couldn't sleep, but I didn't want to be alone with my thoughts either. Avoidance was not a tactic I would prescribe to my patients as a way to deal with their problems. I definitely shouldn't be using it, but I didn't want to think about Nick. The man who used to keep me up for other reasons. How many nights had I fantasized about him? I'm embarrassed to admit how ridiculously steamy some of them were. Those fantasies had now turned into complex and perplexing issues. No steam involved.

Nick won. I placed the latest psychological thriller on my nightstand before snuggling deep under my peach tufted comforter. I had to deal with this. I was meeting him in six hours for breakfast. Beyond that, I would be choosing who to pair him with and I would have to follow up with him about those pairings. That's where it started getting complex. The man on paper was awful. The man in real life was arrogant and rude at times, but the way he was with Skye threw it all into chaos. My conscience grappled with setting him up with so many unanswered questions regarding his character. At least we had done a background check. One of those would have solved so many of my own personal problems. Believe me, if I was ever proposed to again, I was having a background check done and a credit score report.

Hard lessons learned.

So we knew Nick wasn't a bigamist, like Douglas, and he didn't lie about his credentials and money. Those were plusses for Nick and assuaged some of my worry. And he didn't want anything serious, but I knew that could change. We'd had couples get married who had marked that category. Thoughts like those left me to worry if he did end up marrying someone he met through our services and it turned out terrible, would she blame the company? Me? I would no doubt feel some responsibility and guilt over it. Or worse, she might have to suffer in silence because Nick would surely make her sign a hundred-page document stating she would never tell a soul about him.

What if he crushed her soul? I had a feeling he was the kind of man who could. He was like Douglas in that he could pull you in so deep you didn't even know you were drowning in him until it was too late. The worst part was that you'd think it was love because love should be all consuming. It should be, but it shouldn't consume you. Nick's celebrity status and money would only make that more likely. Someone could easily get sucked into the seduction of that lifestyle. And let's not forget how beautiful he was. Even I had to watch myself around him.

But then there was this father side to him. I watched for signs to see if it was fake, but it seemed authentic. Skye showed all the signs of a normal, happy childhood, right down to feeling free to speak her mind and even tease her father in front of others. She didn't seek attention unduly or act out. In fact, she was a delight.

Jack's words also ran through my head about Nick's ex-wife and his taste in women. Did Nick really want a change? Was that why he was using our service? And I'd promised Jack to pair him with the best. Skye deserved that. Every child did. But what if Nick didn't? This was why my head hurt and sleep was nowhere in sight.

Maybe in the morning, or I should say later this morning, I would get a clearer picture. We would meet one-on-one again, and hopefully the casual environment would allow for the clarity I needed to emerge. Perhaps this time he would say more than a few words to me. In the parking lot he proved he could. That was another thing I found odd. Why did he want a real client date when it was obvious it wasn't something he was interested in?

I closed my eyes. I think I liked it better when I only thought about him as a sex symbol and somebody I wanted to father my children. They would have been gorgeous, judging how Skye turned out. *Stop thinking like that Kate.* I needed sleep.

I managed a few hours, not nearly enough to face my task. Look at me, meeting with a former sexiest man alive and referring to it as a task. My eighteen-year-old self just gasped. I couldn't blame her. That poor girl had no idea what was in store for her.

Since I had to go to work after our "date," I dressed more professionally in a white blouse and striped ankle pants with a pair of ballet flats. I was planning on walking to the café, which was only a couple of blocks from my house. It was easier than the hassle of driving in morning traffic and trying to find a parking spot. And the rain was supposed to hold off until late morning. Besides, walking would help me stay calm. I was for sure buying the handbag and comforter now. Two dates deserved two rewards.

It was an overcast but pleasant morning for July in Georgia. I loved the large magnolia trees that lined my walk and the smell of honeysuckle and jasmine in the air. The city streets were already alive with commuters. I met a few joggers and people walking their dogs on my way. I still couldn't believe I was headed to breakfast with Nicholas Wells. It wasn't too far from where I met him the very first time, come to think of it. I always wondered why he had chosen that bookstore, *my* bookstore. Where did he stay while he was here? I suppose I could ask him. I didn't think to last night. Not like I needed to know. All I knew was he didn't complain when I texted him the address last night. His response was, Got it. Nothing polite like *thank you*, or *see you in the morning*.

Not like I expected anything polite. It was not a word I would use to describe him.

I arrived a few minutes early in front of the bustling café. People were leaving with bags full of pastries and cups of coffee. The smell was making my stomach growl. I decided to wait outside, since the café was one of those places that didn't have wait staff. You ordered and picked up your own food, and with luck there was a table to sit at if you were dining in. As a relationship manager it was my job to pay for the client date, so I waited.

Five minutes past seven and I was still waiting. No big deal. He was probably stuck in rush-hour traffic. Ten minutes past, I checked my phone. The courteous thing to do when you're going to be that late is to text or call the person. I should have known better; no message from him.

Fifteen minutes late. Maybe traffic was really bad.

Twenty minutes. Okay, maybe he was an inconsiderate jerk. That fit his profile. I was going with that.

By twenty-five after, I was done waiting and the forecast was wrong—it started to rain. What a way to start my day. I was too tired already, and this didn't help my mood.

I started marching my hangry, tired self back to my place, determined to set him up with exactly the kind of woman he deserved. I turned the corner that led to the nearby residential area I lived in.

Guess whose car was turning toward the café? We both caught a glimpse of each other and I glared at him, now damp and contemplating telling Kenadie that I refused to be his relationship manager. She's the one who made the deal with the devil, so he could be her problem. All my good intentions for wanting to help the company went out the window.

He, on the other hand, stopped his fancy sports car in the middle of the road and almost made the person behind him hit him while he rolled down his window. "Kate!"

I did the mature thing and ignored him while picking up my pace. All I wanted to do was be home and dry. Anywhere he wasn't.

Horns were now blaring since he'd stopped the flow of traffic. I heard a squeal of tires but didn't look back. I would match him solely based on his questionnaire and who came up as compatible for him. My guess was he was getting a prima donna. We had a few for clients. My promise to Jack buzzed around my brain. I tried batting it away, then Skye's lovely face showed up in there too. Nick didn't deserve those two, or any of the nice women we had as clients.

By the time I made it to the next corner, I heard that same velvety-though-irritating voice calling my name, but it came from behind, not to the side of me where the road was. Now I was more than damp and wearing a white blouse, so that added to the fun. I was in no mood for company, so I hustled across the street without acknowledging him.

"Dammit, Kate, wait up." The voice was closing in.

Halfway across the intersection the rain stopped falling on me, but it was still raining. I looked up to see a large black umbrella covering me. The faint smells of amber and vanilla wafted off the man to my right. Not a word passed between us until we were safely across the street.

"Will you stop," he said, more like a command than a request.

I stopped right in front of the mailbox near the corner, but not because he told me to. I looked up into his face that had perfected the short stubble beard. It was darker than his sandy brown hair, but matched his brooding attitude. What did he have to be brooding about? He was dry and looking like a million dollars. I probably looked like a drowned rat or worse, a wet koala bear.

"Is this all a joke to you?"

His tight jawline pulsated while he peered into my eyes, not saying a word, per his usual.

I didn't have time for this, or him. I strode away.

He followed, keeping his umbrella over both of us. "I have an excuse."

I took note that he didn't answer my question and kept on walking.

"Skye had a...woman thing this morning."

That got me to stop. "A woman thing?"

He gave me a look that said he wanted to do anything but explain himself to me. He heaved a heavy sigh. "I bought the wrong kind of...anyway, I can never remember if she likes the ones in the blue box or the green box. I don't even know what the difference is."

I couldn't hide my grin.

"Needless to say, I bought the wrong ones and had to return to the store."

It was my turn to sigh. I hated when I jumped to the wrong conclusion. Not to mention behaved the way I just had. But... "You could have called to say you would be late."

He tilted his head like what I'd said was a foreign concept.

"It didn't even cross your mind?" I inquired.

"No."

"Hmm." I turned to head toward my place.

"What?" He followed me.

"I hope you will show more respect than that to the woman or women you may date using our services."

"Who says I'm being disrespectful?"

"I do."

"It's not like I planned on being late."

"I didn't accuse you of that, but once you knew, the right thing to do would have been to call or text me. I would have understood and waited. But now thanks to you, I look like I entered a wet T-shirt contest and I'm hungry."

"You could have eaten while you waited."

I turned and narrowed my eyes at him. "I was being polite and waiting for you so we could eat together and so I could pay for your meal, since you wanted the *full experience*."

"What do you want me to say?"

"An apology would be nice."

He pressed his lips together as if to say *those words weren't escaping his mouth.*

I figured that was the case, so I kept on walking. The only sound between us for several steps was the pitter-patter of the rain hitting the umbrella.

Why he followed I had no idea.

"You can go home, or wherever you have to be." I tried to get rid of him.

He made no move to change course. "Kate."

I didn't pause or acknowledge him.

"I . . ." he stretched his neck to one side then the other, "apologize." That last word came out like he'd never used it and it hurt him.

I did him a favor and didn't look directly at him or grin. This had obviously been a difficult task for him. "Apology accepted."

"Where are we headed?" he asked, quick to change the subject.

"*I'm* headed home."

"So our date's off?"

Was he for real? "I think that's probably the safest course to take. Besides, now I have to change my clothes and redo my hair before I head to the office."

He gave my body a pat down with his eyes while he walked and held the umbrella.

It made me feel self-conscious. My white blouse was clinging to me like saran wrap. I touched my pulled up wet hair. "I know I look ridiculous."

His eyes smoldered like I'd seen dozens of times when he played Talon Fox. Was that something he was taught to do, or did he bring that to the table all on his own? Judging by his father, I think it might have been an inherent trait. Either way, I felt it down my spine. That wasn't supposed to happen.

"I wouldn't say that." His gaze drifted away from me.

I dared not ask what he thought. I was having a hard time breathing or thinking, which was absolutely ridiculous.

"My place is right there." I pointed across the street. "I can see myself the rest of the way home. Thank you."

"I've come this far, I might as well go all the way."

I looked both ways before crossing the street. "Can I ask you a question?" I figured it was now or never.

"You can ask." It sounded like, *I probably won't answer.*

"Who are you?"

His head turned my way. His eyes questioned my question.

I landed on the sidewalk in front of my townhome. "Are you the man in our office profile or the man who dances with his daughter, makes feminine hygiene runs, and walks women home to keep the rain off them, albeit grudgingly?"

He studied me for a moment before leaning in. "Who do you think I am?"

He kept catching me off guard. I had to back away from him. I shouldn't have any physiological reactions to him. "I'm trying to figure that out."

"Do you really want to?"

Why did I feel like there was more meaning behind that question than I wanted to know? "I need to know so I can do my job correctly."

He gave me a half smile. I doubted he ever fully smiled. "For anything Binary Search related, you can use the man in your profile."

Did he just refer to himself in the third person and as two different people? I was more confused than ever. So much so my head hurt.

He looked over the colonial style three-story structure I called home. "This is your place?"

It dawned on me that he now knew where I lived. I wasn't sure what to think about that. I doubted he cared to know or would ever use the knowledge, but I was always cautious about letting people know where I lived, especially men. Very few men ever made it to the stage where I would invite them over for, say, dinner. I didn't even let a man pick me up for a date until we'd had two successful dates. Since I'd moved here a year ago, no man had ever made it that far. My dad excluded. And here I let some stranger walk me home. A famous stranger I didn't even like.

"Yes. Thank you for walking me home. I'll send a message to you in your client portal tomorrow after our connection meeting regarding who was chosen for you. Of course, after she's signed your NDA. Assuming she will." His celebrity status and requirements added extra steps we weren't accustomed to.

His eyes said he had no doubt whomever we chose would sign it. "I'll look for it."

"Okay. Goodbye."

"Kate." My name sounded too good coming out of his mouth. "You still owe me a date."

"I don't think we should tempt fate." Or me. Not that I was tempted by him.

"Like I said, I want the full experience."

"It's too late now. I'll be busy all day evaluating potential clients and doing research on the best candidate for you." Not to mention all the extra questionnaires we had coming in due to the man next to me. I had to at least do a quick review of each one before we wasted time and money getting a background check done.

"I didn't say today. I'll let you know when."

I'd never known anyone who spoke like there was never a question he would get his way. "But—"

"Binary Search is committed to keeping their clients happy, aren't they?" he interrupted me.

"Yes," I stuttered.

"Now you know what would make me happy. See you later, Kate." He strutted off like a peacock. He only went a few steps before turning back around. "By the way, I didn't begrudge walking you home." He didn't linger to see my reaction.

I stood dumfounded in the rain watching him walk away, wondering what had just happened and telling myself my heart was only pounding hard due to the brisk walk.

Chapter Seven

M Y HEAD POUNDED so much I almost took my emergency stash of over-the-counter pain reliever, but both of my parents' voices sounded off in my head. My chiropractor dad would be telling me I only needed to be adjusted and my...well, I wasn't sure what my mom was, perhaps *naturalist* covered it for this week. She had been everything from a massage therapist to a henna tattoo artist to a professional snuggler. You wouldn't believe what people were willing to pay for that service. Dad put his foot down on that one after only a few clients. I'm pretty sure some people wanted to do more than snuggle. Despite her new hobby/job-of-the-month, she was adamantly against the "poison," as she referred to it, sold at the store.

To please my parents who weren't present, I did a few stretches to relieve the tension before reaching for the peppermint oil. My ibuprofen would stay on standby. While I rubbed diluted peppermint oil into my temples, I continued my research on Nicholas Wells. I'd decided I needed to dig a little deeper into his background before I chose any candidates for him. Plenty of our clients were calling or messaging their relationship managers, jumping at the chance to be paired with him. There were going to be a lot of disappointed women, perhaps including the one he got paired with when she found out that prince charming was brooding, arrogant, and rude.

I knew some women found that attractive and challenging, especially when it came in such a beautiful package, not to mention a wealthy and famous one. My favorite nonfiction book, *The Science Behind Why Good Girls Love Bad Boys*, detailed why as women we were so prone to love the Nicholas Wellses of the world. It was basically biology. Successful, handsome men like Nick screamed *I'll give you strong offspring*, but with rational thinking the urge to mate with such men or engage with them in any way, shape, or form, could be overcome. If only that book had come out earlier, think of the heartache it could have prevented. Now I read it religiously, like some people read their bible. I'd even loaned it out a few times and recommended it to patients. I credited that book with helping me formulate my rules and saving me from another Douglas.

I wondered if Kenadie would allow me to give each potential Nick date a copy. Probably not. Maybe I would casually start leaving my copy out on my desk whenever I evaluated clients. And if someone asked about it, it wouldn't hurt to tell them. It was a plan.

Back to Nick and my yogurt. I was eating lunch at my desk so I could squeeze in more time to research him and his victims—er, dates. Who knew, maybe my initial assessment of him was wrong. I rubbed my temples some more.

I focused my research on the last ten to eleven years of his life, since the end of *On the Edge*. Personally, he was a single dad awarded full custody of Skye. From my brief interaction with them, it appeared they had a strong bond. I had to admit how sweet it was that he was making tampon runs, even going back to get the right kind. It appeared he kept her out of the spotlight as much as possible and even sued a couple of tabloids for taking pictures of her. I could respect that.

On the other hand, he didn't lack for female companionship. Several pictures and stories popped up with him and a slew of different women. He didn't have a type, per se, unless you counted gorgeous. He was interested in blondes, redheads, and brunettes. They were skinny, curvy, tall, and short. But each dazzled on his arm or when they were kissing for the cameras. To think I used to want that to be me.

He had never remarried. One article rumored he and Gisele Starr, a young starlet, were engaged a few years ago. He broke up with her, though it wasn't clear why. Maybe because she didn't look old enough to drive his daughter to school. That was judgmental of me. I'm sure the party girl was lovely. I mean, those pictures of her flipping off the camera and holding bottles of booze were precious. Exactly what every dad should want in a stepmother. I tilted my head to check out her physical assets. Wow. Her legs went on for miles, and if those were her real boobs I was impressed. I looked down at my size 34B chest. It was nothing to be ashamed of.

The moral of the story was Nick loved beautiful women in all sorts of shapes and sizes. That wasn't a surprise, based on his questionnaire. When asked if he had any preferences, he said *the hotter the better*, like some college frat boy. Except for some reason, I couldn't even imagine him saying the word *hotter*; it didn't fit any interview I had ever seen of him or the few times I'd been in his presence. I would at least give him that; he didn't speak like a Neanderthal. Even in the couple of interviews I'd just clicked on—he was discussing one of the charities he was involved in that supported the spouses and children of fallen police officers—he had spoken eloquently, even passionately. I dug more into that aspect.

I was surprised to find several articles about his involvement in supporting law enforcement and our military. Why didn't he put any of this information on his questionnaire? I had to smile when he spoke of how proud he was to have a father who served in the navy. But then I switched back to his recently-out-of-puberty alleged ex-fiancée. I couldn't reconcile the two. Throw in my evaluation and interactions with him, and he had me reaching for the ibuprofen.

I moved on to his professional life.

He was in a couple of short-lived TV shows after *On the Edge*. They each failed to capture the magic of the show that had made him famous. I remember watching the shows and hoping they would be as good. I'd needed something at that time of my life to help me cope with the crumbling world around me. Not only had I found out that I was married to a man illegally and my marriage was considered void and would be annulled, but I'd miscarried at fourteen weeks. Late for a miscarriage. While I was grieving the loss of my baby and the man I thought I loved, I had to prove that I had no knowledge of his wife who lived in Maryland to avoid being charged with the crime of bigamy as well. Not even my crush on Nicholas Wells could comfort me. And honestly, the shows were lackluster. Those new characters, one being a TV lawyer and the other an emergency room doctor, had nothing on Talon Fox. The magic was gone, and so was he from the spotlight. I moved on from my fantasy in both my real life and the make-believe world of Nicholas Wells. Well, mostly. I still ached for my baby. I didn't suppose that would ever go away.

He didn't disappear from Hollywood, but he took on a different role behind the scenes. Like Skye had mentioned last night, he was a producer now. According to my search, he owned a production company with a man named Simon Wilder. The name of the company was, get this, Wilder than Wells. Kind of catchy. I wondered if there was a double meaning there. Not only was Nicholas a producer, but a writer. I was shocked to see he had written and produced one of my favorite romantic comedies a few years ago, *A Step Up*. It was a cleverly written movie about an unlikely relationship involving a stepbrother and stepsister. They didn't grow up together, but had been best friends before their parents took the plunge. It was quirky and witty and now I wanted to watch it again. How did I not know he wrote the screenplay for that? Probably because I was no longer a fangirl. And once again, why didn't he mention any of these things on his questionnaire?

I stared at the picture of him front and center on my screen. *Who are you Nicholas Wells? And why are you using Binary Search?*

A knock on my office door had me clicking out of my browser. "Come in," I called.

Zander appeared on the other side still looking shell-shocked at his impending fatherhood. Yesterday he had kept to himself in his own office, coming in late and leaving early.

"Have you chosen the three candidates for Nick you want to present tomorrow in our connection meeting?" he asked.

Zander had revamped the way we did connection meetings, especially since we had so many new relationship managers. Zander might come off as a laissez-faire sort of guy, but he was anything but when it came to business or his personal life. Not that he didn't like to have his fair share of fun and banter, but he was well organized and savvy. Meg even mentioned how pristine he kept his place, now their place. I wondered if he knew how messy babies were. Zander now asked everyone to send him their clients and choices on Thursday so he could review them before the meeting. Another thing about Zander was his uncanny and innate ability to "get" someone. He was the best relationship manager the company had ever had; his wife was a close second. Maybe that's why they worked. They "got" each other.

Maybe he could help.

"I'm working on it, but I'm...confused."

Zander tilted his head.

"Can I ask you what you think of Nick?"

Zander stepped in and closed the door. I knew it was because he didn't want anyone to hear us discussing our famous client. "I told you, I think he's a player."

"With the number of women he's dated, that could be true, but…"

"But what? How did your client date with him go?"

I sighed. "Well, it didn't technically happen."

Zander took a seat in front of my desk as if he knew this might take a while. I gave him a brief overview, leaving out me walking away in a pouty huff and the fact he walked me home, or dancing with his dad. Basically, I dumbed it way down, but enough to give him valid reasons for my confusion.

Zander leaned back in his seat. "People always tell you who they are, even if they are trying to hide it."

That was actually insightful and true. "Do you think he's trying to hide something?"

"We all are."

Who was the psychologist here?

"You're not helping me." I grinned.

He gave me his signature Zander smirk. "You're intuitive. Listen to that, and if all else fails, give him what he's asked for. He told you on paper and verbally what he's looking for. If that's not really what he wants, that's his problem, not ours. Hell, I'd be happy if he decided to break his contract with us. But Kenz knows what she's doing and she's right, this is a smart business move. Don't forget this is probably business for him too."

Huh. That was a thought. "Do you think he's trying to revive his acting career?"

"I wouldn't be surprised. He kills two birds with one stone this way. He gets exposure and chicks to date who have already had mental evaluations and background checks."

"You think this is a just a ploy of his?"

Zander shook his head. "No way. Kenadie would never allow anyone to use our services who didn't take it seriously."

I raised my eyebrows—that was how she met her husband.

Zander read my reaction correctly. "She didn't know about Jason's motivation for using our services. I don't have Kenadie's scruples."

That was true, but I didn't voice it. "But what if he ends up hurting someone, or worse, it turns into a publicity nightmare and it's my fault because I chose wrong? Or because he really is a narcissist and I gave him a pass because of who he is?"

"Why do women worry so much?"

I was sure that was a rhetorical question.

Zander rubbed his hands together as if he was getting down to business. "Listen, first of all, he's not looking for you to pair him for life and neither are the women you are going to pair him with. Find someone who likes to play the game as much as his profile says he does. We don't offer people guaranteed happily ever after's here. We offer them a chance, a better one than they would have on their own. And for people in Nick's category, we are offering a 'safer' environment. We can't remove every risk. No one can. Second," he flashed a sardonic smile, "you don't know for sure he's a narcissist, and even if he is, that doesn't mean he's a sociopath."

I nodded in agreement. What he was saying was all true and I knew it, but sometimes you needed someone to regurgitate it back to you. "This was helpful. Thank you."

Zander didn't make a move to leave. Instead, he ran his hands through his chestnut hair and uncharacteristically shifted in his seat. "Do you mind if I ask you some questions?"

"Not at all."

He didn't say anything right away.

I let him gather his thoughts. I was pretty sure what he wanted to discuss.

He had a hard time meeting my eyes. "You know about Meg...and me..."

"You're having a baby," I tried to help him out.

His eyes met mine. "At the end of February," he said like it was not far enough away.

"How's Meg feeling?"

He tossed his head from side to side. "She's stubborn, so she's faking it. I think for my benefit, which is why I want to talk to you. Get a professional opinion."

I gave him a warm smile to let him know I was listening.

"I think Meg is under the impression I'm not happy about the—" he swallowed, "baby, so she doesn't want to act happy or sick, even though I can hear her puking in the bathroom. And I know she's excited, even if she won't say. And it's not that I'm unhappy...it's just..."

"You're scared."

He sat back and shook his head vehemently. "No."

I pressed my lips together, trying not to show any amusement at his obvious denial.

He let out a huge breath. "I'm scared as hell."

"That's normal," I tried to reassure him.

"I wasn't expecting this so soon. Hell, I didn't even expect Meg."

"You didn't expect her, but I would dare say your life is better with her. You're happy together."

He nodded. "She gets to me."

A need arose in me to be spoken about like that. I had to push it down. This wasn't about me. Envy never did anyone any good. "You think that will change once the baby comes?"

He looked up to the ceiling. "Maybe."

"Zander, Meg has a great capacity to love. And for most women, their love grows for their spouse when they create a child together." I remembered feeling that way briefly for Douglas. It was hard to remember feeling any love for him at all. "But you will need to share in the process and the experience of it all. Believe me, Meg is scared too. Her body is going through some amazing and terrifying changes. It can be a lot to take in. She'll need all the support you can give her, which doesn't mean you can't be honest about your feelings. You *should* be honest; she'll know one way or the other."

"I don't want her to think I'm a douche bag, especially since I'm the one who knocked her up." Zander had grown, but he was still Zander.

"A little advice," I kept my tone light. "You might not want to say you knocked up your wife, especially around Meg."

His smirk returned.

"Meg knows you and obviously she knows this isn't easy for you. Talk to her. Make sure she doesn't have to second-guess your feelings for her. She doesn't deserve that. She's in a vulnerable state right now."

"I love Meg." He said it so firmly there could be no doubt he did.

"I know you do and she does too, but it wouldn't hurt to remind her more often for the next few months." What I wouldn't have given for that comfort.

He took several more deep breaths. "I don't want to screw this up, or my kid."

"You're going to screw up a time or two." I grinned. "Everybody does. Just make sure to acknowledge it and fix it. And don't forget, this is a fun time in life. You have a lot to look forward to."

He stood up, his confidence was back. "Thanks. I think I'm going to head home and take Meg to lunch."

"I think that's an excellent idea."

"Make sure to email me your top three picks for Nick before the end of the day."

"I will."

Zander left without another word.

I watched him go and had a weird thought of how proud I was of him. I had been wrong about him. I mean, not completely wrong. He was as arrogant as they come, and he had a heavy dose of love for himself, but he was a good man.

Was I wrong about Nick?

We were about to find out. I ran his profile against our database to see what women he was compatible with in our system. And I inhaled and exhaled...a lot.

Chapter Eight

FRIDAY WAS CONNECTION day, which usually meant we didn't see clients in the office, or anyone for that matter. Because we were intimately discussing people's lives, we wanted to be as discreet as possible at least to the outside world. Conversations inside the conference room sometimes bordered on inappropriate. You wouldn't believe some of the behaviors people displayed on their client dates. We had one client who did a nice table dance and removed half her clothing because her favorite song came on. As a sidenote, she had shown up a little tipsy. Another client clipped his fingernails at dinner. Yuck.

I didn't submit the aforementioned Angie-the-stripper as a possible choice for Nick. Though she was quite popular in our not-looking-for-anything-serious crowd. Skye and Jack played into my selection process for Nick, although, based solely on Nick's profile, Angie would have been a good choice for him. Instead I chose Nicole, the occupational therapist; Chanel, the loan officer; and Scarlett, the fitness trainer.

I typically didn't come to the connection meeting, except on rare occasions when my opinion was wanted. I attended the Monday morning meetings where relationship managers were paired with clients so I could report on the evaluations and note anything I thought they should look for on the client dates if I was concerned. We could reject any potential client at any stage. So Nick was adding even more to my plate besides the stress he'd caused me. To unwind last night, I watched *A Step Up*, the movie he had written and produced, paired with a glass of wine. I couldn't believe how witty and endearing that movie was. Maybe he wasn't the only writer. Maybe I should quit thinking about him.

That was going to be difficult for the time being.

Kenadie peeked her head in before I headed to the connection meeting; she looked harried.

"Everything all right?" I asked.

She blew a large amount of air out, making her bangs move. "Yes. It's just been a crazy morning. Momma found out that Meg is pregnant, so Jason and I have received twenty calls each asking why we aren't pregnant yet and giving us pointers. Lots of detailed pointers on how to make that happen." She shook her head as if chasing out the imagery. "Anyway, on top of that, Nick will be in later, so I've been prepping. We're doing a joint interview with Channel 15's lifestyle reporter."

"Here?" That came out as a desperate plea for it not to be true.

Enough to startle Kenadie. "Everything went okay with his client date, right? No more red flags?"

There weren't any more red flags. More like flags of confusion. But Zander was right, I wasn't seeing any sociopath behavior. If anything, I saw a side of him that made me think twice about my initial assessment. Despite him being rough around the edges, bordering on rude, I couldn't really report anything additional. I didn't want to give Kenadie more heartburn unless it was necessary.

"Besides our 'date' being a little unconventional with his dad and daughter there, no, I didn't see any additional reasons for us to be more concerned." Yet. I was still holding out judgment. "Though I didn't really get a chance to talk to him much," I confessed.

"You met his dad and daughter?" She obviously was clinging to the fact that I didn't raise any more red flags and skipped over the part that I didn't have any real one-on-one time with him.

I nodded. "They're both great." Nothing like him. That wasn't true, I think Jack had passed on the ability to charm women and those eyes. Eyes that made you dream of all the possibilities. Oh my gosh, I had to quit thinking things like that. Both men were on the no-fly list as far as I was concerned.

"Huh." She looked impressed. "I was told under no certain circumstances was I to ask about his family. His assistant said he likes to keep his private life just that, private."

"I can understand that, given his career."

"Well, good job, he obviously felt comfortable with you." Her phone buzzed, causing her to pause and roll her eyes once she looked at who was calling. "If Momma leaves me one more message about different positions we should try, I might change my number or move out of state. Jason's already afraid that Momma's been making pornographic movies on the side given her in-depth knowledge."

I busted out laughing. I highly doubted Nan, the epitome of Southern momma propriety, would be caught dead watching porn, much less making it. Not that porn was a laughing matter. I'd seen way too many people at the clinic trying to get over their addiction to it. It ruins more relationships than most people would think. The unrealistic expectations it gave people combined with the violence it perpetuated while lessening the ability to make real life intimate connections was lethal to a relationship.

"Good luck."

"Thanks," she sighed. "I'm going to need it. And a vacation. Momma did recommend that as a way to get pregnant. We haven't told her yet that we're waiting until we've been married a year to try. She and the Nanettes would probably be over here trying to chase some evil spirit out of me if we did." She walked away, ignoring her phone that was now constantly buzzing.

Meanwhile I was hoping the connection meeting either prevented me from having to see Nick or that it got over in enough time I could leave early. I could review all the new questionnaires at home. I should have asked Kenadie when he was coming in. I assumed it would be after the connection meeting. Kenadie wouldn't want Nick or a reporter in the office for that in case someone got a little loud in our meeting, aka Zander or his protégé Dante, who was a recent new hire. He was as loud and opinionated as Zander, arrogant too, as well as an excellent relationship manager.

With Zander at the helm during these meetings, the structure had changed—everything was digital now. No more printing out pictures of the clients we were matching. Zander had them all ready to go in a program he worked with Kenadie to create. Everything flashed up on a screen or we could pull it up on our tablets. It was another reason Zander had everyone send him our picks the day before.

I walked into the conference room to find Cara and Eva already there, sitting next to each other as always, deep in conversation. They had become more territorial since the new relationship managers had come on board. I had thought one or both would have left after the debacle with Meg. They both put their foots in their mouths when Eva decided that she wanted Zander. No one knew how deep Zander's and Meg's feelings had run for each other; I'm not sure even they did at first. But I guess getting paid to take men out on dates to fancy restaurants, while not the only job requirement, was a nice perk. It also came with a nice expense account. It was a cushy sort of job, but one that came with great responsibility and the requirement to be able to read people and situations.

Eva and Cara both looked my way when I entered.

"We are so jealous," Eva said. "We thought one of us would be Nicholas's relationship manager."

"How did you get so lucky?" Cara's tone intimated that it wasn't luck, but that I'd struck a deal with Kenadie or something.

If they only knew how much I didn't want the job. "Legally, it worked better for the company and him," was all I would say about it.

Both of their eyes widened. Not sure if they believed me or not.

Others started gathering in. The room was getting crowded. We had eight relationship managers now. Will and Andy had been there for a while, but our recent hires were Dante, Jade, Todd, and Leah. With the exception of Todd, everyone was in their late twenties and early thirties. Todd was in his forties. It was nice to have his perspective. And it was hard to find people his age to do this job.

Daphne, our receptionist and admin assistant, brought in lunch that consisted of sandwiches and fruit while Zander got the presentation on the seventy-inch screen at the head of the room. It was like a toy for Zander. Sometimes during lunch breaks you could catch people in here watching sports, especially when events like the Olympics were on.

The buzz around the table all centered around Nick. I focused on my food and tried to ignore it, until Jade asked, "So what was it like going out with him? I've been binge watching his show on Netflix. He's amazing."

I refrained from rolling my eyes at the sweet woman.

Zander gave me a smirk, knowing how I really felt about it all and knowing I couldn't voice my true feelings.

"It was..." how did I put it without lying? "It was unusual."

There was a collective let down around the room as if they had all wanted some salacious piece of news. It was like all their bodies said, "Aw."

Everyone was waiting for me to expound and give them one juicy morsel. Again, they were disappointed.

I was grateful when Zander said, "Let's get started. Since you are all so eager to hear about Nick Wells, we will start with him."

I smiled around the table, not sure why I was so nervous. Zander was right, it wasn't like I was setting two people up for the rest of their lives. Though I did worry about how the women might change their tunes if they got a shot at the celebrity. Fame and fortune did funny things to people.

Zander pulled up Nick's picture and the women in the room sighed. Oh, brother. Three womens' heads lined up beneath him, each with a short bio under their profile pictures and their compatibility ratings. Both Nicole and Chanel were forty-eight percent compatible and Scarlett was fifty. There were women who had higher compatibility rates, and typically we wanted them to be above fifty, but these three were who I deemed more stepmother material, in case it ever went that way. At least they were old enough to have given birth to Skye.

"Tell us about the women you've chosen for Nick and why." Zander turned the time over to me.

I faced the screen. "Each woman recently asked to have a new match in our not looking for anything serious group." It was before we announced Nick was using our services, so that played in their favor. "They're each successful and enjoy adventure. Nicole is a motorcycle enthusiast like Nick."

"Nicole and Nick? They would be Nic-Nick," Dante teased.

There was a smattering of laughter before I moved on.

"Scarlett has done some local plays and commercials, so they share an acting background, which could be good or bad."

"Why?" Zander asked.

"She might look at it as a way to get her foot into a bigger door."

Everyone nodded and said things like *hmmm* and *that's true.*

"Chanel and Nick have different political views, but she runs endurance races and I remember her being a lot of fun when I evaluated her. Plus she has a lot of self-confidence." And I didn't voice it, but I thought she would be a good role model for Skye.

"None of them have children and two are divorced, like him."

Nick stipulated that he didn't want to date anyone who had children, which was a major point against him in my book since he had a child. I could understand if he were childless.

"So who do you think would be the best fit?"

He deserves none of them. "Chanel has my vote."

Zander looked around at everyone else at the table, especially the guys who were the women's relationship managers. "Any objections or concerns?"

"They aren't as young as the women he typically dates," Eva threw out there.

"True, but he didn't specify an age." On his questionnaire, all he said was *as long as they look good on my arm.* Insert a huge eye roll from me when I read that.

"They look to have more class than the eye candy I've seen on his arm," Will chimed in.

"That's a bad thing?" I asked.

Will shrugged. "I just wonder if he wants someone a little more vampy."

"Yeah, did you see his ex-fiancée?" Dante said. "Yeow, baby, was she hot and young."

"And," Cara added, "there wasn't anyone with higher compatibility rates?"

"I took into consideration our client date," I said, trying not to squirm in my seat, seeing as it had never really happened.

"That must have been some date." Eva gave me a hard stare.

"What happened?" Cara was dying to get more information.

Feeling uncomfortable with where this was all going, I looked to Zander for support. I promised Jack I would pick well for Skye's sake, but I couldn't reveal that. I wasn't even sure I should mention his daughter since he tried to shield her.

Zander gave me a thoughtful glance and thought for a moment. "Let's go with Kate's gut. She's evaluated every one of our clients, and since Nick is a special circumstance, we need to make some allowances."

There was some disgruntled murmuring, but everyone knew not to argue with Zander, he always won.

I would thank him later.

"Todd, you're Chanel's relationship manager, correct?" Zander asked.

Todd nodded.

"She has to sign the NDA his lawyer provided before he, or most likely his personal assistant, will contact her."

Nick was adamant that he made the first move. Typically we gave each person the other's contact information.

Zander continued. "And she has to do it here in the office so we can verify it's her. It might be best if you send her a message now. Maybe she can come in later this afternoon and sign it."

"Just let me know when she's coming in, and I'll send her information to him," I addressed Todd.

"Don't you go through his personal assistant?" Eva asked in a condescending manner.

Why did she care one way or the other? It's not like it was some treat for me.

Zander intervened before I could answer. "Kate, you're free to go since you have other duties to attend to."

Bless him. I didn't want to be looking over questionnaires all weekend.

Before I could leave, Kenadie came in. She looked polished and pretty, ready for her interview in a smart looking navy dress and wearing her signature killer stilettos.

"I wanted to let you all know Channel 15 will be here around four to interview Nick and myself, so please beware and let's be professional. No fangirl moments please." She eyed Cara and Eva. "Sorry to interrupt." She flitted out as fast as she had come in.

I took that as my cue to make my exit. I hustled to my office, bent on getting out of there as fast as I could to avoid the office celebrity later this afternoon.

No such luck.

Chapter Nine

I MADE MY ESCAPE from the conference room only to be faced with *him*. What was he doing here so early? Where I used to love how open our loft style office was, I was lamenting it now. There was no ducking and hiding from him from where I stood. My office was too far away, and he had seen me.

Daphne, our receptionist, had just finished greeting him in a way too breathy I'll-love-you-forever tone when Nick's and my eyes locked.

He was dressed to steal hearts in a shirt and slacks that molded to him in a way that enhanced his broad shoulders and trim waistline. He knew he looked good by the way he swaggered my way wearing not quite a smile, but a look that said he was pleased. His eyes drifted over my tapered jeans and off-the-shoulder blouse—it was casual in the office on Fridays since we didn't see clients.

I felt self-conscious before I reminded myself that I had no reason to feel that way. I looked fine enough for the office and I wasn't dressing to impress him. I didn't even want to impress him.

"Kate." He never greeted people with simple words like *hello*.

"Hello, Nick." I walked toward my office hoping that was all he had to say to me.

Nope. He followed.

"Can I help you with something?" I asked, trying to make it to the safety of my office.

"I have no doubt you could."

What did he mean by that? I stopped to face him. I shouldn't have. His eyes drew me in like one of those cobras that could put you in a trance before they poisoned you.

He edged closer to me, reeling me in. "Why do I feel like I've met you before this week?"

His question shook me out of my stupor. I had to be more careful around him. "Where would we have met?" I responded with a question of my own, knowing I couldn't own the truth, but not wanting to lie. The woman he met fourteen years ago no longer existed, even if I missed her occasionally.

He inched closer. His scent filled me. I held my breath while he studied me.

His eyes went from searching to frustrated. "Have you ever been to LA?"

I shook my head. "Not yet."

"Yet?"

"I have a mental health professionals' conference there next month." I was looking forward to it. I was extending my visit and planned on doing some sightseeing. And after this new assignment, I was going to need the vacation.

His stare was still trying to place me.

Did he really remember me? No matter. I headed back toward my office. "Good luck with your interview."

"I don't need it."

I couldn't hide the eye roll. It naturally appeared after such a cocky statement.

He arched the one eyebrow. "This isn't something new for me," he defended himself.

"Right. Well, then have a good weekend." I darted into my office.

He didn't get the social cue that I didn't want to continue our conversation and invited himself in. "Speaking of the weekend, I'm going to need you to go on that client date with me tomorrow night."

I held on to my desk for support. "I don't think a client date is necessary." Panic interspersed every word. "I've already chosen your first connection. I'm just waiting to get word that she's coming in to sign your NDA. You can take *her* out," I stumbled over my words.

A pressed-lip smile danced on his face as he approached my desk. "I'm going to pass."

"You haven't seen her yet."

"This event calls for someone... I can trust. Just for this weekend."

I could feel the crease between my brows increase exponentially with that confusing statement. "You don't even know me."

"I have a sense about these things. Besides, I don't know the other woman at all, and this is important to me."

"I'll show her to you and you'll see what a catch she is." I was desperate to convince him.

His hands pressed against my desk while he leaned over it, getting too close to me. "What are you so afraid of?"

"I'm not afraid," my voice shook. "But really, you should take Chanel."

"What if I—"

Thankfully, Kenadie interrupted us. "Oh, good you're here." She stood at my door. "Did Kate tell you who she paired you with?" Kenadie's eyes shone with excitement. She loved seeing a good match made.

Nick stood up straight. "We were just discussing her." He gave me a gratified look. "We can pick up where we left off after the interview."

My shoulders fell before I dropped into my chair. With Kenadie watching I couldn't refuse. "Sounds good." I hoped he heard the implied *I loathe you right now* in there.

By the look of his smirk he heard it loud and clear.

So much for me leaving early.

He and Kenadie walked off together. Kenadie was chirping happily about some of her thoughts regarding the interview. I hoped he didn't disappoint her.

Meanwhile, I was reaching for the peppermint oil and rubbing it into my temples. I was going to my parents' tomorrow, so my dad could adjust me and my mom could massage away the knots in my back caused by Nick, if they hadn't killed each other yet. More than likely I would have additional knots when I left because my visit would turn into a marriage counseling session. I rubbed more oil into my temples.

I sent a desperate plea disguised as a follow-up email to Todd asking him to let me know as soon as Chanel could come in and sign that stupid NDA since Nick was asking about her. So I stretched the truth a tad. I was banking on Chanel running in here waving a pen, ready to sign her life away to have the chance to date the ex-superstar. There was no way I was going on a date with him tomorrow, even a platonic client one. And what was this event that was so important to him? He had to have flocks of women willing to go with him on a moment's notice, even if Chanel happened to not be available. Really, she would be better company for him than me.

I did my best to focus on the mass influx of questionnaires we had received this past week knowing it would only get worse from here, especially once the interview Kenadie and Nick were doing today aired, not to mention the commercial he was doing. Kenadie may need to hire another psychologist if this kept up, or that raise I was getting better make up for the new chaos in my life. I wondered how long his contract was with us. His profile didn't say and when I tried to access it, the information was blocked.

I was so distracted, I only got through two questionnaires in an hour and a half. Before I knew it, I heard the rumblings of a camera crew and unfamiliar voices in the office. I walked over to my door so I could close it to drown out the sound, but before I did, my curiosity got the better of me. I peeked out to see what was going on. They were staging some chairs in front of the wall of bliss where a picture of each engaged and married couple we had matched hung. It was Kenadie's pride and joy.

I observed Nick perusing the wall with interest. That was, before he turned around and caught me staring at him as if he knew I was watching. What gives? Even from the distance, I could tell how gratified he was that he found me paying attention to him. I slipped back into my office and shut my door. I took a deep breath. And another.

I'd barely sat back down when there was a knock on my door. Kenadie popped her head in before I could acknowledge it.

"Hey, Nick thought it would be a good idea if you came out to watch the interview since you're his relationship manager."

I blinked a million times hoping I heard her wrong. I was ready to give her an excuse to why I couldn't, but she didn't give me the chance.

"I think it would be nice too. It would show that we're a team here."

How was that going to be conveyed? I had a sneaking suspicion he was only doing it because he knew it would get under my skin, and that would amuse him. Which, I might add, was a sign of a narcissist.

I reached for the ibuprofen in my top desk drawer. "I'll be right there." I couldn't say no to her. She was lit up from the inside and it obviously meant a lot to her.

She flashed me a huge smile before leaving me to try and remedy my headache. I had a feeling it wasn't going anywhere. Along with the two pills I popped, I took several sips of water, delaying walking out there. I resigned myself to my fate and headed to the crowd gathering near where the interview was going to happen. Additional lighting had been brought in, and there were a few people from the news station prepping. Jason, Kenadie's husband, was there looking on with pride. It was sweet of him to come and support his wife. Zander stood next to him, still looking unsure about his current circumstances, but doing his best not to show it.

The women in our office were in herd mentality and clustered together. They followed every move Nick made, from the way he ran his fingers through his thick, styled hair to the way he flirted with the lifestyle reporter, Dana Zimmerman. I noted how he was like two different people when the spotlight came on. He was all ease and please while talking to Dana. Here was an idea, he could take *her* to his "event" if Chanel wasn't available. Dana certainly looked interested.

Which reminded me. I made my way over to Todd, who was the only other person in this office showing any signs that he was still sane. He was more interested in his phone than the hullabaloo.

I sidled up near him. "Have you heard back from Chanel?"

Todd smiled up from his phone. "I was just checking my email. Not yet."

I smiled back to hide my disappointment. It was almost 4:00 p.m. and we closed at 5:00. I would volunteer to stay late if I had to. "Thanks."

Todd went back to his phone, leaving me on the edge of all the action to watch the man causing me more consternation than I'd had in a long time. Nick glanced my way for a split second while talking to the reporter. Before I knew it, though, he was making his way to me through his admirers.

Every eye in the office took notice.

I stood tall, doing my best to act unaffected and professional about it. "Mr. Wells."

He narrowed his eyes. "Should I start calling you Dr. Morgan now?"

A small smile escaped. Dang him. "No."

He took that as invitation to stand too close. "In that case, I spoke to Kenadie about my dilemma tomorrow night during our meeting."

I leaned away with an air of skepticism. "Dilemma?"

"I'm in need of a date for the charity event I'm attending." He kept his voice low.

I tucked some hair behind my ear. "I'm still waiting to hear back from Chanel." My eyes drifted toward Dana Zimmerman applying some taupe lipstick to her luscious lips. She looked like an exotic beauty with dark hair and skin. She was perfect for a charity event. "You could ask the reporter."

"Now how would that look since I'm using Binary Search?"

He had a point, but... I had one too. "Client dates don't include doing charity events."

"They do now." His blue eyes electrified with his declaration.

My stomach dropped as well as swirled with feelings reminiscent of my twenty-year-old self. His eyes had an effect on me that I didn't wish to acknowledge.

I swallowed. "What do you mean? I just talked to Kenadie. She didn't mention me going." I could barely speak above a whisper.

His head tilted forward in a seductive manner. "I wanted to be the one to give you the good news."

I had no words.

"Kenadie is excited to not only make a sizable donation, but to have a representative at the Fallen Officers Charity Gala supporting the spouses and children they left behind."

"Sounds like a worthy cause," was all I could think of to say that would be appropriate given the audience nearby.

"One that's close to my heart." It was the sincerest thing I had ever heard him say.

I wasn't ready to give in. "I really think Chanel—"

"Sorry to interrupt," Todd was holding up his phone. "Chanel emailed and she wants her brother who's a lawyer to look over the NDA before she signs it." Todd gave Nick an apologetic smile. "Don't get me wrong, she's ecstatic, but she's nervous about signing an NDA."

"Understandable," Nick responded. "Tell her to take her time."

Todd nodded and walked off, leaving me with nothing left to cling to.

Nick gave me a real smile and it was heart stopping.

I had to turn from it. I caught Kenadie staring at us, and she gave me two thumbs up. This was all a great business opportunity for her and I'm sure she thought this was playing into the whole I needed to spend more time with him to fix him angle, which I understood, but...

I looked back to Nick. "I may be polishing my resume after this."

He came dangerously close and whispered in my ear, "I wouldn't be too sure. You haven't seen me in a tux yet."

Oh, I had.

That was part of the problem.

Chapter Ten

I SAT CURLED UP on my couch ripping cherries off the stems and spit-ting the seeds into a bowl after I masticated the delicious fruit. It was satisfying after the day I'd had. And it helped me keep my emo-tions under control while I watched Nick's interview during the late news. I was irritated that they hardly kept a thing Kenadie had said about our company in it. It was obvious that Dana would have liked to pet Nick while she hung on his every word. But come on, Kenadie was a brilliant woman who had written some amazing software. Not only that, but she was successful. That was all skipped over so that Nick was the shining star of the entire thing.

Dana asked him questions like, "So, Nick, tell us what qualities you look for in your ideal woman?" She might as well have asked *do I fit into that category?*

He responded, "It's hard to define, as that changes over time and circumstances." How PC of him. He sounded like a politician who would not be getting my vote.

After that, Dana made a huge deal about the gala tomorrow night since she would be in attendance too, covering it for Channel 15. Oh joy. Another thing I didn't like was that she made it all about her instead of what that event supported.

The only decent thing to come out of the interview was when she asked Nick why out of all the matchmaking services available he chose Binary Search. I will admit to liking his response: "After doing my homework, I liked the personalized attention Binary Search gives their clients, as well as the intuitive software that is used in the process. No other service does what they do."

I clicked off the TV and threw the remote next to me. I leaned my head back against my chenille tweed couch and sighed. I couldn't believe I had to endure more of that man over my weekend. The arrogant man who offered to have his assistant in LA call me for my measurements so he could have a gown delivered to me. What? Was that a thing? I declined. I could pick out my own clothes, thank you very much. And if he thought that would impress me, he was going to be disappointed. All that said to me was he was only thinking about himself. That the way I looked reflected on him. If I wasn't representing Binary Search and I had enough guts to show up in something outlandish, I would contemplate it for the sake of knocking him down a notch or two. He'd probably just have someone escort me out.

I remembered Douglas picking out my clothes for me whenever I attended his lectures. At first, I thought it was sweet. He did it under the guise of buying me a present. For too long I was so taken by the older, debonair visiting professor on the lecture circuit for ancient Egyptian studies that I fell for everything he said or did. He only wanted me to look a certain part. I needed to look worthy to be his girlfriend and then his wife. He saw someone he could mold, and he was right. I gave him so much power and he abused it. Never again could I allow that to happen. It was part of the reason I sat at home alone on a Friday night.

I knew I needed to find a happy medium, someone I could trust enough to be vulnerable around, knowing that they wouldn't be perfect. They would hurt me, and I them. It was inevitable and human. But I wanted—needed—to do all I could to make sure they were worthy of the risk and that they would take every care not to hurt me. I would do the same for them. So I had my rules in place and a list of warning signs. Things I wished I would have had ten years ago. My parents said I was young and I should cut myself some slack. After all, they fell for Douglas's intellectual and charming persona that he knew how and when to portray. It wasn't all that comforting. I was still embarrassed by it. Not by my parents. No. My gullibility.

Lingering embarrassment meant I had never worn the beautiful black gown in my closet. I bought it for a weekend reunion last year in New York with some of my girlfriends from graduate school. The women who were there when I found out my "husband" was a bigamist, making him a felon, and I was pregnant with his child. All this before my twenty-fifth birthday. It was a titillating tale that had gotten around the university. Right in the middle of it all, I miscarried. My girlfriends were fantastic, supportive women, even if a couple made comments like *at least you won't be tied to him forever now.* It was true, but I wanted my baby. The sound of my baby's heartbeat was the most beautiful sound in the world. It carried me through some of my darkest days and reminded me there were good things to come. That something beautiful would come out of the ugly. Its absence was deafening and devastating.

Like a coward, I couldn't face them last year. I didn't want Douglas to come up in conversation. And they were all married now, with at least one child. Meanwhile, I helped people get what I wanted. I was happy to help, truly I was. If only I could help myself.

At least I knew better than to be taken in by Nick Wells, even if sometimes my body forgot. We can't help who we are attracted to, but we can control our behaviors. Believe me, I planned on keeping a tight rein on my natural desires for him. It was all biology. And though some small part of the Nicholas Wells fangirl still resided deep inside me, it didn't mean I couldn't overcome it or think rationally when I saw him in a tux tomorrow night. I wouldn't be the woman who used to watch every awards show he was part of back in the day so I could drool over him.

I patted my copy of *The Science of Why Good Girls Love Bad Boys* that was tucked up next to me. I had been refreshing my memory earlier of what it was that drew women to men like Nick and why we shouldn't engage with them. I had to remind myself to separate attraction from what I really desired. I wanted someone who was confident, but not arrogant. And we as women seemed to be attracted to this ride-off-into-the-sunset sort of guy. I was guilty of this too. But what we truly wanted was someone who would be there to watch each sunset with us. To top it off, I had to be extra careful this time of the month since I was ovulating. My ovaries would lie to me in a heartbeat about Nick and make me think the sexy cad would be an amazing dad and partner. Well...he did appear to be an amazing father already.

That was an aspect of him I couldn't put my finger on.

That was okay—he had so many other things going against him in my rule book, it didn't matter. And it's not like he wanted anything to do with me other than amusing himself. I was only making sure I didn't do anything I would regret or be ashamed of, like ogling him in his tux.

I needed sleep and a pair of dark shades, you know, just in case my eyes wandered.

Though it was a muggy July morning, I walked the mile to my parents' place. Walking soothed me, and I needed all the help I could get today. I took deep, cleansing breaths while I admired all the large trees fit to burst with greenery and the variety of flowers in each yard. My favorite were the hydrangeas. Several people were out mowing their lawns, trying to beat the heat of the day. Still, sweat could be seen pouring off them. I too was a little sticky, even with only running shorts and a tank top on. It was summertime in Georgia and I loved it. I'd known after I graduated that I would never live in cold weather again. I was a warm weather girl. Besides, I loved this community. There was something safe and secure about it.

Before I knew it, I was in front of my parents' two-story brick home with plantation shutters. We moved there when I was twelve. It looked the same, except the trees were taller and the climbing roses my mom had planted back in her horticultural experiment days were overtaking a good portion of the front of the house. Pink blooms could be seen all over. Dad wasn't all that thrilled with the mainte-nance of it all, but Mom insisted they stay. Something about them being a moderator of emotional health.

I skipped up the brick path and only tapped on the door before I walked right in. "Mom, Dad," I called out into the two-story foyer while I shook my head at all the plastic tarps covering the furniture and the lingering smell of sawdust. I didn't even want to know what Dad was up to now.

Mom came walking down the large staircase to the right of the entryway, dressed in a yellow muumuu with her spiky pewter hair sticking up like a crown surrounded by a bright cloth headband. She grimaced at the mess Dad had made before acknowledging me.

"There's my Katie." My parents were the only people who called me Katie. Her arms were open wide, making her look like a muumuu tent.

I move forward to hug her as soon as she finished descending the steps.

Instead of hugging me, she took a minute to look over me. "Your auras are all over the place this morning."

Oh no. Here we go.

"You have some muddy orange right about here." She was pointing to the thin air around me. "You must be worried." She moved her hands all over my body without touching me. "And red, lots of it, and there is some of your usual pink in there." A smile played on her well-preserved face. I hoped I inherited those genes. "You're obviously ovulating and…attraction is rolling off you like a freight train. Care to tell your mother what that's all about?"

I hugged her before she could say anything else. "Hi, Mom."

She patted my back. "You don't want to talk about it."

I gave her one more good squeeze. "There's nothing to discuss."

"Honey, you can't fool your mom; you have some major sexual tension vibes coming off you."

I backed away and waved her off. No sexual tension here. Nope, nada, zilch.

Dad could be heard walking in from the garage. "Stella, do you know what happened to my drill?"

Mom rolled her eyes before he came into view. "Glenn, our daughter's here." She didn't answer his question. Why did I think she had something to do with that missing drill?

My once put together, wear a dress shirt and dress pants every day to his chiropractic clinic dad, was now wearing overalls, and his gray hair was about a month past a haircut. He'd also gained a little weight around his midsection. But his smile for me was as big and bright as it always was. Though his brown eyes told another story. They were subdued. "There's my girl."

"Hey, Dad." I met him in the hall that led to the kitchen and hugged him as well.

"You're tense," he remarked.

"It's sexual tension," Mom said like it was a fact.

Dad pulled away and I wasn't sure if he thought that was good news. On one hand he looked hopeful, on the other he looked like most dads who didn't want to think of their daughters in that sort of way. I knew both my parents worried I would never find anyone again.

"I'm not seeing anyone," I let them down.

Or maybe not. Mom's face lit up like she remembered something. "We saw on the news last night that Nicholas Wells is using Binary Search. Why didn't you tell us?"

I walked back toward the kitchen to get a drink of water. "I'm not allowed to discuss our clients. Except...well..."

"Well?" Mom was salivating. "Does he know you slept with a poster of him above your bed in college?"

I whipped my head around. "No. And he never will." I had been trying to forget about the shirtless poster of him leaning against a red Ferrari. Great, now I was going to have that image in my head.

"Honey, don't whip your head around like that. It's not good for you." Dad was ever the chiropractor. I had him to thank for my good posture.

Before I could reach for a glass in the cupboard near the faucet, Mom was already getting me one. "Don't drink the tap water. I made some strawberry, cucumber, lime, and mint-infused water. It will help with your tension."

"Do you still have a crush on him?" Dad asked.

"Of course not." I was too old for crushes. "He's well...he's just..." I suppose I shouldn't bad mouth him. It was probably against the NDA I'd signed.

"He's what?" Mom handed me a colorful ice-cold glass of water.

"Thank you." I took the glass and downed half of it.

Mom studied me. "What are you not telling us?"

I set my glass on the island, inhaled, then let it out in a pathetic exhale. "I have to attend some charity event with him tonight."

Mom clapped her hands together and brought them up to her face like this was a dream come true for her. "You have a date with him? This explains your aura."

I shook my head with vigor. "Mom, I can't date our clients. I'm going as a representative for Binary Search. Besides, even if I could, I would never date him."

Her hands fell, along with a long sigh. "Which of your rules does he break?"

"All of them." Well, almost all of them, but that didn't need to be articulated.

A look passed between my parents. It was like I united them in worry. I suppose I should be happy that at least they weren't bickering.

Mom rubbed the gemstone chrysocolla that hung around her neck and closed her eyes. She believed chrysocolla gave her wisdom.

Dad held onto the nearest counter, bracing himself for what Mom would say. He wasn't a big believer in the healing powers of crystals and gemstones. Neither was I. And Mom probably wouldn't be in a few months, but you never knew. This particular "hobby" had stuck around for the last couple of years.

I was good with it until she held the gemstone between us. "Here, honey, rub it with me and breathe in and out slowly."

I caught my dad's amused expression. "Let her be, Stella," he jumped in on my behalf.

Mom didn't take kindly to it. In slow motion she turned around, no doubt giving him a stare to be afraid of. "I'm only trying to help her gain wisdom and visualize how a life living outside the rules would bring her happiness and how Nicholas Wells may play a part."

I stepped back, stunned. "What does he have to do with anything?"

She did the air-hand-wave-thing again all over my body. "His presence is flooding your aura like never before. I really need to see you two together. Do you think he could swing by here with you tonight before the charity event?"

What in the world was she talking about? "No, Mom. For one, I'm meeting him there." Which, for some reason, seemed to disgruntle him. He'd offered to pick me up after the whole I'll have a gown sent to you, but I declined. Unfortunately, he pushed the issue, forcing me to tell him that I only allowed a man to pick me up if we'd had two successful dates. Talk about a strange stare. No doubt he thought I was odd.

"Did you invoke rule ten on him?" Mom had numbered my rules.

I reached for her hands and held them. "I. Can't. Date. Him." I needed to say each word, slowly and succinctly. "Actually, it's my job to pick his dates."

Both my parents looked confused.

"I can't really go into detail, but I'm his relationship manager."

Mom squeezed my hands. "All I know is something is off, but...right with you. Almost as if your subconscious has identified your soulmate."

I dropped her hands. "I don't believe in soulmates." You make your soulmate, you don't find them. To think otherwise was dangerous and caused more relationship problems than it helped.

"People used to believe the earth was flat. We can't always be right. Not even you," Mom quipped.

Believe me, I knew how wrong I could be.

Chapter Eleven

I PULLED UP TO the hotel that only had valet behind a line of cars in downtown Atlanta. I kept repeating in my head there was nothing to be nervous about. This was a business meeting of sorts, an obligation, really. Nothing more, nothing less. Except I had never worn a dress like this for a business meeting. I looked down at the one shoulder, A-line dress that hugged and squeezed every curve I owned. The slit was a little too much. What was I thinking when I bought this? I was thinking of having a fun weekend with girlfriends and taking in a Broadway show or two, maybe meeting someone by chance in New York. But I'd chickened out. I wanted to do the same right now.

Too late.

A valet met me at my door and opened it. "Good evening, ma'am." He held out his hand to help me out of my car.

I hesitated for half a second before I took it. I was grateful for it, though. Tight, long dresses were not easy to maneuver in. Once out and upright, I took my valet ticket and headed for the unknown. I had no idea what to expect. Nick said it was a casino night, but that meant nothing to me.

He said he would meet me in the lobby at 6:30. I was five minutes early, so I didn't expect to see him when I came in through the revolving doors, but there he stood.

Dashing. He was dashing. I wanted to dash away. It helped that before he saw me he was accosted by a couple of women in dresses that had cutouts...everywhere. While they fawned all over him, I took a minute to take in the grandeur of the lobby's crystal chandelier and the woman playing a lovely tune on the grand piano. Now I knew why they charged five hundred dollars or more a night for a room here. Opulence dripped on everything from the fine furniture to the marble floors.

Several couples mingled in the lobby and the bar area, dressed to the nines. There were signs directing people to the ballroom for the gala. Many were headed that way. I found myself wanting to melt into the crowd, not to be seen. Not to be here with the guest of honor and keynote speaker. Oh, yeah, he threw in that tidbit yesterday. I wanted to have more fun in my life, but not like this. I liked a quiet, unassuming life. I was thinking more along the lines of trying new restaurants and going to a show or two. This felt more like a Hollywood thing. Not my style at all.

My thoughts were interrupted by a tap on my shoulder.

I turned to come face-to-face with a handsome, dark-haired gentleman who looked to be around my age wearing an alluring smile. "You look lost," he said.

That was embarrassing. I must have gotten too lost in my head. "Just taking in the sights."

"Are you going to the Fallen Officer's gala?"

I nodded.

"I would be happy to escort you."

I didn't know what to say. It had been a while.

"I should probably introduce myself first." He held out his hand. "I'm—"

"Kate."

A shiver went through me. Why did my name on his lips do that to me?

My new almost-acquaintance and I turned toward the voice and the man it belonged to, who now stood by my side wearing a look of contempt. It went well with his tux. I think anything would look good with it, with him. That didn't mean I was attracted to him, it was only the truth. It was plain to see how beautiful the man was.

"Hello, Nick." I looked between the two men who were intent at staring at each other. "This is…" I smiled at the man who suddenly looked disappointed.

"Trent," he answered while rescinding his hand.

"Trent, it's nice to meet you. This is Nick Wells."

"Her date," Nick added in his brusque fashion.

I wanted to disagree with him, but did it really matter now? Trent was sufficiently scared off. I did laugh, though, when he walked off muttering, "What in the hell kind of name was Talon Fox?"

Nick raised his eyebrow at my giggle.

"You have to admit that was funny."

He wasn't admitting a thing. His eyes were busy perusing me from the French roll twist in my hair all the way down to my black heels.

I held my breath while his eyes lingered.

For some reason, I expected a compliment. Maybe because that's what a gentleman would do. I should have known better. All he said was, "So you did have a dress."

I held my shoulders back, stiff. "Glad we've cleared that up." I headed toward the ballroom. "And by the way, you shouldn't tell people I'm your date. It will give them the wrong impression."

He had no problem keeping pace with me with his long legs and me in ridiculously high heels that had me thinking about every step I took. It didn't help that it felt like all eyes were on us, or should I say Nick. The attention made my skin crawl.

Nick noticed the attention too. "Slow down," he said low. He held his arm out. "You *are* my date, Kate."

I put on the brakes, unsure of how to behave. His eyes implored me to take his arm. I shifted my handbag to my left hand, thinking about it.

He leaned in carefully. "I don't bite...until the end of the night."

I think he was telling the truth. My eyes widened while my pulse raced.

He was impatient and reached for my hand.

No. That was too intimate. I didn't hold hands with anyone unless I wanted to pursue a relationship with them. Rule seven, my mom would call it. Holding hands in some ways meant more to me than kissing. It was one of those tender affections I didn't take lightly. I took his arm.

I detected a hint of annoyance at my rebuff, but he quickly recovered. He had to keep up appearances. I could never live a life like his.

"Was that so hard?" he whispered out of the side of his mouth.

"You have no idea." Especially when my hand finally got the message to my brain that we were touching. And it felt...it felt like the first time he touched me at the bookstore. Unbidden passion filled me that I'd never experienced except for that day. No. No. No. So his arm was solid and warm and when he brought his other hand over to rest it on top of my hand clutching his arm, feelings like I was reading that torrid love letter we'd never written, but apparently existed between us, rippled through me.

It meant nothing. I was ovulating and I would admit I was attracted to him physically.

I wanted to tell him to remove his hand that was now caressing mine ever so gently, but people were gaping at him and I didn't want to do anything to disgrace Binary Search. But he really needed to stop doing that. It wasn't fair to me. I reminded myself to be rational. I didn't want the man who held me exactly like I wished to be held, as if he was proud I was on his arm. It had to be an act. He was playing a part and I was only the supporting actress.

In real life, this man and I were completely incompatible. At work we called it statistically improbable. And he went against all my rules, except two. He was a good father and he made my spine shiver. That last one was a weird rule, I know. Nick was to blame for it. He would never know that, but I'd never forgotten how he'd made me feel outside the bookstore. I never wanted to because I wanted to feel that way again. Maybe it was silly, but there was something significant about it. Like this was how a man should be able to reach you. With a touch so deep that it reaches your spine, the very thing that controls most of your senses.

The same kind of touch I was feeling now.

I needed it. But not with Nick.

"Relax," Nick whispered.

I realized I had an iron grip on his arm. I loosened my hold on him. "I don't like being the center of attention," I admitted.

"Why? You look good on my arm."

His comment brought me back to where I needed to be. A good reminder of why he was the wrong kind of man for me, or anyone for that matter. "It's all about you, right?"

He turned his head toward me and I was hit with his eyes that said he didn't appreciate my last comment. "I was trying—"

"Nick, Nick, Nick," a familiar voice called his name, interrupting his thought.

A brief flash of annoyance zipped through his eyes before he reluctantly turned from me and put on his Hollywood charm. "Dana."

Dana wrapped her tentacles around him and suctioned him away from me. "Nick, you look amazing."

She did too. She was wearing a silver dress that shimmered and revealed that her bust was much bigger than mine. Her flawless skin glowed. She completely ignored me.

Nick kissed her cheek. "I could say the same to you."

So he did know how to compliment a woman. I suppose it was just me he wouldn't compliment. I begged myself not to begin comparing myself to the exotic looking beauty with a camera crew trailing behind her. I didn't even care what Nick thought of me.

I melted into the background and watched as more reporters clamored for his attention, asking for interviews and about his involvement with the charity. I should have felt relieved not to be in his company, but feelings of discontent began to surface. Hadn't he invited me to come? Basically coerced me by getting Kenadie involved?

Before my ire got worked up, I took control of the situation. I headed for the ballroom by myself. Nick obviously didn't need my help and had forgotten about me. I shouldn't have expected anything different.

The ballroom looked like Las Vegas had exploded in it. Neon colors flashed in all directions. Laughter and loud music filled my ears. There was everything from blackjack tables to craps and roulette. The room was already filling up. It was nice to see so many police officers there in uniform. Too bad I didn't date cops. Maybe I could find Trent. I headed to the check in table, not sure what else to do. Everyone else had tickets in their hands. Was I supposed to have a ticket? Could I purchase one? Maybe this wouldn't be a long night after all. I mean, if I couldn't get in, I couldn't get in. And I certainly wasn't going to go find Nick or drop his name. I'm sure if I said I was here with Nicholas Wells they would laugh at me and call security.

With some trepidation, I approached the front of the line. The sweet looking woman asked, "Do you have a ticket, dear?"

"You see, I'm here on behalf of the company I work for, Binary Search. I didn't know I was supposed to have a ticket."

She gave me a warm smile. "That's okay. What's your name? Let's see if you're on our VIP list."

There was no way I was on that list, but I gave her my name anyway. It wasn't going to hurt my feelings if I had to go home. "Kate Morgan."

She scanned her list. "There you are."

Bummer.

She handed me a golden ticket. "If you take this to that table over there," she pointed behind me, "they'll give you your chips."

"Chips?"

"You can use them to play any of the games. It's all for fun, though. No real value to them."

"Oh." I was so out of my element. "Thank you."

I looked around the room as I made it to the other table. It dawned on me I was in a room full of all the vices that many of my patients over the last few years had come to me seeking help for— gambling, alcohol, and sex. Not like anyone was having sex there. At least not that I could see, but believe me, I saw a whole lot of hooking up and sexually charged advances going on, thanks to alcohol, I'm sure. It's why I never drank in these kinds of settings. Yes, it was a rule. I believe that was nineteen according to Mom.

Once I got my bag of chips, I had no idea where to begin even if I wanted to. Gambling, even for fun, wasn't really my thing. And I admit to scanning the room for Nick. A very small part of me thought perhaps he would come looking for me. I found him across the room near the stage talking to none other than the governor of Georgia and the mayor of Atlanta. Even from a distance I could see it was a schmooze fest. A ridiculous number of pictures were being snapped. No one wanted to miss their photo op.

With nothing better to do, well, at least nothing better to do there, I headed for one of the blackjack tables with an empty seat at the end. Seven of us sat around the semi-circle table with the dealer in the middle. All the dealers were wearing white shirts with black bowties. It was all so official. The dealer at our table was a middle-aged gentle-man with a mischievous twinkle in his brown eyes. He was flirty with the women and full of banter with the men. He sure handled cards like a pro. He dealt them faster than you could blink. I played a few rounds and even hit blackjack once. It was fun, but not something I wished to do all night.

Once again, I looked for Nick. Surprisingly, he appeared to be looking for me from where he was near the bar area. It looked like he was going to make his way over to me, but he was stopped by a woman who I believed was the chief of police.

I headed for the appetizers. Not that I could eat a lot in this dress, but I had nothing better to do. It was worth the walk over for the choc-olate velvet mousse shooters. I may have eaten two, I was so bored. I gave up looking for Nick, but it didn't matter; the attention was all on him as he walked up to the stage flanked with all the very important people in the room.

The music ceased playing and the noise level dropped to a low hum. The governor was first to speak. It was flowery in true political style, but heartfelt when he spoke about the reason we were there for the night. The mayor's speech was basically the same, but more directed toward those on the force in Atlanta. The police chief was more intimate, even getting teary eyed when she spoke of the fallen officers she had personally known and how each day the men and women in blue put it all on the line. She spoke of the sacrifices their families made. She had me tearing up. Then it was my *date's* turn.

More camera's flashed for him than anyone. He dazzled up there under the bright lights. His smile was the perfect blend of brooding and I'm-honored-to-be-here. The ladies in the audience were eating it up. The number of selfies being taken with him in the background was embarrassing.

"I'm honored to be here tonight," he began. "I was raised in a military home and taught from a young age to respect and honor those who serve not only abroad, but here at home, whether it be in the military or in law enforcement. It was a great privilege to portray an officer, a hero. I was able to go through the police academy right here as I prepared to take on that role."

I remembered reading about that long ago. At the time, I thought it was the most amazing thing. It solidified my unrealistic love affair with him.

"Those men and women became true friends. The instructors and those on the force here taught me invaluable lessons about integrity, honor, and bravery. I've lost two of those friends in the line of duty." He choked up so much he had to pause.

That caught me off guard. By the wave of silence in the crowd, I would say it had the same effect on everyone. In the silence, a thought popped in my head. He was an actor. No. This seemed real. I hoped it was. But I'd been fooled before.

"Tonight their wives are here. Heather and Janelle, we owe you and your children a debt of gratitude for your sacrifice that can never be repaid. You, and others like you, are why we are here. Please, ladies and gentlemen, think of these families without fathers and mothers, husbands and wives. Think of them when you go to bed tonight safe in your homes. Think of them when you kiss your children good night, knowing somewhere there is a child who no longer has a mom or dad to tuck them in. Especially think of them tonight when you are opening your pocketbooks. Think of the opportunity you have to make a difference in their lives."

The names of the women he mentioned floated around in my head. I recalled the news reports about their husbands' deaths. They were partners and best friends. They died responding to a domestic issue. I had no idea he knew them. Regardless, he had me ready to pull out my checkbook.

"I thank you on behalf of myself and all the organizers for your generous contributions already, but we can do more. These families deserve the best we can give them. It is the least we can do for their ultimate sacrifice."

There was some chatter around. "Isn't he so wonderful? I heard he actually visits some of the families and has paid for several college tuitions."

I eavesdropped the best I could.

"And he's gorgeous to boot."

"He's using that techno dating service. I'm thinking of joining. I would love to get a piece of that."

That concluded my eavesdropping session.

Nick's speech ended with thunderous applause. I even found myself clapping for the perplexing man. How could a man do so much good, but be so egocentric? I found myself wanting to dissect him piece by piece and figure out who he really was. See what made him tick.

I thought maybe I would get a little insight once we had a moment to talk. Without even thinking I made my way through the crowd toward him. The festivities in the room had begun again and he wasn't everyone's focus, though many clamored for his attention. I had a feeling the first women who hugged him were Heather and Janelle. Such tenderness accompanied the embraces. Each woman wiped her eyes. There was laughter too. It was beautiful.

I stood back and let everyone get their turn, thinking I would get mine too. After all, he asked me—okay he coerced me, but still, I was his guest.

I waited and waited and waited. My feet ached, I waited so long. Flashbacks of waiting for Douglas hit me with force. Even after we married, I wasn't the first person he came out to greet after his brilliant lectures. I was the last. Always the last. Though I held no place of affection in Nick's heart—one could even say I never did in Douglas's—I knew one thing, and that was I didn't have to be last ever again. At the very least, I didn't have to forget myself.

I turned and headed for the exit, never looking back.

Tonight, Kate remembered herself.

Chapter Twelve

J AMES, PLAY ME some mood music," I called out to my hands-free speaker as soon as I kicked off my shoes in the living room. I'd named him James because I'd always thought the name was sexy, kind of like Nicholas, but I didn't need any more Nicholases in my life. I didn't need the one I left at the event. Not like he noticed or cared. I sighed and pulled out my phone. I supposed the polite thing to do would be to at least tell him I left, even though he was anything but polite to me.

I sank into my couch and stared at my phone while letting the soothing sounds of Norah Jones invade my soul and calm me. What a waste of an evening. Well, maybe not a complete waste. I was able to donate a nice bit of change to a worthy cause. It was the only good to come out of the evening. I debated texting. I doubted he would even see it until he left with some gorgeous woman on his arm. My bet was Dana. She did her best to be wherever he was all night. And it was for more than her job's sake. But despite his lack of manners, I had some.

I decided to call it a night. Thank you for . . .

Thank you for what? Thank you for ignoring me all night. Thank you for the blister on my foot. Thank you for dredging up memories of my ex. Thank you for proving to me that you are the last person in the world I would ever want to be with despite how your touch encompasses all my senses.

I went with *Thank you for the interesting evening.*

I still had to associate with him, so I kept it cordial. I was happy he didn't take Chanel to this thing. She'd be asking for a refund and probably shouting about how awful he was all over social media and then Nick would sue her for breaking her NDA. That wouldn't bode well for Binary Search. So maybe this was a good thing, even though it was the worst date ever. I was starting to feel like a sacrificial lamb. I didn't get paid enough for this.

I tossed my phone on my ottoman and headed upstairs to change. It was going to be an evening of reading and wine for one. I unzipped my gown as I went, happy to be out of the constricting thing. Yoga capris and a tank top were more my speed on the weekends.

I settled into my oversized chair with a stack of books on the small table next to it. A larger than normal glass of red wine accompanied them. A Serendipity bag rested on the floor near me full of books I'd yet to read. I wasn't sure what my mood would be and I wanted some backups ready to go. I could finish the psychological thriller I was reading, or perhaps go with a well-loved classic, or maybe the romances that filled the bag. I would see how it went.

The music, words, and wine began to do their job, relaxing me and pushing out thoughts of Nick. Just when I really settled into my book, there was a knock on my door. I jumped and sat up. I rarely had visitors and it was—I looked on the large decorative clock on my wall—it was almost eleven.

I grabbed my phone in case I needed to dial for help. Maybe I shouldn't read psychological thrillers at night. All I could think was there must be a psychopath on the other side of my door. Be rational.

It was probably some kids playing a prank. Not that a lot of kids lived around here.

Maybe it was my imagination. Another knock. Definitely not my imagination. I crept toward the door and, with great trepidation, I looked through the peephole, clutching my phone, ready to dial 911.

My first thought was right. Psychopath.

I leaned my head against the door. "What are you doing here?"

"Will you open the door?"

I thought about his request. "I'd rather not."

Silence.

Did he really go? Was that all it took? Fabulous.

"Please," he growled.

I didn't even know that word was in his vocabulary. I sighed and unlocked the deadbolt, but only opened the door as far as the chain lock would allow. I peeked out at the brooding but devastatingly handsome man in a tux on my porch. What did he have to be so broody about? By the look of it, he'd had a fantastic evening.

"Why are you here?" I repeated my earlier sentiment.

He rested his hand against the door's frame, leaning forward, eyes dancing brilliantly in my porch's light. There was no mistaking the fire, though, that burned in them. "You left."

"How long did it take for you to notice?"

He pressed his lips together as if not wanting to admit to a thing. "Can I come in?"

"What would that accomplish?"

"Apparently everything I do around you is wrong. I would like to know how to fix that."

I narrowed my eyes at him, unsure if he was in earnest or why he would care. A debate within me raged on whether to let him in or not. And there was the tiny matter that I wasn't wearing a bra,

107

other than the built-in one provided by the tank top I wore. I was flat chested enough it did a decent job, but one accidental bend over and I would be exposed. So no bending over in front of him. That was, if I let him in.

He leaned in, turning on all the charm he possessed, which had to be over the legal limit. A half smile danced on his face, making him more handsome.

Forget butterflies. A flock of birds took off in my stomach. *It's because you're ovulating,* I told myself.

"Are you refusing me?" It was like he blew some type of magical elixir in my face that shut down any rational thought.

"Maybe," I stuttered. I was trying to hold strong. Someday I could tell my daughter I refused to let *People's* Sexiest Man Alive into my house. That was something I could be proud of.

"Let me guess, you have a rule against it." His voice was becoming deeper with a sultry quality to it.

It had me mesmerized. Oh no, no. I was immune. "I did. I mean I do," I managed to say.

"Please, Kate?"

He was good.

I closed the door and slid the chain off. Tapping my forehead lightly against the door. What was I doing? I slowly opened the door.

He stepped in right away as if he knew I could change my mind at any given second.

I wasn't exactly sure what to do with him, but it hit me how tall he was. I looked up at him while I shut my door.

He scanned my place, everything from my empty dining room to the great room and kitchen. It could all be seen from the entryway. I was sure it paled in comparison to his own home or the homes he frequented. He didn't make any remarks. His eyes landed on me as if he was waiting for me to make the next move.

"Would you like to sit down?" I waved toward my great room.

He didn't hesitate and headed straight for my couch, undoing his tie as he went and removing his jacket. He landed on the couch and placed both articles of clothing beside him. He got more comfortable by rolling up the sleeves on his white shirt and unbuttoning a few buttons.

I swallowed from my nearby chair, watching the scene play before my eyes. It was like a nightmare and daydream all wrapped up together. I glanced at my copy of *The Science of Why Good Girls Love Bad Boys* on the coffee table right in front of us. It gave me some strength and a good reminder it was only biology at play here and I should not be listening to my screaming ovaries. In a couple of days, they would be so over him.

Once he was finished making himself comfortable he pointed up. "You like Norah Jones?"

I nodded.

"I saw her live a few years ago. She's impressive."

So we had one thing in common.

I didn't know what to say. My twenty-year-old self would have had a list of questions.

He, on the other hand, seemed very interested in his surroundings. He reached out and picked up the best book ever written from the coffee table with a smirk on his face. "Is this any good?"

"Life changing."

His famous eyebrow arched before he tossed it back on the coffee table. He took note of the pile of books near me on the side table. "You like to read."

"As often as I can."

His eyes shifted down and he saw it. *The bag*. The bag with the bookstore name on it. His eyes widened before they landed on me. They went back and forth a few more times between the bag and my face. I could see the light in his eyes connecting the two. He remembered.

I jumped up. "Do want something to drink?"

I didn't want him to bring up the first time we met. That was mine. All mine. And he would ruin it by saying something stupid about it. I know that didn't make sense, but for some reason I could keep the past and present him separated. My twenty-year-old self needed that serendipitous moment. I never wanted the magic of that day to go away. My skeptical, introspective self needed it.

He studied me for a minute. I could see he wanted to say something about that day. My eyes pleaded with him not to. And somehow, he seemed to be able to read me. He looked at my half empty glass of wine. "I'll take whatever you're drinking."

"I'll be right back." That came out breathy. I darted to the kitchen to pour him a glass.

He took that as his invitation to get up and walk around. I'd never known anyone who would feel comfortable doing so. He headed toward my built-in bookcases and perused the titles, pulling out a few books and flipping through them.

I watched him from my island instead of doing what I'd come in the kitchen to do. Next, he moved to the entertainment console and dang it if I hadn't left out the DVD case of *A Step Up*, and worse, my entire collection of *On the Edge*.

He held up both and faced me with the look of a cat who had caught a mouse. "I thought you weren't a fan."

"I didn't know you wrote and produced that movie when I bought it," I defended myself.

"Right." He held up my collection of his TV show. "What about these?"

I cleared my throat. "I set those out to donate them to the library."

He looked them over with the smuggest grin. "Looks like they've gotten plenty of use."

Had they ever. "I could have bought them used."

"But you didn't." His eyes dared me to contradict him.

I wasn't admitting to a thing. I shrugged before reaching for the bottle of wine.

He placed the DVDs back on the console. "You are determined not to like me."

"That's not true." I said that before I thought. On some level that was probably true. But I didn't need to like him. It was probably better if I didn't. There needed to be a professional line between us.

He walked toward me in the kitchen, taking a seat on one of the barstools around my island. "Then tell me why you left tonight."

I scooted the glass of wine toward him, perplexed as always around him. "Do you really not understand why I had good reason to?"

His blank stare said he didn't get it. Interesting.

"What is it that you expected?" He returned my question with one of his own.

"From you? Nothing."

He didn't appreciate that answer by the way his jawline tightened and pulsated. He stretched his neck from side to side. I'd noticed he did that when he was trying to not say what he really wanted to.

"Let me rephrase my question," his tone had a little bite to it. "How would you have liked to see the evening go?"

"With someone besides you?" I grinned.

"Sure." He took a hefty drink of his wine.

I walked around the island and took the stool next to him after pulling it a reasonable distance from him. My elbow landed on the island and I rested my head on my hand, deciding how to proceed.

He waited. And every signal he gave said he really wanted to know my answer.

It occurred to me that maybe it would help to tell him. This way he could use it with the women he would be paired with.

I sat up and took a deep breath. "Well, for starters, it would be nice if my date greeted me with a 'hello' or 'I'm so happy you could make it. How are you?' Any pleasantry would do."

His brow crinkled. "I greeted you while you were flirting with that man."

"I wasn't flirting with Trent."

"You remembered his name."

"It's a gift."

That got a lip twitch out of him.

"And you didn't greet me. All you said was, 'Kate.'"

He leaned toward me. "I like your name."

I, on the other hand, had to lean away. He was intoxicating, and wow he knew how to deliver a line. "Be that as it may, it would be polite if you said, 'Hello, Kate' or Chanel or whoever."

"I'll try and remember that."

Huh.

"What else, Kate?"

I did like it when he said my name. Moving on. "Um... My date should have realized how uncomfortable I was in an unfamiliar setting without knowing anyone but the person I was there with. Not to mention how ridiculous I felt wearing an evening gown. It would have been nice if my date would have thrown a compliment or two my way and then introduced me to some of his friends. Or, since I was his date, he might have thought to keep me company instead of ignoring me all night. I know what a crazy notion that is." I ended with a smirk.

"First of all—" He reached out and intimately tucked a tendril of my hair behind my ear.

The spine shivers were back, so much so I almost fell off my stool. He couldn't touch me unexpectedly like that.

"I mentioned you looked good."

"On your arm," I added.

"If you looked good on my arm, don't you think I thought you looked good off?"

"Women don't think like that."

"How do you think?"

"What I heard was that I was only an accessory there to make you look good."

He opened his mouth but paused and thought. "I suppose I could see that, but I was trying to compliment you." His eyes locked on me. "You were stunning."

I couldn't breathe. My dumb ovaries. I had to force my eyes away from his. "Thank you," I stuttered.

"You're welcome. Now back to the other charges you've leveled against me."

"You're not on trial."

"I beg to differ, Dr. Morgan. You've been judging me from the moment I stepped into your office."

"It's my job."

"Fair enough, except you already decided who I was before you ever tried to get to know me."

"You haven't exactly made that easy. Each time we've been together, you either don't speak, don't show up, or disappear," I threw back at him.

"I'm here now." There was no edge to his voice, only seductive tones.

I bit my lip. "I noticed."

"Let's get to know each other."

That was a dangerous proposition.

Chapter Thirteen

WE MOVED TO the great room where it was more comfortable, at least when it came to the seating. Him being there was out of my comfort zone.

I sat on my chair, sipping my wine, waiting for him to make the first move. He sat on the end of the couch closest to me. His eyes drifted to that Serendipity bag and back to my copy of *Les Misérables* that could always be found on the table next to me. They finally landed on me. For a split second it looked like he might say something about that day, but he didn't. Instead, he let out a heavy breath and rubbed his neck as if this was not comfortable for him either.

"I'm not used to being around people like you, Kate."

I set my glass on the table. "People like me?"

"Real people," he clarified.

My eyebrows raised. "As opposed to fake ones?"

"In a manner of speaking, yes."

"Can you elaborate?"

"You sound like a therapist."

"Habit. Sorry."

That brittle smile of his appeared. "I didn't ignore you tonight. I did my thing, and I expected you to do yours."

I laughed. "I'm really sorry, but you're going to have to elaborate."

He leaned back into the couch. "Normally when I take a woman to any event, it's expected that we give each other space so we don't overshadow each other. She gets her chance in the spotlight and I get mine."

"I don't have a spotlight, nor do I want one."

"You have one, whether you see it or not. I noticed the way the men in the room looked at you."

I blushed. I hadn't done that in a very long time. "You were watching me?"

"You were my date."

"Client date," I reminded him.

"Regardless, I didn't forget you were there. Though I will admit I can see where you might disagree with me."

"I appreciate your concession. Can I ask you a question?"

He gave a small nod.

"Why do you even bring dates to these types of events if you're only planning on spending the evening apart?"

"Because it's all part of the Hollywood game."

"So tonight was a game for you and I was there to play my part."

His entire body went stiff. "No." The steel in his voice was raw. "I take seriously what I do for law enforcement families. I asked you to come with me tonight because I wanted you to see that."

"Because you think I've judged you." Why did that make me feel a tad guilty?

"And because I know I've given you reason to. I was hoping we could start over tonight, but I only gave you more reasons to think I'm a Hollywood playboy."

116

That and some other things. "Why does my opinion matter to you?"

He captured my gaze. "You are the first person in a long time who hasn't wanted anything from me. The fact that you despise me is kind of refreshing."

A mile-wide grin sprung up on my face. "I'm happy to oblige."

"I have no doubt." He relaxed against the couch again.

"Is that why you're using Binary Search? You want someone 'real'?"

"Something like that."

"You want someone who despises you, too?" I teased.

He gave me a look that went right through me. "Perhaps I do."

I shook my head. He needed to stay out of my insides. "I'll see what I can do."

"Kate..." He paused in a way that seemed like it was for dramatic effect. "I meant what I said on my questionnaire. I won't be committed to anyone I date using your service."

"Don't take this the wrong way. I would ask this of any client. Do you have commitment issues?"

"I have no problem being committed to the right woman."

"How do you know we won't match you with the right woman?"

"You won't."

"Okay." I let it drop.

"What about you?" he asked. "What kind of relationship are you looking for?"

"I'm the one who gets to ask the questions here."

"That's not how a date works."

"Is that what we're on?"

"You do owe me one."

"I've tried three times."

"Not very hard."

I raised my eyebrows. "What do you mean?"

"Two of the three dates, you left before they ever happened. And the first date you flirted with my dad all night. By the way, he would love it if you came to the restaurant for dinner again."

I would love to go to Jack's on the River again. The food and most of the company was amazing. "I like your dad."

"That was apparent." I couldn't tell if that annoyed or amused him.

"Your daughter was right; he's too old for me. But he does make a girl think twice. He reminds me of an old Bogart and Bacall film. Where the man doesn't play any games. You know right away he's attracted to you."

"Is that what you're looking for?"

"You keep trying to make this about me."

"And you keep avoiding my questions."

"Fine." I grinned. "I want someone with class, who's not afraid to have fun. Someone who will make me have some too. Get me out of the shell I sometimes stay too long in."

"Any other qualifications?"

"Lots."

"I've got time."

I took a sip of my wine, avoiding his question again. "I think it's your turn to answer a question."

"What do you want to know?"

I tried to think of something that wasn't on his questionnaire, though I was still having a hard time reconciling the man on paper with the one in front of me. The one where I could see a peek of the hair on his chest. I had to shake my head to refocus.

"Um...Where do you live?" That was so lame. I couldn't think of a single question on the client date check-off list.

There was a sparkle of victory in his eyes. He knew he had unhinged me a bit. "This summer, Skye and I are staying with my dad. He has a little place near the restaurant."

I tilted my head, surprised.

"What?" he asked.

"I don't know. I figured you'd be staying in some penthouse suite or something downtown."

"You pegged me for a penthouse guy."

"Maybe. Are you?"

"It's not really my style. I have a house in Laguna Beach."

"Is it on the beach?"

He shook his head. "It's located in the hills above. It provides a view of the ocean as well as privacy."

I tucked my legs under me and got a little more comfortable. "I imagine that's not easily obtained in your profession."

"It's been challenging at times, but I'm old news now." A hint of loss mixed in with his words.

"You wish you weren't."

He leaned forward and rested his arms on his legs. "Are you trying to diagnose me?"

"Why does everyone think that as soon as they know what I do?" I grinned.

"You didn't deny it."

That's because it was true. I wanted to figure him out. I realized, though, now that I'd relaxed, I was hungry. The only thing I had eaten all night were those chocolate mousse shooters at the gala. "Do you want some cheesecake?"

"Is this your way of evading my question?"

"Yes." I jumped out of my chair.

It didn't surprise me at all that he followed me into the kitchen.

He stood at the island while I retrieved the cheesecake I'd made a couple of nights ago and some strawberries to slice. I turned around to see him carefully observing me.

Suddenly I felt shy with his eyes so intent on me. I placed the spring form pan and carton of strawberries on the island "Did you want a slice?"

He peeked into the pan. "Looks like you eat it straight out of the pan."

"If you're afraid I've contaminated it with my germs I can offer you—"

"Why don't you grab two forks and we'll call it good?"

How did he make that sound seductive? And why did I stop breathing? Breathe, Kate. Breathe.

"Okay."

Never in a million fantasies did I imagine one where Nicholas Wells and I sat at my island and ate cheesecake straight out of the pan. But there we were, stools close together, indulging in sweet ecstasy.

He rested his fork in the pan for a moment. "This isn't half bad."

I gave him half an evil eye. "Was that a compliment?"

"Yes," he replied matter-of-factly.

"You need to work on those."

His brow arched. "Would you like to give me a list of character defects I can work on now, or does that come later?" His tone wasn't curt, but it drove his point home.

I sank some in my chair. "I'm sorry. I didn't mean for that to come out judgmental."

His expression softened. "Don't be. I know how I can come off." He picked his fork back up. "This is delicious."

"I don't know if I believe that now." I nudged him with my shoulder, though I shouldn't have, but it had happened naturally. That weird connection I had to him appeared, making me drop my fork in the pan.

He ceased moving as if he felt it too. Or maybe he didn't think he should be touched. Though he had touched me before.

For a moment we were both still.

He was first to speak. "Do you like to cook?"

I almost laughed at his out-of-the-blue question, but I didn't want him to think I was being critical of him. "Honestly, I'm not that great of a cook. I only learned to bake because my mom's idea of dessert borders on embarrassing and hazmat."

I got the smallest hint of a laugh out of him.

"It's no laughing matter. I lost friends over the whole-wheat-carob-chip cookies my mom tried to pass off as the best chocolate chip cookies ever, and don't even get me going on when she started a house fire when she tried to make bananas Foster. We still don't let her make dessert."

"Are you close to your parents?"

I nodded. "As crazy as they drive me, they're my best friends. How about you?"

Nick wiped his mouth with a napkin. "My mom," he paused, "was everything a mother should be. My dad is all right when he's not hitting on my dates."

"Does he do that often?"

"Only once." He ran a finger down my cheek making me shiver. "I can't say I blame him though."

He had me locked in his gaze. Something inside my brain was buzzing, warning me of danger, but it took me a moment to respond. "It's getting late," I whispered.

"I suppose it is." He didn't move.

For a second I didn't want him to. That was wrong. He was wrong for me. And he was a client.

I leaned away. "We finally got in our client date."

"Is this your idea of a good date?"

"You can never go wrong with cheesecake, wine, and...good conversation."

"I'll keep that in mind." He stood up.

I hoped he did for his dates with Chanel or whoever else he dated using our service. I stood up and followed him to the great room, where he picked up his jacket and tie. He took one more glance at the book bag. Still he didn't say anything.

I walked him to the door and held out my hand, not sure what else to do as this was business. "Have a nice night, or I guess, morning." It was already past midnight.

He stared at my hand with narrowed eyes. "I don't end dates with handshakes."

"Oh." My hand dropped like a cement block. My cheeks flooded, embarrassed. I scrambled to open the door for him.

"Kate." His smooth, deep voice made me pause with my hand on the knob.

My eyes fluttered up. He was standing ever so close, and before I could say or do anything, he bent down and brushed his warm lips against my cheek.

He didn't stop there. He whispered in my ear, "I read the unabridged version of *Les Misérables*." He whispered even lower what happened to the doll. It was a secret only to be shared among those who read the full version.

He had me immobilized and wishing I was still that twenty-year-old who believed in the magic of him, of romantic love.

He stood up straight but held me with his eyes. "I went back to the bookstore several times that summer hoping to meet you again."

I had no words.

He kissed my cheek one more time. "Good night, Kate."

I somehow managed to open the door for him. He strutted out and I watched him walk to his car.

I was right. Getting to know him was dangerous.

Chapter Fourteen

I NEEDED TO RIGHT my world. My "date" with Nick last night had me in a tailspin. I needed research and coffee. Serendipity's it was. I'd missed my normal Saturday visit there anyway thanks to him. There was great irony going to the place where I met him for the first time, but it was my place. And it had the self-help books I needed.

I purchased a stack of books, everything from, *How to Maintain a Professional Relationship with Someone You Are Attracted To*, all the way to *Why Smart Women Make Stupid Choices and How to Stop*. I wasn't messing around.

I ordered a large coffee in their café and sat crossed-legged on one of the chairs in their reading nook and started with *Narcissist or Self Centered*. Maybe I had missed something.

I spent my morning deep in research and making notes in my notebook. One of the big questions on my mind was, was Nick empathetic, meaning was he willing to change his behavior once he was called on it? Or was he accommodating because he knew it would be best for his image?

The biggest question on my mind, though, was why, after everything I knew about him and despite him breaking most of the rules on my list, couldn't I stop thinking about him? Worse, I was his relationship manager and I was having thoughts—lots of thoughts. Thoughts that went way beyond him kissing my cheek. I rested my hand where his lips had been.

I took a break near noon to rub my tired eyes and people watch. My favorites were always the children, their innocence and excitement when someone read to them or when they could read the book for themselves. I loved to watch parents help their children sound out words. There was a little boy there with his father. His dad was making all the sounds, from a choo choo train to an airplane. The boy clapped with delight. Small chubby hands were the cutest. I wanted one to hold. Some days I wondered if I would ever get the chance. My parents had mentioned adoption. It was an option. They'd even offered to pay for it. They were ready to be grandparents, and thought they would be by now. My miscarriage was a loss for them too.

But I wasn't sure I wanted to do it alone. I wanted a partner to share it all with, whether we adopted or had a baby together.

I was about to get up and get a refill on my coffee when my people watching got interesting. Two of the most beautiful people ever headed my way. One with an air of self-regard, the other wishing she was somewhere else by the look of her pouty lips. I did take note, though, of the way Nick put his arm around his daughter and whispered something to her to make her smile.

Why was he here? In my place. Our place? I couldn't think like that. But he had remembered.

I hastily closed the book in my lap and tried to shove the rest in my bag, but I was too late. He was upon me.

"I thought I might find you here." He sounded so pleased with himself.

I looked up and bit my lip. "You were looking for me?"

"What do you think?"

I ignored the chill that gave me and focused on how conceited that was. I chose not to respond to him but acknowledged his daughter. "Hello, Skye. It's nice to see you again. You look very pretty today." Did she ever in a coral sundress with her hair pulled back.

"Thank you." She seemed surprised by the compliment, which surprised me.

"Are you guys just out and about today?" I babbled, trying to keep this all aboveboard and light.

Nick held up a leather laptop case. "I needed a good place to write and Skye," he gave her a meaningful glance, "wanted to...get some books."

Skye gave him a forced smile. Why did I think Skye didn't want to get books? Most kids read everything digitally now. And did he really need to write in a bookstore?

"What kind of books are you interested in?" I asked Skye, playing along.

Skye looked at her dad, not sure what to say.

Nick brought out his acting skills and smoothed it right over. "I thought you might have some recommendations for her."

"Is that why you were looking for me?" Skepticism littered my tone.

"One of the reasons." He had a much different tone. One he shouldn't be using around me.

"Right." I focused back on Skye. "I have some recommendations if you're interested."

Her face soured. She obviously wasn't. "Okay," she resigned herself to her fate.

127

I shoved my notes in my purse before standing up, thinking that was the safest course of action. I needed to get away from Nick. "We can head to the teen section or the classics." I spoke only to Skye. Her dad wasn't invited.

She gave her dad a look like *you owe me*.

"I'll save your seat and write while you ladies peruse," Nick said while perusing me. I was super casual in shorts and a T-shirt. I wasn't expecting visitors at the bookstore, especially not him. He was dressed, as always, to break hearts, in tight jeans and a T-shirt that showed how lean and muscular his arms were. I was surprised he hadn't been accosted yet by a fan. Even I wanted to pet his arm. I seriously needed to stop that line of thinking.

I brushed past him, rolling my eyes. It was better than petting him.

He grabbed my hand.

Oh, no. That was not part of the package.

I held very still, like unnervingly still, telling my ovaries this was not what they wanted even if my body was singing a loud chorus of YES YOU DO.

"Thank you," he whispered intimately.

"You're welcome," I could barely breathe out. I pulled away from him.

Skye waited for me and studied me. I hoped she didn't think there was anything going on between her dad and me.

"Where would you like to head?" I asked her.

She shrugged.

"How about the teen section?" I suggested. It was the farthest away.

She didn't say anything but followed next to me.

I didn't have a lot of experience with teenagers other than having them as patients. I wasn't sure exactly what to say, but I knew teenagers liked to talk about themselves.

"Are you enjoying your summer?"

"Yeah, kind of. I like being with my grandpa, but I miss my friends and my pool."

"That must be hard. Do you have any friends here?"

Her cheeks pinked. "Sort of."

"Sort of?"

"I know this one guy, Liam. We've known each other since we were little."

"That's fun."

She twisted her hands together. "He's a few years older than me and I don't know if he likes me anymore."

I stopped to take a good look at her. "I can't imagine him not."

She blushed again. "Maybe. He's acting weird around me now."

I grinned. "That's not surprising."

She stiffened. "Why?"

"Well, I don't know for sure, but I would say his feelings for you now that you are both older are no longer only friendly."

"Do you really think so?" Her face was all alight.

"I take it you would like that."

She nodded. "But don't tell my dad. I don't know if he would like it."

"Most dads don't. Your secret is safe with me."

There was more of a skip to her step while we headed toward the teen section.

"Are you more of a romance, fantasy, or dystopian kind of girl?" I asked once we arrived at our destination.

"I'm not much of a reader unless it's for school assignments."

"Huh." That was a shame, but I didn't mention it. Maybe I could change her mind. "I could recommend some books I read as a teen that are probably too cheesy now, but one of my patients loves this new YA fantasy romance about dragon shapeshifters." She'd told me it was all the rage now. I promised her I would look into them. I guess now was a good time.

Skye looked mildly interested. "I might read something like that."

"Let's see if we can find them."

She gave me a dazzling smile. "I like you, Kate."

I tilted my head. "You do?"

"Yeah. It's nice that you don't throw yourself at my dad. I never know if someone is being nice to me because they want to get to my dad."

Ouch. That made my heart hurt. "I can't imagine how difficult that is."

"Where we live, you kind of get used to it. Everybody wants a big break or to hand you a resume and a headshot. Or they want to be my dad's next girlfriend."

"You don't have to worry about that with me. I don't like your dad like that, or at all." I gave her a wink.

She giggled. "I think that bothers him."

"Oh, really?"

"He told my grandpa that he doesn't know what to do around you. My grandpa said that was a good sign."

"A good sign for what?"

She shrugged. "I don't know—I turned up the volume on my phone." That sounded like typical teenage behavior.

"Let's go get those books."

It took us no time to find the books and make our way back to her dad, who was helping himself to my books, smirking as he read my copy of *How to Maintain a Professional Relationship with Someone You Are Attracted To.*

"I thought you were writing?"

130

He looked up from the book, amused. "I couldn't resist."

I swiped the book out of his hand.

"Are you attracted to someone at work, Kate? I noticed Todd seemed to have an eye for you."

"He does not. And the answer is no."

"Then perhaps it's one of your patients."

"Perhaps I should go."

"Wait." He sat up straight. "Where do you have to be?" He was so blunt.

"Not that it's any of your business, but I was thinking of grabbing some lunch and going purse shopping." I was treating myself for enduring him all week.

"Ooh, I love to purse shop." Skye beamed.

Her dad and I both turned to her. She was too sweet to be his.

Don't ask me why, but this came falling out of my mouth, "You wouldn't want to go with me, would you?" That was too bold. She hardly knew me and I'm sure Nick wouldn't like it, as he was so protective of her.

"I would love to. Anything but hanging out here." Skye's gorgeous green eyes owned her dad. "Can I, Dad?"

I peeked at Nick to gauge his reaction to his daughter's reaction. The tender smile was one he obviously reserved for her.

I took a deep breath and threw more caution to the wind. "I would love the company, if that's okay with you, Nick."

That tender smile hit me too, and I had to look away.

"Please, Daddy?" Skye flashed her own brilliant smile.

"Okay," he easily gave into her. "But why don't we all do a late lunch together after you're done shopping?" Nick's presence drew me back to looking right at him. "We could head to Jack's. My dad would love to see you again."

131

Skye bent down and kissed her dad's cheek before I could agree or process.

"What say you, Kate?" Nick was doing that thing again where he was looking not at me but into me.

What did I say? I say I was in over my head.

Chapter Fifteen

"WHERE ARE YOU?"

"Well, hello to you too. I'm fine, thank you for asking. Skye's great too." I gave Skye a little wink while we walked out of Michael Kors with our bags. I'd picked out a gorgeous pebbled bag in soft pink.

Skye had whipped out her dad's credit card and bought a few things, including a darling floral lace dress that she looked beautiful in, along with a bag and matching shoes. The total made me squeamish, but she said she had a thousand-dollar-a-month allowance. Yes, I said a thousand dollars a month. We obviously came from very different worlds, but I enjoyed my time with her. She was infectiously upbeat and caught me up on all the new teen lingo like, "that's so extra" and "hundo p," which meant hundred percent sure. Who knew?

She smiled back at me. I sure did like her. The gruff voice on the other end of my phone, I wasn't sure about. At all.

Nick sighed in frustration. "Hello, Kate. Better?"

"Much. How are you?"

"Hungry. Are you still shopping?"

"We just finished. I can meet you at the restaurant with Skye."

"How about I meet you at your place and we can drive together?"

"That makes no sense. We're closer to Jack's, and you would have to take me home if we drove together."

"And?"

"And...that's unnecessary." On so many levels.

"Right. Your rules. Two successful dates before a date can pick you up."

There was that. And there was him. "Yep. And since that will never happen between us—"

"Technically we've been on three."

I cleared my throat and whispered into the phone since his daughter was walking next to me in the shopping center's parking lot. "Technically it's none, because I'm your relationship manager."

"Then the rules shouldn't apply to me."

The rules applied to him doubly.

"I'll meet you there." I wasn't backing down.

"If you must," he growled. "But there's been a change in plans—we're eating at my dad's house."

"Oh. Okay. Why?"

"I thought it would be more comfortable for you that way. You don't seem to like the attention being in public with me sometimes garners."

I paused before I clicked the key fob to unlock my car. "That was actually very considerate of you. Thank you."

"You sound surprised, Kate."

"I am."

"Good. I'll send you his address. See you soon."

I stood dazed for a second.

"Are you okay?" Skye asked, bringing me out of my Nick fog.

"Yes. Thanks for coming with me. It was nice to have a shopping buddy." I lacked in that department. Mom was a no-go for this trip unless I wanted to hear about how I was cruelly slaughtering cows so I could have a nice purse. Meg was dealing with Zander and pregnancy, Kenadie was still in the newlywed phase, and I hadn't really gotten to know any of the other doctors at the clinic I volunteered at. Not to mention my cautious nature had gotten in the way of making attachments. I needed to do better.

"Anytime. I love to shop." Skye sounded like she was volunteering for any future trips where shopping was involved.

We got ourselves and our bags situated in the car. I looked over at Skye and hoped someday I would have a daughter like her to go shopping with. I wondered about her own mother. All Nick put on his questionnaire where it asked about ex-spouses was "out of the picture." Was she out of Skye's as well?

Skye was also good enough to catch me up on the new music kids were listening to. She plugged her phone into my car and I was treated to Ed Sheeran, Drake, and Charlie Puth. She had pretty good taste, but she wrinkled her nose when I played her some Nina Simone. She offered to make me a list of "hip" songs and artists to download. I blamed my "old" taste on my parents and a jazz artist I dated my junior year of college.

We also decided to read the dragon books together. Who didn't need a little dragon shapeshifter love in their life?

So when Nick told me his dad had a little place near the restaurant, he meant he had a mini mansion by the riverfront.

"Is this the right place?" I pulled up in front of the breathtaking, sprawling home set in the middle of the Garden of Eden.

"This is Grandpa's," Skye confirmed.

Skye ran in with her bags while I looked up at the home that reminded me of a *Better Homes and Gardens* cover. The two-story home, white with green shutters, was perfectly classic. The deep porch and second story veranda spoke of its Southern flair.

Jack came out smiling, drying his hands on the dish towel he carried. He had to be the most distinguished looking gentleman I'd ever met. Besides his son, who was his clone.

"Darlin', it's good to see you."

"Hey, Jack." I returned his smile before he embraced me. I soaked in his fatherly warmth. "How are you?"

"Better now that you're here."

I pulled away from him, grinning from ear to ear. "You are a flirt."

"You're worth every effort." He held out his arm to me. "Shall we, darlin'?"

I happily took his arm tattooed with his wife's name, Barbara, and what I assumed was the date of their anniversary. "We shall."

Jack held the screen door open for me. "Nick should be here soon. He stopped by the restaurant to pick up the food."

"I hope I'm not putting anyone out."

"You're not, but even if you were, it would be good for Nick. He needs to think about someone besides himself and Skye."

I looked up at him and decided to be more daring than I usually would be. I wanted to put all the pieces of Nick together until it gave me a clear picture of who he really was. "Would you consider Nick self-centered?"

Jack's laughter filled his large entryway. "I would consider most men self-centered." He took a thoughtful pause. "Maybe Nick is more than most, but..." A twinkle appeared in his eye. "Never known anyone more generous than him."

My brow furrowed.

"What's got you vexed, darlin'?"

I took a deep breath, trying to form my thoughts into words. "He's a walking dichotomy. I can't figure him out."

A sly smile appeared on his handsome, lined face. "Are you trying to?"

Some heat crept up my neck. "It's my job."

"Uh-huh." Jack patted my hand that was wrapped around his arm. "You keep doing your *job*, and I have a feeling you'll both figure each other out."

"That's not necessary." There was a fair amount of alarm in my voice.

Laughing to himself, Jack led me back through his beautiful home to the kitchen that opened up to the large family room. "This is going to be fun to watch."

I was going to ask him what he meant by that, but Nick came in through the nearby garage entry carrying bags that smelled amazing. Unfortunately, the man carrying them looked more so. My ovaries needed to get over him. I got their message—he would give me beautiful babies. No one was denying that.

"*Hello*, Kate."

"Look who found some manners," I teased.

Jack smiled between us. "I'm glad I'm getting a front row seat for this."

Nick narrowed his eyes, confused by his dad's statement.

Jack headed for Nick and relieved him of the bags. "Why don't you show Kate the gardens out back while I put this all together."

"I can help," I was quick to volunteer. Anything to not be alone with his son.

"You are, darlin'. Now get out of here." Jack wasn't giving me an out.

I dared a glance at Nick, whose gaze was already set on me.

My hands found their way through my hair, trying to offset the nervous energy coursing through me as Nick approached. A kaleidoscope of brooding and amusement played in his eyes. "Ready?"

Not at all, but I followed him out the back door that led us to a massive deck that was a garden in and of itself. Strawberries were bursting to overflow several containers. Raspberries climbed the walls. Pots of flowers outlined the perimeter and sat on the small tables near the patio furniture. It was paradise.

"This is amazing. But I thought you said your dad had a small place?"

"You should see my place," he whispered too close to me, causing me to shiver in the hot, humid air.

I had no doubt it would be grandiose. But I would never see it. I took a moment to get my bearings back. He had a way of knocking me off balance. I took in the view of the river below and the garden of trees and flowers. It was breathtaking.

"Did you get a lot of writing done?" I asked, hoping that would help set me straight.

He shook his head. "I was hit with a case of writer's block, and I found I was distracted."

"Did your fan club show up?"

"Other than you? No." His smirk was off the charts.

"Just because I own some of your works doesn't make me a fan. I was given a copy of *Sharknado* once as a joke and that movie was awful."

His eyebrows zoomed up. "Are you comparing me to that drivel?"

I gave him my best patronizing smile. "You can comfort yourself knowing you're better than a movie that mixes cyclones and terrorizing sharks."

"Thank you for that ringing endorsement."

"You're welcome."

He rested his hand on the small of my back, leading me toward the stairs. "You don't have to admit it. I know a fan when I see one."

I rolled my eyes. "Wishful thinking."

His eyes hit me. "Oh, I have some wishes, Kate."

In the name of self-preservation and all that was good for me, I stepped away from him. I cleared my throat. "Don't we all." Like right now I wished he was a thirty-five-year-old surgeon or chemical engineer who had never been married. Statistically speaking, they had very low divorce rates.

"What do you wish for?"

"Um…" I couldn't think. I swore his breath contained some brain-numbing seducing agent. No. No. I had to think. I had this under control. "Tell me what producers do."

The abrupt but much-needed change in subject had him halting on the last step and giving me a look that said, *what?*

I bit my lip and shrugged, not planning on explaining myself to him. "I've always wondered what role producers play. You see their names in the credits, but what do they really do?"

"You are an interesting woman, Kate Morgan."

He had no idea, but I wondered why he thought so. "What makes you say that?"

He leaned against the rail and crossed his arms. "For someone whose chosen profession necessitates her delving deep into the personal lives of her patients, you give away very little of your thoughts." He cocked his head. "Why is that?"

Why was he so perceptive? I swallowed hard. "I have my reasons."

"Some of your rules?"

"They're connected."

"How many are there?"

"According to my mother, twenty."

"Can I get a list?"

I shook my head no.

He pushed himself off the rail and came dangerously close to me. "I guess I'll have to do my best to learn them. *One*," he paused, "*by one.*"

"I don't know why you would want to know them," I stammered, trying to remain calm.

"Something for you to learn, then."

If he was acting, he deserved an Academy Award. I felt every word he said from the top of my head to my littlest toe. He drew me in and made me want to hang on every arrogant word.

"All I want to know right now is what producers do."

His eyes smiled. "Okay, Kate, but someday, I predict you're going to open up to me."

"I look forward to proving you wrong."

His face came within inches of my own. "Me too."

Chapter Sixteen

*T*HINGS I LEARNED *today* was a nice exercise I used to do with my dad when I was growing up. At the dinner table every night, he made me list ten things I had learned and one thing I had failed at. He thought failure was the best teacher. It was a nice exercise, but now, lying here in my bed, it was kind of excruciating because, oh, had I failed today. I had blurred the personal and professional lines by entwining myself with a client's family, which was kind of fabulous, by the way. More importantly, I'd let my pheromones rule my day. They had me feeling like old, naïve me who believed in kismet, serendipity, magical moments, and Nick.

So the biggest thing I learned today was that I was a dolt. Followed by, there were a lot of strange people who got paid to eat bizarre things on YouTube. That knowledge came courtesy of Skye. We watched YouTube videos together while her dad and grandpa cleaned the kitchen. That probably wasn't the best thing to do after eating. One of the guys ate congealed pig's blood. Sadly, she informed me, he made five times what I did.

Speaking of Skye, she was adorable and had her dad wrapped around her finger. When she came down wearing what she had purchased, he beamed and didn't even ask how much she paid for it. Skye also asked if we could do something this week. Of course I said yes. I mean, I might as well do a thorough job of erasing any professional lines that were left. Not to mention the connection I felt to her. Something I'd never felt before, like I'd always known her. It's as weird as it sounded.

My list didn't stop there. Not that this was any surprise, but I had indisputable evidence now that Nick was born with Greek god status. To Nick's dismay, but admittedly to my delight, his dad brought out some photo albums. The Gerber baby had nothing on Nick. His cherub cheeks and big blue eyes had my biological clock in hyperdrive. And he used to smile when he was little, like huge-rays-of-sunshine smiles. That smile had my heart melting and my ovaries begging to let him put them to good use. Then there were the family pictures. Gorgeous. His dad was one handsome sailor, and his mom exuded grace. She obviously adored her son by the way she smiled at him in several photos.

Jack spun a good story. I loved hearing about his days in the navy. He told touching stories of all the men in the barracks singing Christmas songs while lying in their bunks. For many of them, it had been their first Christmas away from home. Jack also had me sold for life on his restaurant. We had *flamiche*, which was like quiche, and the best dessert of my life, *tarte tatin*, which was a fancy French way of saying apple tart.

Nick also gave me the inside scoop on Hollywood. See, producers were involved in a broad range of roles. If you were an executive producer, it meant you probably shelled out some serious cash for the movie or TV show that you'd produced. Producers also raised money, managed books, hired the crew, including the director, editor, script consultants, and casting directors. If you were a TV producer, you ran the show. To get your idea greenlighted to make a movie, you had to create a pitch package that included a treatment, which was a two to five page synopsis, or the broad strokes of the plot line. If the studio liked it, they would send you a contract, but that contract was just the first of many contracts, and at any point in the process they could kill your project. Other steps included outlines and drafts of the scripts. In between, you got notes from the studio executives on what you'd given them. And if you were lucky, in two to three years, you might have your movie made. It was a lot of information. He seemed to enjoy talking about it as we strolled through his dad's flower gardens and along the river walk.

One thing he wouldn't discuss was what he was working on now. He did leave the door open to telling me someday, but only after I confessed all my rules to him. So I would never know. Unless it got made into a movie. But how would I know it was what he was working on now? As soon as he was done using Binary Search, I planned on cutting all ties with him. Except maybe Skye. I would keep in touch with her if she wanted to. And Jack.

I rolled to my side and squeezed a pillow for comfort. Sleep was going to be hard to come by. I hadn't relived the biggest failure of the day. I shut my eyes tight, trying to forget it, but my cheek was still burning from where he kissed me goodbye. I told him he didn't need to walk me to my car, but he'd insisted.

It was there in front of my car that I let him get to me. I should have seen the question coming, but I'd hoped he'd let it drop since he hadn't mentioned it right away. But there we were under the starry Georgia sky, cicadas singing in the background, a light breeze ruffling through my hair. The breeze didn't help with the intense heat I felt from Nick's gaze. It was like being in an episode of *On the Edge.* He was channeling detective Talon Fox, wanting answers and using his wiles to get exactly that.

I wasn't having it. At least that was my intention.

"Good night," I'd said, reaching for my car door and hoping that would be the conclusion of what was admittedly a great day with his family. I hadn't had that much fun in too long.

He had other plans. He pressed his hand against the door and dialed up his searing stare. "I make you nervous." He didn't ask or surmise, he stated it like cold, hard truth.

"No," I breathed out an octave too high. Lying like I'd never lied before. He made me nervous on so many levels, but mainly because I thought I was smarter than to be attracted to him.

The corners of his mouth lifted, but never made it to a smile. "Then why didn't you tell me we'd met before?"

"I…" I couldn't think. That was my moment. We were never supposed to talk about it. What happened at Serendipity stayed at Serendipity. I think it was a rule of serendipitous moments, if not, it was my rule.

"Let me guess, you have your reasons."

That was the perfect answer. I nodded.

"Did you despise me then too?"

And this is where the fatal error occurred. His darn sexy eyes had me mesmerized and before I could stop my mouth, it said, "Not at all."

He flashed a brilliant, self-satisfied smile at me before leaning in and kissing my cheek without warning. Which only spoke of how well he could read a situation and me. He knew he'd never have gotten away with it if I'd anticipated it.

"You shouldn't do that," I whispered.

"Why?"

There were so many reasons why that couldn't be voiced. "I'm your relationship manager."

"Where I come from, it's a natural greeting or parting for business associates ... or friends."

I tilted my head. "You want to be friends?"

He pushed off my car. "That's a start. Good night, Kate." He strode away, whistling low like his character used to do after he'd gotten his way.

I threw myself back against my pillow. What did he mean by that was a start? A start to what? We shouldn't be friends; not even sure we could be. It wasn't only that I was attracted to him physically, but I was confused about what kind of a human being he was. Narcissism was so hard to diagnose and even harder to treat because they could mimic a range of emotions to get what they wanted. Once they got what they wanted was when you had to start worrying.

I knew that from experience. Douglas got exactly what he wanted out of me. A young, naïve wife who he thought he could mold, while feeding off my insecurities. He also got the envy of his colleagues—he had a wife thirteen years his junior who worshipped the ground he walked on. Or at least, I had until his true colors came out. It was terrifying how fooled I was. My only consolation was it wasn't only me. He'd taken everyone for a ride. The debonair lecturer who could deliver a presentation with such finesse and skill it was breathtaking.

Like Nick, Douglas was an actor. Perhaps Nick's hubris wasn't as big as Douglas's, but his self-confidence and self-importance was higher than average. Douglas's was off the charts. My pregnancy was all about him. Having a child with me meant the fake life he'd created with me was bound to come undone. He would be caught in the web he'd spun and tangled me up in. Even when I lost the baby, all he could say to me was he didn't know why I even let him know—it meant nothing to him. *I* meant nothing to him. It was his final blow. He wanted me to feel like nothing. And for a while, that's exactly how I felt.

I would never feel like that again.

The problem was, in my quest to never be with such a person again, something had been lost. Desire, passion, butterflies, all the magic that should exist when you pursue a relationship had disappeared. I'd had some nice dates, good conversations, even some sweet kisses, but nothing that stirred my soul or made me feel.

I brushed my cheek with my hand. I felt the lips that lingered there. That simmering moment where you breathed each other in. Where desire and passion stirred and made the butterflies take flight. Feelings I feared were once gone had erupted. The connection I'd been longing for since that chance meeting so long ago clicked into place. Why must fate be so cruel to give me what I had been longing for all while knowing it was wrapped up in all that I should distance myself from?

Why, then, was I lying in bed thinking of Nick?

The better question was, what was wrong with me?

Chapter Seventeen

M ONDAYS WERE BUSY and for that I was grateful. Less time to think about a certain someone. I came in early to put together my notes on all the clients I had seen last week who were ready for the client-date stage. Each new client would be assigned a relationship manager today. I attended those meetings to discuss any concerns I had. They were minor things. Anything major meant that they would have been rejected unless we were talking about our famous client.

There were a couple of clients who concerned me. One admitted to being a recovering alcoholic, which I gave him major props for. That was no small feat. He'd been sober for five years, but he had confessed it was still difficult for him and he attended regular AA meetings. Obviously, I didn't want his relationship manager to drink in front of him, but I also wanted her to let us know if he drank in front of her. He had to agree to allow us to inform whomever he was paired with that he had dealt with the disease. He was actually relieved that we would. He said it was always awkward to bring it up in conversation.

My other concern dealt with a woman who seemed overtly anxious in my office, though she denied dealing with anxiety or depression.

She made it sound as if those were weaknesses that were beneath her. I wasn't sure if she was anxious or if it was the situation. Sometimes people were nervous to meet with people like me. I needed her relationship manager to see how she responded in a relaxed environment over dinner. We also needed to be sure not to pair her with anyone who had dealt with anxiety or depression since she spoke so ill of the conditions.

There were no perfect people in our databases. We did our best, though, to match imperfections.

I gathered my notes and headed to the meeting. I slipped in right before the meeting started. My workload had me squeezing everything in whenever I could, which meant I didn't have time to come early. Everyone looked my way when I entered, even Kenadie was there. She normally didn't attend these meetings anymore. But there she sat next to Zander, bright-eyed and looking like she'd had a great weekend. Maybe her mom stopped giving her sex tips. That would surprise me, though. Nan was the most persistent woman I'd ever met.

I took a seat across from Kenadie and next to Jade. Everyone was still looking at me. Suddenly I was afraid my blouse had come unbuttoned, so I took a peek. Phew, no wardrobe malfunctions. I smiled nervously. "Good morning, everyone."

There was a low murmur of replied greetings. Kenadie beamed at me. So maybe Nan had laid off the pregnancy badgering.

Wrong.

"Kate, Nick's interview over the weekend was so amazing. Maybe we should make you a full-time relationship manager."

She better be teasing.

Why did I feel like I was the only one who had no idea what she was talking about? I had to play this the right way. I started by laughing, albeit with a fake ring to it. "Oh, no, I'll leave that to the professionals." I gave props and smiles to my colleagues, some of whom didn't look all that pleased, aka, Cara and Eva. Believe me, I didn't want to hone in on their territory.

"Regardless," Kenadie responded, "you obviously did us proud representing us at the Fallen Officers gala. The way Nick talked about Binary Search, I might have to think about hiring more staff and opening another location." Her eyes went all dreamy thinking about the possibilities.

I was going to have to find that interview. "Um…I'm happy it all worked out."

I couldn't think of anything else to say that wasn't a lie. I couldn't tell her the truth about how uncomfortable it was and how I'd left him there. I especially couldn't mention to her how he came to my house or how I spent most of the day with him and his family yesterday.

Kenadie stood up. "Keep up the good work, everyone. Now that we are in the spotlight, we must be more diligent and professional than ever."

I hadn't been all that professional.

"Get out of here, Kenz. This is my meeting now." Zander was ready to get down to business.

"Fine." She rolled her eyes at her best friend before zeroing in on me again. "Kate, drop by my office when you're done here."

Now I was more nervous than ever. Did Nick say something to her? Did she want to talk more about the interview I had no idea about?

I nodded. "Sounds good," I lied. It sounded more like heart palpitations.

Zander gave Kenadie a nudge and out she went. Zander stood up, all business, and wasted no time handing out assignments; there were more this week than last. He seemed to be in a hurry. I wondered why, which made me think I should text Meg to check on her. I should have over the weekend, but I was dealing with things, lots of things. Things I thought I'd prepared myself for but had not. Or had I just not expected a Nick?

"Any concerns, Kate?" Zander got me out of my head.

I focused back on the meeting and voiced my two concerns, as well as gave my normal spiel to report any inconsistencies or if any red flags popped up. We could still reject people at this stage.

Zander flew out of the meeting while I stalled, reading an email on my tablet. Anything to postpone my meeting with Kenadie even though I had a lot of work to do and several psych evaluation appointments. Most of them were women. Not surprising, but soon our dating pool was going to be female heavy.

When I could no longer stall, I made my way to the executive offices where Kenadie, Zander, and I were located. Kenadie's office was at the end of the hall. Her office wasn't exactly what you expected a CEO's to be. She, above all, was the architect of our software, a fact she took great pride in, as she should. It was a phenomenal solution. Her desk looked more like you would expect to see for a software designer, with two large monitors. Her door was open as if she were waiting for me. She was still all smiles.

"Kate, come in and shut the door."

My nerves crept up. I really hoped she didn't want to talk about that interview or Nick in general, but I had a feeling it was about him. Everything in my life lately seemed to be about him.

I decided to direct the conversation up-front. Anything to avoid the inevitable. "Is everything okay with Zander? He flew out of the meeting." I said while shutting her door.

Kenadie gave the smile of a sister who was enjoying torturing her brother. It was fitting of Zander's and Kenadie's relationship dynamics, but normally it was Zander doing the torturing.

"Oh, he's fine," she let out a laugh that had a hint of evil to it. "He's meeting Meg at the doctor. She has her first OB appointment today."

"Is he nervous about that?" I took a seat in front of her desk.

The delight in her eyes was off the charts. "Oh, yeah. Serves him right. Nothing has ever rattled him, well, except Meg, but this takes the cake. They came over yesterday to talk to Jason about having him design them a house. I had to keep from laughing as I watched him become an adult before my eyes. He followed Meg everywhere and must have asked her a hundred times if she needed anything."

"How did Meg handle it?"

"You know Meg. She teased him about it. I think she's hoping he'll relax. I think he's overcompensating because he's afraid he's going to screw it all up. He never saw Meg coming, and he'd probably never say it out loud, but he knows he's the lucky one."

I couldn't help but smile. "I'm excited for them both."

"Me too, except for the grief my momma keeps giving me about it. I need to get her a new hobby, maybe a man."

That caught me off guard. "You would be okay with that?"

She took a breath and thought. "My daddy's been gone for a long time and Momma's never complained, but I think she stays so busy because she gets lonely. It's a little weird to think of her with anyone else, but I don't want her to be lonely."

An odd thought tickled my brain. *What about Jack?* Was I insane? I couldn't suggest that my boss's mom and Nick's dad go out. I pushed that crazy thought out. "Maybe she could use our service."

Kenadie laughed. "Oh, no. I love her, but I value my sanity more. She'd be in here every day trying to retrain the relationship managers. Speaking of people using our service, that's why I wanted to talk to you."

I sighed internally. I would much rather talk about Nan.

"Nick—"

I knew it was about him.

"—has requested—"

Oh, here it came. He probably wanted us to roll out a red carpet, or something along those lines, every time he came in here. Or maybe he wanted more gorgeous reporters to interview him.

"—that we help one of his friends."

That I wasn't expecting. I perked up in my seat. "How?"

"He's paying for his friend Janelle Whitman to use our services. She's already filled out the questionnaire online and he's hoping you can squeeze her in this week."

Janelle Whitman. The name sounded familiar. She was...she was one of the widows at the fallen officer's event. Interesting. Very interesting.

"I rushed a background check. I know it's out of step, but this is a special circumstance."

"It is?"

"Nick is doing great things for us, so I want to return the favor," Kenadie replied.

Favor? He was doing us a favor? "I assumed he was being paid."

Her cheeks were turning rosy. "I can't go into specifics, but we have a mutually beneficial contract that includes him being a client of ours first and foremost."

That eased some of my worries about him. But what were the other specifics? Did he want Janelle to use our services so we would pair them up? Was he trying to win her over in some cute way? He didn't strike me as a man who did "cute" things. But maybe since she was the wife of his deceased friend, he wasn't sure how to ask her. That didn't sound like him either. He seemed to be more of a direct person. He certainly didn't lack confidence.

152

"I'll work her in this week as long as her questionnaire checks out."

"Thanks, Kate." She gave me a grateful smile. "I know this has added to your workload, but you're doing a great job of *fixing* him. The way Nick praised you in his interview was the best advertising on the planet, so thank you."

Right, the interview. I rubbed my neck. "Well, I better get to work. I'll look for Janelle's questionnaire after my appointments this morning." And after I found that interview. I stood up. "Is there anything else?"

"Let me know if you feel like it's getting to be too much, okay?"

I nodded. It was already too much, or at least Nick was. What would Skye say? He was so extra. Yes. Very extra.

As soon as I got to my office, I did a quick search for that interview with the ten minutes I had to spare before my first evaluation of the day came in. It wasn't hard to find after I typed in his name. I clicked on the link and there he appeared in all his tuxedo glory. Flashbacks of the kisses he'd planted on my cheek played along with the interview he'd done with Action News. I was surprised the interviewer was male. At least he wasn't drooling all over him.

The first part of the interview was all about his work with the charity. Nick reiterated a lot of what he had said on stage that night. If all I knew about him was watching the few minutes of him talking passionately about helping those families who had lost so much, I believe I would find myself...what? He was still a client, first and foremost, like Kenadie said. Besides, I knew him to be arrogant and ill mannered. So he was trying to be more polite. And he cleaned the kitchen. Stop it, Kate.

I focused on the screen.

The reporter chuckled. "Nick, we hear you are using the Atlanta-grown dating service Binary Search." The familiarity he used with him was weird to me. I bet they didn't know each other. "Is that true? And what value is there in it for a guy like you?"

That was a pompous question. Who did this guy think he was? This was the twenty-first century. People used dating apps and services all the time. Sure, some were questionable and made only for hooking up, but many places like ours truly wanted to help people.

Nick's darkened eyes said he found no humor or appreciation for the question. "Darius," his tone was patronizing.

Go Nick, I thought before I could stop myself.

"Who doesn't need help navigating the relationship waters nowadays? And Binary Search is unique, as you are given your own relationship manager to help guide you through the process."

Darius did his best to not look taken aback, but his shoulders twitched. "A relationship manager? What exactly do they do?"

"In my case," Nick gave his most debonair smile, "she's given me a new perspective. One might even say, the inside track about how women think."

"Where can I sign up?" Darius teased.

"Anyone looking for some relationship help should check them out online," Nick gave us a nice plug.

"Tell us who you're dating, then."

"I don't kiss and tell." Nick's tight jawline said don't press for information.

That was pretty much it. I wasn't sure what to think about it. I felt like what he'd said about me wasn't all that truthful. I couldn't imagine what he meant by new perspective. And the only insight I'd given him about how women thought was how I thought about him, which wasn't all that flattering. I was at least grateful he painted Binary Search in a good light, especially considering I'd left him at the gala. Maybe he hadn't realized that when he'd done the interview.

I didn't get the chance to mull it over; my ten o'clock was a few minutes early. She walked in wearing an *On the Edge* T-shirt with Nick's face plastered front and center on it. I knew then it was going to be a very, very long day.

Chapter Eighteen

THERE WASN'T ENOUGH peppermint oil in the world to address the pounding going on in my head. If I had to hear Nick's name one more time today I was going to...well, it probably involved eating cheesecake for dinner, except I had to head to the clinic as soon as I was done here. I felt like I'd already been treating mental disorders all day. It was called Nickitis. It was a contagion and everyone had it. Perhaps I should warn the CDC.

My phone rang. I was definitely eating cheesecake for dinner, with a side of hot fudge. Why was he calling me?

"Hello," I growled.

"Hello, Kate."

Now he chose to get some manners?

"Can I help you?"

"By the tone of your voice, it sounds like that might be a painful option for me."

He had no idea. And I had no idea why that made me laugh.

"That's better," his silky voice crooned.

"I'm sorry I snapped at you. I've been dealing with your sycophants all day."

"I'm all ears."

"You know I can't discuss clients, but I did meet a woman today who, from memory, could recite the name of every episode of *On the Edge*, including the special holiday episode you did after the show ended. Not only that, she photoshopped a picture of how your future children together would look. They were beautiful by the way, so mazel tov."

He may have chuckled. Maybe. "Please tell me you're not setting me up with her."

"Well..." I paused. "I thought about it until she showed me her tattoo of you. On her butt. Then I got a little frightened and ill. Needless to say, she's no longer a client."

Too bad peppermint oil couldn't burn that image out of my head.

"What can I say? I'm adored."

And egotistical. I kept that to myself since I was at work. "Is that the kind of attention you like or want?" I asked, because his profile told the story of a man who would, but my interactions with him said something entirely different.

He thought for a moment. It wasn't a hard question. Or so I thought.

"It's the price of fame. Something I've come to terms with."

"So you want someone who worships you?" Figures.

"You make that sound as if it's a terrible thing. Don't you want to be with someone who's devoted and adores you?"

I sat back in my chair, once again caught off guard by him. "I imagine most people would."

"I didn't ask about most people."

"Yes," I whispered. "But hero-worshipping your partner is not healthy."

"Thank you for that insight, Dr. Morgan."

"Now you're mocking me."

"That's not how I operate."

"Duly noted. Is there a reason for your call?"

"Other than the fact I enjoy talking to you?"

"Yes," I breathed out like one of his fan club members.

"I wanted to know why you didn't call me."

What? I shook my head. "Why would I call you?"

"That hurts, Kate. I thought we were friends."

"I don't remember us agreeing on that title."

"Let's agree on it now," he fired back.

"That's not how friendship works," I countered.

"I suppose you have rules for that too."

"Not necessarily," I stammered.

"Then we should have no issues."

I closed my eyes and rubbed my neck. Was someone playing a prank on me? Why did Nick Wells want to be my friend? Or should I ask, was he capable of friendship? Narcissists were not.

"Do we have a deal?" he interrupted my internal struggle of trying to figure out who or what he was.

"You don't broker friendship."

"What would you have us do?"

Was he for real? "Do you want a list?" I was so confused.

"Sure."

"Well...to become friends with someone, you should spend time together, share interests, and have mutual respect for each other."

"Done. Have dinner with Skye and me tonight."

He had to quit lobbing those kinds of things out there. My heart skipped a few beats. "Uh...first of all, Alex Trebeck, you didn't ask in the form of a question." It had sounded like a demand. "And second, I sent Chanel's information to you in your client portal. She signed your NDA, so you should probably take her out. By the way, she's...how did she put it? Over-the-moon excited. A dream come true for her." I'd done my best not to roll my eyes when she had come in jumping up and down.

I swore I could see him stretching his neck in the silence. He let out a heavy breath. "Will you please join Skye and me for dinner tonight?"

"Can't."

"I asked nicely." He didn't hide how grating that was for him very well.

"Yes, you did. I'll put another star in your chart," I teased. "But I'm volunteering tonight at the clinic."

"Right, you mentioned that to my dad."

"You were paying attention that night?"

"More than you know."

Why did everything he say sound like he was delivering a line in a romance movie where I was the unsuspecting female love interest? Obviously it was his job to write those one-liners, and he used to say them with such perfection in *On the Edge*.

I swallowed down the reigniting crush I used to have on him. "Okay, well, let me know if you didn't get Chanel's info—"

"I received it. That was part of the reason I was calling."

"Oh. I'm confused."

"I would prefer in the future if you called me regarding anything Binary Search related."

"Why?"

"As stated before, I like talking to you, and doesn't Binary Search tout individual attention from their relationship mangers?"

"Yes...but—"

"Do you have a problem calling me?"

Yes. A huge one. "I suppose not, but it's not the way we usually do things here."

"I'm not your usual client, now am I?"

"Well, you're certainly more demanding than most."

"Ah," he said with an air of amusement. "Did you expect anything less from me?"

"I think you know the answer to that."

"Yes, but hearing your distaste for me is so refreshing."

I really should have more for him, but there was a part of me that really had anything but distaste for him, which was distasteful. "And you still want to be my friend?"

"More than you know."

He hung up. No *goodbye*. No *I'm sorry for unhinging your life.*

I was about to bang my head on the desk, but a text from Meg saved me.

My baby.

An ultrasound picture came through.

Looks like a peanut, she added.

I remember thinking the same thing when I had my first ultrasound done at eight weeks.

This is so sweet. How are you feeling? How is Zander doing?

The nausea comes and goes for both of us, I think. He can't stop staring at the picture. He says it looks like a boy.

I laughed to myself in my office. *Why do all men think that? I think it would serve him right to have a girl.*

Oh my gosh. That's what I told him. I think that scares him more than anything.

I could imagine. The reformed womanizer having a daughter would be poetic justice. *We should do lunch this week if you're up to it.*

I would love to. You can fill me in on Nicholas Wells. Zander only says he's more trouble than he's worth.

I partially agreed with that statement. He was a pain, but he was good for the bottom line, I would say.

Just let me know a good day for you.

And I would do my best to steer the conversation away from the man who was making me question who I thought I was, or who I thought I had grown to be. I couldn't be the woman who fell for the Douglasses of the world. But was Nick a Douglas?

Chapter Nineteen

Y OU NEED TO challenge your defense mechanisms and turn off that critical inner voice that says you are unworthy to be loved."

How many times did I have to tell myself that after Douglas destroyed my heart?

John sighed and slouched in the chair across from me in the tiny office I used at the clinic. "I want to, but staying home and playing online is safer."

"But is it fulfilling?" *And what do you really want to be doing? Of course I didn't want to be at home. I mean, I'm sure John didn't.*

He gave me a furtive smile. "No."

"What is it that you are really afraid of?" *Yes, Kate, what are you really afraid of? Be quiet, Kate, this isn't your session.*

He ran his hands through his thinning blonde hair. "When I was with my wife, I always knew I loved her more than she loved me. I knew I never lived up to her expectations. I mean, I'm still a fast food manager."

"Do you like your job?"

He puffed his chest, whether on purpose or involuntarily I couldn't tell. "Yeah, I do. And I'm good at it. We're always one of the top stores in the region."

"That's great. So why do you talk down about it?"

He thought for a second. "I shouldn't." He sat up straighter. "I'm proud of the job I do."

I gave him a warm smile. "Don't let anyone tell you otherwise, not even yourself. If your thoughts start to wander in that direction, I want you to list five things you're good at and five reasons you love your job. You need to retrain your thought patterns."

He nodded like he could do that.

"And as far as being afraid of being in an uneven relationship, that is a natural worry. Love is a fickle creature and our feelings for someone we are in a relationship with can change from moment to moment. But you will never be in a healthy or even satisfying relationship if you hold your own feelings back for fear they won't be reciprocated. You need to allow your natural feelings room to grow." *Yes, Kate, you stifle them at every turn. Kate, we can talk about our self later.* "So embrace your feelings, the good, the bad, even the sad ones. They lead to a fuller life."

I lead a full life. I have a great job, I volunteer, I do DIY home projects, I'm well read, I travel some. So, there isn't anyone to share it with. Focus back on the patient, Kate.

His eyes said he wholeheartedly agreed, but his mouth said, "I don't know if I can take the rejection again."

I felt for him and knew exactly how he felt. Part of me wanted to tell him to stay home and play those online games, or maybe he could just be a little more well-rounded. We each had our safe things to cling to. "Are you happy right now?"

Are you happy, Kate?

John took a deep breath and slowly exhaled. "That's why I'm here."

"What do you really want?"

Yes, Kate, what do you really want? I want you to be quiet right now. I need to focus on John.

"I want the kind of relationship my parents have. They've been married for forty years and are as in love as they ever were."

I wished I could say the same about my parents right now. Mom had called me earlier to tell me that Dad was threatening to "update" their bathroom, and if he even touched the faucet she was coming to stay with me.

"Why don't you write down some of the qualities you are seeking, as well as the ones your ex-wife had that you would like to avoid in a future partner. Sometimes we can fall into a pattern of the kind of person we date. You may need to be more cognizant when you begin dating again. But avoid making hard-and-fast rules about relationships—that can cause its share of problems too."

Did I just say that? Crap. That's what I was trained to say. So what if it is true for everyone else but me? Is it getting warm in this room?

"That's good advice, Dr. Morgan."

Yes, it is. I mean, for most people. I bet he wasn't married to a narcissistic bigamist.

"Your homework for the next two weeks is to make your lists and do something social, like attend a party or invite someone to dinner, even if it's a friend. Take it a step at a time."

A step at a time. What was my next step?

....

My next step might be new employment after I read Kenadie's email first thing Tuesday morning.

To my favorite employees,

She was getting way too chipper.

I have some exciting news. The director of our new commercial featuring Nick would like to film some shots here. I didn't want to disrupt our day, so they'll be coming after hours. I know most of you will have client dates set up, but if you're free, you are welcome to stay if you would like.

These are great times for Binary Search.

Keep up the good work!

Kenadie

I had no intention of staying. It was no surprise that most of the evaluations I had today were with women—my Nick quota would be full by the end of the day. We were going to have to start running some half-price deal for men soon to balance it out.

My biggest hope for the day was that everyone kept their clothes on. If one more person showed me their tattooed butt, I was out of there. I didn't care how good the benefits were or how much I valued what we did here. Nothing was worth that.

The first client of the day walked in and I had high hopes when she was dressed in a business suit with no visible Nick tattoos. She behaved quite demure with the way she sat herself and crossed her legs, making sure to hold her shoulders back and keep her posture straight. My chiropractor dad would have given her good marks.

"Welcome, Lyndsey. I'm Kate."

"Hello." She had a sultry alto voice.

I'd already gone over her questionnaire, but I always reiterated some of the questions up-front to gauge how truthful they had been on it before I got into the heavier questions.

"To begin, I have a series of questions for you. There are no right or wrong answers. Just be honest with yourself."

She nodded.

"Your questionnaire stated that you are looking for a long-term commitment. Is that still true?"

Her eyes sparkled. "Definitely."

"What qualities are you looking for in a partner?" I always asked this because everyone wanted to sound good on paper and they always put what they thought were the "right" answers, like loyal, kind, good sense of humor, etc. But I found when asked directly without time to think, I got a clearer picture of their expectations.

She sat up even more. "Good looking, for sure. I love a man with brown hair and blue eyes."

Oh, no. Please tell me she wasn't a...

"And he has to be successful. Really successful."

I tried to keep from grimacing. Honestly, most people who used our service were successful professionals due to the fee we charged. We weren't a run-of-the-mill matchmaking service, but this was over the top.

"I wouldn't even mind if he was...famous."

Great. Another sycophant. Little did she know by saying she wanted a long-term commitment she was totally out of the running.

She flipped her long, ebony hair back. "I do own my own salon, so I can be red carpet ready at a moment's notice. And not to brag, but I was the lead in my high school's rendition of *Seven Brides for Seven Brothers*."

"That's a fun show." I had no other words.

"Oh, and," she continued, "I really want someone who lives on the coast."

"Which one?"

Her eyes looked around my office. "You know...the West."

Normally I wouldn't press, because people were free to say what they wanted, but I couldn't let this go. "Even though you live here?"

"I would totally move for Nick...I mean, the right man."

Don't roll your eyes. Don't roll your eyes. Moving on. "Do you feel emotionally ready to be in a long-term relationship?"

If she nodded any harder, her head was going to snap off. "Yes. I take every quiz in *Cosmo* and I always score high. And I'm so tired of every guy I date leaving after a couple of months."

That statement made this an entirely different type of interview. "Why do you feel like your past relationships haven't lasted?"

She paused as if she hadn't ever given it much thought, but she obviously wasn't going to, either. "They were the wrong guy. I need someone who can give me the lifestyle I deserve. I don't look this good for no reason." Her hand waved over her body.

We did not find people sugar daddies or mommas. I also wanted to tell her that she needed to look deeper inside herself to find things beyond her beauty to love about herself. But I wasn't her therapist, and she wouldn't be a Binary Search client.

At least the next two women weren't as blatant, and there was a man between them who didn't want to date Nick.

By lunchtime I was already looking forward to going home, and then *he* called.

"*Hello*, Kate."

"You get another star for your proper use of a greeting."

"Was that very proper?" he threw back at me.

I wasn't really in the mood to be polite to the man who was making my professional life hellish at the moment, but I mustered up some manners. "*Hello*, Nick. How are you?"

"Better now that I'm talking to you."

Why must he say things like that? When he did, my body took it all the wrong way. My stomach snapped, crackled, and popped. That wasn't supposed to happen, and I was sure he didn't mean it like my body reacted. "That sounds an awful lot like you want something."

"I definitely want something."

Add tingling to the list. "And what is that?"

"We'll get to that later, but for now I'll take you being there tonight when we shoot the commercial."

"Darn. I have a date with the grocery store and my remote tonight. Sorry."

He paused. And paused some more. Normally he was quick with a reply. "You're going to disappoint...Skye and...my dad." That didn't come out as smooth as he normally talked.

"How?"

"Skye's coming along with my dad, and they were hoping to see you. Skye was particularly disappointed you couldn't have dinner with us last night. She wanted to discuss the book you've been reading together."

"Oh."

I was embarrassed to admit how much I liked the shapeshifting dragon book. I'd started it last night after I got home from the clinic and the male protagonist was interesting. At first, he came off as an alpha-male type, but he had this I-love-a-strong-woman side to him. And thank goodness there was no instant love to their relationship. That was a huge pet peeve of mine. I needed a story to give me real reasons for them to be in love. I liked that the heroine had a healthy dislike for him still.

"You'll be there tonight, then." He said it as a statement, not a question.

I sighed, trying to think of a way out. Not that I didn't want to see Skye and Jack. I did. If I thought about it, I realized how much I would look forward to that, but they included Nick. And if I thought about him too much, I would think things I shouldn't think.

"How can we discuss the book while you're shooting a commercial?"

"There's always downtime between takes, and we could do dinner after."

"Don't you have Chanel to take to dinner?"

"Margo, my assistant, is setting something up with her for this weekend."

Margo. Figured he had a woman assistant. She was probably more than his assistant. More like a goddess, I bet, who did his bidding no matter what that was.

"You really should call her yourself."

"I don't have time for that."

"You're calling me."

"This I have time for."

I rubbed the tension creeping up in my neck. "You confuse me."

"The feeling is mutual."

"How do I confuse you?"

"This should be discussed in person. So, dinner tonight?"

I couldn't think or speak.

"You don't want to disappoint Skye again, do you?"

"Well, no, but—"

"And how can you be a good relationship manager if I confuse you?"

"I could quit."

"That doesn't seem like your style. We'll see you soon."

"Agghhh!"

"I heard that, Kate. Goodbye."

Crap. I thought he'd hung up already like he normally did.

I leaned back in my chair and breathed deeply, asking myself the same questions I had last night. What did I want? Why did I stifle relationships, even non-romantic ones? Why did I continue to run from my feelings?

That wasn't to say I had feelings for Nick. Yes, I was attracted to him, but I knew I had to keep it professional, and the jury was still out on his narcissist diagnosis. That book I bought Sunday said if you found yourself attracted to someone you work with, you should let your mind live out every daydream and fantasy but leave it all there in your mind. Those feelings of attraction would come and go. The problem with Nick was I had daydreamed about him for years. Intimate, detailed, burning-fires-of-passion kind of fantasies.

But maybe if all the mystery was gone from him and he proved to be the man who first walked into my office, the confusion would all be gone. I would work him out of my system and my life could go back to normal.

The problem was I didn't want my normal anymore, and I wasn't sure how to make it better. That wasn't true. I was afraid to make it better. And if I was honest, I was afraid of Nicholas Wells.

Chapter Twenty

IT WAS ONE big party at Binary Search. Not only did we have a film crew and Nick, who counted as like ten people with his big head, but Kenadie's mom and niece Lana came. Meg was dying to meet Nick, so she was there too. Zander didn't seem all that thrilled about his wife's obvious doe-eyes for Nick. Zander kept ahold of her from behind and whispered in her ear, making her giggle. They were cute. I also noticed how his hands rested on her abdomen.

Nan, Kenadie's mom, hovered nearby them in mothering mode. Since Meg lost her mother as a teen, Nan had been like a second mother to Meg and really Zander. I think by the way she smiled at the pair she was happier than almost everyone about the baby. I expected Kenadie and Jason, who stood by her side while talking to Jack, would get more sex advice tonight.

I was happy to see Skye and Lana talking. Lana just turned seventeen, I think, so they were close in age. Then there was most of our staff. Funny how many client dates had canceled for the evening, at least all the ones our female relationship managers had.

Oh, and how could I forget the actress who hung on every word and limb of Nick's that she could. I didn't realize this was that kind of commercial. Most of our commercials featured Zander and Kenadie talking about how and why they created Binary Search and what you could expect using our services. They were more like mini infomercials. By the way the blonde was dressed in a revealing red dress, it was shaping out more to be an advert for 1-800-GET-A-MISTRESS-NOW. We didn't take married people by the way, not even if they were in the process of getting divorced.

Nick looked good in a dark suit with no tie. He was in his element and let everyone around him, including the makeup artist, fawn all over him. The director was blocking the scene while a crew swirled around setting up lights and recording equipment.

I stood as far back as I could, taking it all in until all the praise heaped on Nick made me feel ill. I headed toward the cute teen girls who already looked as thick as thieves.

When Skye saw me, she immediately came to me and wrapped her arms around me. Whoa. I wasn't ready for the affection but welcomed it. When I reciprocated, my heart spoke loud and clear saying this is what I needed in my life. I wanted it more than anything. My own daughter to hug.

"Hey, there." I naturally stroked her hair, like my own mother had done on several occasions when we embraced. "How are you?"

She gave me one more squeeze. "Okay. I hate watching my dad work."

I pulled back. "Really?" Why did she come then?

She rolled her eyes. "Do you see the way that woman is pawing him like a cat? Gross. If she calls him bae, I'm out of here."

"Bae?"

"It's a so yesterday word for boyfriend or girlfriend."

"Oh." I needed to brush up more on teen vernacular.

"My dad's last girlfriend called him that. I almost threw up every time."

I laughed at her. "I think you're in luck tonight. I don't think bae is in the script." At least it better not be, or I would object.

Lana joined us.

"How are you?" I asked Kenadie's mini-me. Kenadie may have been her aunt, but they looked like sisters.

She smiled such a sweet smile. "Really good. I'm getting ready to start my senior year and apply for college."

I knew she planned on being a veterinarian like her dad and her deceased grandfather.

"Exciting. How's your family?"

"Great. Kind of weird having brothers now, but Daddy and Renee are really happy, and I like having a momma around."

I noticed a tinge of sadness in Skye's eyes when Lana mentioned her new stepmom. I wondered more about where Skye's mother was.

We were interrupted by Nan in all her glory. She had aged like a fine Southern belle. Hair and makeup properly done, and dressed like she was headed to her monthly Junior League meeting in heels and a pretty ruffled blouse. She had a kiss on the cheek for me.

"Kate, darling, how are you?" She didn't let me answer. She set her sights on Skye. "You must be Nicholas's daughter."

To Skye's credit, she smiled. "The one and only."

"This is Skye, Nan. And Skye, this is Mrs. Marshall, Lana's grandma." I made introductions.

Nan looked between Skye and me with one of her mischievous grins. "You are a gorgeous thing, aren't you? And you and Kate are friends already, I see."

"Kate's the best," Skye responded.

That warmed my heart. I put my arm around Skye. "The feeling is mutual."

Possibilities began to swim in Nan's eyes. I recognized it before when she tried to set me up with her oldest son, Dylan.

Nick didn't help the situation. He picked a horrible time to come over.

"Ladies," rolled off his tongue.

I had to stop myself from laughing at the ridiculous amount of makeup he was wearing. I guess it never crossed my mind watching him all those years that he was wearing makeup the entire time.

"Have you met Lana and Nan Marshall?" I asked instead of laughing.

"I have not had the pleasure yet." He held out his hand to Lana first.

Lana took it and blushed.

Next up was Nan. "Oh my," Nan swooned, "I'm a fan." Of course she was.

Lana and Skye giggled at Nan's reaction before walking off. I loved it. Wished I could do the same.

Then a very interesting thing happened. Jack entered the picture. Jack, who was every bit as debonair as Nick, and from the looks of the Wells smile he gave Nan, he had an eye for her.

"Who is this lovely lady?" Jack took Nan's hand and kissed it, making her blush.

My, my. I glanced at Nick to see what he thought. His eyes seemed to be reserving judgment.

"This is Nan Marshall, Kenadie's mom," I made introductions.

Jack gave me a wink. "How are you, darlin'?" He focused right back on Nan.

"I'm happy to see you."

"Why didn't you say that to me?" Nick whispered in my ear.

And darn if those tingles didn't appear.

I leaned away from Nick. "You didn't ask how I was."

We had an audience in Nan and Jack, who were grinning between us and each other. It felt very warm being under the microscope.

Jack, who still kept hold of Nan's hand, made it hotter. "Maybe we should leave these two alone."

"Good idea," Nan said with her conspiratorial flair.

"Please don't leave on our account. Nick has to get back to... well...whatever he does."

Nick flashed that dang charming Wells smile. "Actually, I do have something to discuss with Kate, if you wouldn't mind."

"Not at all." Jack led Nan away.

Nan giggled like she would when Zander would sweet talk her. Then she left me.

I placed a little more distance between Nick and myself. My coworkers were staring at us. More like Eva and Cara were shooting darts with their eyes at me.

Nick wasn't having it and closed the distance. "You're always trying to get away from me. Why is that?"

I leaned against the wall I was near, begging my heart to quit skipping beats and my mind to not replay any old daydreams of him. I tucked some hair behind my ear. "I'm maintaining a professional distance. My coworkers may get the wrong idea," I whispered.

Nick erased any professional, and almost all personal, distance. He placed his hand on the wall and leaned in. "What idea would that be?" His eyes were as devious as Nan's.

"Do I really need to spell it out to you?"

"I wish you would."

I caught my breath. "Nick."

His eyes grabbed mine and refused to let go. "Kate."

"What did you want to talk to me about?" I stammered out one syllable at a time.

A half smile played on his face.

Another interruption. Thank goodness. No. No. It wasn't good.

The director, Tabby I think I heard someone call her, a no-nonsense roll-up-her-sleeves kind of woman approached and was about to speak, but instead she stared at us before her eyes widened in an aha sort of fashion.

"Yes. This. This is the chemistry we need. What's your name?" she asked me.

"Um...Kate."

"Kate, have you ever acted?" She started touching my hair that I had kept down in beachy waves today.

I shied away from her touch. "No."

"Would you like to? It's only two lines."

I shook my head vehemently no. What about the blonde bombshell they'd brought in?

"Are you sure? You two are like screen gold. The chemistry and angst is rolling off you two."

Now we had a crowd, as in everyone who was there. I wanted to disappear into the wall.

"Nick, try and convince her," Tabby walked off.

I felt every eye on us even though I couldn't face anyone but Nick. How did he become my source of comfort?

Nick surprisingly gave me a sympathetic smile before he faced everyone. "Everyone, will you give us a moment? Kenadie, you should come."

I caught Meg's eye, and she wagged her eyebrows. That wasn't helping.

The three of us moved back to the executive office hall.

Kenadie looked as if she wasn't sure what to make of this turn of events. She would look at me, then Nick. It was if I could see her debate with herself about what might be going on, but then she landed on me and her shoulders relaxed. "How funny is this?"

"Hilarious," I played along.

"You don't really want to do this, do you?"

"I think it might be inappropriate."

She thought for a second. "You're right. Even if it's all pretend, it might look odd to our clients who meet with you if they saw the commercial." Kenadie laughed. "Or they might think it was fun."

"I'm no actress."

We all heard the real actress getting huffy. "You're still going to pay me even if I don't shoot this—it's in my contract."

Kenadie cringed. "We better let the professional do it. I don't want any bad publicity. Excuse me while I go put out this fire."

Now I felt guilty and embarrassed.

I began to follow Kenadie, but Nick caught my arm on the way by. "Slow down."

"Do you see what you've done?" I wanted to cry.

"Kate, I had no idea that was going to happen. But you have to admit there is something between us."

Did the world stop, or was that the aneurysm I was having? "I'm your relationship manager." I pulled away from his gentle hold. "I don't have to admit anything. I mean, there's nothing to admit."

"Say it enough and maybe you'll believe it." He stalked off.

I had to believe it.

Annulment was an ugly word, I repeated, over and over and over.

Chapter Twenty-One

AFTER HEARING THE whiny blonde who couldn't keep her hands off Nick while they were shooting their scenes say, "We want to give you the first kiss of the last person you date," a hundred times, and "Isn't it time you started dating by design?" I found myself at Shasta's, the famed ice cream place Meg, Zander, and Kenadie always talked about.

I knew it was a Friday night tradition for the Marshall and Grainger clan, along with Nan's two best friends, Adelaide and Cissy—aka the Nanettes. But Jack suggested we all go out somewhere to celebrate. He couldn't take his eyes off Nan. Nan suggested we go for ice cream. I think her motivation was showing off Nick and being in her comfort zone. Don't get me wrong, she seemed to like the attention from Jack, but I don't know that she had dated all that much—or ever—after the passing of her husband. I watched them as they sat next to each other and it was cute to witness the little flirtations and touches between the two. Jack knew how to work it and he made Nan the center of his attention. He used those enigmatic Wells eyes to captivate her.

The ice cream shop placed two tables together to accommodate the twelve of us. None of my other colleagues had been invited. Thankfully, I didn't think anyone else knew this soirée was taking place.

I sat between Meg and Skye with Lana across from us while the Nanettes went crazy over Nick. They were petting him like I'd seen them do with Zander.

"Looks like you've been replaced," Meg teased her husband.

"Darlin'," he kissed her, "I'm not worried."

That gave me some comfort. Nick didn't live in Georgia. Someday he would leave. Hallelujah. Unless...What if he fell in love with a Georgia woman? I knew he said he wasn't going to, but like I'd said, he wouldn't be the first person in that "nothing serious" category to find true love. Plus, his dad lived here. I had to think positive thoughts. He was going back to California.

"I hear you guys are looking to build a house," I mentioned to Meg and Zander.

Meg gave a coy smile. "We're thinking about it."

"Maybe," Zander cut in.

Meg rolled her eyes. "I don't think a baby and a bachelor pad go together."

As soon as she said *baby,* the Nanettes shifted gears and surrounded her. "That's right, a baby." Cissy and Adelaide attacked Meg and Zander.

"It's about time one of you had a baby." Adelaide gave Kenadie a serious stare.

"Your momma deserves a baby, Kenadie Anne," Cissy wagged her finger.

"Maybe Rick and Renee will have one," Kenadie sassed back.

Lana's eyes went wide with that news. Kenadie, who sat next to her, gave her a squeeze. "Don't worry, sugar, your daddy isn't having another baby."

"Now who said that?" Nan was deeply offended by the notion.

While everyone argued about babies, I watched Nick for a few seconds taking pictures with the staff working on a Tuesday night in the small town of Flowery Branch. And, of course, any patron who knew of him. It didn't take long for me to get my fill.

I focused on Skye sitting next to me. "I'm loving the book. How about you?"

Her pretty emerald eyes lit up. "Love it. Kieran is so hot!"

"Are you talking about the Dragons Unleashed series?" Lana asked.

"Yes." Skye fanned herself. "Kate and I are reading them together."

Lana sighed. "They're so good. My stepmom and I read them. My daddy makes fun of us."

"My dad says he's heard they are optioning the series for a movie," Skye informed us.

"Really? That would be amazing," Lana responded.

The two girls went on to talk about which of their favorite actors should play Kieran. I'm going to admit I didn't know one. The more I was around Skye, the older I began to feel.

Nick was released from the clutches of his admirers and wouldn't you know it, he made his way over to me. I mean Skye. You don't know how glad I was there wasn't any room on either side of me. The only seat left was on the end.

That was, until Skye took a breath and noticed her dad.

"I bet you want to sit by Kate." She moved over without missing a beat in her conversation with Lana.

She was a traitor.

Nick didn't waste any time taking his daughter's vacated seat. "Don't think I forgot you promised to have dinner with me," he said low enough so only I could hear.

"Don't you mean with your family? Besides, ice cream is perfectly acceptable for dinner. I have many college roommates who will back me up on that." I plucked one of the menus from the middle of the table hoping to distract myself and him.

It was no use.

"This is not how I envisioned this night." He brooded next to me.

I scanned the menu and spoke into it. "How did you picture it?"

"There were a lot fewer people involved."

I turned toward him. "I thought you loved a good crowd."

"This is why we need to get to know each other better." He leaned closer. "You think you know me, but you have me all wrong."

"I read your profile." Several times.

"Like I said, you don't know me."

I tried to ignore the electricity that surged between us. Instead, I looked around to see if we were the center of attention. I was surprised to see everyone talking and laughing like we weren't there. And for half a ridiculous second, I wished we were alone. If we were, I could peer into his eyes that were drawing me in. I could dissect him piece by piece. I could work him out of my system.

"Why do you want me to know you?" I whispered.

He rested his warm hand on my bare knee under the table. That connection was back and coursing through my soul. Why? How did he do that? Why could only he make me react like that?

"Because your lips say you despise me, but your eyes tell another story. I want to read the entire book and see how it ends." He removed his hand and turned toward Skye like he hadn't just upended my world or made me want to give him a library card with free access to my thoughts.

What was I thinking? I shook my head. Did anyone else witness our exchange? If anyone did, they weren't reacting to it. It was like the world had gone on without me. It had felt that way for a long time. I'd stood back after Douglas and watched the world. Being in the world meant real living and getting hurt.

I kept to my status quo and observed. Meg and Zander lived and breathed each other. Between kissing Meg, Zander kept saying they should head home. I ached to have a relationship like that. One so affectionate with visible passion.

Kenadie and Jason weren't quite as gooey-eyed as they had been, but they were still each other's main focus. Kenadie was thrilled about the commercial and spoke of all the doors it might open. Jason gave his wife his full attention and even suggested spending more money on advertising. Kenadie never smiled so widely at her supportive husband.

Nan and Jack laughed and talked about the good old days when life was simpler, when music and movies were better. I had to agree with them there. Cissy and Adelaide couldn't keep their eyes off their best friend and part of their trio of meddlers. From their bright eyes, they seemed to be on board with this new development.

Kenadie and Nick both snuck glances at their parents. Uncertainty, maybe even some melancholy, marked their countenances. I imagined it would be hard to see a parent, no matter your age, taking steps toward a romantic relationship again. Especially since both Jack and Nan had beautiful relationships with their spouses.

When Nick wasn't casting glances at his dad, he was being the ever devoted one to his own daughter. He was happy to give Skye and Lana some of the inside Hollywood scoop, like who he heard may play Kieran. Again, some actor I didn't know, but both girls squealed. Nick let Lana ask any and every question she could think of about all her famous crushes. I think Nick may have disillusioned her some when he revealed how those nice boys on screen were anything but.

And what did I do? I ordered a large hot fudge sundae.

Chapter Twenty-Two

NOTE TO SELF. You are not twenty anymore. Do not eat hot fudge sundaes for dinner. On that same note, you are not twenty anymore and you should no longer have fantasies about Nicholas Wells. But what if he's calling you? Like he was at this very moment.

I stared at his name holding my stomach while I laid in bed not sleeping. Soothing ocean sounds played on James, my hands-free speaker. My twenty-year-old self told me it was okay to believe in magic. My thirty-four-year-old self wanted to believe her, but she argued that there were rules in place for a reason, a valid reason, and he was a client. My twenty-year-old self reasoned that answering his call wasn't breaking any rules, personal or professional.

I pushed the speaker button. "Hello."

"Kate... Hello," he made sure to add in.

I smiled to myself. "I had a feeling you would be calling."

"You are getting to know me better already."

"I don't know about that, but you seemed frustrated tonight that we didn't talk."

"I didn't want to cause you any more discomfort. You obviously don't like it when I pay attention to you in public settings."

"Thank you for recognizing that."

"I am sorry," he had a hard time articulating that last word, "about Tabby today. Even if her assessment was spot on."

"It wasn't your fault, though thanks to her and you, I will be the main source of office gossip for weeks to come."

"I've never met anyone like you."

I rolled over on my back, holding my stomach, but now for other reasons than the hot fudge. "Because I'm a private person?"

"No. Whether you think so or not, I value privacy. What intrigues me about you is that you don't recognize how noticeable you are."

"I'm not—"

"Kate, the first time I met you, you..."

My heart pounded wildly. We weren't really going to talk about that day, were we? "I what?"

"You left an impression."

"Even though you didn't recognize me again when we met?"

"I couldn't place you. There's a difference. And in my defense, you were wearing a hat. The question is why you didn't tell me when I asked you if we'd met before?" He paused. "I know, you have your reasons."

I sat up straight in bed. "Nick." I felt as if I couldn't catch my breath. "That day..." I couldn't do it. "Ask me any other question," I blurted without thinking. What did I open myself up to? I swore I could hear his mind working to take advantage of the power I'd handed him.

"Don't think I won't come back to the previous question again someday, but for now I'll settle for a list of your dating rules, beginning with number one."

"Why do those matter to you?"

"Ah-ah-ah, Kate, you said anything."

I landed back against my pillows. "You're probably going to make fun of them."

"Probably."

I took a deep breath and let it out in a rush. I was just going to get this over with. "The biggest and overarching rule is no narcissists or those with narcissistic tendencies." That would be you, buddy. Maybe. I still didn't know.

"Interesting."

"What?"

"Narcissistic tendencies—it has a ring to it. Like a movie title."

"Narcissism is no laughing matter. A person with narcissistic personality disorder can lead to a trail of emotional, psychological, and even physical abuse, leaving partners and loved ones drained and traumatized."

"Hey, slow down. I'm not saying it sounds like a romantic comedy. I was thinking more along the lines of a psychological thriller."

"Oh. That would be fitting."

"Do you like psychological thrillers, doctor?"

"As a matter of fact, I do. I'm reading one right now called, *Fading Orchid.*"

"Sounds intriguing."

"You should check it out."

"I will when I'm done working on my current project. I don't read while I'm writing."

"Why?"

"I don't want to muddy the waters."

"That makes sense."

"So no narcissists," he went back to rule one. "How can you tell if someone is a narcissist?"

Ooh. This was good. Maybe I could use this to my advantage. "It's difficult to diagnose since most narcissists are highly intelligent and they can manipulate situations to their advantage, make you believe they are something they aren't. Not only that, but they will probably be proud of that accomplishment, and can play the game for a long time in some cases."

"Hmm…Interesting. If you can't diagnose it, how do you know someone has narcissistic personality disorder?"

"You can diagnose it, but people who have NPD don't usually walk into a psychologist worried they might have it. It's usually a partner who recognizes the signs."

"And what are those?" He was so curious.

"I could give you list of questions that you could…I mean, that I might ask someone." I hoped that came out nonchalant.

"That would be good."

I heard some rustling in the background. Maybe some typing. Was he working on his script while he talked to me?

"I'm ready whenever you are."

"Okay. Do people gravitate toward you? Are their first impressions positive, but sour over time?" I paused waiting for him to answer.

"Keep going."

Darn it. I sighed. "Do you take responsibility for your actions or do you play the victim?"

"I know a lot of people like that," he growled.

Like yourself? I wanted to ask, but didn't. I was sure I heard typing now, though. "Are you materialistic and like to show off large purchases? Do you always have to have the best?"

"Have you been to Hollywood?" he snorted, not helping me out at all.

"A narcissist would also be unable to handle criticism and always think they are truly special."

"You just described the better part of Hollywood's population."

"Including you?"

"I really am special."

I couldn't tell if he was teasing or not. "I bet you think you are."

"So do you. I saw your worn-out copies of *On the Edge.*"

"I'm rolling my eyes at you right now, but will admit I may have had a slight lapse in judgment in my late teens and early twenties."

"Now we're getting to the truth. Tell me what your favorite episode was."

"Did I mention that narcissists always make the conversation about them?"

"No. That's a good one though." He was completely unfazed by the question and didn't answer it. And what did he mean that it was a good one? Did he see himself doing that?

"Are we done now?" I asked.

"Not even close. I thought you had twenty rules."

"I do."

"Looks like we have a long night ahead of us, Kate."

He wasn't lying. We talked until almost one in the morning. He got to hear almost every rule, from my no dating entertainers, celebrities, bartenders, dancers, choreographers, massage therapists and police officers because they had the highest divorce rates, all the way to age ranges. The closer in age you were, the better your relationship fared. That went for income and level of education as well.

He listened and made remarks, like how normally staying away from celebrities was a good rule of thumb, but I shouldn't make broad stroke judgments regarding them. But mostly he asked a lot of questions.

"You weren't lying when you told my dad you do your best to keep men away. I doubt if you'll ever find anyone who matches your expectations."

I closed my eyes and pulled my knees to my chest. "I know."

"You would rather be alone?"

"There are worse things than being alone."

"Agreed."

"You speak from experience."

"As do you, I would say. Have you been married too?"

Wow. He tossed that right out there.

I took a moment to answer. "Technically, no." That was one good thing about annulment. In the eyes of the law it never happened. In my case, it couldn't have happened since he was already married.

"Technically?" He was obviously confused.

I wasn't going to elaborate. "I think we've talked enough about me for the night."

"Was opening up so awful for you?"

I thought about it. "It was tolerable."

He laughed, but in a muted sort of way. "There's always next time."

"Next time?"

"How do you expect for us to get to know each other if we don't talk?"

"I suppose that would be difficult."

"I would say impossible. I say we pick it back up this weekend—"

"Excuse me," I yawned. I was getting too old to stay up this late on a work night. My brain was late-night foggy. I must have heard him wrong. "I'm sorry, did you say we should get together this weekend?"

"Yes. Is that a problem for you? I would say a night this week, but my schedule is full."

I rubbed my face in my hands. "Nick, aren't you taking out Chanel?"

"That will only take a couple of hours."

"How do you know? You may really hit it off, and you'll want to keep your weekend clear so you can spend more time together."

"That's not going to happen. Besides, I already know what we should do."

"And what is that?"

"There's a film noir event going on downtown. I thought you and Skye would enjoy it."

"How did you know I loved that genre?"

"I saw several among your DVD collection."

"Nick—"

"I already worked it out with the theater manager. We won't be seen."

"How do you know I'll say yes?"

"It's all in your eyes, Kate."

My eyes and I were going to have a serious talk, as well as my heart that pounded because he had taken notice of my interests. "I need to think about this. It's late, and I have to get to work early."

"Fine." He sounded put out. "I'll call you tomorrow. By the way, Janelle is looking forward to meeting with you."

That's right. In all the weirdness I'd forgotten that his *friend* was coming in today for her evaluation. "Did you sign her up hoping you would be matched with her?" Though I could tell right away judging by their questionnaires they would be considered statistically improbable. On paper she was too good for him.

A patronizing chuckle escaped him. "Janelle and I will never be more than friends. And I don't need a dating service to ask a woman out."

"Then why are you using one?"

"Like you, I have my reasons." His tone said not to press.

"Good night." I was going to hang up.

"Kate…that came out harsher than I intended. I know how all this may appear. I'm hoping you can separate the two. Good night."

I lay staring at my phone in the dark. Separate the two? I didn't know what that meant. I didn't even know if I could separate fiction from reality anymore, because more and more my life seemed like my twenty-year-old dreams.

I guess it was a good thing that I knew better now than to follow them.

Chapter Twenty-Three

THERE WAS A lot of office buzz going around the next day. Unfortunately, I was part of the annoying chatter. I heard things like, "Did you see how cozy Kate and Nick were last night? Maybe she's managing more than his relationships." It was embarrassing for me when I walked out of the bathroom stall and Eva and Cara didn't know I was in there while they gossiped about me.

"Maybe I'm just doing my job." I tried to keep my voice steady.

Both of their faces turned bright red before they rushed out of the bathroom.

I'm not sure if the other relationship managers and admin employees were talking about me behind my back, but I got a lot of those wondering glances. I knew what they were all wondering, and they were wrong. I didn't care what that director thought. There was no chemistry or angst between us. Perhaps that wasn't exactly true. There was something. I felt it each time we touched. I would be a fool to deny it, but I was working through it.

The other bit of news on the grapevine was much more pleasant. At least, I thought so. Kenadie seemed unsure when I overheard her and Zander talking outside his office while I tried to pay attention to Todd asking me my thoughts on his client date the night before. Kenadie was cautious about her mom and Jack, who apparently had a lunch date today. They were bringing along Lana and Skye. I thought that was a cute touch.

Zander had put his hand on her shoulder. "Relax, Kenz. This is good for Nan. And for Meg and me too. Hell, I think she'd move in with us to take care of Meg right now if we'd let her."

Kenadie laughed. "Just wait until the baby comes."

Zander turned a shade of green.

She rolled her eyes at her best friend. "You're going to be fine." In a softer move, she gave him a hug. "You're going to be a great dad."

Zander seemed to take comfort in the hug and words.

I slipped into my office after speaking to Todd. I had to get ready for Janelle Whitman's evaluation. Because I needed more people connected to Nick in my life.

I pulled up the single mom's file. She had three kids ranging in age from seven to eighteen. My heart broke knowing their tragic loss. She was a nurse for a local doctor's office, and from reading her profile and staring at her picture, she gave off the vibe of a beautiful soul. She reminded me of a grown-up Disney princess with cascading brown hair and jewel-toned eyes. She didn't look old enough to have an adult child.

I was more impressed with her volunteer work. She was PTA president, a court-appointed special advocate, and she taught English to immigrants in her spare time. I'm not sure how a mom, much less a single mom with three kids, had spare time. I felt ashamed at how little I gave back in comparison. Maybe I should increase my time at the clinic. I should ask her about becoming a CASA volunteer. It's something I had thought about. I loved helping children at the clinic; this would be one more way.

Janelle was on time and in her scrubs. She was taking an early lunch. Cuteness rolled off her as well as some nerves as she sat in the chair in front of my desk.

"I never thought I would use a matchmaking service." She looked around my office. "I think my Caden would be laughing at me."

"Is Caden your husband?"

She sighed but smiled. "We'd been together since high school. Broke up at least a dozen times, but there was something about him that kept me coming back. He drove me crazier than anyone I know, but I miss him."

"I'm sorry for your loss."

"He died trying to protect someone; I can't fault him for that. But sometimes I want to. I knew the risks of his job, but somehow I never thought it would be us."

"It wouldn't have been easy to live with that kind of anxiety every day."

"Maybe I should have worried a little bit more." There was a hint of Southern sass to her voice. I liked it and her.

"Do you feel like you are ready to date again?"

"Nick sure thinks I am."

My body twitched at the mention of his name. "And you value his opinion?"

A cat-like grin appeared on her pretty face. "Not as much as he thinks I should, but he's been one of our best friends for ages now, and he's helped us more than anyone since Caden was killed."

"Really?" That piqued my interest.

"He flew in as soon as he got the call. He paid for both funerals and anytime my boys need a man to talk to, they call him."

"And you let them? . . . I mean, that's nice."

Her smile only grew. "I know he comes off as a real hind-end of a mule sometimes, but there's a soft side to him. He only needs the right woman to bring it out in him a little more often."

I cleared my throat and tucked some hair behind my ear. "Maybe you'll both find a match here."

She spat out a laugh. "Heather and I have been making fun of him for using this place. Like he needs more women to fall all over him. Rumor has it, though, that one woman isn't all that impressed with him." She gave me a telling grin.

I pointed at my chest. "You don't mean me, do you?"

"You are Kate Morgan, right?"

I nodded.

"You have Nick so wound up." She gave me an appraising look. "I can see why too."

Blushing was becoming a regular occurrence lately. "Our relationship is professional in nature."

"Uh-huh."

"We should probably get back to the interview," I fumbled over my words.

"Would you mind if I gave you some advice first?" she asked in the sincerest way.

I couldn't refuse. "Okay."

"Maybe this is more insight than advice, but Nick's ex-wife really did a number on him, and Skye too, though Nick's done his best to shield Skye from the real ugliness. He hasn't been so smart over the years when it comes to women, but I think it's because he's afraid of getting hurt. He'd never admit it, but I think he chooses the wrong women so he doesn't have to worry about getting his heart broken again."

I found myself leaning in, absorbing what she was saying.

She scooted her chair closer. "Or maybe…" A twinkle flashed in her eye. "He's been holding out for the woman he met at the bookstore a long time ago."

Words. I had none. Feelings. I had a million, ranging from numb to electrified. He was telling people about my moment, our moment. He wasn't supposed to do that.

Janelle sat back in her chair with a satisfied expression. "I just thought you might want to know. Now, ask away."

....

Janelle left my office, but her words and presence lingered. She was as lovely as her questionnaire said she was. I think she was ready to begin dating, and I agreed that starting off in the not-anything-serious category was a good start for her to dip her toes back into the dating scene. She asked if we could reevaluate in a few months and I thought that was reasonable and sensible on her part. Nick had paid for an annual plan for her, so she had plenty of time to test the dating waters. She obviously missed her husband, but she was someone who had a lot to give and she missed companionship.

Her words, though, kept ramming into me like a Viking's ship. Did that moment mean something to Nick? He had read the book and had come looking for me. He also dated Academy Award–winning actresses.

Who was I? I was his relationship manager, that's who, and too smart for the thoughts of Nick that kept popping up like a jack-in-the-box and scaring the heck out of me. Maybe I should suggest to Kenadie that Nick get placed with a real relationship manager. Proximity all on its own could lead to attraction.

What frightened me more, though, was after everything I'd been through with Douglas, and every rule I'd made that Nick broke, I found myself wanting to believe in magic. Not supernatural powers, but an ineffable experience where my heart, body, and soul came together to connect me to another human in a way that was unexplainable. The way I'd felt that day outside the bookstore. The way I felt every time Nick touched me.

Magic was an illusion.

Though many of my fellow psychologists would disagree with that statement. Many of them believed that when it came to being in love, to have the fullest experience you must bring with you your fantasies and illusions. They would argue the magic of love is real.

I used to believe that too. But when you trusted someone and surrendered all your vulnerabilities to them only to have them use them as weapons of war to assail and assault the very essence of who you were, it was a natural conclusion that love shouldn't be so reckless. That I shouldn't have been so reckless.

Magic needed to be taken out of the equation. Love needed to be born out of mutual interests, circumstances in life, friendship, and a healthy dose of realism. My mom called it a sterile breeding ground where love would never bloom. She believed magic was what made love grow, and all the other stuff was what it took to make it last.

Sterile was a good way to describe my life and any relationship I'd had since Douglas. It's not that I didn't miss the passion and emotion, but my heart needed the shelter from the carelessness of my younger days. At times, though, I felt like my heart had grown weak and begged for another chance to call the shots once in a while, or at least to be heard above the sensible arguments my brain was so good at winning—until very recently.

I sat at my desk and rubbed my chest, trying to calm my heart, begging it to listen to reason, reminding it of the damage it had caused. Out of nowhere, my brain turned on me and tossed a zinger out there. *Two wrongs don't make a right.*

Chapter Twenty-Four

"THANK YOU, DARLIN'." Jack kissed my cheek.

"My pleasure." I already had my arm wrapped around Skye.

"Nick's a little over protective and—"

"A little?" Skye complained. "I'm almost sixteen. I don't need a babysitter." She gave me the half smile she'd inherited from her dad. "No offense. I like hanging out with you."

I liked hanging out with her too, and it's why I agreed to it against my better judgment when Nick had asked me last night if I would mind if Skye hung out with me while he did some research at the police department for the screenplay he was working on. I really shouldn't be entangling myself more with his family, but my heart felt more alive around them.

"None taken." I gave her a squeeze. "Have fun on your *date*." I smiled at Jack.

Jack flashed that debonair grin of his. "I plan to."

"Gross, Grandpa." Skye held up her hand. "Don't say anything more. It was bad enough watching you on Tuesday make a fool of yourself with Lana's grandma."

Jack laughed and kissed his granddaughter's head. "You'll understand someday, kid. Love you." He stepped off my doorstep with a spring in his step. "See you ladies later."

Skye and I waved our goodbyes to Jack and watched him drive off. I turned to Skye. "You ready to have our fun?"

"As long as it doesn't involve old people kissing."

My head tilted, surprised. "Kissing?" Jack and Nan were moving fast.

"Not like making out, but more like old people pecks."

"Old people pecks? What are those?"

"You know, where they're like birds pecking each other's beaks."

Not sure if I wanted to, but I tried to visualize it. My parents were around Jack's age, but they never kissed like that. My dad, when things weren't so tense between him and my mom, would press his lips against hers and breathe her in for a small moment. He never parted her lips in my presence, thankfully, but the emotion was always felt. I never doubted how much my dad loved my mom. I wanted a man like that.

"Did they do that a lot?" I was curious.

"Just once that I saw when he walked her to her door, but it was enough."

"There will be no kissing tonight unless you count loving on some puppies and kittens."

Her green eyes lit up. "Where are we going?"

"I talked to your dad's friend Janelle about some volunteering opportunities and she mentioned that her son *Liam…*" I paused to see if that elicited a reaction and it did. I found it interesting that Janelle was the mom of the same Liam who Skye had told me about. Skye's porcelain cheeks tinted pink. I continued, "Volunteers at an animal shelter once or twice a week."

"Is Liam going to be there?" She bit her lip and refused to make eye contact.

"I heard a rumor that he might be."

She threw her arms around me. "Thank you."

I reciprocated and hugged her back. "You're welcome. I thought afterward you and I could do a late dinner before your dad picks you up."

She nodded against me.

I felt a piece of my heart connect while holding her. I wasn't sure if I should back away or hold on tighter. What was it with the Wells family? "We better get going."

On the drive over to the shelter I was able to learn more about Skye. Her birthday was the second week of September, which she hated because she was the oldest person in her class. She was still mad that her dad didn't let her start kindergarten a couple of weeks early. She went to a private all-girls school, which she was also not a fan of. And her best friend's name was Hensley, who she could text incessantly with while she conversed with me. I admired the talent. I imagined she was telling Hensley she was on her way to see Liam.

I hoped it would be okay. I supposed I should have mentioned it to Nick, but the less I talked to him, the better. I was hoping tomorrow night he would hit it off with Chanel when he took her to a Braves game. I guess he hadn't taken my advice. He'd asked what I would like to do on a first date, and I recommended the improv club because it wasn't too intimate, but you could sit at a table alone and talk between performances. Not only that, you could gauge the other person's sense of humor to see if it matched your own.

Topgolf was also on my favorite lists for dates, not like I had a lot, but I'd been there before and the food was good and my date and I had a great time playing the interactive golf games. I mentioned he could even help her with her swing if she needed it. That was romantic. Then there was always Friday night jazz night at the art museum, a favorite of mine. What was better than art and live jazz? Apparently, baseball. I wasn't a huge fan.

What he did was his own business. But I really needed him to hit it off with Chanel. I didn't care that he said he wouldn't. The sooner he found love, the better for all involved. I would no longer have to be his relationship manager and my heart would get the message that he was never a contender, and we weren't breaking the rules, especially the mother of all the rules.

Though I wasn't sure he broke that particular rule. The people in his life, from family to friends, seemed to love him even if they all thought he could use a little work. But who didn't need some work? I wasn't thinking to repair him. And people could only be repaired if they wanted to; no one could do it for them. Sure, you could help. It was my job to help people in that process. But you should never enter a relationship with the intention to "fix" someone. You would only end up broken.

The thing with narcissism was it wasn't curable, and for any change in behavior it would require extensive amounts of psychotherapy. It would be an arduous task. And narcissists rarely felt the need to change.

Regardless of what Nick was or wasn't, we weren't meant to be. My job was to help him find his last first kiss, as the commercial was going to say. And we were never kissing. You should never kiss men like Nick. My books backed me up. There was even a chapter titled, "You Should Never Physically Bond with Bad Boys." You thought ovaries were loud, they had nothing on saliva. The chemical makeup of saliva could tell you if your partner in question would give you beautiful babies.

And really, was that even a question in Nick's case? He would give anyone beautiful babies. I had living proof next to me in the car. So her mom was a supermodel. Nick had passed on plenty of his gene pool to her.

Mix that saliva with all the happy chemicals kissing released in your brain and you'd be throwing out every rule you'd ever made to be with him. And if that didn't do it, the flush of pheromones rushing through the both of you would make the other person seem even more sexy. If Nick got any sexier...well...I couldn't think of it. And unfortunately, I had thought about it, many times in my past, present, and probably my future.

I focused on Skye. "Do you have any pets at home?"

She took a second to stop texting. "We had a cat once. My dad brought her home to me in his jacket pocket," she smiled, but it faded quickly, "after my...mom...Alessandria..."

That was telling. She called her mom by her first name, her only name. I tried not to draw attention to it or react one way or the other. I waited to see if she wanted to continue, and she did after a pause.

"Decided she didn't want to keep pretending to be a mom anymore."

I was able to safely sneak a glance at her and it didn't take a degree to recognize the pain on her beautiful face. "How old were you?" I reached for her hand.

She took it and that bond appeared again. "Six. I mostly lived with my dad anyway..." She tried to sound brave.

"It's okay that it hurts."

She shook her head and looked out the passenger-side window. She was obviously trying to pretend the hurt had healed. "I overheard her tell my dad that if it wasn't for him, she would have never had me in the first place. All I was for her was publicity. Every interview and article written about how much she loved being a mom was all a lie.

She used me," her voice cracked, "to further her career. I hate when people at school show me old magazine covers they've found online with her and me on them."

I gave her hand a gentle squeeze while my heart broke for her. "It's hard when the people we trust most in our lives fail us. You didn't deserve that."

She wiped her eyes. "My dad has always been there for me. I don't need her."

"No, you don't. The loss is hers."

"That's what my dad always says. I think it's why he's so overprotective. I had a nanny until I was twelve." She laughed. "I had to tell him how embarrassing that was. I'm surprised he lets me hang out with you. He's never let any of his girlfriends take me anywhere."

I coughed and swerved a tad. I had to place both hands back on the wheel. "I'm not your dad's girlfriend."

She gave me a crooked grin. I saw a lot of her grandpa in it. "I know. You're *friends*."

"Sort of."

"You like him though, right?"

I had to think about what to say. It was complicated. I didn't not like him, but I didn't want to like him. How did I explain that to his daughter? I didn't. "Yes." It wasn't a lie.

"Good." She smiled.

Did she breathe a sigh of relief?

We needed to change the subject. I couldn't ask about the cat now since she said she used to have one, so that indicated it probably died and it was associated with an awful memory of her mother. That woman now ranked right up there with Douglas for me. Who says that about their child? What Janelle told me two days ago made so much more sense. I even felt sorry for Nick.

"Tell me what you like about Liam."

A dreamy giggle escaped her. "He's so cute, but in that nerdy, glasses kind of way. Do you know what I mean?"

"I think so." I was picturing Clark Kent. Did she even know who that was?

"And he's so nice, but he's really shy."

"Nice is good." Very good, well, as long as it was genuine.

She held her hands together. "He's super smart too. He got into Princeton, but he's staying in Georgia so he can be near his mom and brother and sister. He doesn't want to leave them since their dad died."

"He sounds like a really great guy."

"He is," she let out a wistful sigh, "but things are so different between us now."

"Well, he has a lot of big life changes coming up, and you're still in high school, not to mention you live in California. He's probably being cautious."

"I know, but we're only two-and-a-half years apart and he's come to visit before. He's really into comic books and science fiction movies and books, so my dad took him to Comic-Con last year."

Of course he did. Nick needed to quit confusing me. "Did you go too?"

"Uh, yeah, even though it isn't really my thing."

I smiled at her. I would have done the same thing at her age. "The only advice I have for you is to be yourself around him. If he sees that, maybe he'll relax and maybe someday your friendship can blossom into something more."

"I'll try, but what I really want to do is kiss him."

To be almost sixteen again. I laughed. "He probably wants to kiss you too, but don't rush it."

"How will I know when it's the right time?"

Oh gosh. I didn't know if I was the right person for her to be asking, but maybe she wanted a woman to talk to about it instead of her dad or grandpa. Sadly, I had to think back a ways.

"Um...it's all in the eyes. The way the other person gazes at you, but they don't speak. They may stare at your lips. There may even be some awkward silence. They'll tilt their head and lean in closer. The magic of anticipation will stir between you and you'll close your eyes and before you know it, it will happen."

"That sounds so romantic."

"It isn't always, that's why you should wait and do it with someone who means something to you." Honestly, I was shocked she hadn't kissed someone already. She had to have boys, even men who had no business doing so, clamoring after her. And I'd had patients younger than her who were already having sex and dealing with the repercussions of it. They were too young to handle the emotion of it. Many felt pressured into it. Skye's experience or lack thereof was a breath of fresh air for me.

"Liam means something to me."

I believed her. I watched her interactions with Liam that night as we played with the abandoned puppies and kittens, trying to help socialize them. There was no question that shy, lanky boy with hair of dishwater blond and thoughtful hazel eyes behind thick dark glasses was smitten by the beauty of the girl he thought was way out of his league by the way he gazed at her when he thought no one was looking. It was as if he didn't dare hope that Skye could really like someone like him.

He was selling himself short. Not only did I observe him with Skye, but there were young volunteers there who read to the animals, and he would help them sound out words. He did great animal sound impressions. Skye giggled as he did everything from an elephant to a lion. His smile said he was pleased he could make her smile and laugh, though he turned a few shades of pink.

I enjoyed my time snuggling furry creatures and talking to Skye about our book. It was getting really good. The hero and heroine were locked in a battle of wills. He wanted to protect her, to claim her, and she wanted a choice. They were bound by legend and fate, but she wanted to know she was loved by him regardless. The kissing scenes were A+ too. Sad, how much I was enjoying them.

Skye made an interesting observation while stroking the head of the cutest calico kitten. "How will she ever know the truth?" she asked, speaking of our heroine.

Oh, that was a good question. One I was still searching for myself. If only I could script out my own ending.

Chapter Twenty-Five

NICK WAS WAITING for us outside my townhome when Skye and I pulled up after having the best teriyaki bowls ever and one of the best nights, at least for me. Being with Skye made me feel. I missed feeling.

We got out of the car still laughing about some of the memes she showed me at the restaurant. Apparently memes were a major form of communication between teenagers now. Who knew? Some of them were hilarious, though, like all the ones about the new eyebrow styles. I had no idea you could braid your eyebrows or that there were accessories for them. Not trying either trend.

Nick was leaning against the sports car he was renting for the summer. Flashbacks of that poster above my bed hit me. Thankfully, his tight T-shirt was on, but that was alluring all on its own. I had to think of something else, like the kitten that almost came home with me. He was cute and cuddly.

I bet Nick was cuddly.

Where did that thought come from?

Skye gave me a big hug after we exited the car. "Can we go to the shelter again?"

"I would love to, if it's okay with your dad." My eyes drifted up at the man who was walking our way, taking in the scene with a look of contentment. The snapping, crackling, and popping was back in my stomach. I took a deep breath to stave it off.

Skye left me for the waiting arms of her dad. He wrapped her up and kissed her head. It was the most attractive sight of my life. *I'm his relationship manager*, I repeated to myself.

"Did you have fun tonight?" Nick asked Skye.

"So much," she responded.

He kissed her head one more time. "Why don't you wait in the car? I want to talk to Kate for a minute."

Oh, no, no. We didn't need any alone time.

Skye was too obedient. She waved at me. "Bye, Kate, thanks for everything."

"Bye, honey." That term of endearment came out of nowhere, but it felt so natural to call her that.

Her smile said she liked it.

"Call me tomorrow when you get to chapter twenty so we can discuss." I was a little ahead of her because I had no life.

"I will." She pranced off.

Nick looked between Skye and me; his normally brooding eyes had lightened up considerably. If I wasn't mistaken, he was happy.

I leaned against my car, nervous as he approached. The steamy Georgia night felt more suffocating with each step he took toward me. My back was now flush with the car, my blouse clinging to me. I had nowhere else to go. And he was close, so close.

"Thank you, Kate."

"It was my pleasure. You're lucky to have her."

He glanced back at his daughter. "I know."

"I should probably let you go. We wouldn't want Skye to get hot in the car."

He pressed his lips together forming a smirk while he pushed a button on his key chain making the car start. "What were you saying?"

"Good night."

"We aren't there yet."

"We're not?" I bit my lip.

He shook his head in a mesmerizing manner. "You haven't even asked me how my night was. Where are your manners?"

I smiled, but not because I wanted to—he had this effect on me. "Did you get the research done you needed?"

"There's always more that needs to be done, but yes, it was a productive night. I think I know what direction I need to go in now."

"It seems like more than that. You seem almost happy."

"That surprises you?"

"You surprise me." I was becoming unguarded around him, saying what I felt. This wasn't good.

That earned me one of his rare genuine smiles. "The night was more productive than I thought, then."

He needed to quit looking pleasant. It was more appealing than the brooding sex symbol look he usually wore. "Being productive makes you happy?" My voice was uneven.

"Among other things," his voice became more intimate.

I held my stomach.

He tilted his head, noticing my body language. "Why do I make you so nervous, Kate?"

I swallowed hard. "You are direct, aren't you?"

"I find it's usually the best way to go, but lately I've realized there are exceptions."

"Let's make this one of them."

He took a step back. "Okay, Kate."

I felt like I could breathe again. "Thank you."

"Are we still on for Saturday?"

"I don't ever remember agreeing to it."

"Agree to it now...please?"

"Maybe someday that word won't sound so strangled coming out of your mouth."

"See how much I need you? Come with us on Saturday."

I hemmed and hawed.

"You know you want to."

That was my problem.

"Are you really going to pass up a Bogie and Bacall marathon?"

That did sound like fun, and I said I needed more fun in my life. "Okay, you win."

His eyes sparkled like someone who got their way. I was sure he was used to it. "We'll pick you up at six."

"I can—"

He pressed his finger to my lips. "Unless you think this is a date, your rules don't apply to me." He bent down as if he was going to kiss my cheek. "Do you consider it a date?"

He had me dazed and struggling to find air in the hot end-of-July weather. "No," I managed to eke out.

"Then we have no issues." He closed the small gap and his warm lips brushed my cheek, leaving sparks behind. "Good night, Kate."

I placed my hand over the spot his lips left their mark as if to preserve the electric pulse that remained. It almost felt like...magic. I stood motionless for several seconds until I came to my senses.

"Have fun on your date tomorrow night," I called out.

He shook his head and kept on walking without responding to me.

Skye gave me a goofy grin and wave. I could only imagine what the scene with her dad and me looked like.

My sterile environment had suddenly become contaminated with a flood of emotional bewilderment. I was going to have to make an appointment with myself at this rate.

....

Thank goodness it was Friday. I didn't have to see any crazed Nicholas Wells fans and I didn't have to attend the connection meeting because my *client* didn't need a match. Hopefully we kept it that way. My mental well-being was counting on it. The only downside was my lunch with Meg was cancelled. Her morning sickness was turning into an all-day sort of thing. Poor thing. Maybe it was a good thing, though, since she texted, *I need the down-low on you and Nick.*

I'm his relationship manager.

According to Nan, she has a feeling about you two.

Oh great, Nan and her feelings. I'd heard about them. She had them about Kenadie and Jason and Meg and Zander. I'd more than heard about Meg and Zander, I saw with my own eyes how she did everything in her power to push those two together. So she'd made a couple of good calls.

Is Nan there with you?

Not yet. She had a late date last night.

I admit I was curious to know how that went. *Has she said anything to you about Jack?*

Are you trying to change the subject?

What subject?

Clever, Kate. She's acting pretty giddy. She says she hasn't felt this way since she was a girl and her husband asked her on a date.

That's sweet.

It's fun to watch between puking episodes.

I'm so sorry. Can I bring you anything?

Between Nan and Zander, I'm good. Yesterday he brought home every flavor of popsicle imaginable because I told him they sounded good.

I never thought I would say this, but he's a keeper.

You and me both, sister. I better go, the porcelain god is calling.

Take care! Let me know if you need anything.

I didn't hear back.

I remembered those days. I never thought I would feel better, and just when I started to, it was over. Those were the darkest days of my life. The days where the rules were hatched and started to be honed.

My first rule back then was no men ever. I eased up on it after the dust had settled and my hormones went back to normal. It still took me two years to go on a date. And I'd only had one semi-serious relationship since, meaning we dated for three months on and off. He was a nice podiatrist. We both knew it wasn't going anywhere. There were no sparks. Nick's kiss on the cheek did more for me than any kiss from any man, to be honest.

Why was that?

I rubbed my cheek.

What was it about Nick?

Chapter Twenty-Six

O H MY GOSH, oh my gosh, Kate, you will never believe who texted me." Skye's voice rang through the Bluetooth on my drive home

I was pretty sure I could guess by her excitement level, but I didn't ruin it by guessing. "Who?"

"Liam," she sang.

"What did he say?"

"Hi."

I refrained from laughing. That was anticlimactic. "That's a start."

"What should I say back?"

"I would start with, how are you, so he knows you want an answer back."

"That's good. Then what?"

"I would wait to see what he says back."

"Okay, okay," she kept repeating herself. "Do you think I should invite him to come with us tomorrow to watch those old movies?" She was jumping too far ahead.

"Well...I would wait to see how your conversation goes. But you should probably ask your dad first if he would be okay with it."

A large rush of air came through loud and clear. "I know, but he's kind of overprotective. Do you think you could ask him?"

Her sweet voice had me wanting to say yes, but… "Honey, it would be best if it came from you. Just be honest and tell him why you like Liam."

"Okay," she didn't sound all that okay. "Maybe I won't even ask Liam."

"How about this, if your dad says no, I'll help you convince him." What was I getting myself into?

She squealed. "You're the best. I'm going to text Liam back now."

"Good luck. Remember, nice and slow."

"Got it." She hung up like her dad, without saying goodbye.

Skye's call put a smile on my face. That girl was working her way into my heart, breathing life into it again. I was happy she had called because I needed that boost before I had to face what was at home when I arrived. My mom's Volvo sat in front of my townhouse, empty. That wasn't a good sign. She had a house key, so I assumed she waited for me inside.

With great trepidation, I entered my house. "Mom?" I called from the stairs.

"I'm in the living room," she sobbed.

My heart sank. I trudged the rest of the way up the stairs to the main living level. I found her sporting a sleeveless bright green romper on my couch surrounded by tissues and vegan paleo dark chocolate wrappers. I wasn't sure how to feel about her outfit other than disturbed. My mom was beautiful, but she was pushing seventy. Things weren't as in place as they used to be. At least she was wearing a bra, even if it was the wrong kind for that outfit. The straps were showing.

I made my way to her pitiful looking self and pushed the tissues and wrappers out of the way so I could sit next to her. I took her hand. "Mom, what's wrong?"

"What do you think? He's gone mad and I can't take it anymore. I refuse to live in a demolition zone. He's ruined my feng and shui."

Those went together without the conjunction, but I didn't mention it.

"Not only that, but the cry from all the dead animals he's consuming and bringing into our home is sickening. I hear them everywhere."

I managed to keep a straight face and tried to think up a plan to get the chicken out of my fridge before she discovered it.

"And," she wailed, "he doesn't touch me anymore."

Okay. That was enough. I hugged her, hoping that would silence her. "Mom, it's going be okay. Let's go over and we'll talk it all out."

"I'm done talking. He doesn't listen anyway. Besides, he's flooded the house."

I pulled away. "What? How did that happen?"

She flapped her hands. "Oh, he decided that we needed a new toilet in our bathroom. The idiot didn't even turn the water off, then he busted a pipe. The bathroom's a wreck and the kitchen too. He's ruined the ceiling."

"Did you call your insurance company or a repairman?"

"No!" she shrieked. "He made the mess; he can clean it up. I'm tired of it."

"Mom, you've got to get this taken care of. You don't want mold or rotten floors."

She threw her hands up in the air. "I'm done. He can burn the house down for all I care. We're over."

Tears welled up in my eyes. "Don't say that, Mom."

She turned from me, shedding her own tears and reached for another chocolate bar.

I found myself changing into some old painting clothes and heading over to my parents' to see if I could help salvage the house I grew up in and loved and my parents' relationship that I loved even more. I felt bad leaving my mom, but for now, she was finding solace in vegan chocolate and raiding my wine cabinet. She was going to be fun later tonight.

"Dad," I shouted over the sound of what I hoped was a Shop-Vac. The house didn't smell right. It went beyond musty. I traversed my way to the kitchen. Kitchen chairs and some of my mom's plants littered the way. I wasn't prepared for the scene in front of me in the kitchen. The ceiling was pooling with water and several pieces of drywall had fallen. What must the master bathroom look like? I was afraid to go upstairs and look.

Dad was indeed using the Shop-Vac to clean up the water that covered the tile floor among the soppy mess of drywall. "Dad," I called louder.

He looked up harried, clothes a mess, embarrassed I was there judging by the bright red cheeks and his balding spot. "Go home, Katie."

I pulled the plug on the Shop-Vac. "No. This has to stop. Dad, what's going on with you?"

"You wouldn't understand." He grabbed an industrial strength trash bag and started picking up wet drywall. It was like he had no fight left in him.

"Try me."

"I don't want to talk about it."

"Fine, but I'm not leaving and I'm calling one of those emergency restoration services."

"I don't need help."

I shook my head. "We'll address that lie later, but you're getting some whether you want it or not." I pulled out my phone and googled a company. I chose the one with the best star rating, not caring how much it was going to cost me.

He stared at me dumbfounded.

I dared him with my eyes to try and stop me. All he did was hang his head and start cleaning again.

I wanted to cry, and probably would later. After I called the restoration service, I jumped into cleaning up the disaster. My first job was to dry off the gorgeous dark wood cabinets and cover anything I could in plastic that sat beneath the wet drywall that hadn't come down yet.

Dad and I worked in silence for an hour before the restoration people showed up. I knew better than to push him before he was ready to talk. Besides, I had to concentrate on not gagging. The smell was awful. I opened all the windows and turned the air conditioner to run nonstop. Thankfully, my parents had a couple of fans I made use of, especially in the bathroom where the water made it to the carpet in the master bedroom. Wet carpet was disgusting.

The repairs were going to be costly. I left a message for our mutual insurance agent, who was also a family friend, to see if my parents could file a claim. I didn't know if stupidity was covered, but we would find out.

I was a mess by the time the restoration guys got there. My dad acted for a moment like he was going to protest, but I wasn't hearing it. Though when I whipped out my credit card to pay once they had their estimate ready, he showed he still had some fight in him. He refused to let me pay and handed them one of his own instead. Hopefully we would get some of it back if his homeowner's policy would cover the cleanup minus the deductible. And Dad would only allow them to clean up and dry everything out. He was hell-bent on making the repairs himself. We would argue about it later.

Once the guys went to work, it was my job to keep Dad out of the way. I ordered Chinese takeout and we sat outside on the back porch.

We sat out staring at the pool that I should come over and enjoy more often. Thankfully, he was still paying a pool guy to maintain it.

The air smelled like honeysuckle and barbecue, better than inside, for sure. I stared at my dad. It was the first time I ever thought he looked old. He was going to turn seventy this year. My parents had met later in life and I'd followed soon thereafter. My mom started out as a patient of his after getting whiplash from a car accident. She made up a lot of reasons to come see him, as the story was told, even after the whiplash was gone.

There was so much I wanted to say to him, but I decided to take another tactic. I held up some of my lo mein between chopsticks. "Remember when I was seventeen and you took me to Chinatown in San Francisco and we got fresh fortune cookies?"

"You ate the entire bag." He faked a smile.

I would take it. "You had a few. I still have the picture of the little ladies making them."

"That was a fun trip." He was refusing to make eye contact with me.

"One of my favorite father-daughter trips." We had taken one every year from age ten to eighteen. "We should take another one and bring Mom with us."

Dad pressed his lips together. "I know what you're trying to do."

"What's that?"

"Get in my head."

"Then make it easy on me and tell me what's going on with you," I practically begged.

"Katie, you're not the right person to talk about these kinds of things with."

My heart dropped. "Are you sick? Did your cardiologist say something?"

He shook his head. "I feel fine."

"Then what? Please."

He set his food down on the patio table and patted my knee. "I love you, Katie girl."

"Dad…"

He shook his head. He wasn't going to budge.

I left late that night as soon as the restoration crew left. The house now smelled like a strong antiseptic. It was better than the sewer smell. I begged Dad to come home with me and talk to Mom, but he gave the excuse he should stay home and keep an eye on all the fans going. I began to worry he had fallen out of love with my mom, or that he was having an affair.

Whatever it was, I was determined to find out and fix it. My parents were one of the things I counted on, like the sun coming up every day. They had to be right.

I was canceling all plans for the weekend. I wondered if the Braves game was over or if Nick was still on his date. An odd twinge of jealousy pricked me thinking about that. No, Kate. Don't even go down that road. This was a good thing, I reminded myself.

I noticed I had a few texts from Skye.

Liam hasn't responded.

An hour later. *He just responded, but all he said was good. What do I do now?*

I was sorry I had missed that one.

Thirty minutes later. *I didn't text him back, but he texted me again and asked me if I liked volunteering at the shelter. That's good, right?*

Yes. That's a good sign. I'm sorry I missed your other texts. I was helping my dad.

I better text her dad too. *I've had a family thing come up. I'm not going to be able to make it tomorrow night. And Skye may ask if Liam can come. You should say yes.*

I shoved my phone in my purse and headed home exhausted, worried, and wishing for someone to go home to. Mom was there, but I was thinking more along the lines of someone I could snuggle up to in bed. Come to think of it, I bet my mom was in my bed. Ugh.

On my very short drive home, Nick called. Should I answer it? He would probably keep calling if I didn't. I hit the Bluetooth button in my car. I could hear a cheering crowd in the back.

"Are you still on your date?"

"Where have your manners gone, Kate? No hello?"

"Mine? You shouldn't be calling me while you're on a date."

"You texted."

"I didn't think you would look at it until you were home; that's the polite thing to do."

"I always keep my phone handy in case Skye needs me."

"Oh. Well, I suppose that's a good reason, but I'm not Skye."

"No, you are not."

"Where's Chanel?"

"I left her in the box."

"You should get back to her."

"First tell me why you're canceling on me."

"I told you, I have a family," my voice cracked, "thing."

"Kate, what's wrong?"

I paused, unsure what to say to him or if I should say anything to him.

Before I could formulate an answer, he threw me another curveball. "Is it anything I can help with?"

"Not unless you know anything about home repair."

"Actually, I do."

"Really?"

"I used to work construction while I was trying to break into acting."

"I didn't know that."

"What can I do, Kate?"

Why did he pick now to be sweet? It wasn't helping me keep my emotions in check or out of my voice. "It's more complicated than fixing my parents' house."

"What's happened?"

"I think my parents..." I could hardly say it. "I'm not sure, but I think they might be headed for divorce." Tears streamed down my face.

"Do you want me to come over?"

Yes. "No. No. You're on a date. You should go. I'm sorry I interrupted."

"You're not an interruption."

If it was anyone else but him who said that line, I would be asking him to come over. What a beautiful thing to say to somebody. "Nick, you better go."

"If it will make you feel better."

"Thank you."

"For what?"

"Trying to help. Goodbye."

"Wait," he got in before I hung up.

"What?"

"Does Skye like Liam?"

I laughed through my tears. "I think you should ask her. Good night, Nick."

"Good night, Kate."

I foolishly wished for the kiss on the cheek that usually accompanied those words, and for so much more.

Oh, Kate, why do you always fall for the wrong guy?

Chapter Twenty-Seven

I WOKE UP WITH an awful crick in my neck from sleeping on the couch. I'd been right. Mom made herself comfortable in my bed, and judging by the empty wine bottle on my nightstand, there was no getting her up last night. Sleep was probably good for her, anyway. I sat up and rubbed my neck. I was going to take a long, hot bath, then I was going to get to the bottom of what was going on with my dad.

Mom was sitting on the edge of my bed in her classic muumuu, rubbing her head when I creeped in.

"Morning. I have some coffee brewing downstairs."

"Is it organic?"

"Sure. . ." I had no idea.

She ran a hand through her spiky hair. "How's the house?"

"I thought you didn't care." I grinned.

"It's too early for back talk." Mom encouraged some growing up; she didn't want to stifle me. Dad wasn't all that fond of it.

I sat next to her on the bed. "I called a restoration service, so it's better. It's going to take three to five days for everything to dry out and before repairs to the ceiling and your bathroom can really begin. I also left a message for your insurance agent."

"This isn't your problem, honey."

"Of course it is; I'm your daughter. And you're sleeping in my bed." I tried to keep it on the lighter side.

She laughed but rested her head on my shoulder. "I don't know what to do with him anymore."

I patted her head. "We'll figure it out together." I felt more like the mom now.

"I love you, Katie." She sniffled.

"I love you, too. Do you want to take a shower first?"

"You go ahead, honey. I need to commune with my crystals."

"You have fun with that." I was going to become one with my jetted tub and some music.

I slid into the hot water while the soulful tones of Billie Holiday singing *Body and Soul* filled my bathroom. I tried to clear my head, but all I could think of was Nick, giving myself over to him body and soul. I slipped my head underwater trying to drown out thoughts of him and my parents. My life felt suddenly out of control. Controlled environments were safe, albeit sterile.

I came up out of the water and ran my hands over my face, trying to wipe away the water and thoughts of Nick. He was completely off limits. Not only was it my job to find him a match, but there were rules against me dating him—the company's and my own. He was a young adult fantasy, that was all.

I hoped Chanel knocked his socks off and he was rethinking being in a short-term relationship. I didn't think it would take much to convince her to change her mind by the way she was jumping up and down when she came in to sign the NDA. Maybe after the game ended he took her out for drinks and they stayed up all night talking or doing…other things that were none of my business and shouldn't be making me feel even an ounce of envy. I had to work through it like the book said. Live it in my head and never act on it.

I stayed in the tub until the water went tepid. It was long enough for my neck and back to relax. I had a feeling the knots would be back while I figured out what was going on with my dad and how to get my parents back together. Unless he was having an affair. I felt ill thinking about it. And I didn't want to suggest it to my mom until I knew for sure. She would have said something, though, if she'd been suspicious, right? Mom wasn't the kind of person to sweep things under the rug.

I threw on some cutoffs and an old college tee. I planned on going over to my parents' house to talk to Dad some more and clean up some of his other messes. Mom was right; the house resembled a demolition zone. I wouldn't want to live there right now either. But she couldn't stay with me forever. I loved her, but I knew after a while she would drive me crazy, along with any potential suitors I would probably never have anyway, but one could hope.

My hopes faded even more when I turned off my tunes and the fan in my bathroom once I was ready for the day, meaning my hair was pulled up and I had some mascara on. At first I heard Mom's voice. That didn't concern me too much. She was talking to her crystals. It was a little, or a lot, weird, but that was her. The real problem was when they talked back in a deep, masculine voice that wasn't my father's.

I rushed out of my room and listened for a moment trying to figure out who she'd let in the house.

My worst fears came to light.

"Did you know she kept a poster of you above her bed in college?"

Oh. My. Gosh. I ran down the stairs, but not fast enough.

"Really?" His silky tones rang through my house.

Mom cackled. "Oh, yes. She was so in love with you. She used to write *Kate Wells* on everything. I bet I saved a couple of her notebooks with yours and her name plastered all over them in hearts."

I came to a screeching halt at the bottom of the stairs. There they were sitting at my breakfast bar, drinking coffee. Nick wore the most arrogant grin in the history of smiles, and my mom sat there like she was talking to a girlfriend, pouring cream in his coffee.

"Mom!"

Both heads turned my way. Nick's eyes said *I knew it.*

"Speak of the devil." Mom placed her hand on Nick's arm. "Really she's an angel."

"I can see that." Nick's eyes roved over me.

Mom's head bounced between the two of us, her eyes and smile widening with each turn. "Just as I suspected. Your auras are calling to each other."

"Mom," my voice warned.

She blew that warning right off and squeezed Nick's arm. "Katie, here, has a mostly pink aura, which means she's a romantic and searching for her soulmate. She won't admit it, but don't let her fool you. She loves to be loved and to give it in all aspects of her life."

"MOM!"

She ignored me. Nick did too; he was captivated by what my mother had to say.

"And you," she waved her hand over and over Nick, "have the rare gold aura, which makes you a generous lover and perfect for pink. You enjoy being the center of attention, but you can make a woman feel like she's the center of your universe. And you know what you want, don't you?"

"That's enough." I headed toward the kitchen. "I'm sure Nick has better things to do today than listen to some made-up wives' tales."

"Uh," she tsked, affronted by the insinuation. "This is science, and anyone can see the connection between the two of you."

I cleared my throat rather loudly. "Mom, we have a professional relationship and Nick is dating someone."

"No, I'm not," Nick interjected.

"Yes, you are."

"I would think I would know if I were dating someone."

"You're dating Chanel." I was getting more frustrated by the second.

He gave my mom one of his elusive smiles. "We went out once."

"And you'll go out again."

"I don't think so."

Every part of my body sank. "Why?" He needed to like her for my own mental well-being.

"We'll talk about it later."

Mom with her ridiculous Cheshire grin stood up. "I think I've done my job here. I'm going to go get ready. You two obviously need to talk."

"No, we don't. You can stay. I'll make us some breakfast," I offered, okay, pleaded.

"No. No." She patronizingly pinched my cheek. "I would hate to intrude."

She was well past that.

Nick stood up. "It was nice to meet you, Stella."

Her eyes drifted over him adoringly. "The pleasure was most certainly all mine. But I have a feeling it won't be the last time we meet."

"I hope not," Nick replied.

Okay, maybe it was time for her to go. "You can use my bathroom, Mom." I gave her a little push.

She flitted away like she was Doris Day until she made it to the stairs and turned around. I swore her leg popped. "One more thing, Nick, do you wear boxers or briefs?"

I was dying. Literally dying inside. "Goodbye, Mom."

"Honey, we need to know these things. You aren't getting any younger, and it's important to know about any fertility issues up-front." She zeroed in on Nick, expecting an answer to the very private question.

I was never getting married. No man wanted this. Besides, I would never be able to show my face in public after this.

Nick smirked at me before turning toward my mom. "I've got plenty of healthy swimmers left, Stella."

I couldn't believe he said that. And why were men so proud of that achievement? And how did he know that?

You know, I didn't want to know.

Mom looked ever so pleased. "You look like a virile man, but it's good to check."

Words I never needed to hear my mom say in my presence—*virile* or *generous lover*.

As soon as Nick left, she and I were having a serious talk about boundaries.

She floated up the stairs, leaving me with the large can of worms she opened and a man who couldn't wait to dangle the slimy things in my face.

Nick folded his arms. "Kate. Kate. Kate. My biggest fan."

I narrowed my eyes until I realized he was in tight faded blue jeans with a white tee, my favorite look on a man. And the way he filled them out was a sight to behold. His cocky attitude, however, helped keep me properly disgruntled.

"Believe me, I'm not. You'll never see me with a tattoo of you on my . . . never mind."

He pressed his lips together, but his eyes smiled. "I prefer my name all over your notebooks anyway. *Kate Wells* does have a ring to it."

I was in hell by the way my cheeks burned. "That was a long time ago, and it was a stage that I outgrew."

"Right." He wasn't buying it.

"What are you doing here, anyway?"

His arrogance was replaced with concern. He tucked a loose strand of my hair behind my ear, making me wish for things I shouldn't.

"I wanted to see how you are this morning. You sounded upset last night."

"You could have called."

"I was in the neighborhood."

There was either no oxygen left, or my diaphragm and lungs ceased working. "You didn't have to come."

"That's what friends do."

"Are we friends?" I was finding I so wanted to be, even amongst all my conflicting emotions and rules.

"I'd like to be, but you're a difficult woman."

"I know."

He cocked his beautiful head. "Why is that, Kate?"

I looked up to the ceiling before meeting his eyes. This desire to open up to him welled up inside of me. I had to dial it back.

"I made a big mistake once, and I can't afford to make the same one twice."

His eyes bore in, penetrating my core. "Me, either."

Chapter Twenty-Eight

WHAT WAS MORE embarrassing than having your mom tell Nicholas Wells that you'd wanted to marry him once upon a time and asking him if he could father her grandchildren? The answer was not a thing. But having him help clean up your parents' house while your mom searched for your old notebooks with his name scribbled all over them came in a close second place.

Not to mention how my dad was keeping to himself in the garage. My parents barely even acknowledged each other when we showed up with our famous friend. My dad, like me, was embarrassed to have him there with the state of things, but my mom thought it was a great idea to bring him over here once he offered.

All I could be thankful for was that I had given that poster of Nick to one of my roommates when I got "married." But who needed a poster when I had the living version next to me sweeping up the layer of sawdust that coated everything in the dining room? If you asked me, he was even better looking now, with a few gray hairs dancing among the brown. His features had become more refined, and he still had a body like a god.

I wiped my brow after cleaning the chandelier until it shined again. "Thank you. You didn't have to do this."

"I wanted to see those notebooks."

I rolled my eyes. "I was eighteen. I'm more mature now, and I was infatuated with Talon Fox, not you."

"You know I wrote a lot of his lines?"

"I think I might have read that somewhere. So you based him off your life as a detective?" I teased.

"I only gave him my finer qualities."

"Like stringing Samantha along for years?"

"Everyone would have quit watching if we got together."

"Yeah, well, you were kind of a jerk to her at times."

"That was Talon, not me."

"You said you based him off you." I smirked.

He stopped sweeping and leaned on the broom. "I said I gave him my finer qualities. I don't string women along." He made sure I felt those last words.

I had to shake off his intensity. "Tell me about your date last night." I hesitated to ask, even though it was part of my job, but there was this part of me that didn't want to know because...well...you know. But since we were talking about stringing along women, I thought this was a good time to ask.

His brows came together. "Did you match me with her based on our profiles?"

"Yes. Why?"

"Are you sure?"

"I ran the numbers, and while there were other women more compatible with your profile based on percentages only, that isn't the only factor I took into account."

"What were the other factors?"

The table looked like it needed to be polished again. Now was a good time. I picked up the cloth I'd used before.

"Kate." He wouldn't be ignored.

I met his gaze and bit my lip. "Didn't Kenadie tell you how this all works?"

"I'd like to hear it from you."

I let out a heavy breath and paused. "The reason we have relationship managers is because our questionnaires don't always give us the full picture. That's why we do client dates and have psych evaluations. We use every tool we can to determine the best match for you."

"Based on Chanel, I must have made a very good impression on you."

Instead of being *People's* Sexiest Man Alive, he should have been the cockiest.

I shook my head. "Wait, you like her?"

He shrugged. "She was nice enough, but not what I expected."

"What did you expect?"

"Hmm." He thought for a moment.

It was the first time I'd seen him at a loss for words.

"Someone who aligned more with my profile," he finally answered.

"Is that what you want?"

He did that neck stretching thing again. "Like I told you before, it is my . . . preference through Binary Search."

I threw the cloth down. "You need to think about this. You have Skye's feelings to consider. And she doesn't want your girlfriends calling you bae, whatever that means. And not to be judgmental, but do you really want to be with the young tarts you've been linked with all over social media? Think about what message that sends to your sweet, wonderful daughter about body image and self-respect. She's at a vulnerable and impressionable age right now."

He leaned the broom against the chair before meeting me at the middle of the table. His amusement was apparent, though I couldn't figure out why he seemed to be enjoying himself. He shook his head while swiping some hair out of my face. He really shouldn't touch me. It did things to me. He was too touchy-feely for a friend.

"Relax, Kate. Take a breath."

I did take one, not because he suggested it, but because I needed to. In addition to several more.

"There you go," he said after I took my last deep breath. "I didn't think you could get so worked up. I like this side of you."

I did the wrong thing and stared into his eyes. They were like wells of water waiting to draw you in before you fell right over the edge. "Nick," I said in hushed tones, "please think about Skye."

His features softened. "She has been in every thought I've had for the last sixteen years. Though I like that you are studying me, you can't believe everything you read about me."

"What should I believe?" There was a childlike pleading in my voice. I'd been asking that question for the last nine years. More like, was there any man I could believe in?

He tilted his head, again taking a moment to think before he spoke. "What's right in front of you."

"That hasn't always worked out for me." I picked up the cloth again, ready to get back to work.

"How's the other way working out for you?"

Those words were like a knife in the heart. "You like to cut to the chase, don't you?"

"I like you. And I want to get to know you. You may even find out how much you still like me if you were willing to admit it."

"Or you could be a huge disappointment."

"I've never let my fans down before. By the way, which poster did you have of me?"

"I think we should get back to work."

"By the red in your cheeks, it must have been a good one."

"I bet you think they were all good."

"Is that a question?"

"If we are going to be friends, I'm going to need you to dial your ego back to mere mortal level."

"For you, I will try."

I threw the cloth at him.

He caught it easily with a satisfied expression.

I turned to tackle my next task of cleaning the hutch, but Nick grabbed my hand. "Kate."

I had no choice but to turn toward the man I felt this indescribable connection to. My eyes drifted toward our hands. I swore I could see sparks crackle between the two. And what was it about a masculine hand that was so attractive? Perhaps it was a representation of things hoped for. Someone to watch over you, to walk beside you, lend comfort when needed.

"I need to thank you."

My head lifted. "For what?"

"Your treatment of and concern for Skye."

"Unlike you, she's very easy to like." I pulled my hand away reluctantly.

My slight didn't faze him, but he seemed to regret the loss of my hand by the way his eyes stayed fixed on it until it rested by my side. "You know, she takes after me."

"Uh-huh. I was thinking more like Jack."

"Speaking of my father and daughter, do you plan to play matchmaker for everyone in my family?"

"I only made the introduction between Nan and your dad. He clearly had his sights set on her before I ever said a word."

"How about my daughter?"

He reminded me I should contact Skye. She never texted back last night. I took that as a good sign. "What about her?" I feigned innocence.

"You are aiding and abetting her growing up."

"I'm sorry to say, Dad, there is no stopping that train. And Liam seems like a nice boy, or is that young man?"

"Skye's a minor compared to him."

"I don't think it's illegal for them to see each other; besides, I thought you liked him."

"I did."

"He's pretty shy, so I don't think you have too much to worry about. He could hardly string a sentence together when he was around her."

"It's the quiet ones you have to watch out for."

"And why's that?"

He leaned in, taking an intimate stance. "The ones who run and hide from you have a way of captivating you. They leave you wanting more. You find yourself wondering what's going through their head and how to gain access to their thoughts. It's almost maddening."

I swallowed and stepped back. "I don't think that's Liam ploy, or a conscious effort on his part."

"It's their genuineness that makes them even more intriguing." He stood up straight and went on his merry way, picking up the broom again.

I had to take a moment to reflect. He had this way of dazing me with profound thoughts, whether indirectly or directly aimed right at my heart. Like Liam, I knew I ran and hid whenever I could. I had *genuine* reasons for doing so. But I was beginning to question whether my good reasons were good for me. Or was this the first time I had to put them to the test and I was failing? I watched Nick sweep up a mess he didn't create, using time he could be spending with family or working, all to help me. It was hard not to fall for a man like him. Was he genuine?

"Nick."

"Yes." He turned and met my gaze.

"I know I said it before, but thank you. This means a lot to me."

He did a scan of the room filled with half completed or poorly done projects, like the crown molding that wasn't on straight and hadn't been painted, or the wainscoting that was only done on one wall. "Did you say your dad recently retired?"

I nodded. "Last year, right after his heart attack."

An aha moment lighted his gorgeous eyes. "I may have a hunch what's going on with your dad," he said barely above a whisper.

I walked closer so we could keep what he had to say private between us. I was desperate to hear his thoughts. If he could tell me what was going on with my dad, I would kiss him. No, I wouldn't. But I would want to. I already did want to. Anyway.

"Do you think it's another woman?" This was my worst fear and I wanted to have it dispelled one way or another.

He shook his head. "But I think your mom has something to do with it."

I held my heart. "You do?"

"I think your dad is trying to prove to her that he's still a provider."

I pursed my lips. "I don't know, my parents were never a traditional kind of couple. My dad was the main breadwinner, but he didn't ever seem to pride himself on that."

"That only means he's a good man. But believe me, as men, we want to take care of our families, and our careers are our identity, whether we mean for them to be or not. When those are gone, we feel lost."

"Are you speaking from experience?"

He mulled over his thoughts before speaking. This was obviously a difficult subject for him. "When they told me that *On the Edge* was being canceled, I guess you could say I had an identity crisis. Every show I did, every screenplay and script I wrote immediately after amounted to nothing or, frankly, embarrassment."

"Yeah, that show you did right after was . . ."

"Awful," he finished my sentence. "I know. I did it because I was afraid if I didn't do something immediately I would be forgotten. And I was determined to prove to the studio execs that it was a mistake to cancel *my* show." He cleared his throat. "It didn't work out so well for me."

"What did you do?"

"What I should have done in the first place—take some time, process. Wait for something I was passionate about."

"Have you found that?"

He drew in close enough to whisper in my ear, "I believe I have."

Chapter Twenty-Nine

NICK WAS RIGHT. How had that happened? I was supposed to be the psychologist, or at the very least the daughter. Why did my dad feel okay opening up to Nick and not me? Nick said sometimes all it took was a beer, a garage, and some man talk. I think it might have taken more than one beer since they were out in the garage for some time before they came in talking like best friends.

Now Nick was helping my dad fix the crown molding while Mom and I were sitting on the back porch eating nondairy strawberry ice cream that evening. I was wondering about the perplexing man who used to hang on my wall. Mom was swooning.

"Katie," she fanned herself with her hand holding her spoon, which wasn't the best idea in the sweltering heat. She flicked some ice cream on her muumuu. "The chemistry between you two is palpable. Your aura is singing right now."

"Mom, shhh. He might hear you."

"So what? His aura is calling for you, like it's been searching for years for something it's lost and now it's been found." She cocked her head. "Have you two ever met before?" She immediately waved that idea off with her spoon again, now getting ice cream, or whatever this healthy knockoff was, on the covered patio. "That's silly, you would have told me."

I focused on the pool, not wanting to lie to her. Why did everyone want a piece of that day? That was mine, all mine. I had to admit that it kind of freaked me out that she'd guessed we had met before.

"Maybe you met in a previous life?" She didn't give me time to answer her first inquiry.

I took the out, hoping she wouldn't mention us meeting previously again. "Perhaps."

"I know you think I'm talking nonsense, but there is something about the two of you. I've never felt a connection so strong."

I inadvertently perked up at the word connection. It didn't go unnoticed.

A meaningful smile played on my mother's face. "You feel it too, don't you?"

I took a bite of the fake ice cream and tried to savor it, but I missed the fatty calories.

Mom grinned at me the entire time, knowing I was stalling.

"I'll admit I'm attracted to him," I whispered. "Who wouldn't be?"

"You know it runs deeper than physical attraction."

I shrugged. "Mom, I'm his relationship manager and . . . well . . . you know."

She reached over and patted my bare knee. "I do know, but Douglas," she said his name with such vitriol, as she should, "he wouldn't be in there," she pointed toward the patio door, "helping your dad."

"No. But he was in Dad's study and they would talk for hours about ancient cultures and rituals. He dazzled you with all his knowledge of herbs and tribal remedies. Admit it, Mom, you and Dad both loved Douglas once upon a time. We all did. We were taken in by his charisma."

244

She gave me a disconcerting look. None of us wanted to admit we loved Douglas, but we had. And we all knew it.

"You think all Nick has to offer is some superficial charm?"

"Honestly, I don't know what to think about him, but it doesn't matter. I'm prohibited from dating him, and getting involved with a celebrity is a terrible idea."

She let her spoon fall in her bowl, making a loud clink. "Rule three, right?"

"Four," I replied sarcastically.

"Katie, Katie, I raised you to be a rule breaker, not to follow the crowd."

"You're in luck—most of my friends are married now with kids, and I'm single. I'm a rebel." I smirked.

"Without a cause," she quipped.

"It's not by choice." I stared off into the distance.

She rubbed my arm. "Honey, this has all been your choice. Eventually, you're just going to have to trust someone...or...be alone."

I turned slowly to face her with stinging eyes. "I know, but I can't forget what Douglas did to me."

She squeezed my arm at the mention of his name. "I don't think you're supposed to forget, but you are supposed to learn from it and move on."

"That's why I have my rules."

"Katie, honey, when it comes to love, it's good to have boundaries, but you have to throw out the rule book. Do you think I planned on marrying a doctor and someone as boring as your father?"

I shook my head and laughed.

"Your father and I are like oil and vinegar, but in those moments when we are shaken and come together for a brief period, we make the best salad dressing. You're living proof of that."

"Yet you are sleeping in my bed," I reminded her and prayed she didn't go into further detail about how I was made.

She waved her hand. "That was to prove a point. I would never really leave your dad."

I narrowed my eyes at her. "Are you sure?"

"I'm too old to break another one in, and most of the time I love him. That is, if he doesn't start another home renovation."

"Hopefully, he'll listen to Nick, or at least take his pointers."

"Nick," Mom said dreamily. "He's my hero. And I think he's looking for a leading lady." She wagged her eyebrows.

"I don't think so."

"He's using a dating service."

"I know, but..." I wasn't sure I could elaborate. "Let's just say he's not looking for anything serious."

"He looks at you pretty seriously."

"Mom."

"Katie," she looked down her nose at me. "I know you see it...or is that feel it?"

Her mother's intuition was starting to freak me out. I was hoping her crystals weren't really communicating with her. I would have to rethink everything, then.

I bit my lip. "I'll admit there is *something* there, but as we know, that doesn't mean it is meant to blossom into anything. Sometimes it shouldn't."

"And sometimes we give away what could have been the most beautiful bouquet because we were afraid that we might get pricked by a few thorns. Here's a newsflash, my dear daughter, all roses have thorns, even you. Though yours are few." She gave me a sardonic grin. "Honey, you've got to be willing to bleed a little. I know after Douglas you felt like you needed a blood transfusion, but most men won't suck you dry, not even celebrities."

Maybe that was true, but I had a feeling Nick could leave a woman feeling like she needed life support after he was done with her. "Regardless, my job takes him off the table."

"Like I said, I raised you to be a rule breaker."

She may have raised me to be that way, but I was more cautious, like my dad. Except for once, and that hadn't turned out so well.

"Thank you."

It seemed wholly inadequate to express my appreciation to the man covered in dust looking like every woman's construction man dream. We all had one. Not sure why, but I think there was something we women loved about a man who could fix things. And the way Nick's muscles flexed in his dirty T-shirt didn't hurt. Well, it kind of did since it made me feel ways I shouldn't. I leaned against Nick's car, exhausted, trying not to ogle him. It had been a long day of cleaning and emotional highs and lows. At least my parents were in the house together. Dad had even taken Mom's hand while we all stood and admired Nick's and Dad's handiwork before we left. The crown molding turned out great. But the pride on Dad's face was priceless, as was the way he asked my mom to stay home. It was as if I could see his self-dignity return. And I owed it all to the man who rested himself close to me against his car.

"No thanks are necessary. I told him I would come back next week and help him finish the wainscoting."

I turned and stared at him dumbfounded. "You don't have to do that. I know you're busy and . . . you hardly know us."

"But I want to know you, and your dad's inside information is good."

"You're researching me?"

"You've done your fair share on me."

My cheeks turned from pink because of the warm weather to heat-stroke red. "It's my job," I stammered.

"I saw the notebook, *Kate Wells.*"

I was going to strangle my mother for showing him those once her home was back in order and she was in an emotionally better place. After, I was going to kick myself for thinking how nice that name still sounded and the small thrill it gave me to hear him say it.

"I think I'm going to go now." I pushed off his car.

"Let me take you home," he was quick to offer.

"It's not that far of a walk."

"But it's late and I would still like your company."

It was hard to say no to a man who had spent his entire day help-ing your parents, or to his blue eyes that captured you and held you hostage. From the half smile that played on his face, he knew the captivating power his eyes had. Not to mention that strong jawline with a layer of facial hair that bordered between a midnight shadow and a fine beard.

"I suppose you can drive me home." I yawned.

"Your unenthusiastic response is not fooling me. It's all in the eyes, Kate…and the notebooks."

I rolled my eyes at him but smiled.

He chuckled and clicked his key fob, unlocking his fancy car. He got right in while I walked at a snail's pace toward the passenger side. As weird as it sounded, this was a significant deal for me, allowing him to drive me home. When someone took you home, it meant there was a certain level of trust associated with your relationship. And this was *him.* The man I dreamt of marrying one day and fathering the four babies I'd planned to have. I didn't like being an only child, so I swore I was going to have a house full of kids. Not sure how realistic that was anymore. The four babies, not marrying *him*. That wasn't going to happen.

I slid into the passenger seat, nervous. I focused on all the gadgetry the car had instead of Nick, who looked pleased I'd joined him. "Nice car."

"Not bad for a loaner."

"I hope you're teasing." The car probably cost a hundred grand.

A gloating expression filled his features. "I enjoy getting a rise out of you, Kate."

"Remember what I said about your ego and our friendship?"

He rested his hand, which still had specks of white paint on it, on my knee. His touch was warm and gentle. "I hope we are friends."

His touch clammed me up and muddled my brain. I nodded before I knew what I was doing.

He dazzled me with a full smile, with a touch of conceit for good measure. "I'm happy to hear that, because I need you to do me a favor."

Chapter Thirty

APPARENTLY BEING FRIENDS with Nick meant helping him do research for his screenplay, even though he wasn't willing to share what it was about. Something about nondisclosures and privileged information.

Not sure why he needed my help or what the private botanical gardens with the creepy mansion on the property had to do with it, but that is where I found myself on Sunday along with Skye and Liam, who looked so nervous I was afraid he would vomit. I felt the same way. But how could I tell Nick no after everything he had done for my parents? And I thought maybe I could work him out of my system like the book said. I needed my ovaries to quit screaming about him.

Nick had used his mastery of persuasion with the powers that be, not sure who they were, but they allowed us to tour the property even though they were closed on Sundays. I hadn't even known this attraction, which was an hour from my place, existed. It was well off the highway and nestled back amongst the hills. The greenery around the property was stunning, and the long driveway to access the property was reminiscent of days gone by. The large wrought iron gates at the entrance added to the old-time feel. The mansion itself was covered in climbing vines, giving it an eerie ambiance. The dark stone didn't help, or the large magnolia trees that kept the sun from reaching it.

The four of us stared up at the monstrous turreted home before the man we were supposed to meet dawdled out the front door.

"What do you think?" Nick asked while we waited.

"If you are writing a horror film, then it's perfect."

"Wait until I tell you the history of this place."

I rubbed my arms, chilled from his ominous tone, even though it was blazing hot outside.

Nick took notice. "Don't worry, Kate, I won't let anything happen to you."

His mere presence was already doing something to me, just like Liam's was doing something to Skye. I decided to focus on her. I watched how she stood close to Liam, but not too close, and how her hand hung down wishing to be held. Liam kept his hands in his pockets. He'd hardly said two words in the car. But they could have been texting each other. Their fingers were certainly flying, and they kept smiling at each other.

The cute Mr. Kearns made his way over the deep porch that creaked when he stepped on it. His wispy gray hair blew in the light breeze and he was all a dither to meet Nick. That seemed to be the usual reaction where Nick was concerned.

Mr. Kearns shook hands vigorously with Nick. "Such a pleasure to meet you," he kept repeating. "This must be your family." Mr. Kearns smiled at me.

I stepped back, not sure what to say.

Nick smoothed it over by reaching across me toward Skye. "This is my daughter, Skye, and her friend Liam."

Mr. Kearns smiled wide, showing off his rather large dentures. "Darling girl, so nice to meet you," he addressed Skye. "And you, young man," he referred to Liam.

All eyes landed on me.

Nick touched the small of my back and moved me right back next to him. "This is my *friend*, Kate."

Mr. Kearns nodded like *sure she's your "friend"* while holding out his hand to me. "Lovely to meet you, dear." He had a deep Southern ring to his voice.

I took his hand. "It's nice to meet you."

He gave my hand an extra squeeze before letting it go. He turned to address Nick and handed him a brochure from his suit coat pocket. "We are all set for your visit. Here's a map of the property. Entrance is through the home. You can tour the home and then the gardens. I will be available in my office on the first floor if you have any questions. I hope you will enjoy your visit to the Xavier Mansion." He stepped aside and motioned for us to enter the large double doors with an X carved on them in a swirling script.

Nick had to prod me forward; something about the house didn't sit well with me. The teenagers obviously had no issues, or at least bold and beautiful Skye didn't—she took the lead and Liam followed, probably to stay away from Nick more than anything.

I smiled at the two while Nick shook his head; he may have even growled under his breath.

I leaned close enough to Nick not to be overheard. "I don't think you have anything to worry about. He's petrified of you *and* her."

Skye had filled me in over text yesterday between helping my parents. She sent me screenshots of hers and Liam's text conversation and it was amusingly boring. They basically talked about which was a better pet, a cat or a dog. Skye's vote was for cats and Liam felt dogs were the way to go. They also shared some pet memes. I was so glad I grew up when we still talked on the phone.

"That's not going to last." Nick kept his eyes on his baby.

Liam held the door open for Skye and the rest of us like a gentleman. "Sir," he said shakily when Nick passed. Nick only glared at him.

Liam was quick to enter and join Skye, who was already scoping out the art nouveau style furniture, in particular a large armoire that also had an X carved in it. Several pieces did, including the writing desk in the large foyer and several hand-carved chairs. The dim lighting and light blocking curtains added to the creep factor.

Mr. Kearns bounced on the balls of his feet. "Take your time. I have plenty of paperwork to catch up on."

"Ooh, look at this." Skye pointed to the grotesque looking upright piano in the parlor with carved heads on the lid and half naked women's bodies carved into the side that looked as if they were crawling up it.

"What is this place?" I whispered to Nick.

"This was the home of Xavier Toole. He was a bit obsessive about his name and, as you can see, women."

"Are you writing about him?"

Nick shook his head. "I'm more here for the feel of the place and location ideas."

"Well, it feels unsettling."

Nick tilted his head. "What would your diagnosis of someone like Xavier be, just by looking at his surroundings?"

I did a quick scan of all I could see. "I don't know how accurate it would be; I would need some more information on him."

"Try," Nick urged.

"Okay…" I thought his request odd but walked around the parlor and adjoining rooms studying the pieces of furniture and art on the walls. Several pictures were of women, and they all had two things in common—they were all corseted and blonde. And each had an X in the corner. The man obviously had some sexual compulsions and, I would guess, a fetish.

My blood ran cold. "Are these his trophies?"

"Very good, doctor. Anything else?"

"My guess would be that he was abused or abandoned when he was young, possibly both."

Nick pressed his lips together, forming a smile. "Right again. His father abused him, and his mother was a prostitute and made to forcibly give him up."

"Let me guess—she was blonde."

"You're good at this."

"I wish I wasn't." I shook where I stood. "What is the purpose of this place?"

"They do tours and murder mystery events. Xavier Toole, for all his faults, was a very wealthy man at the turn of last century, and for many years, a pillar of the community, until they found out his secret habit of painting his victims before he killed them and buried them on this property."

I held my stomach. "That's horrific."

"Why don't we go outside? The gardens, I hear, are second to none." Nick's hand found the small of my back.

"Are there dead bodies or statues of women?"

"Not that I'm aware of."

"Lead the way. I want to be anywhere but here."

Liam and Skye weren't as anxious as me to leave. They were taking pictures of everything and probably snapchatting it with weird captions.

Nick wasn't keen on leaving Skye alone with Liam, though, and suggested they come outside with us—more like demanded it. Liam hopped right to it and Skye followed him.

I was happy to feel the sun on my face and take in the well-manicured gardens. For as cold as the house was, the gardens had a whimsical feel to them. There were ponds with lily pads and hanging trees with old fashioned wood swings attached to them. Wind chimes sang in the breeze. Toy trains lined the stone path.

"He was trying to capture his innocence and childhood out here," I said aloud.

Nick gave me a thoughtful look. "You are brilliant."

"I don't know about that."

"There's a maze," Skye squealed and daringly grabbed Liam's hand. "Let's go through it."

Nick's first instinct was to follow, and he would have, but I did something I shouldn't have on impulse. I copied Skye and took Nick's hand. "I wouldn't do that if I were you."

Nick's fingers curled around my own without hesitation. "Why is that?"

I forgot what we were talking about. All my senses focused on how Nick held my hand and how spellbound it made me feel. "Uh…" *Disengage,* my brain yelled. Right. I tugged my hand free. My heart yelled what an idiot I was.

Nick's lip ticked up at my obviously flustered state. "Everything all right?"

No. "Yes." I distanced myself from him. The miniature magnolia tree was blooming and beautiful. A great distraction. I headed for it.

Nick wasn't going to be ignored. "What were you saying about Skye? Who is now out of my sight and alone with Liam."

I lightly touched the petals of one of the blooms. "First of all, Liam thinks of you as a mentor, even a second father, so don't ruin that. And Skye needs to know you trust her. As her only parental figure, that's more important than ever."

I turned and noticed Nick's fist clench.

"Does Skye have any contact with her mom?" I asked nonchalantly. Or as nonchalant as you could be when you ask that kind of question.

"None. I suppose you are going to tell me that it's unhealthy."

"Not at all, as long as Skye understands why and she agrees with it."

"She does," Nick said brusquely.

I silently moved on to the beautiful pond full of lily pads. Two swans glided along the water. There was a stone bench near the edge. I took a seat on it. It was such a serene spot, even knowing a murderer had owned it a long time ago. The swans placed their heads together forming their iconic heart shape.

Nick sat next to me and sighed. "I find myself apologizing more around you than I ever have."

"Are you saying you're sorry?" A smile played in my words.

"I suppose I am. Talking about Alessandria is difficult. I shouldn't have snapped at you."

"You don't need to apologize, I understand." More than I cared to admit.

Nick opened his mouth to say something, but for some reason didn't articulate it. Instead he gazed into my eyes. I could tell he was holding something back.

I turned back to the swans before I got lost in him. "Did you know many swans mate for life?"

"I think I've heard that."

"Most remain faithful partners their entire lives."

"That's important to you." He wasn't asking.

"Very," I whispered.

We both sat in silence taking in the swans for a few minutes.

"What is a post consultation?" He caught me off guard with the question and abrupt change of subject.

"Are you talking about the interview we have with our clients when they want to date someone new?"

"Yes, that."

"It's a series of questions to see where things may have gone wrong, strategies for the next connection, things like that. Do you want to schedule one?"

"Why not do it here?"

"Now?"

He shrugged. "Why not?"

"Are you sure you don't want to give it another go with Chanel? You only went on one date."

"That's all it takes to know."

My eyes narrowed while I studied him. His eyes dared me to contradict him, so I didn't. I wasn't going to give him the satisfaction.

"Okay, fine. Were you attracted to Chanel physically?"

He tossed his head side to side. "She was attractive, but I wasn't attracted to her."

"Did you feel like based on your profile we correctly matched you?"

"No." He didn't even have to think about it.

"I'm going to disagree with you for now, but what would you like to see different in a future connection?"

"How can you disagree with me? You know I'm right."

"Your profile is more than your questionnaire."

A wicked grin played on his face. "So what is your diagnosis of me?"

I rubbed my chest where my blouse was unbuttoned. "I don't diagnose people at Binary Search."

"Sure you do. What is your opinion of me, doctor?"

The floating lily pads became awfully fascinating. "This isn't part of the post consultation questions."

"I think you can make an exception."

He was one big exception. Fine. He wanted to know. I faced him. "Honestly, if it were anybody but you, I wouldn't have allowed you to go on to the next phase based on my initial assessment."

I thought he would be upset, but instead a hint of gratification appeared on his face. "Now we are getting somewhere. Why is that?"

"Because of that right there. You're arrogant and, honestly, you have narcissistic tendencies," I blurted.

He leaned back. "Is that what you really think of me?"

"I don't know," I breathed out. "You're a living dichotomy." I faced the pond, trying to regain my equilibrium that he could so easily steal.

He drew close and spoke barely above a whisper. "Just so you know, you confuse the hell out of me too."

A small laugh escaped me.

"Is this the reason you were made my relationship manager? You were worried about me?"

"Yes," I admitted.

"I'm happy it worked out that way," he whispered in my ear. Not at all upset that I had branded him with a possible disorder.

His breath against my skin made me shiver.

"Carry on with your questions...please."

I took a deep breath, not wanting to ask the next question and more than that, stupidly hoping it didn't apply. "Do you feel like you were...intimate too soon?" I asked the last part in a rush.

He raised his eyebrow. "Is that a real question?"

"It is, but...you know, on second thought, let's skip it."

"Oh, no. I want to hear the good doctor's feedback."

"You were intimate with her?" That made me feel sick to my stomach.

"Is that a problem for you?"

"What you do is your business."

"You didn't answer the question."

"Neither did you."

"You got me." He shrugged. "I kissed her."

"You did?" Jealousy flared inside of me. "I mean, okay, moving on."

"I don't think so." He waved his finger back and forth. "Why is that an issue for you?"

"It isn't."

"You're lying."

I hated he could read me like a book. Even more, I hated that it was an issue for me. More than that, I found myself wishing it was me. This was so wrong.

"If you weren't attracted to her, why did you kiss her?"

"Because she wanted me to, and I thought of it like a parting gift."

I delivered the biggest stink eye ever. "You probably gave her the wrong impression."

"It was a kiss, nothing more."

"Maybe for you."

"She wasn't attracted to me either."

"Are you kidding me? She was turning cartwheels when she found out she'd been paired with you."

He sat up straight, ire filling him. "She wanted Nicholas Wells. She wasn't interested in Nick."

I let that sink in. How was it that he always had me regretting judging him? I blew out a large amount of air and stared out into the distance.

"Kate." He brushed back my hair with his hand.

I turned toward him.

"Do you get this worked up with all your clients?"

"You're my first and last."

"Has it been that terrible for you?"

"You have no idea." I wasn't teasing.

He searched my eyes. "What are your feelings about intimacy? We never got to your rules about it and I'm sure you have some."

That I did. "So are you asking about my personal or professional feelings?"

"I have a feeling for you they are one and the same."

He was right, and it frightened me how well he seemed to know me.

This time I didn't turn from him. I wanted to gauge his reaction. "First, there is a difference between true intimacy and physical affection. Unfortunately, most of us have forgotten that because everything from movies and TV to our peers sell us sex and make us think that's all you need to have in a relationship, and if you aren't having it, something is wrong with you. But having a real relationship means putting in a lot of hard work. We have lost the art of courtship in our culture."

"You want to be courted?"

I nodded. That was exactly what I wanted in a relationship.

"Deep down I think most people do, but they're afraid. And too often they make sex the anchor in the relationship because it's easy, or at least they think it is, but it never carries enough weight to hold a relationship steady. And once it crumbles or wanes, they have nothing left. Now, if they make true intimacy their foundation, meaning they get to know someone deeply and build a place where compassion and commitment can happen, they build a place of safety amid vulnerability. If that is their anchor, then sex gets to be the pleasure cruise it was meant to be."

"I've never heard nautical terms used to describe sex before."

I tucked some loose hair behind my ear. "You think I'm ridiculous."

It was his turn to become interested in the swans and lily pads. "I think you have some valid points. It's easy to mistake sex for love. I've probably done it more often than I would care to admit." He rested his hands on his knees and took a moment. "I certainly did in my marriage."

I also leaned forward on my knees. "Tell me about Alessandria." Whoa. Where did that come from?

His head tilted my way. "Are you inviting confidences? Because that door swings both ways."

I thought for a moment. He was right. It wasn't fair to ask him such a question if I wasn't willing to reciprocate.

His eyes drew me in to the point I found my head gravitating toward him before I stopped myself. Then he asked a poignant, maybe even painful question.

"Are you willing to be open with me?"

"It's not really my strong suit, but believe it or not, there was a time it was."

"Before you were married?"

I jumped up, shocked. "How did you know I was married?" My voice cracked. I began to pace in front of the pond, feeling like I was naked.

Nick jumped up and hesitated for a moment, but before I knew it he'd wrapped me in his arms. "Hey, there." He stroked my hair like I'd dreamed about when I would watch him to do it on his TV show. It felt better than I ever imagined.

I wasn't sure if I was in heaven or hell, but I had never felt so safe and insecure all at the same time. I wanted to pull away, all while desperately wanting to sink into him.

"Your dad told me," he whispered in my ear.

I pulled away, though I still found myself in his grasp. "Why would he do that?" It was something we never talked about with anyone unless it was amongst ourselves, and even then, we rarely spoke of it.

"I think he's afraid you keep scaring off your *friends.*"

I laughed even though I felt like crying. "Technically, I wasn't married."

"I remember you saying that. Your dad mentioned it was annulled."

There was that ugly word again. "Best and worst thing that ever happened to me." I released myself from his clutches and started to walk around the pond. "I still can't believe he told you."

Nick stayed by my side. "I've upset you."

"No. Yes. I don't know. It's embarrassing."

"Why?"

"Because I allowed myself to be so taken in by somebody. Did my dad tell you the guy was already married?"

I saw Nick nod from the corner of my eye.

Out of nowhere, a floodgate opened. I wasn't sure if it was because my emotions so desperately needed to be released or if I'd finally lost my mind. "Did he also tell you that he cruelly used me and left me while I was carrying our baby? And when I miscarried, he shoved the knife in further by dismissing me like I never meant a thing to him. Because I didn't. I was a pawn in the game he played."

The tears that had been pricking my eyes dropped one-by-one down my cheek, forming a tiny stream. I tried to wipe them away, but it was useless; they kept on coming.

Nick stopped in his tracks. This was obviously news to him. Great. I bore the rest of the tragedy without having to. I figured since my dad blabbed about the annulment, he'd given him all the gory details. I was going to keep walking, but my name on Nick's lips made me pause.

"Kate." We came face to face with each other. His gaze zeroed in on my blurry eyes. In his eyes I saw fury. "He's a bastard."

"I agree." I wiped my eyes.

"I'm sorry, Kate."

I shrugged my shoulders. "It's not your fault. But now you know why I have my rules and why I do my best to keep people away, albeit not intentionally. I actually like people." I smiled

He stepped closer. The fury in his eyes was replaced with a low, burning passion. "I like you, Kate."

The fire in his eyes was consuming the oxygen between us, making me feel like I couldn't catch my breath. His next question didn't help.

"Do you like me?"

I do.

Chapter Thirty-One

I DON'T KNOW IF *Liam likes me.*

With Nick and Liam with us all day, Skye and I hadn't had a chance to really talk. I rolled onto my back in bed. I had almost been asleep when her text came in. The Wells family still lived on Pacific Time instead of Eastern.

He's just shy, and your dad makes him nervous.

Are you sure?

Positive.

I saw the way the kid looked when they came out of that maze. He was staring at Skye like she was the sun in his sky. At the same time, Nick was awkwardly trying to wipe away the mascara that had run under my eyes. That was a fun conversation, to explain why I was crying and why it looked as though Nick and I were having an intimate encounter. It had ended with me blathering that I should buy waterproof mascara and I liked babies. It wasn't my finest moment.

Okay. You're the best.

Do you want to get pedicures and Chinese one night this week while your dad is doing one of his workshops?

Yes!!! Please!!!

Perfect. Let me know which night.

I will. Gotta go. Liam texted.

I told you. Good night.

I didn't get a response. At least not from her.

Are you still awake? Nick texted.

If I said, no, would you believe me?

My phone buzzed.

I answered it, "I guess that was a no."

"Hello, Kate."

"Hello." I bit my lip.

"Sorry it's late."

"That's okay. Can I help you with something?"

He paused. "We didn't get to finish our conversation."

"Which one?"

"You asked me about Alessandria and I never got to answer you."

"I probably shouldn't have."

"I'm glad you did."

"You are?"

"I want to dispel anything you may have read about us, about me, during that time."

"Despite what my mother says, I didn't obsess over every detail of your life when I was younger."

"So you didn't cry when you found out I got married?" There was a gleeful, bordering on evil tone to his voice.

Searing heat emanated from my cheeks. My parents were both getting an earful from me, and I was banning them from Nick. "Moving on."

"If it makes you feel any better, I should have listened to my fans."

266

"The breakup of a marriage never makes me feel happy, even when it is a good thing. At least not now," I conceded. I was more than giddy when I learned about the demise of his marriage. I'd had a lot of growing up to do at that point in my life.

"Like you, there never should have been a marriage, but..." he inhaled deep enough for me to hear, "I did what I had to do to save my child."

I sat up in bed. "What do you mean?"

"The only anchors Alessandria and I had were our images and...sex. When we met, it was a PR dream, and we had explosive chemistry. It worked to further our careers. We let being the 'it' couple go to our heads and our bank accounts. Then reality hit. Alessandria got pregnant. She wanted to—" he could hardly say the word, "terminate...the pregnancy."

I placed my hand over my mouth, thinking about Skye not existing. And worse, knowing from the conversation I'd had with Skye that she knew her mother never wanted her.

"I convinced her," he continued, "what a good opportunity this would be for us. We would allow the press access to our wedding and our journey into parenthood. I felt like I had to sell my soul, but my child was my priority."

There was a long pause where neither of us spoke.

"Did you love her?" I braved asking.

He didn't answer right away. "We were too in love with ourselves to be in love with anyone else. But I thought I loved her. I wanted us to be a family. That being said, I didn't know what real love was until Skye was born. From the moment I held her, my life changed."

He had me choking up. "I envy you." I tried to keep my voice steady.

"You want children, don't you?"

"More than anything."

"I hope you get your desire."

"Me too. How about you? Do you want more children?"

"Hmm," he thought. "With the right woman, perhaps."

"Perhaps?"

"Skye will be graduating before I know it, and I don't want to be collecting social security and chasing after toddlers like some of my cohorts back home."

He made me laugh. "You have a ways to go before that."

"All I know is I would choose a better mother next time. And keep the press out of my marriage."

"I hope so, for both Skye's and your sakes." I yawned. "I should probably get to bed. Some of us have to work for a living," I teased.

"Today was a work day for me. I even wrote some when we got back."

"How's that coming?"

"I've never felt so inspired. I think it's the best I've ever written."

"I bet you say that about all your projects."

He chuckled. "If only you knew."

"Good night, Nick."

"Kate, thank you for opening up to me today. I hope we continue to get to know each other. Good night."

Me too. I threw a blanket over my head.

....

Monday felt different after the weekend I'd had. Maybe it was because my mom called me on the way to work and informed me that she'd read my horoscope and been to her psychic over the weekend and they both said I needed to look to the stars.

"Nick is a star," Mom yelled in the phone.

That concluded our conversation. Or perhaps it was the email Kenadie sent telling me what a great job I had done matching Nick. She attached a picture of Chanel kissing Nick's cheek at the Braves game. Nick didn't look all that thrilled in it. To be honest, I found myself not appreciating it. The picture had been posted by a local newspaper which touted Binary Search. Kenadie sent me the link to the article as well.

My stomach churned. How was Kenadie going to feel when I told her that Nick wanted to date someone new already? Should I tell her he helped my parents and I went to that creepy Xavier house with him? Maybe she already knew because of Nan. Nick mentioned Jack went to church with Nan yesterday and had lunch at her place. They were getting cozy quickly. Nick seemed to be all right with it. Ugh. How had my life gotten so complicated?

I blamed one person.

The only thing I could do was to find him the perfect match, even if he wasn't looking for anything serious and my twenty-year-old self begged me to break the rules and try him out for myself. I took a breath. We were only going to be friends. And as his friend, I was going to find him someone terrific—a woman he couldn't refuse. A woman who would be a good mother to Skye and any future babies.

I popped a natural peppermint candy in my mouth to help with the upset stomach I was giving myself thinking about it all. I had a feeling I better stock up on those.

Zander's knock on my door was a good distraction. When he walked in, I noticed he looked queasier than I felt.

"Are you okay?" I asked.

He took a seat in front of my desk. "It was a rough weekend. Meg was in the emergency room yesterday morning."

My heart began to pound. The worst scenario running through my mind, remembering my own emergency room visit when I was pregnant, but then it dawned on me before I said a word that Zander wouldn't be here if the worst had happened. He would be with Meg like the good man he proved to be.

I calmed myself. "Are she and the baby all right?"

He ran his hands through his hair. "She was dehydrated from vomiting, but she's better now after some fluids. Nan is with her this morning." He looked wiped out.

"How are you?"

He acted as if he was going to say *fine*, but he blew out a large breath. "Hell, I don't even know anymore. I'm constantly worried about Meg, and now I have to take care of her damn cat I don't like because it's bad for the baby if she changes its litter box." He took a breath. "Then there's diapers, my nightmare of living in the suburbs and growing old and turning out like my parents. Said parents visiting more often now that I'm going to have offspring. And how much should I save for college?"

I tried to suppress my smile, but I was awful at it. "The good news is morning sickness usually goes away in the second trimester, and you are a long way off from paying for college."

He didn't look as if that helped.

"Why don't you pay Lana to take care of the cat? She loves animals."

He perked up a bit. "That's a thought. Now how do I get rid of my parents?"

I laughed. "You're on your own there. I have my own intrusive parent issues."

He stood up and rubbed his neck. "Thanks for the talk, doc."

"Anytime. Tell Meg I'm thinking about her and let me know if I can do anything."

"Will do. By the way, any issues we should talk about with the batch of new clients before I assign them a relationship manager?"

"Besides that they are mostly Nick sycophants? No."

Zander's lips curled. "I'll be happy when he's either found some-one or moved back to La La Land where he belongs."

"He already wants to date someone new." I grimaced.

A smug smile filled Zander's face. "I told Kenadie last night that he wasn't into that chick. That picture of them said it all."

I was glad I wasn't the only one who thought so. I was afraid I'd let my personal feelings cloud my judgment of it. I was afraid of a lot of my personal feelings, come to think of it.

"I guess it's back to the drawing board," I lamented.

"According to Nan and her new 'boyfriend,' you should choose yourself."

I almost choked on the peppermint candy in my mouth. I coughed and spluttered.

"Exactly. Kenadie and I both told her you're way too smart to get mixed up with a guy like him."

I held my chest and took a deep breath after my little episode. I gave Zander a weak smile. "Yeah. Way too smart."

"He won't stay forever, and then you can be done 'fixing' him."

Right. Who was fixing who again?

Chapter Thirty-Two

NICK WAS AS mesmerizing on stage as he was on the small screen. No one could deliver a line like him and make it so believable. I was in time to witness him perform a small scene from *Field of Dreams*, showing his students how it was done. All I'm going to say was, if he built it, I would come.

What made him even more captivating was the way he helped his students. All I could do was stand at the back of the theater and be entranced by him.

I was supposed to be picking up Skye—she sat in the front row watching her dad—but I couldn't move. I watched him coach a kid who I would guess was around Skye's age. Nick walked him through his monologue, helping him visualize his character, suggesting where he should pause, asking him what physical reactions his character might have delivering a particular line or even one small word. He patiently blocked the scene with him and praised him when he suggested something out of the box. Nick patted him on the back and said, "Now you are becoming your character." The kid's beaming smile shone brightly.

I don't know how Nick knew I was there, or how he even saw me in the large auditorium where I had seen plays like *Into the Woods* and *Wicked*, but he was about ready to call up his next student when he looked up to where I stood and we locked eyes.

"Let's take a ten-minute break," he called.

His class consisted of about fifteen kids, all teenagers. Several of them only grabbed their phones and got lost in them, but a few scattered and left the auditorium. Nick made his way off the stage. He spoke to Skye, alerting her to my presence. She turned and waved at me but didn't join her dad when he walked up my way.

I probably should have met him halfway, but I was still buzzing from his performance as an actor and teacher. It wasn't helping me work him out of my system. I was afraid I was becoming more entrenched by the second. All while I was setting him up with other women. I think I had found three excellent candidates to present tomorrow at our connection meeting. This go-around I went with a more yin and yang approach. After spending more time with him, I felt like I was beginning to know him better. And where he enjoyed being the center of attention, I believe he wanted a woman who didn't love the limelight, someone to ground him.

He'd made a comment last night when we were at Topgolf together. Yes, we were hanging out. Friends did that sort of thing. That's what I kept telling myself while he helped me with my swing in our private bay. He may have mentioned that I smelled nice.

And maybe I could still feel the way it felt to be in his arms, his warm breath against my skin when he whispered, "Keep your left hip over your left foot." I didn't know golfing tips could sound or feel so good.

Anyway, back to his comment. He'd said, "It's nice to be with someone who isn't parading me around and who doesn't want to be seen with me."

I kept that in mind when choosing this batch of candidates. It was tricky, though; they all bordered on being statistically improbable according to the numbers, which I knew was going to cause some heated discussions in our connection meeting, but they matched the person I was coming to know. And Nick had said he might want to be with someone who despised him. He found it refreshing.

He sauntered toward me with that stiff smile of his. "You came to see me in action."

"I came to pick up your daughter... but I did enjoy what I was able to see."

His eyebrow arched. "A compliment, Kate?"

"I actually have another one for you."

He sidled up next to me. "I'm all ears."

He too smelled good. That amber and vanilla scent drove me mad. Paired with his tight jeans and T-shirt, it was going to make me insane.

I had to steady myself before answering. "I stopped by my parents' place before heading over, and the wainscot looks amazing." I turned and lifted my head so I could meet his eyes that were already set on me. "Thank you, Nick. I know you're busy and my parents are crazy," I smiled, "but you've probably single-handedly saved my father's dignity and my parents' marriage. I can't tell you how much that means to me."

"The insider information made it all worth it." He didn't sound like he was teasing.

I shook my head at him. "I can only imagine how embarrassed I should probably be right now."

"I got to keep those old notebooks of yours as payment."

My eyes widened. "No."

"Yes." Too much delight danced in his gorgeous eyes. "I'm thinking of posting them on my fan club page."

I nudged him. "You wouldn't."

"I may be willing to negotiate."

"Negotiate?"

"You agree to come to Mobile with Skye and me on Saturday for some more research, and I'll think about not posting the page where you wrote our wedding vows. I particularly loved the line—"

I placed my hand over his mouth. "Don't even say it."

He easily removed my hand. "Come on, Kate, you promised you would always be my number one fan and you would let me steal the covers from you every night without getting mad."

My face must have been turning every shade of red, judging by how much it burned. "I'm leaving now. With your daughter."

He chuckled and grabbed my hand and pulled me back. "Don't go. I didn't even get to the good part about all the passionate kisses you promised."

"Please stop." I was dying of embarrassment inside.

He tilted his head and tugged on my hand, pulling me closer. "Kate," his tone rang sincere, "I'm flattered."

"I was silly and young."

"You were sweet and innocent. Qualities I should have valued more."

"I'm not that sweet or innocent anymore."

"I beg to differ."

"So will you give the notebooks back to me?" I pulled my hand away.

He shook his head. "But...I will keep them private."

"I'll pay you to burn them."

"Like I said, I'm willing to negotiate if you come with us this weekend."

"That's a long drive. What's in Mobile?"

"A decommissioned battleship."

"What are you writing?"

"Someday I will tell you, but for now, come share the experience with me, with us."

A day with Nick and Skye doing research for a movie was enticing. He was enticing. He was my client. He was my friend. And...I did need more fun in my life.

"What time should I be ready?"

<hr />

I had sensory overload when we arrived in Mobile on Saturday. Behind me, sleeping beauty was curled up in the backseat looking angelic as she slept. We had left at 5:00 a.m., so I couldn't blame her. She was chipper for about half of the five-hour drive, but had dropped off midsentence somewhere along the way. She looked so innocent clutching her dragon shapeshifter book and phone, leaning against the window, probably dreaming of Liam or maybe the hero in the book, Kieran. A smile played on her natural ruby lips.

Then there was her father, who surprised the heck out of me this morning when he showed up clean-shaven. I had never known him to be that way, not even on his TV show. I wasn't sure which version of him was more attractive. Perhaps the reason for it made him more attractive. He was using it as part of his "disguise" today, along with a hat and sunglasses. All because he knew how uncomfortable the attention made me. He'd tried to get a private tour, but the timing was too short. I felt guilty but was touched by the effort he had gone to.

I had this overwhelming desire the entire car ride to reach over and run my hand across his smooth cheek. I was in over my head. I needed to bring in some reality.

"I think you are really going to connect well with Thea," I said before our exit to the battleship memorial park.

He glanced my way and grimaced. "I doubt it."

"Did you talk to her already? She seemed really down-to-earth when I met her yesterday when she came in to sign your NDA."

She was surprised too. She didn't even know Nick was using our service, which totally played in her favor. Even though like I'd predicted, our connection meeting got heated because no one but me thought it was a good match and Chanel was apparently devastated Nick didn't want another date with her.

Todd had pressed me for me details, and I wasn't sure what to say. Zander was even tough to convince of my choice. But no one there knew him like I did. They didn't see the man who fixed crazy people's homes—aka my parents—and stopped three times on a five-hour trip because I had to pee a lot in the morning. He may have made fun of my small bladder, but he never complained. And they didn't know Skye, a beautiful, wonderful girl who deserved good women in her life.

"Margo is contacting her," he sounded irritated.

"What are your plans with her?" Squeamish feelings erupted thinking about them together, but this was reality.

He flashed me another look with narrowed eyes. "I haven't given it much thought."

"There's a really good Italian restaurant that opened last month downtown. They have opera singers come in during the evenings to perform."

He kept his focus on the road, quiet for a moment. "Is that something you would like?"

"Yes, it's pretty romantic."

His brow crinkled. "Did you go there with a date?"

"My mom and I checked it out. They have a great vegan menu."

His lip twitched. "Good to know. Maybe I'll take what's-her-name to tour the College Football Hall of Fame."

"Her name is Thea, and I'm not sure she likes football." I knew it wasn't something I would be interested in, and Thea and I had a lot of other similar interests, like DIY home projects, classic novels, and music.

Nick shrugged. "Let's not talk about her."

"But I'm your relationship manager and it's my job to make sure—"

He silenced me by reaching over and rubbing my bare knee. "Your only job today is to enjoy the day with me and my daughter."

I'd already been enjoying myself. When Skye was awake, we talked a lot about the book we were both reading, and once she dozed off, Nick and I talked about psychological disorders and my career. He was happy to let me ramble on about personality disorders, manias, addictions, and impulse control issues. He asked a few questions here and there, but was mostly content to listen. He was particularly interested in personality disorders, wanting to know the cause. That was the million-dollar question. There was no way to pinpoint it. So many factors could play a role, anything from biological to environmental.

It was nice to have someone take an interest in me. Nicer that I felt comfortable talking to him. Conversations flowed freely between us. I hadn't experienced that in a long time.

"I think I can manage enjoying the day." I smiled at him.

"You don't know how happy I am to hear that."

Chapter Thirty-Three

NICK HAD OBVIOUSLY done his homework about the USS *Alabama*, which was a good thing since the place didn't offer tour guides; it was all self-led with a map they gave you when you paid to enter.

It didn't escape my notice that Nick paid cash, not wanting anyone to see his name on a credit card, I'm sure. He also paid for me, which he had been doing all week. I always offered to pay my own way, as that's what friends would do, but he wouldn't hear of it.

I did hope the aviators, black ball cap, and clean-shaven face did their job. So far so good. The line to enter had been long, and not one person seemed to recognize Nick. No phones pointed his way or random people asking for autographs or pictures with him. Oddly, it felt normal standing there in line with Skye and Nick like all the other families. Sleepy Skye leaned on me while we weren't moving. During our wait, we perused the brochures and all the souvenirs that lined the path to the ticket counter.

Once we were on the main deck feeling the sticky gulf air and sunshine, Nick showed off his knowledge, and his fantastic legs. He should wear shorts more often. That was my observation, not part of the tour.

"The USS *Alabama* only took two years to build and was commissioned in 1942." Nick walked toward some of the large weaponry the deck boasted.

I looked around, amazed at the magnitude and grandeur of the ship. I couldn't believe it only took two years to build.

Skye yawned, uninterested. "How long is this going to take?"

"This is important history, honey," Nick admonished Skye.

She rolled her eyes and took out her phone.

I, on the other hand, was Nick's captive audience. I loved history and I was intrigued with what this ship had to do with the screenplay he was writing. And him.

Nick sighed at Skye's lack of enthusiasm but pointed to a large gun and said, "This could shoot a twenty-seven-hundred-pound shell and hit a target twenty-one miles away."

"That's impressive."

Nick gave me a smile that said he appreciated my attentiveness and interest. He continued with his tour. "Not one person died on this ship due to enemy fire."

"Really?"

He nodded. "They called this ship the Lucky A."

"Sounds more like a miracle."

Nick walked toward one of the ladders leading to an upper deck. "I suppose it was. Five men did die, but it wasn't combat related." Nick began to climb the steps.

One thing about him was he wasn't the most chivalrous man, not that it mattered for the kind of relationship we had, but I wondered if his dates were turned off by it. I, on the other hand, took advantage of it and watched him climb up the metal ladder with his powerful legs and tight butt. Whoa.

I let Skye go before me, though she gave me a look like *please save me*. I gave her a squeeze before she made the climb. "Someday, I promise you will look back on this with fond memories."

Her pouty lips said she wasn't so sure. I had no doubt about it. I cherished all the boring events my dad took me to when I was younger, like embassy tours in Washington D.C. Now I would love to do that again. Maybe I would.

I met the Wellses on the next level. Nick was waiting for me, and he made me take back my earlier thought. He reached for my hand and helped pull me up securely to the next level. Very chivalrous. His grip was firm, and we ended up in a narrow space and close to one another.

"Thank you," I breathed out, unsteadily.

He tightened his hold on my hand. "That's what friends are for."

Yes. We were friends. I dropped his hand.

He let out a heavy breath. "Follow me."

That was my plan for the day. My heart beat hard, and not from the climb or maneuvering to the other side of the ship. It was all Nick.

Nick showed us the only bullet hole on the entire ship, and he informed us it was from the ship's own gun.

We wound around and made our way back down so we could reach the lower decks. It was amazing to me that over two thousand men lived on this ship, especially as we descended into the depths of it. I'd been on a cruise before, and this ship was nowhere near as spacious. Every bit of space was used. It kind of freaked me out how close some of the artillery was kept to the engine room and where they all slept. And was I ever grateful for having my own room after seeing their living conditions. Beds stacked four high and lined against walls in cramped quarters. Privacy was nonexistent. Even the officers' bed-rooms were tiny. The captain had the largest room, and even that was small, but at least he was by himself.

Then we got to the sick bay. I knew right away this is what Nick came for. Nick looked around to see if anyone was near before he lifted his shades. His blue eyes looked alive.

"Look at this." He pointed to an X-ray machine. "This was a fully functioning hospital. They performed everything from tonsillecto-mies to appendectomies here and brought sailors from smaller ships to receive treatment here."

I took it all in, from the hospital beds to the creepy looking dis-pensary with replica "drugs" of the day in different bottles. It looked like a chem lab for an evil scientist. That had nothing on the surgical instruments.

"It's amazing anyone survived back then," I commented.

"They did things down and dirty," Nick replied.

I shook off the thought of having to be treated in such a place. "What is your interest here?"

Nick wagged his eyebrows before putting his shades back on; more tourists were upon us. "It lends a certain air of mystery, don't you think?"

"Are you writing a mystery?" I whispered.

"What do you think?" he mouthed.

"I think you are teasing me."

"I think you're right." He dazzled me with his half smile.

Meanwhile, Skye was snapping pictures of everything and saying things like, "Ew," and "OMG." That pretty much summed up the sick bay for me.

I did take a cue from Skye, and while Nick was reading one of the placards, I snapped a picture of him with my phone. For posterity's sake. This way, one day I could prove that I was friends with him, you know, in case this new movie of his won an Oscar or something. I could say I was there when he was doing his research for it.

Nick waved me toward the recovery area. "Do you know how they treated mental illness in this time period?"

I gave another shudder. "Yes, and some of it wasn't pretty. They used psychosurgery, where they would cut out what they thought were the malfunctioning parts of the brain. Or sometimes they would disconnect the frontal lobe or use shock therapy. The cure was worse than the disease. But a lot of good did come out of that time period, especially after the war. They started taking mental health more seriously. I think it was 1946 when they passed the National Mental Health Act."

Nick looked at me in awe. "You are smart *and* beautiful. A lethal combination."

I bit my lip. "I love what I do."

"Do you ever think you will go back to private practice?"

"Maybe. If the right opportunity presented itself. But I feel like I'm doing something important where I'm at."

He tilted his head. "Helping people find love using technology?"

"I suppose, but I think that's only part of it. We allow people to take a step back and evaluate themselves. To see what they've been missing or what's really important," I added.

"And what about you?"

"What about me?"

"Have you ever stepped back and reevaluated your rules?"

I swallowed hard and rubbed the back of my neck. "You love to throw those kinds of questions at me, don't you?"

"I love it more when you answer."

"It's complicated, Nick."

"Your rules are definitely complex and . . . I would say, unrealistic."

I turned and looked at one of the operating tables. "I'm just trying to prevent any past events." I didn't have to spell out which one.

"And, I would say, any future relationships."

"Probably," I admitted, refusing to look at him.

He ran a finger lightly down my arm, blazing a trail of sparks. "Is that what you really want?"

I shook my head.

"Kate." His voice lured me to look his way.

I turned to him to see myself reflected in his aviator lenses. In them, I saw my own confusion staring right back at me.

He leaned in, dangerously close. I could smell the hazelnut coffee we had drunk on our way down.

I wouldn't mind getting a second taste of that.

"Maybe it's time to change the rules," he spoke intimately between us.

I wanted to break each one right there and close the small gap between us.

Thank goodness for Skye.

"Can we go yet? I can't text my friends down here." Which translated into Liam.

I jumped away and tried to shake off what just happened. At this rate, I was going to get fired. Or worse, break every rule.

Chapter Thirty-Four

"PETRA IS A no."

"What?" I stared at my phone on speaker, wanting to bang my head on my desk. Then I noticed the time. He was supposed to have met her at noon for lunch and it was only 2:00 p.m. That was shorter than his date with Thea last week.

"Nick, you're making me look bad. This is the third woman in almost four weeks, and you haven't even tried to go out on a second date with any of them."

"Why bother when I know it's not going anywhere?"

"You're not giving them a fair chance. What was wrong with Petra? She's brilliant and gorgeous."

"Kate," he sighed. "I told you I'm not looking for anything serious with these women. And not one of these women have matched my profile."

"And you're welcome for that."

He groaned. "I know your reasoning and I appreciate your concern for Skye and myself, but will you just trust me?"

"Absolutely not. You're going to end up with Angie the stripper if I do that, and I won't let that happen to Skye... or you."

"Take a breath, Kate."

I inhaled deeply and blew it out. "Please give Petra another try."

"No."

I rubbed my face in my hands. "Fine, you can have Angie the stripper, because I'm leaving for LA on Sunday for my conference and I don't have time to keep looking for the perfect match for you on top of interviewing all your undying fans who want to be 'your last first kiss' who have been filing in here since that stupid commercial aired a couple of days ago. And I'm tired of my colleagues questioning my judgment. But I warn you, Angie is not stepmother material. And I will not have a post consultation interview with you about it, so don't even ask. You can do whatever it is you apparently want to do with the women who match your profile."

My stomach hurt thinking about it. I popped a peppermint candy. "Are you finished?"

My head dropped to my desk. "Yes," I croaked into the phone.

"Kate," he paused, "I didn't have any physical relations with Thea or Petra, in case you were wondering, not even a kiss, although they were angling for it." He sounded pretty cocky there at the end.

My stomach felt better. "You're free to do whatever you want with whomever you want." My insides twisted with that statement.

"If only that were true... maybe someday."

I raised my head. "What does that mean?"

He sighed. "Can we just forget about your job for now? The main reason I called you was to tell you that I'm heading back home this weekend for several days."

I sat up straight. "To Laguna Beach?"

"Yes."

"Why?"

"My partner, Simon, and I have decided my screenplay has the potential to attract big money and a bigger studio. We were going to front the cost at first, but some things have changed, and we've been able to score a couple of meetings with some big studio execs."

I wondered what had changed, but didn't ask since he'd been so tight-lipped about his project. "That's fantastic. Congratulations."

"Thanks. That said, I've been distracted here and haven't gotten in as much writing as I thought I would have. I need to go into my writing cave so I have something solid to present."

Guilt seeped in thinking about the past few weeks and all the time he'd spent helping my parents, not to mention all the nights we had spent hanging out, like last night at the theater. Nick arranged for me to finally get my Bogie and Bacall marathon. We had the theater to ourselves, Skye and Liam included.

Poor Skye had been lamenting over text today how Liam still hadn't held her hand. There was no way that was happening last night since Nick and I sat behind the two. Nick watched every move the kid made.

"You should have said something. We didn't need to hang out."

"I don't regret any time spent with you."

When he said things like that I wanted to break all the rules, even the one at my job that precluded me pursuing him. But reason prevailed, not my ovaries. We were now on the second cycle with him. They were screaming louder than ever. It was probably a good thing he was leaving.

"I wish you safe travels and happy writing thoughts."

"I don't leave until Saturday. You're still coming to the performance on Friday night, right?" He sounded worried.

"Yes, if you still want me to. And my parents would probably kill me if I didn't. They are excited to see your students in action."

I was too. His students were each performing the monologues they had crafted during Nick's classes. It was a graduation of sorts.

"I want you there, Kate."

"I'll see you Friday, then. I better get back to work. I have more sycophants, I mean clients, to interview."

A small chuckle escaped him. "Have fun with that."

"Goodbye."

"Kate, hold on."

I paused and held oddly still.

"You know, I'll probably have meetings in LA when you're there. When does your conference run again?"

"Um...Monday through Thursday, but I'm staying until Sunday to do some sightseeing."

"I'll work something out."

"I don't want to interrupt—"

"You won't."

"Let's just see how it goes." I wasn't going to lie, I was hoping I would meet someone there, someone else in my field who matched all my dating criteria. Someone who would help me get a grip on reality. And the reality was I didn't belong with the handsome celebrity. How could I?

"I'll make the time. Goodbye." He hung up before I could say a word.

I stared at the phone, wondering why all of the sudden two days seemed like a long time before I would see him.

⋯⋯⋯⋯

Bringing my parents out in public, or at least my mom, was probably the worst idea ever. Especially since Nick was involved. I had to search her for notebooks or any of my other old belongings before we left their house. And I couldn't technically uninvite them since Nick was the one who had extended the invitation. Mom was all in a dither and brought out her sequined jumpsuit that I was sure came from the seventies. Dad was looking sharp in a dress shirt and slacks and back to his old self, including a nice, clean-cut haircut for his thinning hair. They were cute, holding hands to my right in the auditorium that was beginning to fill with family and friends of Nick's students.

I owed that scene to Nick. I prayed, though, they stayed cute and quiet. Mom, all the way over in the car, was going on and on about my aura and how I was glowing. And she had it on good authority from her crystals that Nick was indeed virile and would father her grandchildren. I begged her not to mention that to anyone. Especially everyone to the left of me. Skye was right next to me, followed by Liam, his mom, Janelle, a happy client of Binary Search from what I'd heard, and then her two youngest children. Janelle and I kept giving each other knowing glances while observing the teenagers between us.

I had told Skye to play it cool tonight. Not hard to get, but only friendly. Poor thing was waiting for Liam to ask her on a real date with no parents or me involved. Though she must have liked me because she leaned her head on my shoulder.

"Do you think Kieran will get his powers to shapeshift back in the next book?" she asked me. We had finished the first book in the series and it was a cliffhanger ending.

"Probably, but I bet it won't be until the end," I responded.

"I hate that Kieran and Elondra broke up."

"Yeah, that probably won't resolve itself for a while either."

"Why can't she just trust that he wants her, and not because they were bound by a legend?"

I thought for a minute. My first instinct was to say it added tension and kept you turning the page, but then I thought better of it.

"I can't say I blame her. Her parents lied to her about who she really was, and the man she was betrothed to before she met Kieran was a cold-blooded killer. Makes it kind of hard to trust someone."

"Yeah, but Kieran really loves her. He gave up his powers to save her."

"But she doesn't know that yet."

She sighed wistfully.

I kissed the top of her head. "It will all work out. I believe a happily ever after is on the horizon."

"Me too." My mom joined the conversation and patted my hand.

I turned toward my mom and gave her my please-don't-say-another-word eyes. It didn't work.

She smiled as wide as the Grand Canyon when she realized Skye's head was on my shoulder.

"Skye," she said ever so sweetly. "I'm so happy you and my daughter are friends."

Skye sat up straight. "Me too."

That would have been a good place to end, but that was wishful thinking.

"I hope we can be friends too, maybe even more than friends someday." Mom winked at her like she was being covert.

Skye looked at me confused.

"Mom, please," I begged.

She was about to respond, but we were saved by Nan and Jack arriving.

Jack had his arm around Nan, who was dressed to the nines in a smart-looking pant suit. She was beaming by Jack's side. Jack was smiling like he was the luckiest man in the room.

We all stood up and stepped into the aisle to greet them. I introduced my parents.

"Jack and Nan, these are my parents, Stella and Glenn Morgan."

Jack wrapped me up in his arms. "Darlin', how are you?"

"Doing well. Looks like you are as well."

He released me, and his smile said it all. He was doing more than fine. "I keep telling Nick he needs to bring you around again. But I can't say I blame him for wanting to keep you all to himself."

Oh, that was the worst thing that could have been said. Nan and my mom glommed onto that statement and each other like a child to candy. It was as if they were instant bosom buddies attached at the hip with conspiracy theories dancing in their hopeful eyes. The men were smart and dispersed, Jack to greet his granddaughter and Janelle's family and Dad back to his seat, leaving me to the pair of hungry wannabe grandmothers.

I was going to follow Dad and Jack, but Nan and Mom sucked me in like a Hoover. Both their industrial strength hoses—I mean hands—were on me and not letting go.

Nan took the lead. "Sugar, I keep telling everyone I don't care what they say; there is something between you two, or there ought to be."

"Thank you!" Mom said, vindicated. She waved her free hand all over me. "Can you see the sexual tension oozing off her?"

Did we have to use the words *sexual tension* in public? Thankfully we were toward the back so the moms and dads of performers could have seats up close. I had no words. And the harder I tugged away from them, the firmer their grips became.

Nan looked me over. "You're right. It's palpable."

That was it. "We are—"

"Let me guess," Nan laughed patronizingly, "just friends. I've heard it from Kenadie and Meg. And look where they are now. Y'all just need to listen to the mommas—we know a thing or two."

"Amen." My mom somehow gained a Southern accent all of a sudden.

I almost dropped down on my knees and gave praise when the lights lowered, signaling it was showtime. Even better, Nan and Jack sat in front of us, separating the troublesome women temporarily.

The man causing all the drama in my life walked out onto the stage to loud applause. The stage loved him, as did his clothes. Even from a distance, it was easy to see how perfectly snug his dress shirt and jeans fit him. His fine beard was back already, and I think I decided I liked the stubble over the clean-shaven.

Mom squeezed my hand like him gracing us with his presence should be significant for me. I was doing my best to feel like it meant nothing. I wasn't doing a good job. Feelings of being proud of him arose as he spoke about the journey he had taken with these kids and how much they had grown. And when I looked over at Skye, thoughts of wishing the three of us were more than friends filled me. I knew I would miss their presence when they left tomorrow. Almost as if a piece of me were leaving.

I shook my head. Those were crazy thoughts.

The performances were a semi-good distraction, albeit a little depressing. A couple of the monologues dealt with death, one with divorce, and one with infidelity. Thankfully, most of them were comedic in nature. There was quite a bit of talent up on the stage, and I wasn't talking about Nick.

I found it very cute when he came out and they all did a scene together where he played a lost blind man and each kid played a part in helping him find his way home. But the blind man was actually helping each of them to see. It was poignant.

Once the performances were all over, there was a mass rush to the stage to greet the performers and Nick. Everyone around me did the same, except for Janelle; she took the seat next to me where I was observing. It was what I did.

"You've been good for Skye," she began.

"I don't know about that, but I've enjoyed getting to know her. I'll miss her when she leaves tomorrow."

"You aren't the only one." She grinned and nodded in the direction of Liam.

"Poor kid looks so nervous."

"He's had a crush on her for a long time. But you didn't hear that from me." Janelle pretended to zip her lips.

"I had a feeling."

"I don't think Skye and Liam are the only crushes going on this summer." Janelle wagged her eyebrows.

"Oh, not you too."

She laughed while standing up. "I don't blame you for being cautious, but I think you've been good for Nick too. See you later." She started to walk off.

I caught her before she took a few steps. "How's it going with Preston?" He was the man she'd been paired with.

She turned back my way with that smile you get with new infatuation. "I'm being cautious." She winked and turned away.

Cautious was good. Wasn't it?

After a good half hour, the auditorium began to empty and the man who should have caution tape plastered all over his body made his way to me.

"You didn't leave," he sounded surprised as he approached. "I've been trying to make my way to you."

"You are admired, and my parents refused to go," I teased.

He threw himself in the chair next to me, while our family and friends below were all trying to pretend they weren't watching us, but they were doing a horrible job of it. I tried to ignore them, instead fixating on Nick's hand resting on my bare knee.

"Thanks for coming, Kate."

"You're welcome. Your students did a good job."

"They did." His hand began to caress my knee.

 Suddenly it was getting warm.

"Um ... It's getting late. You have an early flight, right?"

"We do." He squeezed my knee. "Kate ..."

"Yeah?" I turned to meet his eyes, which were poised to draw me in.

His hand moved from my knee and tucked a tendril of hair behind my ear. He didn't say anything for a moment, as if he was debating if he should speak or not. "I'm going to miss you."

Oh. Did that sound more than friendly to anyone else?

My wildly beating heart said yes. My mouth said, "I'll miss you too."

Chapter Thirty-Five

I LAID MY HEAD on my propped-up hand, which rested on the table in front of me, holding back a yawn and my drifting thoughts. The doctor espousing new wave treatments for children and adolescents kept getting off topic, making me do the same. It was the same topic I'd been thinking about for days. Nick. I absentmindedly wrote his name on my notebook. Oh my gosh, what was wrong with me? I scribbled it out and sat up straight. I was an adult now. And we hadn't talked in six days. I knew we wouldn't. He was going into full writer mode, no distractions.

At least I'd had contact with Skye. We had talked every night after I got back to my hotel room. Which was usually right after dinner. I hadn't met anyone. Though I'd had dinner with a psychiatrist from London last night in the hotel restaurant. Loved the accent. Him, not so much. He drank like a fish and talked about his patients as if they were there for his entertainment. And, admittedly, I kept comparing him to Nick. Nick chewed with his mouth closed. And Nick didn't laugh like a hyena. Nick rarely laughed, but when he did, it was deep and masculine. Nick would have paid the tab. Not that I expected

Rupert to, but he had asked me to dinner. Nick asked questions about me; Rupert talked about his brilliance. Okay, Nick did that too. But all Rupert wanted to know was my hotel room number. Not happening.

Skye was enjoying being home with her pool and friends, but she too was missing someone. Liam and she were texting, but he was getting ready to start at the university there, so he was busy. Skye wasn't sure what that meant for them. Liam had yet to even hold her hand. I didn't know what to tell her. I was as confused as anyone when it came to relationships. It was much easier for us to discuss the fictional one of Elondra and Kieran. They were currently locked in a dungeon together. Skye and I were both rooting for a reunion kiss. I would find out tonight when I picked it back up.

Today was the last day of the conference. And it had been good. I picked up some new research to study in both of my jobs. Some interesting research about attraction and the key to successful relationships was discussed in one of the sessions yesterday. I picked up the presenter's book they were selling after. I also was intrigued with some of the new cognitive therapy research and approaches that I could use in therapy sessions. I was even proud of myself for not only having dinner with Rupert, even though that was a bust, but I also ventured into LA with a group to have dinner and walk around two nights ago. I was trying to be less closed off.

That said, I was looking forward to curling up in bed tonight with my dragon shapeshifter book. And maybe hearing from Nick. He said he would call tonight or tomorrow depending on how much he had written and on his meeting schedule. I knew I was crazy for anticipating that so much. Part of me thought I should text him and tell him I was renting a car to do the tourist thing, so we couldn't see each other. That was the rational and probably right thing to do, but I didn't want to.

Inside, I was shaking my head at myself. I tried to focus back on the speaker. It was useless.

After closing remarks, I decided room service and reading sounded divine. The introvert in me needed the downtime. And you never knew when someone might call, like my mom. She had called every day to see if Nick and I had seen each other. She was highly disappointed.

I sat on my bed picking through the pecan chicken salad I'd ordered for dinner, wrapped in my silk robe, reading and doing my best not to check the time. If he was going to call, he was going to call.

At nine my phone buzzed. I took a breath before I picked it up to see who was calling. My heart leapt when I saw the name on my screen. I stared at it while it buzzed a couple more times. I didn't want to seem eager to answer it. I had to remind myself that despite how blurred my personal feelings were at the moment, we also had a professional relationship that needed to be maintained, though I knew his call had nothing to do with Binary Search or my role as his relationship manager.

This seemed different somehow, away from Atlanta and on his home turf. Away from those professional boundaries. But he was the name and face of Binary Search. I answered anyway.

"Hello." I did my best to keep any breathiness out of it.

"Kate." His voice wore my name too well.

"No hello?" I could picture his pressed lips and arched brow.

"See what six days without you has done to me?"

"I see you are back to your ill-mannered self."

He didn't disagree. No, it was much worse.

"Hello, Kate."

It was like my name had been dipped in the deepest, richest dark chocolate. I wanted to dive into the chocolate fountain where it swirled.

He was an actor, I told myself. He was trained to sound like he was the world's best word chocolatier. *I will not be tempted. I will not be tempted.*

"How's Skye?" Not like I didn't already know, but I was nervous and Skye was safe. Sweet, not sinful like her father.

"She misses you."

"I miss her too."

"I can remedy that."

Why did part of me feel like he could fix so much more? "What do you have in mind?"

"Would you like to join us at Universal Studios tomorrow?"

"No," I blurted without even thinking.

He paused. "I thought your conference was over." He sounded disappointed.

I closed my eyes, embarrassed at my lack of finesse. "It is. It's just... I can't go to an amusement park with you."

"Let me guess—this is on your list of rules."

"It's not a rule, per se, more like a guideline."

"Care to fill me in?"

I threw myself back against the bed in my hotel room. How did I put this?

"When you engage in thrill-seeking activities like riding roller coasters with, let's say a friend, sometimes the rush of adrenaline you get when doing such activities may cause you to feel more for the other person than you might normally."

And I didn't need any more help feeling things for him I shouldn't.

He did something he had rarely done in my presence. A low rumble of real laughter came through the phone. "Do you believe yourself in danger of such feelings for me?"

"Of course not," I stuttered while my heart pounded out what a liar I was.

"Your concern lies with *my* well-being, then."

"No," I eked out.

"Then tell me, Kate, what are you afraid of?"

Him. Most definitely him. "I don't want to do anything to jeopardize Binary Search's reputation."

"Right." His disappointment came through loud and clear. "Lucky for you, I have meetings there all day tomorrow. It would just be you and Skye, as well as her friend Hensley, thrill seeking, as you put it."

"Oh." Why didn't he just say that in the first place?

"Is it a date then? We can pick you up at nine. Where are you staying?"

"I'm at the Marriott near the airport in Burbank. I think they have a shuttle that goes to Universal if it's out of your way."

"It's not."

"Okay. How's your writing going?"

"Well."

"No distractions?"

"Just one."

"I'm sorry."

"You should be."

My cheeks burned. "How do you figure?"

"I think you know."

I held my stomach.

"Kate."

"Nick."

"I don't need a roller coaster to produce a rush of adrenaline when I'm with you. Good night."

The adrenaline was rushing. I buried my head in my pillow. What had I gotten myself into?

I didn't sleep well and was up well before I needed to get ready thanks to the phone conversation with Nick and debating all night with myself about what I was doing. I knew we'd crossed a line last night. But we both knew we couldn't act on it, right? He was my client, for goodness sake. And he was him and I was me. Safe in my rules. Lonely, but safe.

I stared at myself in my hotel mirror. I wore a pale pink tank top with scalloped edges and casual shorts that showed off a lot of leg. It was supposed to be a warm day in the mid-80s and I knew we would be in the sun most of the day, so I wanted to dress accordingly. I had to say I was loving the California weather. Hot but not humid, and at night it cooled off. It wasn't sweltering like Georgia in late August. I had thrown my hair up in a messy bun. I'd almost curled it but didn't want to seem like I was trying too hard.

By ten minutes to nine, I couldn't take it anymore; I headed for the lobby to wait for Nick and Skye to arrive. The lobby's furniture and décor were done in serene tones, but it wasn't helping my nerves. I kept staring out the large double glass entrance doors to see if Nick had arrived. At five till the hour, Skye texted.

Dad wanted me to tell you that we are going to be ten minutes late. Traffic is bad.

I smiled at his thoughtfulness that not long ago didn't seem to exist. *See you soon.*

Can't wait.

Me either.

I meant it too. I missed Skye and Nick. I tried to relax on one of the lobby couches, but it was no use. Nick Wells was picking me up. My twenty-year-old self was having her moment, and she wanted to lay down on the couch and kick her legs in the air. I stopped her before she could.

At ten after the hour I walked outside, and within a minute, a 1966 Mustang convertible in springtime yellow pulled up with its top down carrying two people I was coming to really care for, along with a girl with striking blue hair and a nose ring, who I guessed was Hensley. I dug her style.

The car suited Nick, and I was in love. With the car. Not him. Before I could ogle him too much, Skye jumped out of the passenger seat and ran around the car to hug me.

I held her tight and kissed her blonde head. "Hey, pretty girl, I missed you."

"Me too." She squeezed tighter. "I kept telling Dad we should have come sooner."

This girl owned my heart.

Her dad pierced it. He stood waiting for Skye and me to end our embrace. As soon as she was in the backseat with her friend, Nick made his move.

He didn't hesitate to kiss my cheek. "You look good."

I missed those kisses and the way his facial hair rubbed against my face.

"Thank you." I sounded shy. "You do too." And did he ever. He was dressed to impress in dark slacks and a blue dress shirt that played well with his eyes.

"Are you ready to go?" he asked.

I threw my small purse around my shoulder and nodded.

Nick did something he had never done before. He followed me to the passenger side and opened the door for me.

I stood astonished. "What's this?"

His eyes took ahold of me. "The way it's going to be between us from now on."

Oh.

Chapter Thirty-Six

WITH NICK BEING who he was, we got super-secret access to the back lots of Universal Studios. It was there I got to meet Margo, his assistant, who I assumed was a lingerie model. I was wrong yet again. I mean, maybe she was at one time, but the elegant woman with silver hair that sparkled like a crown in the sun was at least in her late fifties, I would guess. And she was fully clothed in a conservative wraparound dress. She screamed propriety, and you could tell by the way she walked she was no-nonsense, even if she wore a warm smile.

Margo, carrying a designer looking bag, must have been waiting for us since she was almost to the car by the time we parked.

"You're running late, Nick." She opened his door for him and immediately pulled out a gray tie that matched his outfit perfectly. It was like a song and dance watching them. She tied his tie for him while he introduced me.

"Margo, this is Kate."

Margo peeked around Nick while still working on his tie. I was out of the car, but standing by the passenger side door. The girls had hopped out and were nearby me.

Margo gave me an appraising look and smiled. "It's nice to finally meet you." She turned her focus back to Nick. "You're right," she said to him.

"I know," he said cryptically.

What did all that mean?

I wasn't sure if I should join Nick or stay by the girls, who were excitedly chatting about which rides to hit first. Harry Potter was on top of their list.

Honestly, I wasn't sure about a lot. The way Nick kept giving me heated stares on the drive over had me feeling like I should be reciting *The Science Behind Why Good Girls Love Bad Boys*, but I couldn't remember a single thing I'd learned from it. I hadn't even brought my copy with me. Maybe I should have packed it.

While I contemplated my crisis at hand, Nick and Margo came around and met me. Margo started handing me VIP passes for the park and a credit card with Nick's name on it.

"You're authorized to use this." She was so matter-of-fact.

I tried to hand the card back. "I don't need this."

Margo wasn't taking it; she kept on task. "The passes will allow you entrance onto any ride with express access to them. You can also eat in the VIP dining room."

I looked to Nick and tried to hand him his card.

"Margo, will you give us a minute?"

"You can have one minute; you and Simon need to prep." She stepped away.

Nick took her spot but he drew much closer than her.

"I don't want your credit card. I can pay my way."

His brittle smile appeared. "You are taking care of my daughter and Hensley today, so use it."

"I can pay their way too."

"Kate, don't be stubborn today."

"Thirty seconds, Nick." Margo meant business.

Nick wrapped my hand around his card. "Please don't argue about it." He kissed my cheek. "I'll see you soon."

All I could say was, "Good luck. Or do you think you don't need it?"

"I do today. Thank you." He gave me one more kiss on the cheek before saying goodbye to Skye and Hensley.

Margo was practically dragging him away, but she had time to call out, "Skye has my number if you need anything. I'll check in on you all later."

I wanted time to process what had just happened, or at least to touch my cheek where Nick's lips had lingered, but I had two eager girls staring at me, ready to hit the park. Skye was doing more than staring, she was giving me a hopeful smile. I had a feeling I knew what she was hoping for. It was the same thing I feared and had wished for almost half my life. What an odd thought that was.

I decided it was best to focus on Skye and Hensley. I handed them each a pass to place around their necks. "Where to, ladies?"

"Harry Potter," they answered in unison.

"Sounds good to me. Lead the way."

I was excited to enter the world of Harry Potter. I remembered when the first book came out, sucking me into its magical world. I believe I was thirteen. My friends and I went to midnight release parties and dressed up as witches and wizards.

Skye took my hand and pulled me along. "You're going to love this place. We have to get butterbeer after we do the ride."

"I love the frozen kind the best," Hensley commented.

Frozen sounded good, as it was getting warmer by the second.

The park was already crowded as we wound our way through what looked like a town complete with dozens of stores and restaurants to shop and eat at. The girls were on a mission and we were double-timing it to our first destination. It didn't take us too long to reach Hogsmeade and for the Hogwarts castle to come into view. My geeky heart leapt. I always knew my acceptance letter to Hogwarts had gone missing.

I listened to the girls chatter about who they would rather date, Harry or Ron. It was no surprise Skye chose Harry. She liked a boy with glasses. Hensley chose neither—she was all for Fred or George. I laughed because I had thought the same thing growing up. The trouble-making twins would have been fun. I liked the semi–bad boys from the start.

The line was long to get into the castle and ride. It made me feel bad that we got to bypass it.

"Dad missed you," Skye mentioned as we waited in our very short line to gain access to the castle. Her smile said she knew what she was doing.

"Did he say that?" Did that sound juvenile?

She nodded and giggled with Hensley. I felt like I was in high school again. I was having the do-you-think-he-likes-me conversation. And I had this overwhelming desire to ask Skye everything he said so I could dissect it. I held back.

"Did you miss him?" Skye asked brazenly as we moved forward.

"How would you feel if I did?"

She stopped and tilted her beautiful head. "I would be happy."

I put my arm around her, realizing how much her happiness meant to me, and not because of her dad. It was all her. I gave her a squeeze. "I missed you both."

She leaned into me before she and Hensley were off trying to get to the front of the ride. The indoor virtual-type rides were a new experience for me. As thrilling as it was to feel like I was living out my Harry Potter dreams, it was disconcerting not knowing where you were as you whizzed through the ride.

Butterbeer was next. It was a test of whether I would use Nick's card or not. It seemed awfully intimate to use a man's credit card. Did he give out his credit cards all the time? I would never unless I really trusted the person, and even then, I would have some serious reservations. Did Nick trust me? Did I trust him?

I paid for the butterbeer using my own card. I couldn't bring myself to use Nick's card. Nick had already paid for my ticket, which was astronomical. And he'd been paying for me all summer. It was the least I could do.

The girls had me going all over and almost wetting my pants in the Walking Dead haunted house. I found myself wishing Nick was with us. I would have had good reason to cling to him. Listen to these thoughts of mine. Was I willing to risk my heart and job for him?

I didn't have time to think about it as we rode everything from Revenge of the Mummy to Transformers. Some of the rides we did more than once. I must have been getting old, as I found myself getting queasy easier, but I didn't let it stop me from enjoying the day with Skye and Hensley, the two peas in a pod who loved to talk about each cute boy we passed and who had an insatiable appetite for screaming on the rides.

During the heat of the day, we headed to the Jurassic Park water ride. I didn't realize how soaked I would get, but it did feel good to cool off, even if I did look like a drowned rat. It was then that Margo called Skye and asked us to meet her where they start the studio tours. I wondered if she had set a time for us to join one of the tours, which I was looking forward to. Or if Nick asked her to make sure I was keeping his child alive and well. Maybe both. We hadn't seen him in five hours. I hoped his meetings were going as planned.

Margo stood waiting for us looking at her phone. I could see the wheels spinning in her brain. I bet she was always a woman on a mission.

She smiled up at us as we approached. "Oh good, you're here. Skye and Hensley, you are coming with me on a regular tour and," her smile turned mischievous, "Nick is waiting to take you on a *private* tour."

I swallowed hard. "Um...he is?"

"Right this way," she started to move.

I grabbed ahold of her arm. "Wait."

She gave me a good look over. "You look beautiful wet, if that's what you're worried about."

That didn't even touch the tip of the iceberg of my worries. "When you said private, do you mean only me and Nick?"

"Joe will drive the trolley."

"But what I really need to know is—"

"You're going to be fine." She patted my cheek.

I didn't share her sentiment. Neither did my stomach that was snapping and popping more than ever. "Margo—"

"Darling," she cut me off again, "let's not keep him waiting any longer."

I followed Margo numbly with Skye and Hensley trailing. I could hear their giggles and whispers behind me. I didn't even pay attention to where I was being led, my head and heart were having a conference about what we should do. My mom's voice was also joining the fray, telling me she hadn't raised me to live by the rules. But rules were good and there was a reason for them. I couldn't remember any of them now, but I knew they existed.

Before I knew it, there *he* was, leaning against a single car trolley. Normally there were several cars attached. His tie was gone, sleeves rolled up, and shirt unbuttoned enough for me to get a peek of what my poster of long ago showed off. He was my dream, or was that nightmare? Heart and mind conferred, and they were going with dream.

"Enjoy yourself." Margo turned to leave with the girls.

My first instinct was to go with them, but Nick sauntered toward me, waving goodbye to his daughter, who was giggling louder than ever with her friend. My sandals felt like they had melted into the asphalt. I stood transfixed by Nick.

"Are you ready?" His question resonated with a double meaning.

I shook my head no.

That didn't deter him. He took my hand—our fingers intertwined naturally. Our magical connection crackled between us.

"What are you doing?"

He pulled me to him and we came face-to-face. With his other hand, he caressed my cheek. "I'm doing what I've been doing for the last several weeks."

"And what's that?" I stammered.

"Courting you, Kate."

I must have lost my hearing, because all I could hear was a ringing in my ears and something about us dating. How had I missed that? "No... We can't... I'm your—"

"Shhh." He placed his finger on my lips. "Forget about your job, your rules. We're good together, Kate."

All our time together ran through my mind like a film on fast forward. All my favorite places he had taken me to. The help he had given my parents. Our late-night phone conversations and soul bearing moments. All our research trips, not to mention all the time I'd spent with his daughter and dad. So many sweet memories that made me smile.

I gazed up at him with that same smile on my face.

He mirrored my smile. "Are you ready now?"

I thought I was. I nodded.

He wasted not a second and pulled me toward the waiting trolley. With us as the only passengers I thought we would sit up toward the front, but we sat on the very last row. Nick left not an inch of space between us, holding my hand and placing his arm around me. All felt right in the world by his side.

"We're ready, Joe," Nick called to the man wearing a large grin and a red beret at the helm.

"You got it, boss," Joe responded. "Hold on tight." The trolley lurched forward.

Don't mind if I do. I squeezed Nick's hand.

This was real, right? Nick's finger running down my arm leaving goosebumps as he went felt real.

"How did your meetings go?" I asked.

Nick kissed the side of my head. "Better than expected."

"How so?"

"They loved the entire pitch package, including what I have written of the rough draft. Their lawyers are drafting an initial contract as we speak."

"That's amazing—congratulations."

"It's the first step of many, but it feels good."

"I'm proud of you, Nick. Is that weird to say?"

"Not at all." He raised my hand and kissed it.

Joe interrupted us, or should I say, I paid attention to what he was saying as we began to drive by actual movie sets. Joe pointed out the Psycho house and Bates Motel. For added effect, he screeched out *Norman!*

I was dazzled with all the sets, from *To Kill a Mockingbird* to *Jaws*. Joe was good to give trivia tidbits about each movie, like the shark they made for *Jaws* weighed more than 1.2 tons. And that Gregory Peck won an Academy Award for his portrayal of Atticus Finch in *To Kill A Mockingbird*. I knew that, but I didn't know the book was originally going to be called Atticus.

What I enjoyed most was being with Nick. That was, until we pulled into what looked like an abandoned studio and the doors automatically closed behind us when the trolley stopped on some tracks. It was spine-tingling dark.

"Ready to feel some adrenaline?" Nick whispered in my ear.

"What do you mean?"

He didn't have to say a word. The ground felt like it was shaking, and then water began to rush in. Joe was saying something about this being the set for a television show. But then fire flared up around us and a semitruck dropped from the ceiling.

I jumped while a tiny scream escaped me. I clung to Nick, who pulled me onto his lap and held me tight. The fire around us reflected in his eyes and added to the heat that was palpable between us. Adrenaline was coursing through me as never before.

He leaned in and his lips began to tease mine, first with a light brush. So light, I wasn't sure it happened, but my lips were tingling.

He ran his hand through my damp hair, causing it to fall out of the messy bun. "You're beautiful," he whispered before his lips crushed mine.

Oh, I felt *that* amongst the jolting and crashing going on all around us.

His lips were warm and pressing. His hand tangled in my hair, pulling my head closer as his tongue urged my lips to part.

My lips complied and tasted what he had to offer. It came wrapped in a package of what could only be described as ambrosia. I indulged in the sweetness of him while he groaned and pulled our bodies flush.

Though I was literally in the middle of a catastrophic accident, all my senses were wrapped up in him. My hands explored his rough face and ran through his soft-textured hair. With my every touch, his tongue prodded deeper until I felt as if I was only breathing him in.

When the fire around us began to dissipate, his kiss slowed to a warm simmer. He gently swept my lips with his own. "Kate," he whispered my name. "I've been wanting to do that for a long time."

I had waited for that kiss for almost half my life, and I couldn't have imagined it being as magical as it was. I ran my hand across his cheek.

Joe interrupted our moment. "Looks like it worked, boss. You ready to go?"

Nick grinned at me and waved Joe forward.

I leaned my forehead against Nick's. "You planned this?" My tone was light and playful.

"From the first time we met, Kate." His lips consumed me once again.

Chapter Thirty-Seven

THE UNEXPECTED DAY continued as I found myself at Nick's home. Nick had to get Hensley home, and neither of us was ready to say goodbye. Nick and Skye convinced me to come home with them to have dinner. I didn't realize that meant an almost two-hour drive one way in the worst traffic I had ever been in. Atlanta had nothing on LA. It was almost like being in the middle of that crash simulation, minus the kissing.

The kissing. I should be embarrassed how much kissing happened on that trolley with poor Joe as a witness. But it had been a long time, and I'd never been kissed like that before. Nick was a professional. Come to think of it, maybe he had been taught to kiss, but it went well beyond technique. There was an emotional aspect I'd never experienced before. His uninhibited nature flowed through me, allowing me to feel a comfort and connection that had never been present with anyone else.

I looked around one of his guest bathrooms, which had more windows than any bathroom I'd ever been in. His house seemed to be made more of glass than anything, but I couldn't blame him—the

I let out a big breath, not sure what to make of any of what he did and didn't say.

"You are the only woman I want in my life. Trust me...please."

"That's difficult for me."

He sweetly kissed my forehead and lingered. "I know."

"What do we do?"

"We don't worry about it, because it's all going to work out. And I don't want to waste another second of our time together this weekend talking about things that don't matter."

"I didn't know we were spending the weekend together." I smirked up at him.

"Now you do. I'm going to play tour guide."

His seductive tone sent a shiver through me. "Is that so?"

He nuzzled my neck. "We are going to start right here." He lingered, driving me mad, until he kissed his way up my neck to my lips. "Next stop is here." His warm lips teased and pulled on mine until they gently brushed them a few times.

I wrapped my arms around his neck, giving him permission to continue his tour.

He picked me up and placed me on the counter. I drew him as close as I could by wrapping my legs around him. His lips came crashing into mine before he deepened the kiss and explored every available space in my mouth. The torrid love letter between us was finally being written, and I knew I wanted to reread it as often as possible. His hands once again undid my hair and it fell around us.

"Is something burning in here?" Skye yelled.

Yes, my body. Wait. Something was burning. There was smoke and an acrid smell. How did I miss that?

Nick and I broke apart. While I jumped off the counter, embarrassed to be caught passionately kissing Skye's dad, Nick swore and quickly took the pan of burnt peppers off the stove.

Skye stood there, towel-drying her hair after her shower, with a mix of amusement and I'm-grossed-out playing on her face.

I tucked what I was sure was messy hair behind my ear.

"I'm happy you're together, but can you save the PDA for when I'm not around?" Skye didn't give us a chance to answer—she walked right back out.

A look passed between Nick and me that said the tour would continue later.

As much as I enjoyed the private tour Nick had given me, I loved it even more when I found myself between Nick and Skye on the most comfortable, stylish leather couch of all time watching one of Skye's favorite movies, *Pitch Perfect,* on what had to be the biggest personal screen you could own. Who needed a movie theater?

Plus, the food here was way better. Nick made the most amazing braised chicken with peppers. He didn't burn them the second time around. I had no idea he was such a good cook. I thought he'd have a personal chef on staff. He mentioned he used to when *On the Edge* was at its height.

I was snuggled against Nick while Skye got comfy by resting her head in my lap and prostrating herself on the couch with her feet propped up. I played with her hair while she talked over the movie.

"So, Hensley wants me to go to San Diego tomorrow with her parents. Is that okay?"

Nick mulled it over. "What are they doing there and how long would you be gone?"

"They're going to Coronado Island, you know, to do the tourist thing. We'll be gone all day. Please, Daddy, I've hardly seen Hensley all summer. And you trust her parents." She had the cute pouty-lip thing down.

"But Kate's in town," he countered.

Skye smiled up at me but spoke to her dad. "Yeah, I know, but don't you want some alone time? And we can all have dinner tomorrow night when I get back. We can take Kate to The Loft. You'll love it," she addressed me specifically.

Nick did the total dad thing and acted like he was debating all while I knew, and I was sure Skye knew too, that he was going to say yes.

"I suppose," he relented. "But I'm making reservations for seven, so make sure you'll be back in time for that."

"Thank you, Daddy." She focused back on her movie and sang along with it.

Nick kissed the side of my head. "Looks like it will only be you and me tomorrow. Can you handle that?"

I was going to try my very best to. "I think so."

"We've made progress."

Chapter Thirty-Eight

I HADN'T INTENDED TO fall asleep in Nick's arms on his couch with Skye snuggled against me also sleeping soundly. It felt amazing, but when I realized I was at his home and it was late, I stirred and turned, ever so gently to not wake up Skye, to find Nick awake and gazing at me in the semi-dark.

"Why did you let me fall asleep? You were supposed to take me back to my hotel," I whispered.

His only answer was to brush my lips with his own. "Stay with me, Kate."

I hadn't received that kind of invitation in a long time. My heart was beating double-time even thinking about what that meant. "Nick, I can't...we can't...yet."

"I'm not inviting you to my bed. I promise you, the anchor will come before the pleasure cruise."

"You listened to me."

"Every word." He stroked my cheek. "Please stay."

"Even if we aren't going to sleep together, I don't have my stuff with me. And how will it look to Skye?"

"It will look like I finally let her have a sleepover. We'll all stay here on the couch," he said as if that was a logical solution.

"And she's not going to think it's weird that you let your *friend* stay the night?"

"You can say it like it is and call yourself my girlfriend. Skye already does."

"Does she now? And where did she get that idea?"

"I think everyone but you knew."

"That's not true. Kenadie and Zander said I was too smart to fall for you."

His brows furrowed together. Something about Kenadie rubbed him the wrong way. "What do they know?" he grumbled.

"Regardless of what I am or not, I don't have my things." I grinned. Honestly, I was happy to think of myself as his girlfriend.

He shrugged. "Everything you need will be here in the morning."

That gave me some pause. "Do you keep a closet full of women's clothing for 'occasions' like these?"

"What are you implying?"

"I don't want to be anyone's conquest." My vulnerabilities were coming out.

"Kate." He rested his forehead on mine. "Despite my reputation, I'm not that kind of man. I don't see women, especially you, as conquests. Yes, I've made mistakes—you know that. But you're different. We're different. I knew from the first time we met, you would be."

"The very first time?" I eked.

He kissed my nose. "Yes."

"How could you know then? We barely had a conversation."

"Only because you ran off, which seems to be how you operate. Why did you leave?"

"Your fans mauled you and pushed me out of the way. It looked like you were kind of busy."

"Busy trying to get away from them so I could see what your plans were . . . for the rest of your life."

Time and my lungs stopped working with that confession. "Really?" I breathed out.

"Really." His eyes tried to convey how sincere he was. "When we touched it was like—"

"A torrid love letter," I whispered.

"You felt it too."

I nodded.

"Why did you refuse to tell me we'd met before?" He was not going to let that question go.

I looked up to his high ceilings and bit my lip. "Because I didn't want you to ruin the magic of that moment for me. I was afraid if I ever told anyone about it, it wouldn't be real. The connection I felt that day was so overwhelming. I've wondered if I would ever have it again. But even if I never got to experience it again, I needed it after everything I went through. Something to hope for. As silly as that sounds."

"What you're saying is you needed me." A smile danced in his eyes.

"In some way, I suppose." I rested my head on his shoulder. "Honestly, though, as magical as that moment was, it made me realize that as much as I had dreamed about you, you and I weren't meant to be. You were a newly single father of a toddler." I stroked the hair of that toddler, now all grown up, who rested against me. "A man who could have any woman he wanted, and you didn't need another coed fangirl vying for your attention. I knew I couldn't compete. I didn't even want to try. So I hung up my dreams and got involved with a nightmare."

He held me tighter as if trying to protect me. "You had my attention for far longer than you've known. I wanted you then and now."

His words filled me with such pleasure, but a hint of worry played in the background. "Nick, I'm not the girl who wrote your name in my notebooks or ogled you on my wall."

"Kate, I'm not looking for a fan to share my life with. I want the woman who looks past my fame and who's not afraid to keep my ego in check. You do both well."

I laughed softly into his shoulder.

"But if you want to hang me up on your wall again, I wouldn't stop you. I'd be happy to hang a picture of you on my wall." The last part sounded sincere, maybe even the first half.

I snuggled closer to him. "Nick, is this crazy?"

"No." He tilted my chin up and our lips met. Feelings of serendipity swirled around us. His kiss was warm and gentle this time. He barely parted my lips and only lingered for a stirring moment. He brushed his hand across my cheek and through my hair. "Stay with me."

I took a deep breath and nodded.

He swiped my lips one more time. "Good night, Kate."

I settled back against him, feeling connected and whole for the first time in a very long time. Peaceful sleep engulfed me.

....

I woke to the sound of Skye frantically shouting about how she was going to be late.

Nick and I both sat up lazily.

"I better make us something to eat." Nick yawned.

"Do you want me to see if I can help her while you do that?" I was afraid to overstep bounds and wasn't sure how and where I should insert myself as Nick's girlfriend. Was that ever weird to say or think. Weirder that we had all slept together on his couch. The crick in my neck I was starting to feel was worth every second of it.

Nick paused and peered into my eyes. A thoughtful expression filled his gaze. "Kate," he paused, then opened his mouth to say something, but it never got articulated. I did get a peck on the lips. "Yes."

It was a good way to start the morning. I rushed off to find Skye to see if she needed my help. Light streamed in and illuminated every surface of the magnificent house. It was a weird observation, but his hallways were a lot wider than any home I'd been in, but I was happy to find that it was a normal house of a teenager—Skye's things cluttered the hall leading to what could only be called a suite. Skye's glitzy and sparkly bedroom was every teen girl's dream, right down to the huge lighted mirrors, four-poster white bed, and poufs galore that filled the space. It was also a mess, with clothes strewn about, an unmade bed, and empty strawed plastic smoothie cups.

"Hey, pretty girl, can I help you?"

Skye was frantically tossing clothes all over. "I can't find my new Abercrombie shorts."

"What do they look like?"

"They're denim with embroidered flowers."

"We'll find them," I assured her.

"And I need to do my hair and my makeup." She was starting to panic.

The mom gene appeared, and I easily found the shorts lying next to her bed under some T-shirts with tags still on them. No need to mention how pricey they were. I held up the shorts. "I'll help you with your hair while you do your makeup."

She rushed to me and took the shorts but not before hugging me. "Thanks, Kate."

Her private bathroom was as dreamy and messy as her bedroom. I was jealous of her clawfoot tub.

I brushed and smoothed her hair while she sat at her vanity and applied moisturizer to her flawless skin. "I can do a braided twist."

She met my eyes in her mirror. "You're a godsend. I love you."

Huh. Those words pricked my heart. I rested my hands on her thin shoulders and the most beautiful feeling fell upon me. "I love you too, kiddo."

Her face was all smiles. "I'm really glad you and my dad are together."

"Me too." I began to piece her luxurious blonde hair into strands.

"I wish you lived here."

Oh. Whoa. About that. "Your dad and I will have to work out when we all can see each other once the summer is over. I'll come visit and you guys can visit me."

Her cute nose scrunched. "It won't be the same."

"It won't, but I live near Liam."

Her cheeks pinked while her shoulders fell. "He told me that he thought it would be better if we stayed friends."

"What? When?"

"A couple of days ago."

"Why didn't you tell me, honey?"

"Because it's embarrassing. I mean, why doesn't he like me?"

I set the brush down and squeezed her shoulders. "I don't know that he doesn't. Sometimes it's the timing of it all. He's starting college and you're still in high school. Maybe he doesn't want you to miss out on any opportunities."

"That's what he said." She sniffled.

I smiled at her through the mirror. "He's a good guy. The kind that if it's meant to work out, it will. But you are young, and you should date around and get to know lots of different guys before you ever settle on one. Most importantly, you should get to know yourself."

"Is that what you did?" she asked innocently.

Her question caught me off guard. I had to think for a moment. "Something like that."

I wasn't quite ready to tell her about Douglas. Someday, if this ended up being permanent, we would have that talk. And I would make sure to do my best to see that she never had a Douglas in her life.

"I hope it doesn't take me as long as you to figure it out," she said without any guile.

I laughed. "Me too."

Chapter Thirty-Nine

WITH SKYE OFF, it was only Nick and me, looking frightful in the clothes I'd worn the day before.

Nick pulled me close to him in the kitchen. "We have a busy day ahead of us. Why don't you go take a shower," he groaned. "While I try not to think about you in there." He buried his face in my neck and soaked me in.

My fingers tangled in his hair. "What are we doing today?" I stuttered. He was driving me crazy in the best sort of way.

"I'm going to give you a taste of our world here. See how you like it."

I leaned away from him.

He read my mind. "I'm not the novelty here I am in Georgia. No one is going to bother us or give a damn who you work for." His expression softened. "What do you say?"

"I can't think of anything I would like more, but I have nothing to wear."

"I've taken care of that too." He took my hand and pulled me along. "You will have everything you need when you are done showering."

"How?"

"That's my secret."

I let him keep his secret while I relaxed in one of his guest bathroom showers that doubled as a sauna. I had died and gone to heaven. I was with the man of my dreams in his dream house. How did this happen? My twenty-year-old self said *told you so*. My thirty-four-year-old self was trying to revel in it all while remaining cautious. I was me, after all. And there were things to work out—we lived on opposite sides of the country and my job. My younger self begged me not to ruin this moment for her. *Okay, fine*, I told her while I steamed away the kink in my neck.

There was a knock on the bathroom door while I was combing my hair, wrapped in the softest towel imaginable. I needed to find out the thread count on it. I slid the door open, but only enough to peek out.

Nick stood there with a smug grin on his face holding a large bag with a boutique name on it. "This is for you."

"Thank you." I reached my hand out for it.

He pulled it away from me, making my bare arm extend farther. "Just a little more, Kate."

"Nick."

"You can't blame a guy for trying." He took my hand and kissed it before handing me the heavy bag.

"What's in this?"

"You'll see. I'm going to get ready. By the way, I prefer the red one for the beach."

What did that mean? He strode away before I could ask. When I knew he was gone, I opened the door more and pulled in the bag, which was filled to the top.

The first layer was clothing. I laid each piece out on the counter, touched and uncomfortable by his generosity. I carefully examined each beautiful article from the intimate items all the way to the iconic-looking, cream off-the-shoulder sundress. How he knew my size, I had no idea, but he was spot on, even the bra size. Not sure I wanted to know how he gained that talent.

The comment about the "red one" made sense when I pulled out two bikinis, one red, one white. I rolled my eyes. They were tasteful, but they were bikinis.

Since it appeared the beach was involved, I wore the red bikini under the white safari shorts and V-neck T-shirt. I threw my hair up and only wore a hint of makeup. Nick had thought of that too. In the bottom of the bag were an assortment of high-end cosmetics.

Nick had been busy while I got ready. He had a cooler and beach bag ready to go while looking like a million bucks in his blue swim trunks and tight, white tee. Maybe I would stay in California. Getting on that plane tomorrow afternoon sounded like the last thing I wanted to do.

Nick's garage was more like a car museum. Along with his beautiful Mustang, he owned a Porsche, Range Rover, two motorcycles, and a BMW.

He headed for the Mustang again. It was my favorite.

"Tonight after dinner, we'll cruise the PCH—Pacific Coast Highway—on my bike. It's the best way to experience it." He pointed to the black motorcycle in the corner.

"I'm game."

Nick smiled and placed the cooler and bag in the trunk before opening my door for me.

Before I stepped into the car, I stood on my tiptoes and kissed his cheek. "Thank you for everything."

"You're welcome, but that bikini was for my pleasure."

"You may not think so once this top layer comes off."

"Kate," he leaned in, "there is no one more beautiful to me than you." He kissed me.

The emotion his words evoked spilled out through my lips and I pressed them firmly against his.

"Mmm," he groaned in pleasure. "If you keep kissing me, I'm going to be tempted to take you back inside or lean the seats back in the car," he spoke against my lips.

"I'll save some for later," I backed away and took my seat.

"I can't wait." He shut the door and sauntered around.

And we were off, heading down his long, hidden drive, the sunshine bearing down on us in his convertible. Frank Sinatra was on the stereo and I was falling deeper and deeper.

The roads were windy, but Nick handled them with ease while holding my hand.

"I forgot to ask you how your conference went." He had to use a raised voice to combat the wind whipping through his convertible.

"It was good. I have a lot of studying to do and organizing my notes, but I think I gleaned some good information for both my jobs."

"Did they talk about narcissists?" he teased with a smirk.

"You have to admit that's how you came off, but as matter of fact, they did."

He glanced my way. "Are you going to tell me what they said?"

"You really want to know?"

He squeezed my hand. "I want to know everything about you."

I took a moment to appreciate that sentiment and him. He didn't know how much that meant to me, especially after being with someone like Douglas, who only cared about himself.

"There is some new research that indicates when treating NPD as a therapist, you should work together with the patient to examine their problems from their perspective and to especially focus on their self-esteem."

"Don't narcissists have high self-esteem?"

"They portray that on a grandiose scale, but really they're vulnerable and struggle with it."

"Interesting."

"It is, but I don't want to talk about narcissists today. When are you coming back to Georgia?"

He stretched his neck from side to side. "I'd like to go back with you tomorrow, but I have a lot to get done in a short amount of time and you are—"

"A distraction?"

"The best kind."

"I feel bad I'm taking you away from your work right now."

He pulled my hand up kissed it. "Don't. I hated being away from you this week, and don't think I wouldn't drop work for you in a second if you asked me to."

I smiled over at him. He had a way of making me feel wanted.

"You know, you could stay here." He tossed that out there not so casually.

That gave me something to think about. "I appreciate the invite, but like you, and because of you, I have a lot of work to catch up on. I'm going to be interviewing new clients 24/7 when I get back."

He grimaced. "Let's not talk about work today, yours or mine."

I tilted my head. "Nick, is there something you want to tell me about Binary Search?"

"Not today." His voice wasn't curt, but he made his point.

"Okay." I took in the magnificent coastline coming into view. The aquamarine water played at the shoreline, darkening to the deepest blue the farther out it went.

Nick released my hand and rested it on my cheek. I naturally leaned into it.

"Kate, I've been waiting to have you to myself for so long. I only want to focus on us."

I wasn't sure what to say. I hated unresolved issues.

Nick must have clued in. "I promise you, there is nothing to worry about. My agreement with Binary Search has nothing to do with us."

"Promise?"

He pulled into a metered parking spot near the beach before turning his head toward me. His eyes bore deeply into mine. "Yes."

I took a deep breath of *I'm going to trust you.*

He decided to take my breath away by leaning over to kiss me. He capably cupped my face with his hands before pressing his lips against mine. He held them steady and simmered there. I took in his scent and taste. It had to be the best natural aphrodisiac known to humankind.

"Let me show you my world," he whispered.

I bought a first-class ticket for his tour.

I was surprised how normal it was being with Nick. I mean, he used public metered parking and he was right—no one stopped him. A few people may have glanced at him more than once wondering if he was someone they should be interested in, but there were no interruptions or phones pointed our way.

Nick held my hand, and we behaved like any couple would walking down a crowded sidewalk. We smiled at each other, well, I smiled, he did his half-smile thing. Nick weaved us deftly in and out of people to our first destination while I took in the storefronts and boutiques that lined downtown Laguna Beach's main thoroughfare. I was already half in love with it. There were eclectic beachy boho shops that blended with small café's and higher priced boutiques. Palm trees lined the path, and there were several independent vendors selling everything from jewelry to handmade artwork.

Nick led us into what looked like an alleyway, but instead it was a quaint cluster of shops, complete with a fairytale-looking tree growing in the middle of the courtyard that connected them. The knotty branches were sprinkled with green leaves that danced in the light breeze.

"Where are we going?" I asked, fascinated with my surroundings.

"Right in here." He opened a door with a sign that read, *Swirls of Silk.*

We stepped into a world of colorful silk scarves in all sorts of patterns, shapes, and sizes draped on lines and hooks as far as the eye could see. Standing in the middle of it all were several wooden basins filled with water and bottles and bottles of paint surrounding each basin.

A woman with an ethereal presence appeared from the back. Her hair was blindingly white. It contrasted with the brightly colored paint smattered across her smock. She glided when she walked, and when she spoke, she sounded otherworldly. My mom would love her.

"Nick," she elongated his name when she pronounced it. "It's been forever, darling." She opened her arms wide.

Nick briefly left my side and hugged her. "Zabrina, how are you?"

She stepped back and surveyed me first before answering. "Not as well as you, I see. Who is this?"

Nick took my hand and tugged gently until I was by his side. "This is Kate."

Zabrina walked around me, eyeing me carefully, making me feel self-conscious. "Your mother would approve."

"I know," Nick responded to her, but zeroed in on me. "Kate, Zabrina was my mom's best friend."

"Since we were girls." Zabrina took my other hand and led me to one of the basins. "I take it you came in to make a scarf?"

I looked at Nick, not sure what to say.

"If you have time," Nick answered.

"For you, I always have the time."

"Did you make all these scarves?" I looked around. "They're beautiful."

"Yes, but not as beautiful as the one you will make."

"I'm not that artistic."

"You don't need to be." She placed her hand on my heart. "I can tell you have a good one of these."

"You can?"

"It reflects in your eyes. The windows to your soul are clean and pure. Exactly what this man has needed." She nodded toward Nick.

Seriously, she and my mom were meant to be best friends. And I was touched Nick wanted me to meet his mother's best friend.

I smiled at Nick. "I hope so."

Nick kissed my cheek. "I know so."

"Lovely, lovely. But let's get to work. I have a group coming in an hour."

Nick helped me pick out some colors. We went with classic blues, reds, and cream. Nick also helped me drop the paint in the water. There we watched it swirl. Then we used combs that were really pieces of wood with nails hammered into them and skewers to fine-tune our design. It was so fun to watch the pattern take shape and to listen to Zabrina talk about Nick's mom, Barbara. I knew from Jack she was an angel, but Zabrina told some stories about their wilder single days of skipping school and using fake IDs to get into bars. That's how Jack and Barbara met. I didn't see that one coming. Or the fact that they eloped.

"Please don't tell Skye those stories," Nick begged.

Zabrina waved him off. "She's a good girl. You worry too much." Zabrina carefully dipped the long silk scarf into the colored water, making sure it was straight. Within seconds, she pulled it out. I was amazed how easily the pattern transferred onto the scarf.

"So lovely," she admired it before rinsing and hanging it up to dry. "You can come back later and pick it up. I'm sure you have better things to do than listen to an old woman ramble about days gone by."

I could have stayed all day. I hugged her. "Thank you."

"Yes, you're a good one." She squeezed right back. "Be sure you deserve this one," she admonished Nick.

"I'll do my best." He kissed Zabrina's cheek. "We'll see you later."

And we were off on our adventure. The next stop was an amazing gelato place that was next door to Zabrina's place. We shared a cup of raspberry gelato with chocolate chunks as we walked toward the car and the beach where we would spend the rest of our day.

California beaches were different from the Gulf beaches with fine white sand and warm water that I was used to. The sand here was coarse and rough on the feet. The water was frigid. But the cliffs and coves here made up for it. And the view on the beach blanket was well worth the price of admission.

Did I mention I got to slather Nick in sunscreen? Touching each defined muscle and his taut skin. His poster never did him justice. It was almost as good as him bathing me in sunscreen with his strong hands and light touch, repeating over and over again how beautiful he thought I was.

Best. Day. Of. My. Life.

And just when I thought it couldn't get any better, while we lay there soaking in the rays and stealing kisses, Nick pulled out a fourteen-year-old copy of *Les Misérables*, purchased on the recommendation of one cheeky twenty-year-old in a ball cap.

"Shall I read to you?" Those were the most seductive words ever.

Yes, please. For the rest of my life.

Chapter Forty

BRONZED, EUPHORIC, AND feeling like I'd been soaked in sea salt—I suppose I had been; the cold water was worth it with Nick by my side—we returned to his place to get ready for dinner. We walked in with my legs and arms around him while he easily carried me. Our lips and tongues were as tangled as my limbs around him. I could still taste the lingering mango nectarines we had eaten for lunch. It was my new favorite fruit.

"It would be so easy for me to walk you to my room," he said between labored breaths and kisses.

I pulled away abruptly. "Nick." My hands moved to his cheeks. "I don't want easy."

His penetrating eyes fixed on mine. "I promised we would build the anchor first, and I meant that. At least tell me you want me, too."

"So much…but I need time and commitment."

"I'm committed," he countered.

"You know what I mean."

"How long do you think that is all going to take?"

"As long as it needs to." I pecked his lips.

He groaned and returned the kiss, but it was much less passionate this go around. "Maybe several states between us is a good idea."

"Do you really think so?"

"Not at all. We're going to have to work out a plan."

"Agreed, but I need to get ready first so I don't smell like an aquarium."

"I like the way you smell." He buried his face in my neck.

His breath tickled, making me laugh. In between, I got out, "Nick, thank you for today. You have a beautiful life here."

He stopped and looked up. "I want you to be a part of it."

I swallowed hard and blew out a heavy breath. "That's um...I mean..." I couldn't articulate a thing.

"I know we're just getting started, so we have time, but think about it."

I would be, for hours and days. That was a huge, life-changing decision that necessitated a commitment. I slid down his tall frame. "I'm going to take a shower."

He kissed the top of my head. "I'm going to get in a few lines before I jump in."

I nodded and walked off numbly. Did Nick Wells just ask me to think about moving here? I turned around quickly. "Nick?"

He stopped and turned.

"What if I—"

"We would make it work in Georgia." He didn't say another word. He didn't need to. Those were the exact right words. I needed to know he was willing to make the same sacrifice. It meant all the world to me. Douglas never would have.

I hurried to get ready because I didn't want to waste a moment away from him. I was even considering changing my flight to a red-eye and going straight from the airport to work Monday morning. Anything to prolong my time with Nick and Skye, who I was anxiously awaiting to return. She'd texted earlier to say she had some news. My assumption was it was boy related.

I wore the cream sundress with my new silk scarf draped around me. I let my hair fall loosely in romantic curls. It reflected my mood. With the last swipe of lip gloss, I headed out to find Nick. Our reservations were in an hour.

He was easy to find; he was already headed my way, firmly gripping his laptop. He stopped in his tracks and perused me. "Mmm. I have a sexy girlfriend." He pulled me to him for a kiss.

"You haven't showered yet." Which was fine by me. I could still smell the ocean air on him. And mixed in with his natural scent of amber, it was intoxicating.

"I got lost in my screenplay. You're inspirational."

"I am?"

"Very." He stepped back, still in his swim trunks. "As much as I would like to continue here with you, my partner, Simon, is dropping by in fifteen minutes. He insisted on bringing over the studio contract with our lawyers' mark-up on it. He wanted to discuss a few points in person, if you don't mind."

"Not at all."

"Just in case he shows up early, don't be shocked if he walks in without knocking. I'm still trying to house train him."

"Okay," I laughed.

"And Skye's running late, so I changed our reservations," he called, hurrying to his room to shower and change.

I didn't even make it to the kitchen where I was going to grab some water when I heard a strange man's voice. "Nick, man, it's me."

I walked toward Nick's grand entryway. "Nick's in the shower. He should be out in a few minutes," I said nervously. I realized how this represented a footstep into Nick's world.

Simon was a walking stereotype of what you thought Hollywood people looked like. He was tanner than tan, with sparkling white teeth, dark hair slicked back, wearing sunglasses in the house, and his shirt could do with being buttoned up a bit. As nice as his chest was, it looked ridiculous hanging out of his dress shirt graced with gold chains. Their company name, Wilder than Wells, was making much more sense now.

Simon whipped off his glasses, revealing his grey eyes alight. "What do we have here? Nick's muse in the flesh."

I tilted my head and held out my hand. "I'm Kate."

He took my hand and kissed it instead of shaking it. "You *are* the muse then."

"Muse?" I pulled away my hand.

"Yes. And thank you. This screenplay is going to be huge for us. It's brilliant, and we have you to thank." He hardly took a breath. "Here I was sending him out to Georgia to pretend to use a dating service—like he needed one—but we needed an inside man. Filling out that questionnaire was hilarious, but it fit the whole romantic comedy idea we originally had."

Suddenly I couldn't breathe and my legs felt like jelly, but I had to stand there to hear the ugly truth of it all.

Simon didn't care that I was probably pale as a ghost or that I wasn't responding. He kept on going.

"But then," he waved his hand up and down, "he met you and BOOM!" He made me jump. He grinned at my reaction. "It was like Oscar gold. Psychological thriller wrapped up in a romance about a beautiful but broken psychologist being hunted by a serial killer. Even the working title is genius, *Narcissistic Tendencies*." He smiled to himself as if he had thought it up himself.

I felt everything I'd eaten today bubbling up in my stomach.

"And you were not only the muse, but a built-in reference. You're one smart cookie, from what Nick says."

Every conversation we'd had all summer now became vile and twisted. He was using me. This entire weekend was probably a setup to get more information out of me. No wonder he asked about narcissists in the car. I don't know why he needed to ask. He could look in the mirror and get all the answers he needed.

When I could finally catch a breath, I eked out, "I'm sorry, will you excuse me?"

"Sure, sure. I know my way around. Hey," he did the finger-gun thing, "it was nice to meet you. I'm sure we will be getting to know each other better. Nick has big plans for you."

I'm sure he did. Too bad for him I refused to be used.

I rushed to the kitchen and grabbed my purse and phone. I looked down at my beautiful scarf. It suddenly felt caustic against my skin. I threw it on the counter and backed away as if it would bite me like a snake. I would take off the dress and shoes and get back into the outfit I'd come in, but leaving was the most important objective.

I hustled past Simon, who was loitering in Nick's office, but stopped with a thought. "Do you know the address here by chance?" Uber typically used GPS to find you, but occasionally they required an address.

He gave me a funny look but didn't ask why I wanted to know. He spouted off the address.

"Thank you."

"Sure thing."

I ran out the door, pulling up my Uber app as I went. It was proving difficult due to how hard I was shaking. Once I was able to type in my destination—my hotel's address—the tears began to fall, first one-by-one then by the dozens as they streamed down my face. I could hardly see the name of the driver when his name popped up for how blurry my eyes had become. I traversed Nick's stupidly long driveway haphazardly, only caring to be as far away from him as possible. If I tripped, so be it. It couldn't hurt worse than the pain I was feeling inside.

My chest was heaving, but I was trying to hold back the racking sobs. He didn't deserve the tears that I'd already shed. What was wrong with me? I'd read the books, been down this road before, yet here I was again. Never again would I break the rules.

Minutes seemed like an eternity while I waited at the end of the drive, leaning on one of the stone entry posts, all my strength drained from me.

My hell turned into an inferno with the sound of my name being called. Where was that blasted driver? There was nowhere for me to escape to unless I wanted to take my life into my hands. There were no sidewalks, only a busy two-lane road.

"Kate," Nick's voice was filled with pleading and panic.

"Don't waste your breath! Stay away from me!" I refused to look at him.

"Kate, listen to me." He grabbed my arm gently.

I yanked it away and gave him the foulest look. "Don't touch me."

His hands dropped, but he refused to move away from me. He stared at my pathetic state with only his dress pants on and wet, mussed hair. His blue eyes bore down on me with disquiet. "Please, it's not what you think."

"No, it's worse. Not only did you use the company I've worked so hard for, but you used me. And I fell for it all. You must be congratulating yourself for breaking me all the way. You can write that into your screenplay."

He reached out to touch me but pulled back and flexed his hand. "You have it all wrong."

344

"Actually, I was right about you to begin with." I closed my eyes, trying to hold back the tears, but it was as if trying to hold back the rough waves we'd experienced earlier. "I was wrong to let you ever pass that evaluation."

"Hell, how I wished you wouldn't have! Do you think I wanted to use that damn service?"

"How else were you going to do your 'research'?" I mocked.

His nostrils flared. "When I approached Kenadie last year about a mutually beneficial deal in which I would do some advertising in exchange for some insider information, she refused based on the proprietary nature of what she's created."

Good for her, I thought.

"The fact of the matter is, what you do there is unique, and I felt it was the best fit for what we initially wanted. I approached her again, and after some considerable vetting on her part, she agreed, but only if I would use the service for real. She feels strongly," he stretched his neck, "about the integrity of her company."

"I'm sure that was hard for you to understand, since integrity must be a foreign concept for you."

A flash of anger rippled through his eyes. "Why do you think I embellished the damn questionnaire?"

"Did you?"

"Yes," his voice was strained. "I knew by doing that I was going to get someone who didn't care if things worked out between us. I didn't want to knowingly hurt someone."

"Except me."

He blew out a heavy breath and ran his hands through his hair. "Kate, I didn't count on you, and I couldn't tell you the truth because despite what you think, I'm a man of my word, and as much as I didn't like it, I entered into the agreement with Kenadie."

"And when were you going to tell me?"

"When I could."

"But after you made sure you got all the material you needed from me. What was this weekend? Crunch time? Let's see if we can get Kate to break all her rules? Were you going to seduce me next? That would make a great plot line. A little sexual healing with some meaningless sex for the broken doctor. Maybe some pillow talk about narcissists and diagnosing psychotic killers." I rubbed my hands in my face, feeling like I was about to lose it. "You played me the entire time. Just. Like. Douglas." I removed my hands to find him stone-faced. "But you're worse. You used your daughter to get to me."

"Stop right there, Kate, before you say more things you'll regret."

"The truth hurts? Or, let me guess, you don't believe it, because like a true narcissist, you don't see anything wrong with your behavior. You probably think this is all my fault or in my head."

His face turned the deepest shade of red.

My ride finally arrived.

"What's this?" Nick looked over the Toyota Corolla that had pulled up beside us with disdain.

"My ride."

"Kate," he took my hand, panic played in his eyes. "Don't leave... please."

I looked down at our clasped hands one more time, sick over the connection I felt with him. I pulled away. "I should have never come." I opened the car door and jumped in.

Nick grabbed the door, preventing me from closing it. He leaned in and first focused on the young driver, who looked worried that he'd interrupted a domestic dispute.

Nick scared him even more. "If anything happens to her, you will wish you never lived. Take her straight to her destination, eyes on the road, and take the shortest, safest route. Got it?"

The poor kid nodded like his life depended on it.

Nick reached into his pocket and pulled out a money clip. He threw several one-hundred-dollar bills in the front seat.

"You are not paying for this." I was never taking anything from him again. And I certainly didn't need his pretend chivalry.

Nick ignored my protest. Instead, he leaned in more, coming within inches of my face, making me push my back against my seat.

"The truth is, Kate, you're never going to have the magic you've been searching for because you keep running scared from it every time it finds you. Every time I find you."

It felt like ice cold water doused my spine.

"Goodbye, Kate." He slammed the door.

Chapter Forty-One

WHAT DO YOU do when someone comes in, kicks their shoes off, props their feet up on your coffee table, and makes themselves comfortable in your life before you ever know what is happening? And brings their family along with them? And then, just when you get comfortable with it, they smash the table and leave muddy footprints behind on your heart?

Going back to life before Nick destroyed my house, figuratively speaking, seemed like an impossible task. Especially since I knew that even if he wasn't present, he would be invading my days at work. One thing I knew for sure was that I would not be his relationship manager. I would quit if Kenadie refused to release me from that responsibility. I went in on Monday determined to at least remedy that situation.

I got to work before anyone else. The thought of seeing anyone made me feel embarrassed, like they would all know what a fool I'd been. That everyone had been in on the joke and I was the last to know I was only a means to an end. Kenadie had assured me this was all for real. Had she lied too? Everyone was now suspect in my mind. I was desperate for someone to blame because I couldn't stand looking in the mirror knowing exactly whose fault it all was.

Worst of all were Nick's haunting parting words. Did he speak truth, or was he getting in his last jab? That's what a narcissist would do. Look at me, trying to explain away his behavior. Maybe I should find another profession. For all my schooling and life experience, I had learned nothing.

I kept my door shut in hopes of keeping people away as long as possible. Besides, my inbox was bursting and I had a stack of files on my desk for potential new clients that rivaled the Sears Tower.

I almost laughed maniacally at the poor women, who I'm sure represented a large portion of the stack, who wanted their shot at Nick. Then I wanted to cry because how could I, in good conscience, allow them to hope when I knew it was all a hoax? And how could I tell Kenadie I knew? I would have to admit to dating a client. I would have to admit how utterly naïve and stupid I was to believe in magic, to believe in Nick, and worse, to believe my judgment could be trusted.

I was just going to be honest and let the cards fall how they may. But would that cause legal complications for Nick? Why did I care? I didn't. That was a lie, but I wished I didn't. I wanted a button to turn off everything good I'd ever felt for him.

To get through the morning, I was downing ibuprofen and coffee, along with rubbing enough peppermint oil into my temples to make my office smell like a candy factory.

Halfway through the morning, Kenadie interrupted my no person zone. I supposed since she was the boss she could. She knocked before peeking her head in. "Welcome back."

"Thanks," I said dryly.

She tilted her head. "Are you okay? You look a little...tired."

That was putting it nicely, I knew. My flight was delayed yesterday and I didn't get home until midnight, which didn't really matter since I'd hardly slept anyway, and I'd been crying on and off since Saturday night.

"Long trip," I responded.

Kenadie stepped in. "How was your conference?"

"Good. I have some new research you might be interested in."

"I love new research." She inched closer, studying me. "Are you sure you're okay?"

I sat up as straight as I could and lied. "Never better."

"Oh, okay. It's just, I got a call from Nick."

I did my best not to react one way or the other to his name.

"He mentioned that his daughter had been trying to reach you but hadn't been able to. He wanted to make sure you arrived home safely. I told him you were here and buried under work, I'm sure." She smiled at the stack of files on my desk.

Skye's name pricked my heart. I'd shut my phone off Saturday night and I hadn't dared turn it back on. Now I felt guilty. I bet she'd texted. Or maybe Nick was lying, because he was, after all, a liar.

"It's sweet," Kenadie continued, "that Skye's so fond of you."

"The feeling is mutual," I finally articulated a response.

"Um . . ." Kenadie shifted on her feet. "Nick also mentioned," her voice got higher, "that he thought it would be better if you were no longer his relationship manager." She said the last part in a rush.

I pushed a paper clip around on my desk, not making eye contact. "That's probably a good idea."

"I know you tried and you did a . . . good job," she stuttered. "But maybe since he's asking for a new date every week and you're so busy with your other responsibilities, this is a good thing."

Fantastic. On top of everything else, Kenadie thought I was incompetent. And it was my own fault, thinking he was worthy of so much better than his questionnaire gave him credit for. But it didn't really matter, did it? He wasn't going to stick with anyone we chose for him. Or so he said.

"I agree."

"Great." She twisted her hands together. "Now that that's settled, I'll let Cara know she's taking over his account. I mean, she will be in a couple of weeks. He informed me this morning that due to business and some personal obligations, he has to remain in California."

I could at least breathe a sigh of relief over that. "Okay," I said flatly.

"Kate," she said uneasily. "You're amazing in *your role* here. And I really appreciate you spending extra time with Nick to make sure there weren't any issues, but…" She didn't finish her thought. "Thank you for all your hard work. I'll let you get back to it."

I think what she wanted to say was *keep your day job, you were a terrible relationship manager.* I supposed there was some truth to that. Before she could go, though, I had to ask. "Kenadie, you really believe that Nick is serious about using our service?"

She looked taken aback. "Yes," she was adamant. "I wouldn't…I mean, I think he just needs some matches that better fit his profile." A hint of worry creeped into her tone.

I didn't disagree with her one way or the other. She obviously believed Nick was in earnest when he said he gave his word about using the service. "Well, I have a lot to catch up on."

"Good luck with that." She walked away but turned around at my door and gave me a strained smile.

I was too tired to pretend, so I didn't even try to return it.

As soon as she left, I pulled out my phone from my bag and turned it on. Within seconds of it coming on, I had several texts and voice message notifications pop up. Several from Nick. I ignored those for the time being and went straight to Skye's. He wasn't lying about her contacting me.

I miss you.

I don't know what happened between Dad and you, but he's really upset. I hope you're okay.

Dad says we aren't going back to Georgia. What happened? He won't say.

Well, of course he won't because he's a jerk.

Kate, I love you. Please text me back.

I lost it. Tears rolled down my cheeks as I responded.

Oh, honey, I'm so sorry I missed your texts. I needed a break from my phone. I love you too. Maybe you can call me tonight, if it's all right with your dad, and tell me your news. I'm here for you anytime.

I tapped send.

I reached for the box of tissues on my desk and used one right after the other. The tears and assault on my heart felt never ending. The masochist in me thought I might as well listen to Nick's messages.

"Kate." There was a long pause where I could only hear his breath. He eventually hung up.

"Kate...it's me again." That was it.

"Will you pick up your phone? I just want to know if you made it home."

Why did he care?

"Kate, will you at least text Skye back?"

That was it. No apologies. Not like I expected one. He saw nothing wrong with what he had done.

Meanwhile, I sat here feeling the ripple effect of his charade both in the personal and professional arena. I was sure my colleagues had discussed my supposed incompetence amongst themselves. And they were right. I was incompetent. And absolutely heartbroken.

I wiped my cheeks some more. Here I was, thinking that maybe he was the guy worth leaving my life here for. That maybe we could build a life together. And, bonus, he came with a daughter. A girl that owned my heart.

353

I gazed at the large stack of Nick worshippers and it hit me. I knew nothing about relationships. And if I didn't know, how could I possibly help someone find one? I felt sick about being the gateway to a fantasy world. These women stood no chance. They shouldn't even want the chance to be with Nick.

The moral of the story was, it was time for another chapter. I would go home and start polishing my resume. I was good at doing research, not so good at listening to it, so maybe it was time for me to head back to the world of academia. I had been a research assistant while I was a grad student. The pay was terrible, but now that I had a doctorate, I could supplement with teaching.

First, though, I needed my mommy.

I cancelled my appointments at the clinic and drove straight to my parents' home after work. It probably wasn't the best idea. The dining room with Nick's signature all over it was front and center, taunting me. It looked better than before, with perfectly styled wainscot and beautifully placed crown molding. It was even clean. Not a power tool or speck of sawdust in sight.

It had all been part of the façade, I reminded myself.

"Mom, Dad?" I croaked out. My throat was raw from all the tears.

"I'm in the kitchen," Mom called. "Dad should be back soon with dinner. You can join us."

I walked back expecting to see the fallout from the disaster Dad had created with the water leak, but there was new, unpainted drywall in the ceiling and again, no dust, not even a power tool in sight.

Mom was at the sink filling a vase of water in her normal attire, a muumuu. Some roses from her bushes outside lay nearby.

"Hey, Mom."

"Katie, I'm so happy you're home." She turned to greet me, but instead she grabbed onto her heart and stood terrified. "Honey, what's happened to you? You're cloaked in a black aura."

For once, I believed her about auras. I gripped the island while a trickle of emotion leaked from my eyes.

Mom rushed forward and wrapped me in her muumuu.

I clung to her. "Everything is wrong."

She patted, stroked, and didn't say a word. She did all the right mom things.

I did my part by sobbing.

After several minutes of that, we ended up in the family room on the couch. I assumed the fetal position with my head in Mom's lap and she continued with the hair stroking. It was not lost on me that a similar but much happier scene took place a short two days ago, except it was at the beach and my head was in Nick's lap while his entrancing voice read one of my favorite books. That reminder only made the tears fall faster and more furious.

"Katie, honey, did something happen with Nick?"

I quieted. "Why would you ask that?"

"The only time I've ever seen you this upset was after... Douglas," she hesitated to say his name.

"Nick and Douglas are two peas in a rotten pod."

"What do you mean?"

I vomited out the entire ugly affair, starting with my and Nick's very first meeting to all that transpired over the weekend, all the way down to Cara and Eva, my coworkers, waving my incompetency in front of my face today like a bright red flag and gloating that Cara was Nick's new relationship manager.

"Oh, Katie, I'm proud of you for trying again, but honey, Nick's right."

I sprung upright, sniffling in righteous indignation. What did she mean, Nick was right? She was supposed to be on my side and tell me what an evil pig he was.

"I know that look." Mom tried to stifle her smile. "You think you're right. And granted, what Nick did was stupid, even careless, but he's no Douglas. Douglas never chased after you, never cared one second for your well-being. He certainly never would have jumped through the hoops Nick did to get your attention. All you have to do is look at this house to realize that."

Mom wiped away some straggling tears. "And Nick's right, you're afraid of magic because deep down you know the magic of love isn't created in a moment, it's forged with blood, sweat, and a lot of tears. And you, my sweet girl, have shed more than you deserved to. It wasn't fair what Douglas did to you, and I hate to see what he has continued to do to you, but honey, you are the only person who has the power to end his reign of terror. If you want a future, you have to move on from the past."

I fell against Mom's shoulder, fighting within myself. What she said rang true, but I didn't want to believe it. I wanted to hate Nick.

"He lied to me," I said out loud.

"Did he really? Sounds more like he was stuck between a rock and a hard place."

"Mom," I was getting irritated now. Why was she refusing to see my point? "He used me for information and wrote a screenplay based on me."

"Have you read this screenplay?"

"Well...no."

"Then how do you know you have anything to be upset over?"

"Well—"

"That's what I thought." She kissed my head. "If you ask me, I think it's a pretty romantic gesture."

She talked to crystals. What did she know?

Chapter Forty-Two

O N BOTH MY parents' advice, I decided not to hang up my boots quite yet at Binary Search. They reminded me that knee jerk emotional reactions rarely ended well. It was a good thing I spent eight years in school learning that just to have my parents point it out again.

The next two weeks, I kept mostly to myself at work. I only engaged if I had to, or with Zander asking about Meg. She was having some good days now. Zander's mood reflected that; he was more his upbeat self in the meetings I had to attend. Thankfully, it was only assignment meetings. No more connection meetings for me.

But the office gossip was that Nick was coming into town for the weekend, so he was getting a new match. Eva and Cara were unbearable talking about how Cara had three women lined up who all matched him seventy to eighty percent. I refrained from taking the bait. They could match him one hundred percent and it wouldn't have mattered.

Skye and I were texting frequently. We never talked about her dad. It was for the best. Nick hadn't tried to contact me again, and I was too confused to contact him. And I figured since he was coming into town and I didn't know about it, that seemed pretty final to me. That hurt more than I wanted to admit.

That's why, when I came in Friday, I was more than surprised to see a white box on my desk tied with a red ribbon around it. There was no note or card. It wasn't my birthday and I couldn't think of anyone in the office who would buy me a gift, especially given the atmosphere during the last couple of weeks.

I shimmied the ribbon off the box and took off the lid. I gasped and ran to shut my door. I didn't need to ask who the box was from. When back at my desk, I removed the perfectly bloomed red rose out first, drinking in its fragrant scent before resting it on my desk. Under it rested the clue as to whom the box came from. The scarf Nick and I made together at Zabrina's lay there as beautiful as it was almost two weeks ago when I'd left it in a lump on Nick's counter.

I pulled it out and draped it across my shoulders. Wafts of amber and vanilla tickled my nose. Had Nick worn this? I laughed to myself. It sure smelled like he had. I soaked it in. I'd missed that smell. I'd missed him. And I wasn't sure if I was an idiot for missing him or not.

Under the scarf was a sealed white envelope with my name carefully scripted in Nick's handwriting sitting on top of a manila envelope. I plucked up the white envelope first and sat down in my chair. I took several breaths, eager yet afraid to open the contents. With shaky hands, I managed to open it. Inside was a linen piece of paper folded in half. I carefully unfolded the letter. I admired his penmanship before diving in. It wasn't every day that someone wrote you a letter, especially with today's technology. And it wasn't every day a girl got one from Nick Wells.

Dear Kate,

I found this scarf. It belongs to you. In fact, you left several things behind that belong to you, including me.

Tears sprung up. That was quite the opener.

I know you are furious with me and you have every right to be. But perhaps you could see it from my point of view. Each time we were together, I debated over breaking my confidentiality agreement with Binary Search. I knew withholding the truth from you posed a risk, especially given your cautious nature and life experience. But I'd hoped by the time I could tell you, you'd already be convinced of my feelings for you and would share them. I thought someday we could laugh about your attempts to set me up with a "nice" woman while all along the only one I wanted was you.

In the same vein, I believe you were misinformed by my possible ex-partner about a certain screenplay that I wrote. Kate, I never saw you as broken and wouldn't dream of using you. Were you my inspiration? Yes. I was hoping you would take it as I meant it to be, a torrid love letter.

Now I was ugly crying.

The first draft of my love letter to you is finished. I believe, professionally, it is my crowning achievement, but it means nothing to me if I lose you in the process. I've enclosed a copy of Narcissistic Tendencies. *Read it for yourself and see what you think.*

Kate, one word from you and I will destroy it. I've refused to sign the studio contract until you give your approval.

I'll be waiting to hear from you.

Your number one fan,

Nick

I reread the letter several times. I was snapping, popping, and crackling everywhere. I could hardly think. All I could do was put everything back in the box and rush out of my office. I ran into Zander talking to Todd in the hall. They looked alarmed at my state, but in true male fashion, they weren't touching it with a ten-foot pole.

"I need to go home," was all I shouted as I ran by.

"Are you all right?" Todd called, but I could tell he didn't really want to know.

I had no time to respond anyway. I had some serious reading to do.

Once home, I curled up on my couch wrapped in my silk scarf, and dug into *Narcissistic Tendencies*. I still couldn't believe he was using that as a title.

The opening scene was of Sloane, the female protagonist, taking off a wedding ring and placing it in an envelope and throwing it in a mailbox. You don't know who she's sending it to. She's distraught, but it's an act of bravery.

Flash forward several years and the male protagonist, Detective Foster Carmichael, shows up at psychologist Dr. Sloane Alton's office with the wedding ring. It was found at the scene of a murder. Sloane recognizes Foster from many years ago. A chance meeting at a bookstore she'd never forgotten. She helped him find a book he was looking for. He asked for her number, but she was engaged. For Foster, there was a spark of recognition, but he couldn't place her.

I was intrigued already.

It only got more captivating as the story progressed, revealing some of the emotional damage represented by the ring—a mentally and physically abusive ex-husband and Sloane's feelings of worthlessness. But now she had to face her past to help Foster solve a string of murders that might involve her ex-husband.

I hadn't gotten very far when there was a knock on my door. I was irritated at the interruption but curious as to who would show up at my house in the middle of a Friday morning. Probably a solicitor. But I got up and checked anyway.

My day was full of surprises. Kenadie and Meg stood on my doorstep. How very unexpected.

I opened the door, not sure what to say other than, "Hello?"

Meg was to me in a second, throwing her arms around me. She felt lighter, like she'd lost some weight, but her hug was tight.

"What's this?"

Meg continued to squeeze, while Kenadie gave me an uncomfortable smile. "Kate, I think I owe you an apology."

"Why?"

Meg let go and gave me a devious smile and shook her head. "You and Nicholas Wells. I can't believe it."

My heart stopped while I cleared my throat. "It's not what you think," I stuttered, focused on my boss.

"I think it's exactly what we all think." Kenadie's smile was warm and completely disarming.

"Come in." I waved them in. Obviously, there was plenty to discuss.

"How are you, Meg?" I asked first while they took a seat on my couch.

"Today's a good day, but never mind me. What's going on with you?"

I looked to Kenadie.

"Do you mind if I say something first?" Kenadie asked.

"Please do." I wanted to know what she knew before divulging anything.

"Well, between last night and this morning, I've had some interesting, maybe not-so-pleasant conversations with my momma and... Nick."

I was all ears. I crossed my legs and sat up attentive on my cozy chair.

Kenadie bit her lip, embarrassed. "My momma was at Jack's last night when Nick arrived. And in true Momma fashion, she grilled him about you. Zander had mentioned to her that you'd been acting off the last couple of weeks ever since your return from California. She put two-and-two together. Nick didn't..." she tucked some hair behind her ear, "mince words, and expressed his displeasure with our agreement. Momma is blaming me for keeping you apart."

"Kenadie, it's not your fault. I broke the rules."

"I've been there." She held up her hand and flashed her wedding ring. "But Nick had a point—you can't force a relationship on somebody, you shouldn't. In my defense, I really thought if he tried our services, he would see how amazing it was and he might be surprised. I was trying to protect my company. I had no idea I was hurting him or you in the process. You have to believe that."

I reached for her hand; she took it for a moment. "I do. And really, Nick is a big boy, he knew what he was signing up for."

"True," Meg offered, "but it must have been difficult for him to have found his match knowing he couldn't have it."

"Um..." I rubbed my lips together. "Yeah, he's not all that hung up on those kinds of rules."

They both laughed, but Kenadie interjected, "Believe me, I know. He asked to meet with me early this morning and we renegotiated a new agreement."

"You did?" I asked.

Kenadie nodded. "He is no longer a client, but he will still appear in two more ads. Kate," Kenadie took a deep breath, "I'm so sorry if I made you feel like you weren't doing your job. You were doing exactly what you should have done as a relationship manager. Nick mentioned his questionnaire wasn't an honest reflection of himself, but you saw past that. And I'm sorry I doubted you."

"I've doubted myself more than anyone over the past couple of months. Past several years actually," I admitted.

Both women gave me curious glances. I wondered if it was time to finally let my friends in. To have real friends again. What did I have to lose? If anything, my time with Nick had proven to me how lonely my life truly was.

"I was married briefly, or at least I thought I was, a long time ago."

Shock registered on each of their pretty faces.

"It was annulled because he was already married."

"No!" Meg exclaimed. "Who does that?"

"A true narcissist."

"Not a Zander or Nick?" Meg gave me a sly grin.

"Not them." I grinned.

"Kate," Kenadie interjected, "I may be dense about a few things, but I can tell you this, Nick cares deeply for you. He was willing to be sued by me for breach of contract so he could be with you."

Meg placed her hand over her heart. "That's really sweet."

"You want to know something else?" I decided to go all in. I hoped Nick didn't mind. "He wrote me a screenplay. Do you want to read it with me?"

"Oh my gosh, yes," Meg replied.

Kenadie looked touched that I had asked.

I got out some fruit and chocolate and we did it right. I handed them the sheets of paper I'd already read and passed them a new sheet whenever I was finished reading it. We were all enthralled with the story of Sloane and Foster. I recognized the references to the Xavier house and the battleship. Sloane's ex-husband, Corey, was raised by an abusive father who was in the military. Clues to solving the murders were left at each location, like a baby rattle and an empty bottle of antidepressants.

Nick wrote creepy so good. My spine was tingling. I even jumped a few times while they were on that ship together. They kissed for the first time on the ship, after getting locked into the boiler room by the man who they assumed was the killer. Sloane was intelligent, and Foster was in awe of her. Yet she kept secrets.

Several clues led them to believe the "narcissist" killer, as they were calling him, was targeting women through matchmaking services. Each dead woman fit the same profile, and each used a matchmaking service. Eerily, each dead woman looked similar to Sloane.

We hardly made a sound as we read, it was that engrossing.

And just when I thought I had figured out who the killer really was, I was shocked and impressed at the twist. It was Foster's ex-wife, Dalia, who had killed Sloane's ex-husband, Corey, unbeknownst to any one of them.

Dalia had been Corey's first wife, who he was married to when he married Sloane, though Sloane had no idea she existed. But Dalia, the first wife, was previously married to Foster. They had married young and only for a brief period of time. Dalia had suffered with psychotic episodes and NPD. She wanted her revenge on Sloane for taking both the men she thought she loved away from her. It was so well executed.

I had to take a moment to process when we were all finished. It was the best love letter I had ever read.

Meg was the first to speak. "Wow. I loved how they were healing each other through it all, emotionally and even physically. That scene at Sloane's baby's grave." Meg teared up. "That is probably the sweetest thing I've ever read."

It really was. It was as if Nick was giving me hope that someday there would be more than an empty womb for me. I didn't mention that to my friends. One step at a time.

"I loved that Sloane wasn't a damsel in distress. That they both rescued each other," Kenadie mentioned.

"I loved that too," I responded. I couldn't think of anything I didn't love about it.

"So, what are you going to do about it?" Meg asked with a knowing grin.

I knew exactly what I was going to do.

As soon as my friends left, I called Nick. He answered immediately.

"Where are you?" I asked before he could say anything.

"How impolite of you, Kate." His dark chocolate voice came through sinfully smooth.

"I'm sorry, but I seem to have left some things behind, and I was hoping you could help me find them."

"I'm at Jack's on the River waiting for you."

"I'll be right there."

"Hurry."

He didn't have to tell me twice. All I did was remove my mascara stains and touch up my makeup before I flew out the door.

The traffic was ridiculous, but it was late Friday afternoon. Didn't they know they were getting in the way of my future?

After what seemed like an eternity, I pulled into Jack's restaurant. The parking lot was already starting to fill up. I meant to use some decorum, but I found myself jogging in my wedges toward the entrance. I flew in like I was late for the most important appointment of my life.

Jack was there to greet me with the biggest smile. "Darlin'." He wrapped me up in his strong arms. "It's about time you showed your face around here again."

"Where is he, Jack?"

"Right this way." He took my hand and led me out to the patio.

Nick stood waiting alone, wearing my favorite outfit, faded blue jeans and a white T-shirt, surrounded by a floral shop of red roses in vases of all shapes and sizes. Dean Martin played on the surround sound.

"Have fun." Jack gave me a little nudge forward.

Nick was to me in a second, and there I found myself wrapped in his arms, swaying to the music, feeling connected as I never had before.

Is this what moving on feels like?

At first, we didn't speak. It felt right to only cling to one another.

Nick kissed my head then my cheek. "I'm sorry, Kate," Nick whispered in my ear.

I held onto him tighter. "I'm sorry for the horrible things I said to you."

Nick leaned away and gazed into my eyes. "Kate, I would never think of trying to seduce you. When the time is right, and I take you to *our* bed, it will always be to make love to you."

Ripples of heat washed over me. I pressed my lips against his.

He parted my lips, but only briefly. I barely tasted my ambrosia bliss before he pulled away. "I take it you liked the screenplay." It wasn't a question. He knew very well I did.

"It's perfect. You have to sign that contract."

"Only if you're part of the deal." He skimmed my lips with his own.

"Can I get a kissing clause added to it?"

"Mmm." He groaned against my lips. "All day, every day if you want."

I tugged on his shirt and pulled him flush against me. "Sign me up."

"Is that a lifetime commitment, Kate?"

I sure hoped so.

Chapter Forty-Three

Five Months Later

I BREATHED IN ROSE'S baby scent while cradling her against me. It was the perfect name for her. Her petal-soft pink cheeks and beautiful, intoxicating smell had my ovaries promising they could produce one just as wonderful with the man sitting next to me holding on to her tiny little hand. Nick had come with me to drop off a baby gift while he was visiting me for Valentine's Day weekend. Little Rose had come a few weeks early.

"You guys do good work—she's beautiful," I complimented the new parents sitting across from us in their mostly packed apartment, surrounded by boxes. They would soon be making their foray into suburbia and home ownership.

Zander kissed Meg's head. "She does take after me."

Meg smacked him with the back of her hand. It landed on his chest in a big thud.

Zander laughed and got up. He took Rose right out of my arms. I could tell he'd been itching to since we arrived and Meg had handed us the baby. He held her like a pro and gazed upon her tiny head.

"Thank God, you look like your mom." He kissed her head before returning with her to sit next to his wife. They made the cutest family.

Nick took my hand now that it was free.

"How are you feeling, Meg?" I asked.

"It feels good to breathe and eat normally again. I swear she lived in my ribs the last few weeks."

"Well, you look great."

"Thank you." She yawned.

"We should probably let you get some rest."

"I'm sorry. This little one," she gently swiped the dark hair on her baby's head, "has her days and nights mixed up."

Nick and I stood together.

"Congratulations again," Nick offered.

Zander and Meg both went to stand up. Nick and I motioned for them to stay seated.

"You all rest, we can see ourselves out."

"Ooo, wait," Meg said. "Did you hear Kenadie and Jason are expecting?"

"We saw Nan last night at dinner with Jack. It was all she could talk about." I grinned. Little did she know she would have something else to talk about soon. I'd helped Jack pick out an engagement ring for her last week. He was waiting to pop the question until her older son Dylan could fly out next month. He wanted all her kids there for the occasion.

"How long are you in town?" Zander asked Nick before we could leave.

"Just for the weekend," Nick replied.

Meg gave me a commiserating look. She knew how hard it was on both of us to be apart so much. But it was the way it had to be for now. Nick was busy casting for *Narcissistic Tendencies*. And I didn't feel good about moving to California without a solid commitment. Like the kind Jack was making to Nan. Nick hadn't even said he loved me yet. I hadn't either, but only because I was waiting on him. He acted like he loved me, but he'd never articulated it.

Our drive back to my place was mostly a silent affair.

Nick held my hand and caressed it while he drove. "You okay over there?"

"Yeah," I spoke into the window.

"You look good with a baby in your arms."

I sighed wistfully.

"You still want one?"

"Yes," I whispered. So much.

"You know, I can help out there." His tone bordered on teasing and volunteering.

I turned toward him, not sure what to say. I wanted nothing more than to have a baby with him, but it wasn't something I felt like I could say at the moment.

He flashed me his half smile. "I know you want to be married first."

I did. Was he ever going to offer that? We talked often of our future, and we were always together in it. But we always skirted around the topic of marriage. Even Skye was asking me about it lately, wondering if that was going to happen. She told me she already thought of me like a mother. Oh, how I loved that girl.

"Do you want to pick up Skye before we head to my place?" She and Liam were "hanging out" at Janelle's house. Skye wasn't sure what their relationship status was, but over Christmas break, Liam, in a surprise move, asked her on a date while Skye was visiting me. Nick had joined us for half the time. Skye was doing a good job of playing it cool when it came to Liam. I was proud of her.

Nick brought my hand up and kissed it. "I want to spend some alone time with you."

"I would be amenable to that."

Time alone meant a fire burning low in my fireplace, wine, my head in his lap while he stroked my hair and read *Les Misérables* to me. We were only a third of the way through. Normally I felt content in these moments, but I fidgeted and tossed about a bit tonight.

Nick lowered his tablet and looked down at me. "Is something bothering you?"

I thought for a second. "I miss you."

"I miss you too," he said blandly before going right back to reading.

I was bothered even more. I didn't listen to a word Nick said, which was unfortunate because he spoke the French names so beautifully. I sighed and blew out large amounts of air.

Nick lowered his tablet again, this time with his signature smile. "Are you sure there isn't anything you want to talk about?"

I gazed up into those eyes of his I loved so much. I loved the rest of him too. These past several months had been the best of my life. I hated the separations, but we talked every day, and every other weekend we saw each other most of the time. Our time together was filled with art museums, jazz concerts, cooking together, long walks on the beach, helping Skye with homework, and giving advice about boys and the best tampons. Nick was so grateful I always knew the right ones to buy. There was lots of laughter. Nick even joined in most of the time. And on the weekends Nick came here, he usually tried to help my dad with some harebrained project, like installing toilet seats that automatically lowered.

"Nick, how do you feel about me?" I braved asking.

He ran a finger down my cheek. "I'm quite fond of you. Why do you ask?"

That was sweet, but not exactly what I was hoping for. I bit my lip. "Well...I mean, we've been together for a while now."

"Yes, we have." A flash of amusement lit up his eyes before he turned back to his tablet again.

"And you're happy?" I couldn't let this go.

"Very." He didn't even bother looking at me. "Can I proceed?"

I was getting more frustrated by the second. "No."

He set his tablet down on my side table. "No?" He was more than amused now.

"Nick...I...I...love you," I breathed out, somewhat annoyed. Though it felt incredible to finally say it out loud.

"It's about time." He was practically laughing.

I sat up, upset. That wasn't the response I was looking for. "What do you mean it's about time?"

He smirked. "I mean, it took you long enough."

Oh. I could play his game. I straddled myself across his legs and leaned in, my lips hovering above his.

"I like this arrangement better." He moved in for the kill.

I backed away. "No touching my lips until you tell me how you feel."

"I already told you how fond I was of you." He leaned in again.

I pressed my finger against his lips. "No deal, buddy."

He removed my finger and kissed it. "I'm not your buddy, Kate."

"Then what are you?"

He rested his forehead against mine. He let our emotions simmer between us until they boiled. Our torrid love letter scripted another line. "I'm the man who wants to take pleasure cruises with you," his hand crept up my shirt and rested on my bare abdomen, "and have babies with you."

"You do?" Tears stung my eyes.

"I do." He brushed my lips. "I love you, Kate. I think I've loved you from the very first time we touched. I haven't said it because you've been skittish in the past."

I laughed. "That's one way to put it."

He caressed my cheek and held me with his enigmatic eyes. "Do you think you could handle a lifetime full of magic?"

Crackling currents of electricity ran through me. "I think I could manage that."

"I was hoping you would say that." His hand moved from my abdomen to between the couch cushions.

"What are you doing?"

"Give me a second." He dug a little farther until he pulled out a small, intricately carved wood box. He held it between us with a genuine smile. "Open it, Kate."

When did he put that there? You know, I didn't care.

The tears didn't wait, they trailed down my cheeks while I opened the beautiful box. I smiled, recognizing the ring. Jack had asked me what I'd thought of it when I'd helped him pick out Nan's ring. I told him if I could pick any ring in the world, I would choose the vintage heirloom ring with the stunning round diamond.

Nick gently took the ring out and placed it on my finger, kissing it once it was in place. "Share my name, my life, and my daughter with me?"

My twenty-year-old shouted inside *yes!* The more demure, older me took a moment to revel in it before I answered, "I would be honored to."

I pressed my lips to his, soaking in our connection. It was the most beautiful moment of my life.

Nick took my face in his hands. That smile was back in his eyes. "Are you going to use the same vows you wrote in your notebook?"

"No, but I promise to passionately kiss you every day, and if you're really good, I'll let you steal the covers too."

"Kate, with me around, you're never going to need the covers."

Oh my.

Epilogue

"OUR NEXT GUEST hardly needs an introduction. We all loved him on the hit TV show *On the Edge*, and now he's making waves on the big screen as a director and writer. His film, *Narcissistic Tendencies*, is currently up for two Golden Globe Awards—Best Motion Picture-Drama, and Best Screenplay. Ladies and gentlemen, welcome Nicholas Wells."

The crowd went wild. If only they could see the sight before my eyes. The faint glow of the TV light flickered in our bedroom. Nick was propped up against his pillows beside me on our bed with our son, Nicholas Jr., or Nicky as we loved to call him, curled up on his daddy's bare chest, soundly sleeping.

Our oldest baby was next to me clutching her phone and sleeping restlessly. She and Liam had just broken up and she was heartbroken. His reasoning was they should explore other relationships. From a parent's point of view, that was a wise choice, but I hated seeing our daughter's heart ache. My heart ached too, thinking that she wouldn't be here much longer to invade our bed. She was graduating in five short months. She had yet to decide where she was going to school, but I was angling for in state. Nick and I were constantly touting all the good schools in California she could attend.

"You looked good," I whispered to Nick.

He stretched out his arm, inviting me to snuggle in next to him. I did so with tired pleasure. It was way past my bedtime, but ever since Nick was on the press junket, I'd been staying up late to watch every talk show he and his cast had been on promoting *Narcissistic Tendencies*. I was so proud of him. The movie had made it to number one the third week after it was released in November. It was considered a sleeper hit. The word of mouth and critical acclaim had been amazing. He was home now for Christmas. The show we were watching had been recorded earlier in the week.

Nick kissed my head. "I've missed you. I want you and the kids to come with me next week when I go to New York to promote the film."

"Our parents will still be here." They all insisted on being here for Nicky's first Christmas, and my mom and Nan were worried about me being all alone with a baby and Skye, so they had been here for two weeks already taking over every aspect of our lives from cooking to cleaning. It was fun to watch them debate about whether meat was good for you or not. They both agreed to disagree, so my mom was making a tofu turkey while Nan was making the real deal for Christmas dinner. Poor Dad would have to eat Mom's, and he would be the only one.

But honestly, they didn't have anything to worry about; I was managing fine. Nicky was an angel baby and had been sleeping through the night since he was two months old. Now at six months, he was the happiest kid in the world as long as he was fed, dry, and constantly paid attention to, which was no problem. I almost felt bad thrusting another Wells man on the world with his enigmatic blue, blue eyes and his already killer toothless smile who, like his daddy, already knew if he flashed it he would get his way. He was so adored, we fought about whose turn it was to hold him. Nick got dibs tonight since he had been gone for several days in a row.

"They can still be here. I want you with me." Nick ran his fingers down my bare arm.

I took a deep breath and sighed. "Okay."

"I know what I'm asking of you, so thank you."

Being Nick's wife was wonderful. Being Nicholas Wells's wife was sometimes difficult for me. I hated the spotlight, and I was surprised how many people there were trying to thrust me into it. I could hardly go to the grocery store without someone stopping me or taking my picture. And the number of requests I had from magazines and news organizations for interviews and pictures of our children was ridiculous. Now we had to have security with us at times when we went out as a family, like next week in New York. All this while I was worried about leaking breasts and if I'd packed enough diapers.

The late show host interrupted my thoughts with his laugh. "Rumor has it this movie is a love note to your wife. What I want to know is what kind of man writes his wife a love letter about a narcissistic psychotic killer?"

The audience roared with laughter. That had been a big talking point, and each host had gotten plenty of mileage out of it. It didn't matter, Nick and I knew exactly what it all meant, and Nick was tight-lipped about his personal life. All he would ever say was, "I owe my wife a great deal, and without her, this movie would have never happened."

As much as we tried to keep our family life private, a picture of Nick holding Nicky when he was only a few weeks old at the studio flashed on the screen. The audience gave a collective, "Aww."

It really was a sweet picture. Nick never looked so attractive as when he held our baby, like right now.

"And here's Nick showing off his domestic skills," the host quipped. "How's it being on diaper duty at your age?"

"It's great at any age," Nick responded.

I was glad to hear that and thought maybe this was a good time to discuss a little matter. "How would you feel about extending diaper duty for a while?"

Nick muted the TV. "What do you mean?"

I made circles with my finger on Nick's bare chest. "Well... remember last month when I surprised you at your office for lunch?"

"Yes," he groaned with pleasure. "I'd like a repeat right now. I'll put Nicky in his crib and you get Skye into her room."

"Hold on, tiger, we'll get there."

"Is something wrong?"

I kissed my son's head and breathed in his scent. I smoothed his baby soft caramel hair. Such love filled me.

"Not at all. You gave an Academy Award-winning performance, and to show for it, we are going to have another little trophy next year."

"What?" Nick sat straight up, startling our son and daughter.

Nicky started to cry while Skye sat up like a drunken sailor, swaying and incoherent. "What's going on?" She fell back on our bed and was out again.

I took Nicky out of Nick's arms and gently lulled him while Nick stared at me wide-eyed. "Are you sure?"

I nodded. I was more than sure and surprised. We weren't planning on another one so soon.

Nick shook his head and blew out a large breath. "How are you feeling?"

"Same as last time—good, but tired."

While the news sunk in, he ran his hands through my hair and over my bare shoulders, taking me in with his eyes and touch. "I love you, Kate Wells." He only used my full name when he was trying to convey the depth of his feelings for me.

It still took my breath away when he said it. "I know."

"You probably should get some rest."

"I will later." I gave him my best wicked grin. "I'm a huge fan of your work."

About the Author

JENNIFER PEEL IS the award-winning, bestselling author of the Dating by Design and Women of Merryton series, as well as several other contemporary romances. Though she lives and breathes writing, her first love is her family. She is the mother of three amazing kiddos and has recently added the title of mother-in-law, with the addition of two terrific sons-in-law. She's been married to her best friend and partner in crime for a lot longer than seems possible. Some of her favorite things are late-night talks, beach vacations, the mountains, pink bubble gum ice cream, tours of model homes, and Southern living. She can frequently be found with her laptop on, fingers typing away, indulging in chocolate milk, and writing out the stories that are constantly swirling through her head.

If you enjoyed this book, please rate and review it on
Amazon & Goodreads

You can also connect with Jennifer on
Facebook & Twitter (@jpeel_author)

Other books by Jennifer Peel:
Other Side of the Wall
The Girl in Seat 24B
Professional Boundaries
House Divided
Trouble in Loveland
More Trouble in Loveland
How to Get Over Your Ex in Ninety Days
Paige's Turn
Hit and Run Love: A Magnolia and Moonshine Novella
Sweet Regrets
Honeymoon for One in Christmas Falls

The Women of Merryton Series:
Jessie Belle – Book One
Taylor Lynne – Book Two
Rachel Laine – Book Three
Cheyenne – Book Four

The Dating by Design Series:
His Personal Relationship Manager – Book One
Statistically Improbable – Book Two
Narcissistic Tendencies –Book Three

The Piano and Promises Series:
Christopher and Jaime–Book One
Beck and Call–Book Two
Cole and Jillian–Book Three

More Than a Wife Series
The Sidelined Wife – Book One
The Secretive Wife – Book Two (Coming Soon)
The Dear Wife – Book Three (Coming Soon)

A Clairborne Family Novel Series
Second Chance in Paradise
New Beginnings in Paradise – Coming Soon
First Love in Paradise – Coming Soon
Return to Paradise – coming Soon

To learn more about Jennifer and her books, visit her website at
www.jenniferpeel.com.

94376607R00233

Made in the USA
Lexington, KY
29 July 2018